DOG ROSES

A Novel

ANTHONY MCDONALD

Anchor Mill Publishing

www.anthonymcdonald.co.uk

Anchor Mill Publishing

4/04 Anchor Mill

Paisley PA1 1JR

SCOTLAND

anchormillpublishing@gmail.com

The cover illustration shows *Portrait of a Young Man with Open Collar* by Henry Scott Tuke. Cover design by Barry Creasy.

In memory of Tony Linford

And for Steve Gee,

And Reed Thomas

Acknowledgements

I am grateful to John Newberry as always, for his helpful insights into the mysteries of painting. Also to Chris and Liz Pattenden.

And to Charles Coussens, Nigel Fothergill and Sarah Parnaby for 'musketeering'.

Author's Note

If in the course of the following story I seem to poke fun at the office of mayor in French provincial towns and villages, may I make it clear that I have done so in a spirit of friendly affection. I have met several French village mayors and they have all been very nice to me. I have never met any mayor, past or present, of St-Philippe-d'Aiguille, Ste-Foy-la-Grande or Castillon-la-Bataille. The *maires* of these real places, mentioned or depicted in this book, are entirely fictional, as is the rest of the cast of characters.

Part One

1987

Crisis? What Crisis?

ONE

Christopher didn't paint.

He painted the hulls of boats and their cabins and their fittings. But he didn't paint in the way that Tom did. He wasn't a painter in the sense that Tom was.

Yet Tom didn't consider himself a painter in the way that some of their friends were painters. Those friends who made their livings as artists, and saw their work exhibited in the galleries of the Rue de Seine in Paris. Tom was just an amateur, a dabbler, he told everyone. Just an amateur, he told himself. He made his living helping to manage a boatyard in Boulogne-sur-Mer in northern France. Just as Christopher did.

Christopher always praised Tom's canvasses. 'They're very saleable,' he often said.

And sell they occasionally did. The wall inside the big hangar that was the boat shed was a good place to display the occasional big framed canvas with a price tag attached. Suitably dark for most of the time, the wall was lit spectacularly by the light of day whenever the big doors were slid open. And from time to time a customer who had arranged to have his boat re-painted, taken out of the water for the winter, or re-rigged, would be caught off his guard by the sudden appearance of Tom's latest work in oils and reach into his wallet there and then. Most of Tom's paintings were of boats.

But today, for a change, he was showing Christopher a painting he'd just completed whose subject was a large crab atop a heap of mussels and other assorted molluscs.

'Like in a fish shop,' Christopher said. 'And yet it's not. A still life, but the life isn't still. It's all going on happening.'

'Like in the market,' Tom said. 'You know how the crabs totter about and fall off the table tops. I got the idea from there.' For the crab at the centre of the composition was very much alive. It was rearing up from behind the heap of motionless mussels and reaching up with its gaping pincers. It might have been begging for its life, or else shaking its fists at fate in the manner of Beethoven. It would depend how the viewer wanted to interpret it.

'It's brilliant,' said Christopher encouragingly. 'You can see the glint in its little eyes. The life in its mouthparts… And you say you're not a proper painter because you can't paint the human face…'

'It's not the same,' said Tom patiently. 'A crab's face is like a Darth Vader mask. You can't see the personality behind it. And then there's the question of likeness. I can paint a face that's clearly human; that's no problem. And this is clearly a crab; no question about that. But I haven't had to capture an individual likeness. Nobody's going to worry about which particular crab it's meant to be. It's not someone's aunt.'

That was the day the letter arrived from John.

Christopher had been thinking – just this day, at work in the boatyard – that there were times in life when nothing seemed to change. Day after day everything stayed the same. It was like the middle section of a voyage. The places you'd left behind had vanished from view; the places you were going to were not yet in sight. There was just the seemingly unending sea around you, wave repeating after wave…

Tom opened the letter. 'Oh Christ,' he said. He turned to Christopher, his face drained of everything that was recognisably himself. 'John's writing from England. With news of Angelo. He says Angelo's got aids.'

'I don't believe it,' Christopher said. He got up from the office desk. His movements felt unreal, as if they were being made by someone else. He walked round to where Tom stood, on the floor of the big shed, surrounded by boats and bits of boats, but now Tom looked somehow punctured by the news, crumpled like the paper he held in his hand. He seemed to hang in the huge space like an empty set of clothes.

'It can't be true,' Christopher said. He arrived at Tom's side and peered over his shoulder at what he was reading; Tom held it slightly towards him so that he could more easily see it. Tom's hands shook slightly as he held it. Silently they read the two-page tragedy that had been typed by their friend John. Their TV-scriptwriting friend John Moyse, whose more usual written output consisted of successful sit-com scripts.

TWO

Aids had touched everyone eventually. If only with the long tentacles of uncertainty that fringed the black hole at the centre of it. At first it only frightened gay men who had a lot of casual sex. Then it turned out that heterosexual people could catch it. Drug-users who injected and who shared needles with friends in the interest of economy. Babies in the womb. You could get it from a blood transfusion: public spirited people who, unknown to themselves, were infected by the virus had donated it along with their blood. Many happily married western women discovered that their faithful husbands were actually promiscuous bisexuals, and those that didn't discover that still worried whether perhaps that might be the case. By the time Margaret Thatcher's government launched the Don't Die of Ignorance media campaign in Britain some experts believed that the whole population of Africa could be wiped out by the pandemic. And the passing of the years had taught gay men who were in stable relationships that a recent history of monogamy was no protection against the fallout from an adventurous past.

'How long is it since we had sex with Angelo?' That wasn't the first question that Tom and Christopher asked each other when they'd finished reading the bombshell letter. All the same it was in the top two or three. When someone close to you disappeared into the black hole you quickly found yourself wondering how near to catastrophe you were yourself.

'How long is it since we had sex with him?' The question was on the tip of Tom's tongue but it was Christopher's tongue that got there first.

'Our first term together at Oxford,' said Tom immediately. 'Twenty years ago. Give or take a few months.'

'You fucked him,' Chris said neutrally.

'So did you,' said Tom. 'At least you said you did.'

You knew what your lover had told you. You could never know what he had not.

'He didn't fuck me, though,' said Christopher. 'And I never sucked him off.'

'All that went for me too,' Tom said. 'His sperm never got inside me.'

'Nor in me,' Christopher added, anxious to underline the point. 'I tossed him off…'

'Any open wounds on your hands at the time? Cuts and scratches?' Tom's question sounded equally anxious.

'Not that I remember. You…?'

'Ditto, ditto,' said Tom. 'Yes, I did pull his cock and yes, he did come over me. I don't remember any gaping wounds, though.' Yes, Tom thought, but would I remember a scratch?

Christopher breathed out audibly. 'So we're both in with a good chance of being safe.'

'It's twenty years, Chris,' Tom said reasonably. 'Twenty years. I think we're over the incubation period now.' But were they? The disease had only been identified half a dozen years ago. Did anybody, could anybody, know what the incubation period was?

Christopher said, in a voice that had turned gravelly, 'We're both thinking about ourselves, you notice. Shouldn't we be thinking about Angelo a bit?'

'Where does John say he is?' Tom picked up the letter again and re-read it carefully. 'Um… He says he was working in a remote parish in the fens. Somewhere near Ely. But that's where he *was*. He doesn't know where he's gone to now.'

'Are his parents still alive?' Christopher asked.

'It doesn't say in the letter,' said Tom a bit curtly.

'I didn't mean that,' said Christopher. 'I meant, do you remember? Did either of us know if his parents…?' He left the question unfinished. 'He had a sister, didn't he?' His mind went back to a chance meeting with the whole family twenty-five years ago on the steps of the cathedral right here in Boulogne.

'Yes he did,' said Tom, grasping firmly at a more insistent memory. Of the thirteen-year-old Angelo waving to him from the window of the family car, sitting alongside his sister in the back – Tom remembered that detail clearly – as the family drove down towards the ferry port. That had been the morning after the meeting outside the cathedral. It was lodged painfully in Tom's memory because Tom had been embracing Michel out on the pavement of the Rue Hamy at the time. Michel had been wearing nothing except a dressing gown. And Tom, who was a teacher at the school in England where Angelo was a pupil, would have to face the boy in a few days' time at work.

'We need to talk to John,' said Christopher. 'We need to phone him.'

'Yes,' Tom agreed. 'But not right this minute. Tonight, when we've had time to collect our thoughts.'

'Do we tell the others?' Christopher asked. He was three years younger than Tom. Even now that he was forty-four that remained the case, and he still deferred to Tom's opinion out of habit. Most of the time at least.

'Of course we tell the others,' Tom said. Then a customer appeared in the doorway of the office with a question about spray-paints and the discussion came to a temporary halt.

The others meant Michel and Armand. They lived in a large sea-facing apartment at Wimereux, a couple of miles up the coast. That was where Tom and Christopher drove to that afternoon when they finished work.

They would have phoned to say they were coming over, that there was something they needed to talk about, but as it happened Michel phoned them first. It was Tom who picked the phone up.

'Any chance you could drop by later?' was Michel's opener. 'We're moving some things around. Pictures. Furniture. We could do with your thoughts. Actually…' Michel's voice softened, became more candid, 'we could do with your muscles, truth be told. Help with the big stuff.'

Tom laughed. 'Of course.' He went on to say that he'd been just about to phone Michel. There was something they needed to talk about. He left it at that.

The drive to Wimereux took less than ten minutes from the part of Boulogne where they lived. The road joined the seafront then climbed the limestone cliff. When the weather was good the road showed you England across the sea for a brief moment, and green fields and hills to landward, then dropped down abruptly to deposit you in Wimereux's neat, bourgeois seaside streets.

Michel and Armand were already halfway down the stairs coming to meet them by the time Tom and Christopher started climbing up. Michel, tall – and filling out a bit these days – coming down first. Armand, three years younger and still willowy in his early forties, a couple of paces behind and higher, grinning his welcome over the top of Michel's head.

The summer afternoon's light flooded the room they were shown into. Sky and sea, sun-silvered, filled the big windows that opened onto the balcony. They would be out on the balcony later. But first there was furniture to shift.

'We've bought one of those tall fridge-freezers,' Armand said. 'We've had to take down the big picture in the utility room. And now we have to rearrange everything before we can hang it back up.'

'Where do you want it?' Tom asked.

'The picture? In the second bedroom,' Michel answered. 'But the bookcase will have to go in the hall.'

'Where there isn't room at the moment because of the chest…' said Christopher.

'Well spotted,' said Armand. 'We need to move that.'

It was like one of those mathematical-spatial puzzles, Tom thought. Or was it what people were starting to call the domino effect?

The four of them spent the next half hour sorting the puzzle out. Sometimes Tom found one of his hands cupped intimately over Michel's or Armand's as together they hauled awkwardly shaped pieces of furniture about. You could never forget that a particular friend had once been a lover. You didn't say anything about that subject as your hands came into accidental contact but at those electric moments you each knew precisely the other's thoughts.

And that old relationship, part of the thing they now thought of as 'the big boyfriend swap' was relevant to the situation Tom and Christopher had come over to talk about.

They were sitting over espressos on the balcony, relaxing after their furniture-moving exercise, when Tom at last brought the heavy subject up.

'So very sorry,' both Michel and Armand said when Tom told them of Angelo's fate. In all the years of knowing Tom and Christopher they had never actually met Angelo. But they knew only too clearly how important a role he had played in things. How his existence had impinged on all their lives. Now there was a new connection. A potential new connection at any rate. When it came to sexually transmitted diseases you didn't need to have a personal connection with every link in the long chain. It was another example, Tom now thought, of the domino effect.

'We thought we'd led a charmed life,' said Armand soberly. 'The four of us. All of us here in Boulogne. And Benoît and René, Thierry and Robert…' A sudden worry showed itself on his face. 'Did you ever…?'

'No,' said Tom firmly. He looked at Christopher.

'No,' Christopher said. 'Not with any of them.'

Tom looked enquiringly back at Armand. 'No,' said Armand and then, 'No,' Michel said. There was silence for a moment.

'There were all those people in Paris,' said Christopher in a very flat tone of voice.

'Again it was years ago,' said Michel. 'It can't go endlessly back.'

'It was before we went to Oxford,' said Christopher. For the moment no-one picked up on the significance of that.

No paintings hung outside on the balcony, but they were everywhere else in the apartment. They were Michel's paintings of course. Armand, like Christopher, didn't paint. Though, like Christopher and Tom, he'd often been painted by Michel – nude when younger – and the evidence of that was displayed quite openly on several walls of the apartment among Michel's other work. Those nude paintings sometimes caused a widening of the eyes and a few sideways glances from unsuspecting men who came to read the meters or to service the central heating equipment.

Michel was a little bit famous as an artist. His early seascapes had given way to portraits, and pictures of naked boys and men. Those had been the preserve of his teacher Gérard previously, but in the public's mind the terrain was now firmly Michel's. But even the very famous are only famous among the people who know they're famous. Michel was famous when he attended exhibitions of his own work at the Gallerie Laval in Paris; but he was just a man who had a problem with his boiler when someone came to fix it, casting uneasy looks at the naked youths depicted in oils all round the place. There was also a third, in-between, case. Among the market traders of Boulogne, and the fish-stall holders Michel was vaguely known to be a little bit of a celebrity. A little bit famous for something, though none of them knew – let alone cared – for what.

The other thing about fame that Michel had discovered was that you couldn't actually eat it. It didn't work the way a luncheon voucher did. He still had to paint new work to earn his daily crust.

'Are you still in touch with those Paris guys?' Michel asked.

'No,' Tom answered. 'None of them. Well, Gérard of course…'

'So you don't know if any of them…' Michel began, but Armand cut him off.

'We don't need to cross our bridges before we come to them.' (We, Tom thought.) 'If you're worried, go to Paris and get a test.' Armand thought for a second and did the obvious calculation. 'Perhaps we all should.'

'Perhaps,' said Tom. 'But first we need to get in touch with Angelo. Find out from John exactly where he is. Just … well, make contact with him. For friendship's sake.'

'Who's John? Remind me?' Michel asked, shaking his head.

'John Moyse. Our only link with Angelo these days. They were fellow pupils at the school where we taught. John makes a living writing TV scripts.' Tom saw a certain look on Michel's face. 'He isn't gay,' he added quickly. 'His friendship with Angelo was never like that. John's married, with a wife.'

'So I should hope,' said Armand, smiling again at last. 'A bit odd to be married without a wife.'

'The thing is,' said Christopher, 'that when it comes to contacting Angelo and getting tested, the test ought to come first.'

Tom looked at him. 'Um … why?'

'We keep trying to reassure ourselves that we couldn't have picked the virus up from Angelo. But, all those years ago when we … you know…'

'When we had sex with him…'

'We'd lived in Paris and done all that stuff first.'

Tom thought for a moment. 'You're not saying Angelo could have picked it up from one of us?'

Christopher nodded. 'I think perhaps I am,' he said.

THREE

They were still out on the balcony an hour later, though they'd moved on from coffee to glasses of Pastis with ice and water. 'Of course you've never met Angelo,' Tom said, and wondered as he said it whether he was using an appropriate tense.

'I saw him once,' Michel answered. 'Waving from the back window of his parents' car when he was a kid.'

'Yes,' said Tom. 'With his sister next to him. Turning round and looking at us. It's engraved on my retina.'

Michel frowned. 'You didn't actually see that,' he said carefully. 'You had your back to the scene. I told you about it after the car had disappeared down the Rue Faidherbe. They were going to catch the morning ferry, I think.'

Tom sat silent and thoughtful for a moment. Then he said, 'You're right, of course. I never saw Angelo wave to me. I never saw his sister sitting next to him. It was only because you mentioned it … and because I'd seen him with his sister and his parents outside the cathedral the day before… But … somehow … the scene is lodged in my memory. Because the moment was so important, I suppose. I've thought back to it so often over the years. It's turned itself into a visual memory – as if it was my own…' He stopped, and returned to looking thoughtful.

'That happens to artists,' said Michel, a sly smile tweaking the corners of his mouth. 'Talking of which, how's the crab painting coming?'

'He finished it this morning,' Christopher answered for him. 'In between phone-calls and varnishing someone else's deck. It's very good.'

It was good, Christopher had no doubt about it. But he no longer liked it. The news about Angelo had come too close to it. The image of the crab – whose Latin name after all was cancer – had become one with

Christopher's previously vague mental image of the aids virus, so that that now had a physical shape. It was up on its eight spindly legs, rearing up, stalking about, its gaping pincers brandished aloft… *querens quem devoret* – seeking whom it might devour. Like the Devil in the psalm. *Tamquam leo rugiens circuit* – it goeth about roaring like a lion. *Cui resistites, fortes in fide.* But you, well-grounded in the faith, resist it.

But there was no resisting the aids virus, Christopher thought. No amount of grounding in the faith could help you resist the virus once you'd caught it. Your faith – Angelo's faith – might defeat the Devil, but was powerless against the virus.

'I don't suppose it makes it any worse,' Armand's words cut in on Christopher's meditation, 'but it does give an extra awful frisson: the fact of Angelo being a priest.'

They didn't phone John that night. They did it the next morning – actually Tom did it while Christopher stood nervously next to him – from the office phone at the boatyard. Somehow you felt stronger making a difficult call seated at your office desk than you did standing in the hallway of your apartment.

'So sorry to drop that on you by letter,' John's voice said once his wife had brought him out to the phone from his writing den. 'I should have phoned really.'

'Don't think about it,' Tom reassured him. 'That would have been even more difficult for all of us. Look, the thing is, Chris and I will want to come over and see Angelo. You said he was working near Ely but now you don't know…'

'The order is being very secretive. Which is highly understandable. The press would have a field day if this got out.'

Tom sighed. He could see the headlines in his mind. *RC Priest AIDS Shock.* He knew that John could see those headlines too; he didn't need to spell them out. 'Are you saying they won't tell you where he is?'

'That's about the size of it,' John said.

'His parents,' Tom said. 'Are they still…?'

'Both dead.'

'Perhaps that's just as well.' Tom remembered that Angelo's QC father's uncompromising attitude to his son's early homosexual exploits had had a major impact on all their subsequent lives. 'His sister?'

'Still around, apparently. But I don't know her number or address.'

There was silence from Tom's end. John had to ask, 'Are you still there?'

'Yes,' Tom said. 'I think we'd still like to come over anyway. See you at least. Try and track Angelo down if we can. But there's something we need to do first.'

'What's that?' John asked.

'For reasons that you won't need to be told, Chris and I would like to take an aids test. It means a trip to Paris.'

They bought a copy of that week's Gai Pied and found the Paris clinic listed among its Useful Phone Numbers. There was no need to make appointments, they were told when they called the clinic: they had just to turn up.

But they couldn't just turn up in Paris. Gérard would be deeply upset if he heard from some other source that they'd gone to the capital and not gone to see him. So Christopher phoned their old benefactor, told him they would be travelling to Paris one day later in the week, though not why, and asked if they could look him up. Yes, Gérard told him. He was sure to be in, whichever day it was. In the big old house where, now over eighty, he still lived as an almost recluse.

The streets of Montmartre would have been raw-edged with memories for them both, had not more recent, more casual, visits knocked some of the corners off. So that going to see Gérard in the crumbling house in the Rue St-Vincent had become simply one more trip to a place they often visited – rather than a brutal re-encounter with a place in which they'd lived with a gaggle of art students, had sex with too many of them, and then felt obliged to move out of. Leaving under a cloud they called that.

They pushed open the gate. The garden was a jungle these days. It had been wild and unkempt twenty years ago, but in the way that delighted Edwardian poets. A place where – as Octave Charpentier had put it, *blackbirds, sparrows and chaffinches greet the dawn with a joyous fanfare. Lilac, ivy, hop, vine and clematis make cradles for their hidden nests.* All that was still true, and the birds certainly loved the place none the less. But it was no longer a garden that aspired to Bohemian wilderness; it was a wilderness with scarcely a hint of garden about it. They walked up to the front door, along the line of what they had once thought of as the path, and knocked. Then they waited patiently for Gérard to descend the stairs and let them in.

Gérard was in slippers and dressing gown, though with socks inside the slippers and with trousers, shirt and cardigan beneath the dressing gown. September wasn't finished yet and the sun still had some strength in it. What would Gérard do to ward off the cold when it began to bite seriously in December? How many dressing gowns did he have? But they had wondered that for the past five years – since the death of Gérard's partner Henri. Yet each spring Gérard somehow managed to re-surface, like a tortoise that has spent the winter underground in a hay-filled box.

He was delighted to see them. Wine and glasses appeared on the kitchen table with exemplary dispatch. He wanted news: that was the big thing; it always would be from now on; as time passed so he had less and less news of his own to impart.

They had to tell him what had brought them all the way to Paris. *'Bon Dieu,'* he said and shook his head. 'Time was when one of the privileges of being homosexual was that you couldn't catch anything you'd die of. That and the fact you couldn't make your partners pregnant by accident, of course.'

'You couldn't make them pregnant on purpose either,' Tom couldn't resist pointing out.

Gérard made a noise in his throat. It was what these days passed for him as a laugh. He said, 'Well, you could if you took certain steps – like going to bed with a lady – but I take your point.'

Drinking at this kitchen table... It seemed like only yesterday they'd sat here with the others. Young Alain and Marcel. And Charles, who hadn't seemed quite so young back then but now, with twenty-five years' hindsight, did. The furniture around them hadn't changed, just grown a bit decrepit; the familiarity of it was nice. The only thing that seemed difficult to connect with among a host of memories was the fact that they'd both been to bed with Gérard and, all those years ago, had all had sex.

'I shan't be taking the test myself,' said Gérard suddenly, as though he'd been travelling along the same uncomfortable line of thought. 'Too late for me at my age. I'd rather not know. Something will get me some time, and if it's SIDA so be it. I won't be passing it on to anyone else.'

Most acronyms were the same in French and English. They anagrammed each other; that was the only difference.

'On which subject,' Christopher said, trying to make this sound casual, though for him at that moment it was anything but, 'Have you heard anything of Charles? Of Alain and Marcel?' Either Tom or he would ask this question every year or so, it was a ritual part of the conversation. The answer had been no for some ten years now, and it was no this time. The only difference about the question today was the reason for asking it.

'They none of them persevered,' said Gérard. 'They all had talent as artists.' He looked at them both rather intently for a moment. 'But as you know, talent is not enough.'

Was he thinking about his own case? Christopher wondered. Forty and fifty years ago – before they knew him – Gérard had been the darling of Montmartre, his work the talk of the Parisian art-buying class. Then Michel, his pupil, had risen from the ranks some twenty years ago to steal his general's epaulettes. Gérard's young male nudes were out of fashion suddenly, while Michel's, which were extremely similar in style and character, were now the saleroom favourites. Gérard had accepted the capsize philosophically. That was how the world went, he'd say if anyone asked him about it. If the upset had been a blow to his pride or self-esteem he'd never shown any sign of it, while as for his pocket … he'd been lucky to have Henri for a life-partner. Henri who was a high-up at the Banque National de Paris. And though Henri was now sadly dead he had at least left Gérard very comfortably off. Christopher peered around the shabby kitchen as these thoughts ran through his head. Gérard was indeed well off but, looking at the kitchen with its ancient gas stove and sink, you could see no evidence of the fact.

Gérard stood up. 'Come see the pictures,' he said. It was a fair enough command. There was little point having a house stuffed full of paintings, your own and other people's, if you didn't look at them yourself, or if you didn't show them off to those who came to visit you, even if they'd seen them a hundred times before and knew every brush-stroke by heart.

So they rambled around the crooked corridors, went into musty bedrooms. The bedroom in which they'd once slept. The bedroom that had been Charles's, the one inhabited then by Alain and Marcel, who were partners. All were untenanted now and would probably remain so until Gérard's death. Then what would happen to the house? Christopher wondered. He pushed away the disrespectful thought.

When Michel in the course of his career as a painter had moved away from his old subjects of ships, seascapes and townscapes, and entered Gérard's territory of young male nudes Gérard had headed across to Michel's old stamping ground and had busied himself with painting ships. Among the many canvasses that Tom and Christopher now found themselves looking at there was a fairly evenly balanced selection of both types. And among the male nudes, inevitably, were pictures of themselves, on the beach at Audresselles and in other places. Themselves at the age of twenty or less, and disconcertingly slim and lithe.

Tom thought about the matter of likeness as he looked at the pictures of Christopher and himself. A portrait painter was expected to capture the fugitive essence that was called likeness in his subject's face. But did the same rule apply to everything else? Throughout history the legs of kings and rulers had been depicted as impressively muscular and well-shaped. But had this always been an accurate rendering of the truth? He looked carefully now at his own and Christopher's painted legs. Gérard had done a good job back then, Tom thought. Even if you were to hold something up to mask their two faces Christopher's legs (and arms and chest) were recognizably Christopher's, and Tom's were recognizably his.

The focus of Tom's attention now homed in on their two groin areas and in particular their two cocks. Tom was well aware that in the twenty-six years he'd known Christopher and was used to seeing him naked the physiognomy of their two dicks had altered less than that of any other part of them. He also knew that he would recognise them both anywhere and always be able to tell t'other from which, the way a mother of identical twins could always (it was said) tell her progeny apart.

Not that Tom's dick and Christopher's were identical – though both were similarly uncut. Tom's was slightly bigger and neither of them had a problem with that. Tom was, after all, a slightly bigger chap. He looked carefully now at Gérard's depictions of their two organs to see if his brush-strokes had reflected this. In fact they had, Tom noticed. Where size was concerned Gérard had got the detail right. As far as anything else went… Well, Tom had to admit he couldn't really tell the difference between them. It was like his picture of the crab's face. You weren't expected to care exactly which crab it was. Tom smiled wryly to himself as he thought back through the career changes he'd made during his life. From teacher to shop assistant. From barman to personal assistant for Michel. From there to the joint management of a boatyard. And where painting was concerned he'd gone from being an artists' model to trying his luck as an amateur painter himself. Thanks to Michel's encouragement.

Michel. In pinching Gérard's territory, however unwittingly and innocently, Michel had also pinched his models. None of them would forget that the painting that first brought Michel to public notice was his first nude study of Christopher and Tom. That Gérard had borne no ill-will towards Michel or Tom or Christopher, either at the time or in all the years since, was a measure, they all thought, of the man's great good-heartedness and generosity of spirit.

'And now you must see the two biblical chaps,' said Gérard at last. They knew exactly which picture Gérard meant by that. It hung in his own bedroom in pride of place. The huge canvas that Molly O'Deere had painted – her signature and the year, 1962, were clearly visible in the bottom left-hand corner of it – and whose subject was David and Jonathan … and for whom the models had been young Christopher McGing and Thomas Sanders.

'Hmm,' said Tom as he confronted it. There wasn't much more to be said. That picture had haunted their lives and dogged their footsteps. Although neither of them appeared naked – except as to their chests – the picture had caused a sensation that Molly, art mistress of the Star of the Sea prep school where Tom and Christopher had both taught, had hardly envisaged when she painted it.

The picture had hung in a public exhibition in Canterbury cathedral. The Kent Messenger had reviewed it in startling terms, its critic for the occasion gushing, *Young male beauty at its most virile is here celebrated with unrestrained passion and delight. Passion and delight also illuminate the faces and inform the figures of the two young men, their mutual enchantment plain to see.* The arresting qualities of the painting had even been picked up by the nationals: it was reviewed by the Times under the headline 'Libido in the Cathedral'. It had caused the thirteen-year-old Angelo to make a pass at his friend John Moyse (not until later would Tom and Christopher learn that) and had played no small part in Tom and Christopher's resignation from their posts and their urgent flight to France.

There had been a time when they had jokingly indulged the fantasy that the picture might have grown old while they stayed young, but on catching up with it some years after it was painted and seeing it again it had been borne in on them most forcefully that the opposite was the case.

The David and Jonathan had become theirs briefly – a gift from Angelo, of all people; he'd found it while clearing a monastic cellar out – and they in turn had made a gift of it to Gérard, who had always wanted it. Looking at it now, hanging here in Paris, neither Tom nor Christopher would have been able to say how they felt about it. It wasn't just a painting. It never had been. It was a time capsule that encompassed their lives before and after its execution. And – you only had to look at it, as the Times art critic had noted publicly – to see that it told the world the truth about their love.

FOUR

It would have been easier if they'd had a definite appointment; a time to keep. As it was Gérard kept trying to make them stay. To have another glass of wine and then another one… They had better not, they eventually said. They were going for a blood test. More coffee, then. Or tea – seeing as they were still English despite more than half a lifetime each of living in France. The clinic wouldn't be closing its doors any time soon, Gérard thought. No, they said, but they needed to get back to Boulogne – it was a two-hour-plus train ride – before tonight. Why not stay the night? Gérard offered. Return to Boulogne refreshed… Work, they answered. They had taken one day off from the boatyard; they were expected back. Their master shipwright Luc was managing the place for them today. He would need them back in the morning. At least they told Gérard he would.

They walked down to the bottom of the hill of Montmartre. Past the Sacré Coeur and down the picturesque Calvary Steps. Those near-vertical, tourist-familiar steps held big memories for them both but they didn't want to think, let alone speak, of them at this moment. They caught the metro train at Place Pigalle. The carriage was full and they had to stand, hanging from straps. Christopher glanced at Tom's face. It wore a haggard look, like the face of someone on his way to face a firing-squad. Christopher wondered if his own face wore a similar look. Neither of them spoke.

It was seven stops. It might have been seventy times seven. Or a mere fourteen, like the Stations of the Cross. Whatever it might have been, the company of an ageing man, company that had grown increasingly uncomfortable as their visit extended from a Tom-and-Christopher-planned one hour to a Gérard-acceptable two, and from which they had been only too eager to escape, now seemed infinitely preferable to this journey underground – as their destination grew closer with what seemed like a thumbscrew's agonising slowness.

Belleville was workaday, rough old Paris; few interesting buildings graced it. It was a corner of Paris, east of the Gare de l'Est, that the tourists rarely saw. But the clinic was housed in a clean modern building that was bright inside and seemed somehow full of hope. 'We've come to take tests against aids,' Tom announced, speaking for them both. *'...Tests contre le SIDA.'*

The friendly young lady nurse who had greeted them now corrected Tom's choice of preposition. *'...Tests* ***pour*** *le SIDA. On ne peut rien faire* ***contre*** *le SIDA.'* Tests *for* aids. There was nothing that could be done *against* it. She smiled and looked them up and down. Her eyes twinkled with something that lay between compassion and amusement. 'Why do you think you need testing?' she asked them both.

Christopher decided it was his turn to say something. This would often happen when Tom had been leading the conversation for a bit. 'A friend of ours has been diagnosed with aids in England. We both had sex with him.'

'How recently?' asked their nurse gently.

'Nineteen years – or twenty,' Christopher said. Even as he uttered the words they sounded silly.

The nurse shook her head lightly. 'Then there is practically no risk at all,' she said. 'Which is good news, don't you think? Come on, let's get you tested.' She added, 'One at a time, I think,' when both men tried to barge through the door together behind her.

A gloved hand. A needle-prick in the thumb. Then it was over. They were out in the streets of Belleville again, under a bright afternoon sky that was crowded with plane trees. Some of the leaves were beginning to turn yellow. It gave the place a festive look they hadn't noticed when they'd arrived from the metro fifteen minutes earlier.

They had to wait a fortnight for the results. It was good that their own belief that the risk they stood in was minute had been confirmed officially. But even so, a risk was a risk and a fortnight was a fortnight. There might be only a one-in-twenty-million risk that you'd die in an accident this morning. But if you were that one person in the twenty million… It felt like a very long fortnight.

Christopher's envelope arrived by post on a Saturday. There was no envelope for Tom. Tom stood silently while Christopher tore open his envelope. It was only when his breath came out in a noisy puff that Christopher realised he'd been holding it for long seconds. 'I don't have aids,' he said to Tom. 'I'm HIV negative.'

They couldn't celebrate properly. Tom still didn't have his results. It was a cruel chance that Christopher's letter had come on the Saturday. There was no post on Sunday. Tom had to wait till Monday. They spent the Sunday doing odd jobs at the boatyard; it seemed the best thing to be doing. Then, when the post came on Monday morning there was an envelope for Tom and a re-run of Saturday. Only this time it was Tom who slit the envelope while forgetting to breathe and Christopher who stood stock still, watching. 'It's good,' Tom said. 'I'm negative.' Only then did they contact Michel and Armand. The four of them went out for a restaurant dinner to celebrate.

There was no need for Michel and Armand to get themselves tested, they decided. No need for Tom or Christopher to try and track down Charles or Marcel or Alain, or anybody else for that matter. They did call Gérard and he expressed his satisfaction with the news, although he was hardly surprised by it. It now remained, though, to contact John about trying to find Angelo. They phoned him late that evening.

John said how happy he was to hear about the results of their aids tests. But he had news of his own. It was less of a cause for celebration than Tom's and Christopher's, but more surprising. He said, 'I've managed to track down Angelo's sister.'

'How?' asked Christopher who was doing the phoning.

'She works at the BBC. I'll explain how I found her when I see you. The bad news is that she doesn't want to talk to me about Angelo. I rang her and she put the phone down on me.'

'Ah,' said Christopher. He thought, how like a woman, but didn't risk lowering himself in John's estimation by saying it. 'Perhaps we can make some progress when we come over.' This sounded very presumptuous in his own ears. 'Sorry,' he said at once. 'I didn't mean that we could succeed where you…'

'It's quite OK,' John interrupted him. 'When are you thinking of coming?'

'We could travel in a couple of days' time. Malcolm's coming here tomorrow. With his car. We could go back with him, make our base at his place… Mind you, we haven't told him yet. Can we confirm with you tomorrow?'

Malcolm was Tom and Christopher's boss. He was the owner of the boatyard. He was also one of the people whom Christopher would not now be obliged to contact in connection with the result of his aids test. This was a matter of some relief to Christopher. It was something that Tom didn't know about: the fact that Christopher and Malcolm had once, though only once, together had sex.

For some reason Malcolm had decided to cross from Dover to Calais rather than coming directly into

Boulogne from Folkestone. It was swings and roundabouts, though. Dover was nearer to his home in Sandwich, and perhaps he rather enjoyed the scenic switchback drive along the Opal coast on the French side, past Caps Blanc and Gris Nez, He liked driving, as he enjoyed sailing, and always ran an old Jaguar. Every time one of them lost the will to live, Tom and Christopher used to say to each other, he replaced it with an even older one.

He pulled up on the quayside at the Bassin Napoléon in the middle of the afternoon; the lavender blue XJ6 proclaimed his nationality just as loudly as his accent would do the moment he opened his mouth and tried to make French come out of it. At fifty-five Malcolm was still big, muscular and handsome, though his Duracell copper thatch of hair had inevitably dimmed and greyed a bit. He smiled as he walked towards the boat shed and when Tom and Christopher walked out to meet him, greeted them both with a hug. He was that sort of boss.

He didn't visit Boulogne often. Twice a year at the most these days, since the demise of his big old boat, the Orca. He trusted Tom and Christopher to run things honestly and smoothly. He had another boatyard to run in Sandwich; that one he managed himself. His visits to the Boulogne boatyard were in the nature of friendly audits: a chance to catch up with what was going on, to discuss any problems that had arisen in the previous six months. There was never any talk of expanding the business further. Malcolm's acquisition of the Boulogne outfit ten years earlier had been the limit of the business's operational potential.

Another reason for Malcolm's visits was frankly social. He liked the company of Tom and Christopher (even without the complication of sex), and had done since they'd met twenty-five years ago, long before he'd thought of employing them as staff. Michel and Armand too, whom he'd known for almost as long.

The five of them dined together that evening in Tom and Christopher's apartment near the fish market. Christopher cooked. He did a Spanish-style dish of hake with white wine, parsley and garlic.

'Seems like I'm taking them away from you for a few days,' Malcolm said to Michel and Armand. 'Think you'll be able to cope?' He smiled. The smile of a well-fed tom-cat, Christopher had always thought.

'I think we'll manage,' Armand said, smiling back. Though the boatyard would of course be run in their absence by the more than capable Luc, their shipwright.

Earlier that afternoon, while Malcolm was admiring Tom's portrait of the crab rearing up from its bed of mussels, Tom had explained the need for him and Christopher to spend a few days in England; he had asked if they could have seats in his car for the journey there and a bed for a night or two at the house he shared with his partner in Sandwich. All of which Malcolm had said yes to without so much as raising a ginger eyebrow. Now, between mouthfuls of hake, he asked the French pair, 'Did you two know Angelo?'

'No,' Michel said. 'It just feels like it.'

Malcolm gave a wry half-laugh. 'Same here. Half-Italian, isn't he? I never met him, but I seem to have known him all my life. Follows me around like a shadow, I sometimes think.'

'Not for much longer, perhaps,' said Christopher and then thought – as he often did – that before opening his mouth he should have thought first. Because that remark certainly put a damper on the conversation for the next few minutes.

At last Malcolm came up with a new subject 'There's something I ought to get off my chest too,' he said. 'And I may as well do it with all of you here. Roger's sixty-five now.' Roger was Malcolm's long-time partner. In addition to Malcolm's two boatyards the two men ran a pub. Roger was the owner of the pub. The significance of the number sixty-five was not lost on the others. They listened with ears pricked up for what was coming next. 'We're going to get out of the pub. In other words, sell it. And I'm thinking about… Only thinking, mind, but I want Tom and Chris to be in on my thoughts… I'm thinking I might sell the yard at the Bassin Napoléon. Just hold on to the one at Sandwich.'

There was a bit of a frisson in the room. 'It's only maybe,' Malcolm quickly added. 'And it wouldn't be yet in any case. I just thought you should know. All of you.' The 'all of you' was not out of place. Malcolm had originally bought the Boulogne boatyard during the era of the big boyfriend swap. It hadn't been Christopher and Tom who had managed it for him back then but Christopher and Armand. It was also during that period that Malcolm had for the one and only time had sex with Christopher. It was only since that event that he had taken to calling Christopher Chris. Apart from Tom nobody else – not even his mother – called Christopher Chris.

FIVE

It was seven the following evening, a few minutes before sunset, when the three of them set off for Calais, Tom in the passenger seat alongside Malcolm, Christopher in the back. Christopher had a twenty-five-year-old memory of sitting in a car's front seat while Malcolm drove it. Tom hadn't been there to keep an eye on things then, though he was here now. All the same, Christopher thought it wise to sit in the back.

They had decided to eat when they got to Calais, then catch a ferry that would get them to Dover around midnight. Sunsets always looked magical from the coast road but there wasn't much of a sunset this evening. Instead a bank of dark cloud in the distant west rose above the sea like a wall of black. By the time they reached the point at Cap Gris Nez the dark cloud had been swallowed by the oncoming night and flashes from the lighthouse, one every six seconds, provided the only occasional outside light.

The road turned sharply east after the cape, following the roll of the coastal hills along the cliff to Calais. As they crossed the summit of Cap Blanc Nez fifteen minutes later the lights of the town and the port came suddenly into sight, spread out ahead of them, below them. And at that point, flump, flump, flump, flump, flump.

'Shit,' said Malcolm. He slowed the car to a stop. 'Just what we need.'

The puncture was on the nearside – which was safer at least – and at the back. But it took a while to change the wheel. One of the wheel-nuts had an anti-theft device, a wheel-spanner within a wheel-spanner, which had to be rummaged for in the boot. And then the nuts themselves, un-tampered with for years, were stiff. It was fortunate that they were three men together. Three sets of muscles to take turns with the wheel-spanner. And a hammer that Malcolm kept handy in the boot. Even so, by the time they were on the move again – driving rather slowly because Malcolm wasn't sure if the pressure in the spare tyre was equal to that in the wheel opposite it – they were running seriously late.

They drove straight to the ferry terminal but were now too late for the ferry they intended to catch. The next one, they were told, would sail just after midnight. That gave them time, though, to drive back into the town centre and get something to eat.

A wind had been blowing in Boulogne that afternoon. Coming from the west it had followed them to Calais. They'd noticed, when out on the roadside, changing that wheel high up on Cap Blanc Nez, that that wind had strengthened. It had also become oddly warm. Now here it was again, funnelling along the streets in the centre of Calais. It seemed to be getting warmer by the hour. Which was odd, considering that it was after nine o'clock on a mid-October night.

They ate in a restaurant they knew well in the Place D'Armes. It was a restaurant where all the waiters knew them, and were sympathetic when they explained their reason for turning up so late. 'Last meal in France for a few days,' Tom said, pointing out the rather obvious. But even after all his years of living here he still felt there was something a bit special about meals in France. The waiters allowed Malcolm to use the restaurant's phone – Malcolm gave them a token few francs – to phone Roger in Sandwich, to tell him they would be late, not arriving until the small hours, and he was not to wait up.

The wind hadn't dropped when they returned to the ferry port. It had grown stronger if anything. 'Reckon it's going to be rough?' Tom asked Malcolm. Malcolm was the real sailor among the three of them. They might be managers of his boatyard but they deferred to his knowledge of the sea and ships.

'Could be,' said Malcolm, economically hedging his bets.

The queue of cars ahead of them began to move. A moment later they were driving across the link-span and into the cavernous upper one of the ship's two vehicle decks. Christopher peered out and up, looking for the name of the ship. 'It's the St Christopher,' he said. He had a special affection for the St Christopher. It shared his name for a start. And, that name in any case meaning Christ-carrier, it had connotations of reliability, safety and strength.

Over their years of living in France they had crossed the Channel more times than they could count. Sometimes in the old days with Malcolm and Roger in their sailing smack the Orca, more often by ferry. Boulogne to Folkestone; Calais to Dover. They knew all the ships. The Free Enterprise sister ships on the Calais Dover run, The St Christopher and the St Anselm on the same route. Then the two sister ships, the Hengist and the Horsa on the Folkestone Boulogne route. It was a bit odd, calling them sister ships, Christopher sometimes thought. When Hengist and Horsa had been the Saxon warrior brothers who, fifteen centuries earlier had conquered Kent. Anselm and Christopher were also boys' names. But ships were always she. There was no point worrying about the occasional discrepancies. That was how things had always been and that was that.

They made for the bar once the car was parked and locked. What else did you do on a ferry travelling through the dark in the middle of the night? The crossing took only ninety minutes; these short-crossing ferries weren't equipped with passenger bunks.

The captain's voice came over the public address speakers. 'It has been reported to me that all watertight doors are sealed and secured for sea. We will be departing in a few minutes.' There were safety announcements. Then the captain spoke about the weather ahead. A south-westerly gale was blowing up in the Channel, he told the passengers. The second half of the crossing might be, 'a bit lumpy.' And that was that.

The three men bought pints of English beer: the compensation for the fine cooking of France that they were going to miss. They were all experienced sailors. Even in a force nine gale they were unlikely to be sick. Not even aboard a sailing boat. Certainly not on a vessel of seven thousand tons. A pint of beer, then, was hardly a serious risk.

The beginning of the journey to Dover was something of a retracing of their evening steps. The route followed the coast westward, past Blanc Nez and halfway towards Gris Nez, before turning northward across the open sea towards Kent. Open sea described the Strait of Dover perfectly when a south-westerly was blowing up. For while the landmass of the two capes sheltered the water just off the French coast (it formed a lee shore, as sailors put it) the situation was different once you'd turned north and left the protecting capes behind you. If a wind had been picking up speed as it funnelled into the Channel from the Atlantic you were now exposed to the full force of it.

So it was that night. The first half hour was gently rocky, and curtains of spray swished across the windows of the bar from time to time. But the passengers were very conscious of the change of heading when it came, the northward turn. The ship made it very clear that she was doing this by rolling viciously to the right. Glasses slid across tables and had to be caught. One or two, somewhere across the lounge, could be heard to smash.

The ship returned to the vertical within seconds and began its northbound leg. But the going began to get rougher almost at once. Malcolm was the first to refer to it. 'Hmm,' he said. 'Another whole hour of this.'

By the time even a quarter of that hour had passed Christopher was beginning to wonder about the beer he'd bought. Half of it was already inside him, the other half still inside the glass on the table top. Prudently he wasn't letting the glass out of his hand, but the glass's contents were beginning to slosh around rather a lot. Back and forth. Back and forth. He tried not to think about the beer he'd already swallowed. Whether that was doing the same sort of thing inside his stomach. He wondered whether he would actually want to finish his pint. Malcolm and Tom were also holding tight to their glasses, not drinking very much. Christopher wondered whether they felt the same as he did. He thought about asking them this but decided against it. He had a feeling that whatever they might answer it would only make him feel worse.

Back and forth, back and forth. When the captain had announced that all watertight doors were sealed everyone in the bar had fallen silent for a second or two. They were all thinking the same thing, remembering the same event. The reason why the announcement was being made. Six months earlier the Herald of Free Enterprise, another Dover-based ship, had overturned in Zeebrugge harbour. Despite the shallow water of the harbour over a hundred people had perished. The ship had left its berth with the bow doors still open. As it picked up speed its bow-wave had begun to break over the sill of the car deck. As the quantity of water built up it sloshed about. Back and forth, back and forth. It hadn't taken much. Anyone who had ever tried to carry a roasting pan filled with liquid for even a short distance could have predicted the result.

Tom's voice broke in on Christopher's thoughts. 'Are you feeling OK, Chris?'

'I think so,' Christopher said. Then Tom leaned towards him across the table and put his free hand over the hand that Christopher wasn't holding onto his beer with. He left it there for a second without saying anything, then withdrew it. It wasn't a gesture he would normally have made in the course of a cross-Channel hop.

Some passengers were moving around. Perhaps some were going to the duty-free shop. Christopher rather hoped so. But he suspected that most of them were actually heading towards the toilets rather urgently, in order to be sick.

As the motion increased so did the noise. Groans and thumps were coming from below their feet as cars chafed against their brakes and lorries fidgeted in their chains on the vehicle decks. The waves that were now lifting them several feet every half minute and then dropping them abruptly down again were giving off some of their limitless energy in loud bangs like thunder-claps as they hit the ship. And the tops of the waves that broke against the windows no longer swished like curtains, they smacked against the glass like collapsing walls.

Tom looked at his watch. 'We've been going an hour,' he said. He added optimistically, 'Just thirty more minutes and we'll be in dock.'

'Only if we're making good speed,' said Malcolm. 'And I rather doubt that.'

'We could go and look for a forward-facing window,' said Christopher. 'See if we can see the lights of Dover yet.'

'We won't,' said Malcolm. 'There's mountains of water everywhere. The air will be thick with spray. We wouldn't see through that.'

'We could take a turn around the ship, anyway,' said Christopher hopefully. 'Stretch our legs.'

'I think we're better staying here,' said Malcolm. He looked around. The few people who were up and on their feet were clutching at the pillars and tables to stop themselves falling as they moved about. Then in a gesture more indicative of bravado than prudence Malcolm downed the remainder of his pint. 'Who wants another drink?' he asked.

At that moment the ship experienced a juddering shock. There was a bang like Armageddon. It felt as if you were in a lorry and had run into a solid stone wall that was in front of you and also on your left. Then the whole ship tilted, its port-side rising up, its starboard pitching down towards the depths. There were screams. There was a rumble of moving crockery and furniture, a cacophony of metal against metal from below. Terrifying bangs and thumps through which you nevertheless could just still register the fact that the engines had stopped. All the lights went out.

Christopher abandoned his beer-glass to the fates and held tight to the table instead. From all around came the cries and thumps of the passengers who hadn't managed to do that and were falling, crashing to the floor and sliding down the tilting deck. Women continued to scream above the sound of glass breaking in the darkness. Men were screaming too, but at a lower pitch – emitting the sounds that men prefer to call shouts.

'We're going over!' Tom yelled suddenly in the blackness and nobody contradicted him for a moment. The noise of breaking glass seemed to go on for ever. How ever much glass was there to break? Then, very slowly you could feel the ship's roll lose its downward thrust. Eventually the downward movement stopped. Then, after a second that seemed an eternity it began to come back up. You couldn't see this happening, just feel it in the weight of your limbs and with your inner ear sensors, in the dark. At last the floor was level, but it didn't stop at that. Without pausing the whole ship now began to roll to port. A lesser roll this time, though. When it came back up from that pendulum swing the next roll to starboards was even smaller. Christopher, hearing Tom call his name in panic, was able to think, as he answered Tom and then called out, 'Malcolm?!' that, for the next few seconds at least, they were safe.

'Here,' said Malcolm from the floor beside Christopher. Christopher felt Malcolm's hand touch, then clasp his calf.

'I'll help you up,' said Christopher, and then the emergency lighting kicked in at last, dim and shaky, but at least showing you where you were and what was what.

Tom lay spread-eagled over the table, clasping with white knuckles the rim on Christopher's side of it. Christopher's free hand – the one that wasn't reaching out towards Malcolm – was around the table's solid single pedestal leg, which was mercifully bolted to the deck. Malcolm was the only one of them who had lost his perch. His chair lay a little way away, one of many, many overturned pieces of furniture, and Malcolm was one of many, many people crawling towards their friends and families, or getting un-confidently to their feet.

The sound of breaking glass was finished. The noises from below deck had all but ceased. There remained the sound of the waves outside, combining with the roaring of the wind to make a din so terrible that you wouldn't want to hear it again as long as you lived. But through the row could just be heard the grinding rumble of the engines trying, and trying again, to re-start.

All around people were picking themselves up, looking to their companions, to their nearest and dearest, checking that those they loved were all right. There was a mumble of talking from everywhere. No more screams, but a few people were crying out of fear and shock.

Malcolm was on his feet now, standing up. Holding on to the shoulders of both the others he leant down and kissed first Tom, then Christopher on the lips. None of the three men spoke just yet. Then suddenly one of the engines caught and fired up. Seconds later the other two followed it back into life. The main lights came back on. The mess around them was indescribable. There was a smell that was rank. Of spilled food and drink. Of human sweat. Of more unpleasant bodily excretions, that were also symptoms of fright.

A young male crew member materialised, walking among the tables with a first aid box and a face as white as a sheet. 'Is anybody hurt?' he began to ask everyone. He looked in sore need of treatment for shock himself. It was his appearance, so young and vulnerable – he looked no more than nineteen or twenty – that caused something inside Christopher to well up. He looked for a second at the gaunt faces of Tom and Malcolm and guessed that something similar had happened to them.

Christopher turned back towards the young crew member and looked into his face. He realised that he was not only young and small but also beautiful. 'We're all OK here,' he said to him. 'But what about you? Are you all right?'

SIX

Some of the people who had been thrown to the floor of the lounge regained their seats, others chose to remain where they were, lying flat or reclining against the side of a seat or a wall. The storm outside had not abated; it continued to throw the ship around like a child playing with a bath-time toy. You couldn't know that what had just happened was not about to happen again, with more catastrophic results next time.

But what had happened? As the minutes passed, so news began to spread. From crew members to other crew members, then from crew members to passengers, then among the passengers themselves. The ship had been hit by a monster wave. That had caused the awful roll. More than thirty degrees. Thirty-nine to be exact, someone said… That information had either come from the bridge, from someone monitoring the instruments, or had been made up by someone on the spot. The bow door had been stoven in. What? Like the Herald of Free Enterprise? People began to panic when they heard that. With the bows wide open just above the flat-sea waterline… With waves running twenty to thirty feet high, the ship would sink in minutes.

It wasn't quite as bad as that. The St Christopher had two car decks. The lower one lay deep in the hull, like the car deck of the Herald that had flooded and caused the ship to sink. But the upper vehicle deck of the St Christopher was housed in the superstructure. That was the one whose front door had been broken open by the water. That was the one where Malcolm had parked their car…

Malcolm, Christopher and Tom were among the small crowd bold enough to venture along the constantly moving corridor to the top of the stairs that led down to the car decks. A notice said that no access to the vehicle decks was permitted while the ship was at sea. Nevertheless, among a little group of other people they started to walk down. They didn't get far. The bottom of the stairs was mangled by the cab of an articulated lorry that had fallen almost completed onto its side. Protruding from beneath it was the buckled bonnet of a car. A crewman shouted up at them. 'Stay away. You can't come down here!'

The little group of people backed silently up the stairs. 'Jesus Christ,' said Malcolm in a ghost of a voice. 'Our car's down there.'

There was something wonderful, Christopher thought, something to be picked like a flower from this moment of terror and awfulness, about the fact that he'd said 'our car' and not 'my car'.

Minutes passed and still the St Christopher didn't sink. She rolled unceasingly and violently. More heavily to starboard each time than to port. Terrifyingly she pitched. Announcements came at last from the bridge. They more or less confirmed the word-of-mouth reports. There was further information. They were still in mid-Channel, Cap Gris Nez eleven miles astern, Dover still eleven miles ahead. They were making a little headway but not much.

The darkest hour was just before dawn. But dawn still waited six hours ahead. There were six hours of darkness to undergo. How many of those would they spend on this nightmare ship, adrift at sea, buffeted by waves and winds that no-one, not even among the crew, had ever experienced?

You thought of The Raft of the Medusa, the painting by Géricault. Bodies huddled, groaning with sea-sickness among debris. The bars were shut. No-one minded. Everyone had gone far beyond the stage of needing food or drink.

More rumours circulated as the minutes turned to hours and still the hurricane winds yelled nature's fury outside the windows in the darkness. A Mayday call had been put out by the Hengist as she battled giant waves off Folkestone. A coaster struggling to enter Dover harbour had foundered, smashed against the breakwater. Men had died, falling from the coaster into the waves. The port of Dover – for the first time since the Second World War – had closed. Even if the St Christopher survived the eleven-mile journey to the Kent cliffs there would be no sheltering harbour for her, nowhere for her to dock when she arrived.

Tom, Christopher and Malcolm hardly spoke. They clung to their table and to their chairs. From time to time they clutched one another's legs or arms. They did that at those moments – those moments that kept recurring like the spinning of a room in the head of a drunken man – when the roll or pitch of the ship was big enough and frightening enough to make them think this was the last pitch or roll of their lives. When the movement made them think that within seconds they would be coughing and choking in freezing water, sinking into the eternal dark beneath.

None of them said it, but they were all remembering a time, twenty-five years before, when, sailing from the Kent coast to Boulogne aboard the Orca they had been terrified out of their wits by a twelve-foot wave that reared up at them from the darkness of the night just off Cap Gris Nez. Malcolm and Tom, and Roger who was with them, had managed not to show their fear but the nineteen-year-old Christopher had given way to it. Drenched by the overwhelming wave he had thrown himself round Malcolm and begged him hysterically to take him home. Tonight, each of the three of them, reliving the experience, undergoing the terror for the second time in their lives, seemed determined to outdo the others in their shows of stoicism and strength. None of them was going to be the one who fell to pieces this time. Christopher was perhaps the most determined of all of them.

Time had no meaning now. It served no purpose. There was nothing you could do with it. You might as well be trying to make sense of time on Mars or Jupiter. Were minutes passing now? Were hours? The inexpressible length of the dark night of the sea.

Nobody dared to think it at first, let alone put it into words. But could it be that the storm was weakening slightly? The squid-ink-black windows turned imperceptibly to dark blue. Then to battleship grey. This was the greyest of grey dawns. But it was dawn all the same. It brought with it the hope, if not the promise, of a new day. The ship continued to rear and plunge. But it reared and plunged like a feisty ship now, not like a dying one. A palpable change of spirit, unspoken but deeply experienced, was percolating the stinking de-furbished ferry. Everyone had felt the brush of death that night, a touch or a breath that had come up fearsome and fiery against his or her own skin. Everyone had been reminded with hideous force that they would have to die some time; but the feeling was growing stronger by the minute, as dawn lightened the swell around them, that that time might not have to be today.

The storm was abating, the bridge announced eventually. Slowly the distance between the ship and the coast of Kent was narrowing, but the port of Dover remained closed. It wasn't safe to come close to the harbour piers, and docking was still impossible. The captain attempted to reassure the passengers that, even with a stoven bow door the safest place for a ship to be during the next few hours would be at sea. When they arrived off Dover they would heave to, bows into the wind, until the port could re-open. It would be a rough time, but a safe one. The St Christopher was no longer at risk of being lost on this voyage.

There was other news. The south of England had experienced a major weather event. There had been a lot of damage. Power and telephone lines were down. Roads and railway lines were closed. The Hengist, her moorings broken in Folkestone harbour, had been forced to put to sea. She'd been thrown against the shore at Folkestone Warren close to the railway line and now lay aground there. Her crew had been rescued with line and ladder by the Fire Brigade, who rarely had to deal with ships. No-one aboard her had been killed.

'Roger,' said Malcolm. 'He'd better bloody be OK.' Who knew yet how the town of Sandwich had fared? 'He'd better be OK.'

Christopher was trying to get his head around what had happened. They had planned to cross the Channel to find and give comfort, if they could, to a friend who was dying of aids. It was a fine intention. But they had nearly perished themselves in the attempt.

The air had cleared of spray. Dover cliffs could be seen, looming high and white a few short miles away. The bars had been re-opened, deep falls of glass swept from the floor, and coffee was being served. As they sat out the next few hours, gazing over a still heaving but no longer threatening sea, they began to wonder what had befallen other people they knew. How had Boulogne survived? Were the boats in the boatyard OK? And the people they knew? People in England too. Roger at Sandwich. Parents miles inland… There was no way they could find out, and there was nothing they could do even if they did.

The half-expected announcement came. It made grim news. No-one would be driving off the ferry. The vehicle decks had been pumped free of water but many vehicles had overturned, or were too damaged to be moved. When the ship eventually berthed the passengers would be allowed to retrieve baggage from their cars or else leave it in situ to be collected later. They would all be leaving as foot passengers. Some buses were running in Kent, apparently, but no trains were operating.

Around midday came the news that they were going into Dover harbour. An hour or so later they found themselves looking at the forlorn remains of Malcolm's Jaguar, crushed beneath a truck. There was no way they could pull their luggage out of it. They had to leave it there. They made their way along the link-span, among a crowd of more than a hundred car passengers and lorry drivers. They were refugees, all of them, some carrying cases, others like themselves with nothing but the clothes they wore. This was the second time in their lives, Christopher thought, that they'd arrived on shore after a challenging night at sea, with almost nothing, and nowhere very obvious to go. It gave him a very powerful sense of déjà vu.

Once they had cleared customs (that was a bit of a joke today) and were out of the port on the other side there were suddenly cars. There were taxis, and other motorists were stopping, giving lifts to total strangers out of the goodness of heart that is kindled somehow in the wake of catastrophes.

'Sandwich?' said Tom to the driver who had stopped beside them.

'Get in,' said the driver. 'It's on my way. I'm going to Margate.'

It took two hours. Fallen trees were everywhere and traffic stopped regularly while massive trunks were cut into manageable pieces and dragged out of the way. They passed houses with missing ridge tiles, fallen chimneys and holes in their roofs. Malcolm kept repeating, 'I just hope Roger's OK.' They couldn't use a call-box. All the telephone lines were down.

There were damaged houses to be seen even on the outskirts of Sandwich, although the little town was a couple of miles from the sea. The house where Malcolm lived with Roger was in the centre of the town. Their driver dropped them at the roundabout and went on his way. He had his own anxieties to face at Margate; it was reasonable of him not to want to get involved in other people's troubles on the way there.

They walked through the town centre. It was mid-afternoon by now and piles of debris – roof tiles, small tree branches still in leaf, shattered glass – had been swept to the sides of the streets. Shops were open and people were walking about as though under a spell; when they acknowledged one another they seemed to be calling from the depths of a hollow private space.

Coming round the last corner they were at last in sight of Roger and Malcolm's house. They sighed their relief. The house appeared to have come through the night unscathed. Not a tile had blown from the roof. At least not from the front of it.

Although the house was in the heart of Sandwich it lay by the river and had a small garden at back and front. They approached the front door along a short brick path. The door opened before they got to it and Roger came out. He looked worn and haggard. His thick hair looked very much greyer. But Christopher and Tom quickly realised that this was because they hadn't seen him for over a year: the change hadn't happened overnight.

'Where's the car?' Roger asked his partner. 'The phones are down. I thought you might be dead.' Then he and Malcolm embraced solemnly, standing on the garden path. They didn't speak, they didn't cry; their feelings seemed to be too deep for that. At last they broke apart. Roger swept his hand quickly across the top of Malcolm's head, and then they both lightly laughed. 'Come in,' said Roger over Malcolm's shoulder to the other two. 'The house seems to have escaped damage. But there's no electricity. No radio. No newspapers...'

'No car either,' said Malcolm, deadpan.

SEVEN

During the days that followed normality began to come back. Not, alas, for those who had died. Nor for those who had seen their houses demolished. But, give or take a written-off Jaguar or a toppled chimney, things returned to the more or less normal for everybody else.

A picture of the Folkestone Boulogne ferry Hengist, washed up by giant waves, lying on the beach near Folkestone made the front page of the newspapers. The story of the St Christopher's ordeal at sea was also reported in the press. Millions of trees had fallen in a great swathe across the south east of England. Boulogne had, by a mile or two, escaped the worst. The damage in France had occurred mainly across the Cotentin peninsula in Normandy, and in the western parts of Brittany around Brest.

Once the Kent telephone lines were back in service there were calls to be made to Malcolm's car-insurance company, and to the Port of Dover. It would take some days to clear the St Christopher's vehicle decks, they were told. It was being done with cranes and fork-lift trucks. They could come and collect their belongings from the ruined Jaguar in the middle of the next week.

In the meantime Tom and Christopher needed to get in touch with John Moyse. When it came to tracking down Angelo John was their starting point. For the moment they didn't even know if John was alive and safe. But they phoned him and yes, he and his family were all OK. Tom and Christopher arranged to travel by train to see him at his home in Godalming. As soon as they'd got their crushed luggage back and had changes of clothes to wear. For the moment they were wearing Roger's and Malcolm's clothes and they didn't really fit.

They travelled in the end by a combination of train and rail-replacement bus. There were still trees lying in awkward places, and damaged sections of railway track. But at last they found themselves in the commuter-belt town of Godalming, walking from the station, knocking at the door of John Moyse's rather imposing 1930s detached house.

They hadn't met face to face for years. They looked at John and John looked at them, all thinking how much older the other or others looked but not saying it. John was alone at home. His wife was at work and his young teenage children at school. But home was where John the TV scriptwriter worked.

In the living room stood a shiny grand piano. It was open and there was music strewn across it. They were pleased to see that. They remembered John playing classical piano as a schoolboy. He'd been extremely good at it. At Oxford he'd been musical director of revues and other theatre shows that involved music. John saw his old friends looking at the piano and answered their question before either of them could ask it. 'Yes, I still play,' he said. 'When the writing muse fails me for ten minutes I come down and thump on it. It's the non-smoker's equivalent of a cigarette break. Talking of which, do you want tea or coffee?'

'You said you'd found Angelo's sister,' said Tom when they were settled down behind steaming mugs. 'That she worked for the BBC. She put the phone down on you…'

'Bit of a coincidence,' said John. 'She was pointed out to me in the canteen at the Television Centre. A new lady working in production accounts. The person I was talking to didn't introduce us, he had no reason to. But he'd met her, probably fancied her, and decided for some reason to tell me what he knew of her. That her name was Izzy Dexter – Izzy short for Isabella – and that her father had been a High Court judge. Well, I knew that Angelo's sister had been Isabella, Izzy for short, and I knew what their father did. Though I remembered him as a QC. I didn't know he'd become a judge. But it was obviously her.' John paused just long enough to take a sip of coffee. 'I decided not to rush over to her and interrupt her coffee break with a surprise query about her brother. But I found her office extension number on an internal list and a few days later I rang her on it. To no useful effect. As I told you, she simply hung up.'

'Do you mind if we try to contact her?' Christopher asked.

'Of course not,' said John. 'I can give you the number.'

Tom said, 'I thought we might try and see her face to face. Now I'm thinking, maybe via the BBC canteen?' He got a startled look from Christopher. 'Can you take visitors in on some kind of pass?'

John too was surprised for a moment. 'Well I suppose I could get you in there.' He looked down at the table. 'But now you make me feel I haven't done a very good job of dealing with her myself. You've had to come all this way to take something on that I should have got sorted better than I have.'

'Bollocks,' said Christopher. After four days back in his home country his vernacular English was coming back. 'Sometimes three heads work better than one or even two. We might not have better luck than you did but we can give it a go at least.'

'How did you know that Angelo has aids?' Tom asked John a little later. 'If you didn't know where he was.'

'He wrote it in a letter,' John said. 'He hadn't written for ages and he hasn't written since. The address was the parish priest's house in the little town where he was. Soham, near Ely in Cambridgeshire. No,' he added in response to the others' blank looks, 'I hadn't heard of it either.' He resumed. 'He said he was about to be moved away to somewhere and that he didn't know where that was going to be. The phone number of the Soham parish priest's house was on the letterhead as well as the address. I didn't write back. I phoned instead. That very night. But an unfamiliar voice answered.'

'Male?' Christopher asked.

'Yes,' said John. 'I assumed it was the new parish priest. The days when Catholic priests in parishes had live-in housekeepers are long past. It was this chap, this priest I suppose, who told me I couldn't contact Angelo. That he wasn't at liberty … yes, those exact words … to tell me where he was. I told him I would write to Angelo care of the Soham priest's house and asked if he would kindly forward that. I did write, but I never got a reply from Angelo or anyone else. I've no idea whether the priest forwarded my letter.'

'Which leaves us rather where I thought we were,' Tom said.

They stayed the night at John's house. One of the daughters, Nerissa, moved in with her sister Anna so that Tom and Christopher could have her bed. The boy, Tarquin, was undisturbed by the arrangement.

John had phoned the BBC, had managed to get hold of someone at the reception desk who he was on friendly terms with, and explained that he had two friends from abroad who wanted to see the place where he sometimes worked. Could visitors' passes be arranged for the morning? Happily they could.

They went up to London by train in the morning, as did pretty well everyone else who lived in Godalming. Then they took the tube to White City and the Television Centre. If you wanted to doorstep someone who worked there then the famous canteen was the usual place to do it. It was like Piccadilly Circus: if you waited there long enough the whole world would come past.

Now, as the three men nursed their coffees in the career-making, career-breaking hallowed spot John drew their attention from time to time to well-known figures who daily entered the nation's living rooms via the small screen. But Tom and Christopher neither recognised nor had heard of most of them. Living outside the country for so many years they had lost contact with the world of British television. That source of easy conversation – Did you see such and such last night? – was lost to them. While as for the famous who bestrode the canteen that day… As they well knew from knowing Michel and Gérard, you were only famous among people who already knew you were famous. To everybody else you were just another member of that same great group, *everybody else*.

But some of the people who came into the big room were known to John and he to them. He would acknowledge those with a wave or a word and his relief when that happened, that affirmation of his role here, that evidence of his legitimacy, was picked up by Christopher and Tom. One or two people he actually introduced before they moved away to have their important over-coffee meetings and briefings, conscious no doubt that John Moyse was also in the thick of an important meeting with the two newcomers to the canteen. Which of course he was.

'Oh my God,' John whispered suddenly, urgently. 'That's her. There she is.'

There was a palpable excitement among the three of them, as is always felt when a plan that no-one has very high hopes of actually begins to work. At least they had agreed in advance what they would do if this point was reached.

Izzy Dexter had come into the canteen alone – an additional piece of luck – and was now sitting at a table by herself, stirring a coffee. Evidently she took sugar, though she had the enviably slim figure of someone who didn't.

Christopher got up and walked over to her table. He had been entrusted with this task as he was closer to her age than Tom was. John was even closer to her age but his first attempt to make contact with her hadn't gone too brilliantly. Christopher had the advantage of a clean slate.

'Izzy Dexter?' he asked, standing a couple of feet off.

She didn't say yes or no; she looked up with big Italian eyes – eyes she shared with Angelo – and said, 'You being…?' She didn't smile as she said it.

'Christopher McGing. We met once a long time ago. Your brother was a friend of mine.' He stopped for half a second but for no longer than that. 'We had sex together. I need to see him.' Then he stopped.

Izzy continued to look at him steadily. After a second's hiatus, 'Are you the person who phoned me up?' she asked. Still she didn't smile, but now Christopher did. A bit diffidently.

'No, I'm not. Someone else phoned you on my behalf. I don't live in this country. It's been difficult…'

'I see,' said Izzy. 'It's been difficult for me too.'

Christopher had left it unclear what had been difficult. The tactic, if it had been a tactic, seemed to have worked. After another small pause Christopher asked gently, 'Do you happen to know where Angelo is?'

'Yes,' Izzy said. Then her poise and feistiness deserted her and she became the young teenager Christopher had met on the Boulogne cathedral steps. 'I'm not supposed to tell anyone.'

Christopher smiled again. Again the smile was understated. 'Maybe we could find a way round that.

Although for the moment I can't quite think what the way is.'

At last Izzy did smile at Christopher. But cautiously. 'Will you sit for a minute?' she asked.

Christopher sat. There was a silence during which neither of them looked at each other. Then Izzy said, 'If you did go to see Angelo, what would you say to him?'

'I don't know exactly,' Christopher said. He took a breath. 'In fact I have no idea at all. Though at some point… In fact at this point I need to say this to you, Izzy… I would tell him … and now I'm telling you … that I'm lucky enough not to have the aids virus. I was tested quite recently and I'm HIV negative. So, just in case you were worried, well. I wouldn't be telling him that I might have caught it from him. And I wouldn't be having to confess I might have given it to him either.'

'I was worried, actually,' said Izzy in a quiet voice. 'I'm glad that's not the case.' She clarified. 'I mean I'm glad for you.'

'Our lives have been tangled up in quite major ways,' Christopher said. 'Mine and your brother's. But we're not connected by the virus. …Quite by chance.'

Izzy looked at Christopher carefully. 'Are you one of those two teachers who…?' It seemed that she had no idea what words to end the sentence with. She stopped dead.

Christopher rescued her. 'Yes, I am,' he said. 'I mean, I was.'

'And the other teacher?' Izzy asked hesitantly. 'If I dare ask?'

'Ex-teacher these days. He's sitting at that table there.' Christopher nodded his head towards the place where Tom sat, trying not to watch what was going on between Izzy and Christopher but failing in the attempt, and failing also to conceal that. 'And the person sitting with him is Angelo's old friend John Moyse. From school and university. It was John who rang you up that day – on our behalf.'

Izzy looked puzzled. 'On our behalf?'

'Mine and Tom's,' said Christopher. 'Tom, sitting there. The other teacher. Ex-teacher. He's also HIV negative.'

They talked about the hurricane. The four of them, now all around the same table. It was less than a week in the past and so everyone, especially in England's south-east, was still talking about it. Izzy had her own tales to tell – everybody did – but was ready to admit that, compared to being stuck on a damaged ferry in mid-Channel her own adventures paled into insignificance. But even their tale of endurance on the St Christopher paled into insignificance if you compared it to actually dying in the storm as some had done. If you compared it to dying of aids… To death of any sort…

'His order of friars don't want it to get about what illness it is exactly that he's dying of,' Izzy said.

'That's totally understandable,' Tom said.

'As far as his parishioners are concerned he may as well have disappeared off the face of the earth. They've been told he's ill with an incurable disease. That he won't be coming back. They know he's being treated somewhere, but under an assumed name. No-one in the place he's at will ever know he was a priest.'

'Was a priest?' John queried.

'Is a priest,' Izzy corrected herself. They had all been brought up as Catholics, whatever they might call themselves now. Once a priest, always a priest. They all knew that. They knew the rubric of the ordination rite. *Thou art a priest for ever, according to the Order of Melchizedech.* 'The ladies and gentlemen of the parish have been told not to make any enquiries as to his whereabouts.'

'That's awful,' Christopher said.

'It's Mother Church's way,' said Tom. Izzy could decide for herself whether she thought he was being ironical or not.

Izzy didn't give away her immediate thoughts about that. 'It's not so different from what happened to you two all those years ago,' she said. 'Just abandoned to fate – disappeared like in Argentina – when you became an embarrassment, a minor inconvenience.'

Neither Tom nor Christopher wanted to talk about that just now. They were in reach of the prize they were after: the knowledge of Angelo's current whereabouts. This wasn't the moment to let it slip from their sights by getting sidetracked.

'Presumably they had to let you know where he is because you're his next of kin,' Tom said smoothly.

'Yes,' agreed Izzy. 'They have to do that.'

Christopher itched to say something here but held off. Sometimes he managed not to intervene, and so let Tom run with it. Tom was the shrewder negotiator. Sometimes Christopher's self-restraint at these moments paid off.

'What do you say,' Tom began very slowly, weighing his words to the nearest gramme of nuance, 'to extending the idea of near of kin to include sexual contacts?'

Izzy looked at him for a moment. Her expression gave him nothing. Then, 'I think it might be reasonable if … if in hindsight I decided I'd thought that.' To everyone's relief she gave a little laugh. 'OK,' she said. 'I'll tell you where he is. But I'd appreciate it – and I think he would also – if you didn't all three pounce on him at once.'

'That's OK,' said John. 'Assuming he's not actually at death's door at the moment I'll hang back till these two have gone back to France.'

'Then … would it be OK,' asked Christopher, 'if Tom and I went together? We only meant to be in England a couple of days. But the storm and so on… We really need to be getting back to France to work.'

'I think I'd be OK with that,' Izzy said. 'But he does tire easily. Promise me that you'll…'

'We promise,' said Tom.

'Have any of you got a piece of paper and pencil?' Izzy asked them. John, the professional writer, had both those items in an inside pocket. Izzy gave them Angelo's address.

EIGHT

They travelled from King's Cross. Just the two of them. The North-East Main Line took them across a flattish countryside that gradually grew flatter and flatter. Less than a hundred miles separated their train's destination, Peterborough, from London, but after the disorienting experience of measureless horizons and infinite skies they felt as far from home, stepping down onto the platform, as if they'd landed on a different, entirely flat, planet. The towers and spires of the cathedral reared above the level city's rooftops. 'Perhaps have a look round it on the way back?' suggested Christopher when Tom said, for the sake of making conversation, that it looked rather splendid.

'Hmm,' said Tom. 'Perhaps. We'll see how we're feeling about God by then.'

'You don't need to have an opinion about God to enjoy a work of art made in His honour.'

'That sounds very clever. Did you think it up?' said Tom.

'I had plenty of time for thinking on the train,' Christopher said.

They found the bus station and got on the bus to Ramsey, the isolated habitation where Izzy had told them Angelo now lived.

The land they travelled over was so flat, so vast and un-peopled – a vista of arable fields, now in the process of being ploughed, that went on for ever, criss-crossed by drainage dykes – that the market town of Ramsey took them quite by surprise when at last they reached it. It was bigger and busier than either of them had imagined it. It also amazed them by being there at all, in the middle of the empty fens, raised above them, as Venice is raised above the sea, by a mere but crucial couple of feet.

To reach the place where Angelo was they had to walk past the gatehouse of the ruined abbey. Benedictine monks had settled on the remote island more than a thousand years before and the town had grown around the buildings they raised and the community they set up. Now the community had gone, the buildings had gone, and only the little town was left.

Christopher rang the bell beside the front door of the hospice. When it was opened Tom spoke. 'Angelo Taylor,' he said. 'He's expecting us.'

Angelo sat, in jeans, trainers and a cosy pullover, on a sofa in the spacious lounge. Behind him long windows would open onto a garden when the weather was nice. Angelo, his dark hair re-grown to its natural thick and curly state, no longer looked remotely like a friar and a priest. It was nine years since they'd last seen him, short-haired and in monastic habit and sandals. Then he'd been Brother Michael. More recently, Father Michael, since his ordination as a priest. Now he was back to Angelo again, though he'd lost his surname as though in some weird bit of plea-bargaining. In this phase of his life Angelo Dexter didn't exist any more than Father Michael did. He would be Angelo Taylor for what remained of his life.

There was a compensation, Christopher thought. Angelo once again looked like the handsome young man he'd been at university. It was a pleasant discovery, though Christopher knew that his pleasure in it was selfish.

Tom said, 'Don't get up,' as Angelo did exactly that. They shook hands, then, after a moment's hesitation they embraced. Tom put his arms very carefully around Angelo, the way he would have embraced a very old person, fearing to hurt him, afraid almost that he might break. But Angelo had plenty of strength left for hugging, and held Tom firmly for the two seconds of their embrace. They didn't kiss, but exchanged a laugh instead. Then it was Christopher's turn and the embrace was the same as Tom's had been in every detail. Christopher thought about this for a fleeting moment, wondering whether, twenty years ago, the same had applied when Tom and he had each had sex with Angelo, separately and in private.

'I'm very touched,' Angelo said. 'To go to the lengths you did…'

'We couldn't have done any less,' Christopher said. 'Although it was a bit of a Pilgrims' Progress.'

'Izzy said on the phone that you'd been caught in the hurricane. On a ship…'

Between them Tom and Christopher gave an account of their trip back from France.

Then Angelo told them how things stood with him. Sometimes he was ill, he said, but mostly he was well. 'Today for example.' He smiled happily. 'And I have a dual role here. When I'm ill I'm a patient. But when I'm well I'm a carer. I help to look after others who're in a worse state.'

Tom began to say, 'That must be a bit…'

Angelo stopped him. 'That's how it works here. It's a very special place. Several of us here have that dual role. At least … for the moment.'

'Do you..?' Tom wasn't sure how to put this. 'Do you still practise as a priest?'

'No,' Angelo said. 'Nobody here knows that's what I am. I'm Mr Taylor to anyone who doesn't call me Angelo. My faculties have been withdrawn.'

They looked at him with puzzlement on their faces. Angelo laughed. 'Sorry. I'm not talking about my mental health. It's a bit of priestly jargon. It means I'm no longer expected to say Mass every day, nor can I marry people or hear their confessions or baptize them – except in exceptional circumstances. If someone's at death's door perhaps… It's not a punishment. It's a dispensation. A relaxation of the rules. It's often given to elderly or "infirm" priests. And I don't have to say the Divine Office every day. Although I usually do, in fact.' Tom and Christopher exchanged a glance after Angelo said that, both unsure exactly how they felt about it.

They sat and talked. They drank coffee. They walked in the garden. Tom and Christopher stayed for lunch. They were introduced to other … residents. There wasn't a better word. Little distinction was made between those who were patients and those for whom this was a place of work. But the people they met did not stay around for long conversations or polite social chat. All carried heavy baggage. You would probably need to be in for the long haul with someone here to want to start unpacking it.

After lunch Angelo said, 'I was going to suggest a walk around the town. I sometimes do do that. With one or two of the others.' He paused and looked down for a second, then looked back up. 'We bond very closely. It's a big thing to have in common.' Neither Tom nor Christopher had the insensitivity to say anything in response to that. 'But I feel knackered suddenly. It's the excitement of seeing friends. Nothing bad about that, though. It's something I like.'

'Fine,' said Christopher. 'It's time we headed off, though. Left you in peace.'

'No. Don't go,' said Angelo. His voice tugged at their sleeves even if his hand did not. For a moment he was the bright-eyed thirteen-year-old they had known at first. 'Can we just sit and talk for a bit before you go?'

Tom said, 'Yes, of course,' and they did that, in the slanting autumn sunshine that flooded into the lounge, all three of them together on the same sofa. And there they had their walk around the town, a virtual tour of Ramsey, as Angelo told them what to see, what to look at, and a bit of the history of the place. 'The whole of the fens grew around the monasteries,' he said. 'The monks drained the land in the Middle Ages and turned it into farmland. The ruins of those abbeys litter the place.' He talked of Thorney Abbey, and of Crowland, and of Ramsey Abbey itself. His store of information on the subject became a bit of a monologue, which the others could only respond to with nods and interested-sounding grunts.

'But the Reformation, of course…' They nodded again. They probably knew as much as Angelo did about the dissolution of the monasteries under Henry VIII. Twenty-six years ago they might even have taught him about it. Smaller abbeys and priories gone in 1536, the bigger ones – Ramsey included – in 1539…

'And then, in World War Two the fens became as full of Air Force bases as they'd once been full of religious houses. Duxford, Brampton, Abbots Ripton, Kimbolton…' Christopher and Tom went on politely nodding, until Angelo startled them with this: 'A parachutist landed here at Ramsey. A German spy he turned out to be. He was imprisoned in the Tower of London and executed there. The last person in history to have that particular fate. …Up to now at any rate.

'And talking of executions in the Tower,' Angelo went on without pausing, 'I've been reading the writings of Thomas More. They're very … inspiring, perhaps. For someone in the place I find myself.'

'I suppose,' Tom dared to interrupt at last, 'that it was in the Tower that More found his true voice, his true self.'

'You know, you're right,' said Angelo, flashing Tom a very piercing look. 'And it's here, doing the work I do – when I'm well enough to do it – that I've really found myself.'

'You really think that?' Christopher was unable to stop himself blurting it out.

Angelo looked at him strangely. 'It's God's plan for me. It's what he intended all along, apparently, but mercifully didn't reveal to me before this moment in my life.'

'God wanted it?' said Tom, sounding as appalled as he felt.

Angelo was unfazed. 'Remember what More said to his daughter in the Tower, when she visited him, full of horror and pity for his state. He reassured her. "Me thinks God maketh me a wanton, and setteth me on his lap and dandleth me."'

'Is that what you really think…?' Tom tried to say, but the words would barely come out. And at that moment Angelo's eyelids dropped shut and, between them on the sofa, he fell quietly and suddenly asleep.

Christopher and Tom looked at each other, their gazes meeting in front of Angelo's relaxed and thrown-back head. 'Perhaps that's just as well,' said Christopher in a half-whisper, and Tom understood perfectly that he was referring to Angelo's falling asleep. 'I don't know what I would have said.'

'I know,' said Tom, and they sat in silence for a moment, both wondering whether to tiptoe away and leave Angelo at that point, or to stay until he woke up.

Angelo took the decision out of their hands by waking up after less than half a minute. Tom told him they had realised it was time they went – they'd tired him out. Angelo didn't disagree, but neither did he return to the subject of his relationship with God. Both his visitors were relieved about that.

'Time you had a lie down and a proper sleep,' Christopher told Angelo as they began to stand up, and Angelo didn't disagree with that either.

'We'll come and see you again very soon,' Tom said. 'As soon as we're back in England again.'

'Long before that, you'll get a visit from John Moyse,' said Christopher, somehow finding a cheerful tone of voice. 'Now that he knows where you are…'

They escorted Angelo to the door of his bedroom and he invited them inside. 'I don't get undressed if I have a nap this time of day,' Angelo said matter-of-factly. 'I just take my shoes off.'

'Lie on the bed,' said Christopher. 'I'll take your trainers off. He and Tom both gave their old friend a hug, almost certain this was their final shared embrace. But Angelo had one more thing to say to them after that, looking up at them from the bed.

'I'm happy for you that you're both HIV negative.' His nodding head confirmed the truth of this. 'But I need to ask your forgiveness for something else. I somehow managed to mess up both your lives. Twice. At two different times in the past.'

'You didn't,' Christopher said sturdily. '*If* our lives were messed up – and I absolutely wouldn't say they were – then it was ourselves who did it.'

Angelo smiled, almost cutely. 'I said something stupid to my father. I told him you were lovers, and what you had told me, Christopher, about having sex with boys when you were a teenager yourself. That got you kicked out of the school.'

'You were only thirteen,' Tom said gently. 'Your words to your father were innocent. You were also under terrible stress…'

'You'd been kicked out of the school yourself,' said Christopher. 'In the worst of possible scenarios.' Angelo had been caught in flagrante, in bed with his friend and fellow house captain Simon Rickman. 'And I'd been very careless with my words to you. Tom hauled me over the coals for that at the time. I was nineteen, and a teacher. I should have handled the situation better myself.'

Angelo touched Christopher's hand. 'Everything you said to me that morning was absolutely right. You should be proud of that.' He looked at Tom and a twinkle came into his eyes unexpectedly. 'Whatever Tom may have said at the time.'

'There were other reasons why we had to leave the school,' Tom said. 'The picture. David and Jonathan. The review in The Times. Don't forget that.'

'There was Paris.' Angelo was getting very tired now. He clearly wanted to get everything off his chest and have done with it. 'My behaviour. I got you chucked out of the house you were living at.'

Christopher said, 'Only because you wanted to have sex with everyone who lived there. Because we'd been doing that. You were an impressionable teenager. You only wanted to copy us…'

'It was me who got us chucked out,' Tom said. 'I threw a punch at Charles, after Chris had already done it. Totally over-reacted.'

'Stop, please stop!' Christopher spoke with such intensity that the other two did shut up. 'There's nothing to forgive between any of the three of us. No apologies to make. When everything else has gone the only thing that matters is love.' Angelo had fallen in love with Christopher in his mid-teens. They all remembered that. That was why he had come over to Paris. Christopher was on the point of saying that, anyway, everything had turned out for the best. Fortunately he stopped himself. For Angelo that was hardly the case. Unless you were to believe his assurance that, like Saint Thomas More in the Tower, he was having the time of his life. 'Love,' Christopher repeated instead. 'Just love.' Then he bent down and embraced Angelo again and kissed him on the cheek. Against all his beliefs he said, 'Go with God.'

Tom then embraced Angelo, but wordlessly. Though he too kissed Angelo on the cheek, and Angelo kissed him back.

They left Angelo then. They walked quickly away along the bright corridor. They left the hospice, signing out beneath the understanding gaze of the nurse at the desk.

Outside, the sun felt wonderful as it warmed them with a livelier heat than the artificial warmth inside the place they'd visited. Christopher felt himself shiver involuntarily. As though a shadow had flitted across the sun's life-giving face.

They didn't take Angelo's recommended walk through Ramsey's historic streets. They took his word for the beauty of the place. They made for the bus back to Peterborough instead, and saw quite a bit of the town anyway on their journey out of it. They were in a subdued mood as they tracked back across the fens' flat emptiness. They hardly spoke.

At last Tom said, 'That was a bit difficult to deal with.'

'What was?' Christopher asked.

'You know what I'm talking about,' said Tom. 'Angelo's thing about his relationship with God.'

'He's a priest,' said Christopher. 'It's natural that he should think like that.'

'He wasn't a bit religious when we knew him at Oxford,' said Tom. 'When he was at prep school he went through the motions… Like we all did.'

'How do you know he was going through the motions?' Christopher said, with more than a hint of disagreement in his voice. 'There's no way to see how much religion other people have. Until the chips are down. Until Sir Thomas More jokes with the executioner on his way up the scaffold steps and lays his beard out of the way of the descending axe because the beard hasn't offended the king. Until Cranmer holds out the hand that signed his recantation towards the flames that will extinguish his life…'

Tom stopped him by finding Christopher's hand with his own and taking it. 'OK,' he said. 'Enough now. We're both upset.'

They came into Peterborough at last. Again the cathedral appeared, lofty above the house tops, a stern yet somehow comforting profile of towers and gables. Christopher looked at it, pointing to its spirelets as they got off the bus. He turned to Tom. 'Want to go inside it while we're here? Or not.'

Tom thought for a second. He looked at his watch. 'Yes,' he said. 'Might as well. Who knows when – or if – we'll be in Peterborough again.'

The cathedral's west front was magnificent. They knew it from pictures, of course. The three rearing pointed arches springing from columns that rose without interruption or decoration from ground to hundred-foot-high roof. Unique in form, nothing like Peterborough's west front had appeared in English Gothic architecture before or since.

The interior was warm and womblike, despite the space's great height. They chose a pew at random, shuffled along it and sat side by side on it, beneath the soaring painted ceiling eighty feet above their heads. As they sat quietly Tom wondered how long it was since he had last sat inside a church. He couldn't remember. He thought about Angelo's apparent continuing belief in God, his keeping of faith with his Church. Despite what had happened to him.

Things that had happened to Christopher years ago had caused him to lose his faith. While Tom had never believed in the first place. Only while he was still a child had he pretended to have faith. But he wouldn't be arguing with Angelo. It wasn't just a question of politeness. Angelo was dying. If he needed his faith and the love of his God in his dying months then he needed those things and should have them. That was more important than whether God existed, or whether the tiny speck in creation that was Tom believed in Him or not. Tom became aware that something was happening inside Christopher. He could feel it in his shoulder's touch. He turned and looked at him. Tears were coursing silently down Christopher's cheeks. He didn't turn to look at Tom, and for the moment, made no move to dry his face. Without saying anything Tom laid his arm around Christopher's shoulders like a comforting scarf.

Part Two

1987 – 1988

Goodbye to Boulogne

NINE

It began with books, as things often do. Cyril Connolly wrote in rose-tinted prose about his travels around south-western France in the nineteen-twenties and -thirties. Freda White produced her best-selling Three Rivers of France in 1952. The rivers in question were the Lot, the Tarn, and the Dordogne.

It was a part of France that Tom and Christopher didn't know well at first. For over twenty years their holidays usually took them back to England, to spend time with Roger and Malcolm on the Kent coast and with their two sets of parents further inland. But one year in the early eighties they travelled to Majorca – it was temptingly cheap at the time – to spend a week in the late autumn sun. They travelled from Paris by plane. A novelty for the pair of them.

On the return journey the sky was strikingly clear. The blue Mediterranean passed beneath them and then the icing-sugar peaks of the Pyrenees. A city that straddled a river came next; they pored over a map together later and decided it was Toulouse. Somehow you could see the westward movement of the water in the river. Chris, sitting closest to the window, felt compelled to follow it with his eyes. The river was the Garonne, though he didn't know that at the time. After a little while another river joined it, at an angle, like a slip road joining a motorway. It was the Tarn, swelling the Garonne's waters and glinting silver, moving steadily across the green landscape like a thread of mercury, towards the north-west, towards the sea.

More rivers came down from the Massif Central to join the Garonne, all in parallel, solemn in their inexorable progress, their glistening crawl, towards the west. Their names were printed on the map that Tom and Christopher consulted later. They included the Lot, the

Dropt and, biggest of all and merging spectacularly with the silvered Garonne just downstream from Bordeaux, the Dordogne.

The Dordogne. Aquitaine.

'I never thought about it before,' Christopher said. 'No wonder the Romans called the region Aquitania.'

'Land of waters,' translated Tom, squinting past Christopher's window-blocking shoulder at the view. 'You can see why.' The city of Bordeaux was slipping from sight beneath the wing. The merging rivers were widening into the estuary called the Gironde, funnelling towards the horizonless silver sea.

Both men remembered that sight for years. That glimpse of the beauty of south-west France came to mind every time they heard, or read, of yet another British person who had succumbed to the lure of the region and moved lock, stock and barrel to the Dordogne. For though the Dordogne was the name of the river; it was also the name of an area, a Département of France and of the Province of Aquitaine.

Books began it for many. For Tom and Christopher it had begun in a plane with a view. But books took them on from there. They read Freda White's Three Rivers. Their favourite chapter, The Spring at Beynac, they read over and over again. They read Cyril Connolly too. Connolly had drawn a circle on the map of south-west France – it extended roughly between Limoges in the north and Toulouse in the south, between the edge of the Auvergne in the east and the edge of Bordeaux in the west. Around the rim of the circle Connolly had written the words *Quod Petis Hic Est.* He was fond of Latin quotes. *What you seek is here.*

They were reminded of that aerial view of the rivers once again when they returned from England after their sobering re-encounter with Angelo in the hospice at

Ramsey. Among the little heap of post waiting for them was one handwritten envelope: the handwriting was Tom's mother's. Tom read:

Darling Tom,

I didn't mention this when you phoned last week. You seemed to have so much else on your plate. Surviving a storm at sea, when I had only lost a few roof-tiles in the hurricane. Visiting a sick friend. But I have come to a fairly major decision. I plan a move to the Dordogne. Dominic knows and, after a bit of discussion, has found he supports my idea...

Tom's mother had been widowed some four years earlier. Dominic was Tom's elder brother. 'Good God,' said Tom as he finished reading the letter. That evening he got on the phone.

'It makes such good sense,' his mother told him. 'I read an article in the Telegraph. And I've done a lot more research since. Our house here would make seventy-five thousand, I've been told. I could get something in a village down in the Dordogne for six thousand. Even allowing for some refurbishment and the cost of moving I'd have a very tidy sum to add to your father's money and my pension. Everybody says how much cheaper it is to live down there.'

Bang goes my inheritance, Tom thought. And Dominic's. He didn't say that. Instead he said, 'Mummy, don't even think it. Six thousand pounds would buy you a ruin. You'd be taken for a ride by unscrupulous builders. You don't know anyone down there…'

'The Pattersons moved down there last year,' said his mother, quite unfazed by Tom's horrified reaction. 'They're having a gorgeous time, they say. Besides, you and Christopher live in France.'

'About five hundred miles from the Dordogne. We wouldn't be any use as neighbours. You don't speak French. Please…'

'Actually, I thought you and Christopher could help me find the right place. Then help to do it up. At least you'd be able to talk to people. Find out who the good tradesmen were and then deal with them. And of course I'd pay you both.'

Tom remembered too late that the best way to ensure his mother did something was to advise her not to do it. He guessed that his brother had fallen into the same trap. Yet his mother's apparently harebrained idea that he and Christopher should travel down to the south and restore some ruin for her had chimed with something else. For Malcolm had told them just the previous day that he was indeed planning to sell the Boulogne boatyard. Unless the new owners required the services of two English managers as well as that of Luc the master shipwright, they would at some time in the next year or so be out of a job.

The return from Ramsey to Boulogne by way of Sandwich had been a sober experience. Both Tom and Christopher were still feeling a strong sense of their own mortality, and of the fragility, brittle and empty as a Christmas-tree bauble, of their own shared existence. They still felt occasionally the awful movements of the ship in which, a week earlier, they had faced the possibility of death. Felt it physically. The lurch, the plunging, and the prickles of terror along the skin that accompanied that. For the second time in their lives they had suffered mortal terror on the sea. Yet on both occasions they had survived the experience. The big wave that had broken over them aboard the Orca twenty-five years ago had not washed them overboard or sunk the boat. Therefore, with hindsight, you had to say that it hadn't been going to sink them. In which case the situation hadn't been remotely dangerous, it had just felt like it. The same thing went for the experience aboard the St Christopher. The ship hadn't sunk. Therefore she hadn't been going to sink. The fear they'd felt had been out of all proportion to the danger involved. They weren't going to die that night; it was just an impression they'd had.

But then they'd met Angelo. He was going to die; there was no doubt about that. His foot had slipped through the painted surface on which they still stood – as E. M. Forster had written about someone else. Angelo's confidence that he was slipping away into a better and more abiding world was of no comfort to them, unbelievers both, pleased though they were that Angelo took comfort from his certainty.

Returning to Sandwich they had found Malcolm poring over adverts for used Jaguars, and Roger talking about plans for semi-retirement. The pub on the cliffs at Pegwell Bay, the Admiral Digby, had already been sold. There was no mention for the moment of plans for the Boulogne boatyard. Instead the older men listened gravely to the news of Angelo. 'At least he's being well looked after,' Malcolm said. 'Sounds as though he's in very capable hands.'

'The most capable imaginable, apparently,' Tom said. 'He says he's being taken very good care of by God.'

'Well, there's no answer to that,' Roger said. 'Except to say that's good to hear, and leave it at that.'

The younger pair were staying one night at Roger and Malcolm's before returning to France. In the evening they went out for a meal. 'We have an Indian restaurant in Sandwich these days,' Malcolm said. 'Are you OK with that?'

'Definitely,' Tom answered. 'There aren't any in Boulogne. We find one occasionally when we go to Paris. It's something we miss in France.'

It was over the onion bhajis that Malcolm had broken the bad news: Roger and he had been discussing their future plans carefully and, as Malcolm had warned them might be the case, he would be putting the Boulogne boatyard on the market within a month. Of course that didn't mean it would find a buyer within a month. Malcolm had stopped at that point and both he and Roger had looked searchingly at Christopher and Tom. They wouldn't like to buy the outfit, would they?

Tom had said no for both of them. They too had been discussing the possibility of the boatyard's being put up for sale over their heads. But they didn't have the money to put down a deposit on the place, or the will to take on the mortgage that would go with that. In which case, Malcolm said, assuming the new owner didn't want to keep the two of them on, there would be an appropriate financial settlement. A decent redundancy package. The new situation wouldn't affect their friendship, Roger and Malcolm both hoped. Tom and Christopher both said that of course it would not – each privately wondering what they would do for the remaining twenty years of their working lives. Though they had attacked their various curries with undiminished appetites.

The crossing from Folkestone to Boulogne had been uneventful in the extreme. The sea had been as flat as a billiard table and almost as green. Even so, all the tiny movements of the ship, the little tilts she made as her heading was adjusted from time to time, filled them with alarm – as if she might not right herself after a few seconds but continue to list, down and down, and not come back up. It was good to see the French coast move slowly towards them, to pick out the dome of Boulogne's cathedral crowning the familiar skyline high above the town. It was good to sense the reassuring embrace of the harbour's breakwaters as they glided into port. Best of all was the feel of the solid concrete quay beneath their feet at the moment they landed from the embarkation steps.

Tom's mother, whose name was May, got her own way. As Tom had had years to discover, she usually did. It meant Tom taking another week off from work, less than a fortnight after returning from England, and leaving the boatyard in the hands of Christopher and the master shipwright Luc while he escorted his mother down to the Dordogne to look for a property there. Tom met his mother off the ferry and together they took the train to Paris, crossed the city by taxi, and caught another train, this time to Bordeaux. The plan was to hire a car and spend the week driving up and down the Dordogne river and département. May would be calling the shots while Tom translated her wishes into French. Christopher would join them for the weekend.

It was late evening by the time Tom and his mother reached Bordeaux and they checked into a hotel for the night. They got up extremely early the next morning (May's idea, that) and, returning to the station, equipped themselves with a rental car.

May had been doing her research thoroughly, it appeared, and Tom was glad of that. The Dordogne was a big area to cover if you were looking for a house. But May had read newspaper articles, borrowed books from the public library, and talked at length on the phone to her friends the Pattersons, who had established themselves some way up the Dordogne valley near a village called Trémolat. She'd learnt – Tom was very glad to know – that the upper reaches of the Dordogne, where the landscape and the villages were the most picturesque, were fearsomely cold in winter. They were places for summer holidays, not somewhere for a seventy-five-year-old English widow who didn't speak French to live. May knew, she said, that the lower reaches of the river, nearer Bordeaux, had a flatter landscape. That the villages were more run of the mill, but that there was a better winter climate. It was a question of finding the right compromise, she told her son as they set off that morning, Tom driving, his mother with the map spread open on her lap.

The first bit of road took them on a straight but roller-coaster track across the region that appears on wine-bottle labels as Entre Deux-Mers. The heavily rolling landscape was, as May put it, 'wonderfully beautiful – but extremely big.'

Then they crossed the river on a rattling iron cage of a narrow bridge and the spires of St-Emilion came in sight above a sea of vines from which the grapes had recently been stripped. 'Now this would be nice,' May observed as they looked around the pretty stone-built wine town. Built on a hillside, with only an ancient town wall between the houses inside and vines beyond, its streets were alternately cobbled alleys and flights of twisting steps.

'It would be nice,' Tom agreed, 'but I'm not sure you'd get much for your six grand.' They looked in estate agents' windows at the prices. Tom's guess was proved right. After a coffee they headed into deeper countryside among vineyards. May insisted on stopping at frequent intervals to get out and peer into the windows of tumbledown cottages. 'Old people die and the property goes jointly to all the children,' May explained knowledgeably. 'They all have lives and jobs in Paris; they can't agree what to do with the old houses, or don't have time to think about it, and they go to rack and ruin.'

'So people like the Pattersons can buy them up,' Tom said.

'Not only the Pattersons,' said May.

'Hmm,' said Tom.

They got as far as Ste-Foy-la-Grande that morning. They spent the afternoon talking to estate agents in their offices and making plans to see various properties in the immediate area the following day. They stayed in a hotel in Ste-Foy for the night.

The days followed a pattern after that. Journeying to the next town on the river. Looking in estate agencies, visiting a few properties, then moving up-river after a night in whatever the town offered by way of a hotel. They did Bergerac, Le Bugue, and eventually got up as far as Sarlat – after paying a courtesy call on the Pattersons at Trémolat.

Tom had half-expected that his mother would find fault with every property she looked at. But he actually had no experience of May in house-hunting mode; his mother had lived with her late husband in the same house for all of Tom's life. What actually happened now was almost the reverse of what Tom had thought would be the case. 'Oh, but this is gorgeous,' May would exclaim as they walked round yet another un-modernised peasant farmhouse. 'It's just so perfect. So quaint.'

'Mummy, there's no light,' Tom would point out. Windows tended to be small and high up in these old cottages. Peasants who had spent all day in the open air of the countryside would have had enough of it. They didn't want the un-weeded landscape following them indoors when they went home for the night.

Or there would be no indoor toilet – a privy at the bottom of the garden having been considered enough of a luxury for most of the previous century and a half – and no bathroom. No bathroom of any sort. It fell to Tom during this week of exploration to bring such details to his mother's attention. For Tom the little adventure turned out to be as much of an exploration of his mother's mindset as it was of the Dordogne valley itself.

They met Christopher off the train at Libourne on Friday night. Meeting at Libourne cut off a corner for everyone, saving them all the forty-mile trek to Bordeaux, by road and rail in parallel. 'It's all sorted,' was the first thing Tom said to Christopher after a quick greeting of hug and kiss. 'Mum's got a house.'

'She hadn't when you phoned last night,' said Christopher.

'It fell into place this afternoon. Very suddenly. Very quickly. It's at a place called Castillon-la-Bataille.'

'Wherever that is,' Christopher said.

'About ten miles up-river from here,' said Tom. 'You'll see it tomorrow. It's almost on the riverfront. We're staying tonight in St-Emilion. Halfway between there and here.'

'Ah,' said Christopher. 'Where the wine comes from.'

'Exactly,' Tom said.

In the morning they drove to the market town of Castillon. It was a workaday, businesslike place, though with a centre that was pretty enough. Its main charm was that the Dordogne river ran through it. There were stone-built quays and promenades along the water and some very fine houses lining them. The one they had come to see was a little way from the town centre, though no more than a ten-minute walk. It was made of stone and stood a little higher than the riverfront promenade, with a small terraced garden in front of it as well as a slightly bigger one at the back.

Inside there was one main living area, with a kitchen behind it. Upstairs were two good bedrooms. There were no bathroom or toilet facilities. There was a privy at the bottom of the long narrow back garden, which was sandwiched between the garden of a neighbouring house and a little meadow that marked the edge of town and the beginning of open countryside. The house hadn't been lived in for over a year, Tom explained to Christopher. That was why it smelt a bit damp.

Despite the lack of facilities that most people had taken for granted for two or more generations, the house made as good an impression on Christopher as it had on Tom and his mother. 'You're not getting this for six thousand pounds, surely?' Christopher asked May with some surprise in his voice.

'No,' she answered. 'Because of the location I've had to offer eight. Subject to survey, of course.'

TEN

The boatyard didn't sell at once. Tom and Christopher continued to run it. It was something of a job-share. It kept them busy part-time in the winter, full-time in summer. It had always been like that. Neither of them had ever become a master shipwright. They did the paperwork, negotiated with the customers on Malcolm's behalf, and then did the less skilled manual jobs around the place alongside the other employee, Luc, who was the only one of them qualified to do major repair work on the hulls and rigging of other people's boats. It was an unusual arrangement but somehow it worked. And the experience of doing unskilled work assisting an expert who was actually their employee was shortly to stand them in very good stead – though they didn't know that yet.

The survey of Tom's mother's new property in Castillon discovered nothing amiss. The surveyor, who knew the estate agent, also knew a builder who was well qualified to design a bathroom extension as well as to carry out the work, and they all knew the mayor of the town. This last connection was a very important one. It was the mayor who decided who got planning permission for building projects and who did not.

Later that autumn Tom and his mother paid a brief visit to Castillon. In the office of a notaire (who knew the mayor, who knew the builder, who knew the estate agent) May handed over money and signed papers and became the owner of a property in France. She told Tom that he had the winter in which to get the house into a habitable state, ready for her to move into in the spring. She then returned to England to spend her last winter in the small town in Buckinghamshire in which she lived. It wasn't true that she spoke no French, she told her son. She'd studied it for many years at school. It was simply rusty with lack of use. She would spend some of her time during the coming months taking lessons and brushing it up.

'It all sounds very easy,' Christopher said when Tom, back home in Boulogne, told him how things had gone in Castillon. 'It's something we could do ourselves if we wanted to. Buy a small place in the south and do it up.'

'We could if we had the money,' Tom said.

'Six thousand pounds isn't very much,' said Christopher. 'Or even eight.'

'It is if you haven't got it,' said Tom – as Christopher knew he would. 'And we haven't. Or hadn't you noticed that?'

When you visit a friend in hospital or ill at home you feel you've done your duty if you've done it once. Unless you're very near kin or a lover. But when a friend, even one you haven't seen in years, becomes terminally ill it gets a bit more intense than that. Angelo was without doubt a terminal case but on the evidence of that October visit he wasn't going to die just yet. Tom and Christopher wondered together – in other words they discussed the question – how soon he might expect a second visit from friends who lived on the other side of the Channel.

They were lucky in having a proxy in the shape of John Moyse. He had visited Angelo just a few days after Tom and Christopher had, and reported back in the course of a phone call. A fortnight later he'd driven up a second time, round the newly completed M25 and up the A1, and again spent a comfortable couple of hours with Angelo, seeing him off to bed after he'd had his lunch. John had also run into Angelo's sister at the TV centre again and they'd had a friendly chat. Izzy travelled up to see her brother quite regularly – accompanied by her husband once or twice. She told John that Angelo still seemed in remarkably good spirits, though he went on losing weight and was getting more and more tired as the weeks passed. The days on which he woke up feeling strong enough to care for his weaker fellow residents were becoming rare.

Tom and Christopher decided they would try and get over to see Angelo again before Christmas. Christopher needed to pay a courtesy call on his own parents around that time anyway, although fitting it in this year was going to be a bit more tricky than usual, with the boatyard up for sale and with increasingly frequent trips down to the Dordogne to plan. Once work started on Tom's mother's bathroom extension those trips would extend into stays of some length.

One chill day at the end of November the office phone rang just as Tom was locking up the boatyard for the night. He almost didn't answer it but then, after a moment's hesitation, keys in hand, he went back inside and picked the phone up. It was John Moyse. He didn't sound his usual self. He sounded agitated and upset.

'I wanted you to know at once,' John's voice said. 'Angelo's died.'

'Oh no,' Tom said.

'You need to know,' John went on, 'that it was what people used to call a very good death.'

'Death's never good,' said Tom abruptly, then wished immediately that he hadn't.

'I mean that he died without pain,' John said. 'As far as I could tell, that is.' There was a pause during which Tom registered John's use of the first person and its significance. 'He died in my arms actually.'

'Oh God.'

'I'd rather like to talk to you about it, actually.'

'Well, yes,' said Tom. 'Of course…'

'I meant come over to Boulogne and have a proper talk.'

'Oh right, of course,' said Tom, feeling a whole consciousness-stream of emotions, including surprise at John's request. 'Come any time. We can put you up if you want to stay a night.'

John arrived two days later. Writers and painters are among the few groups of workers who can rearrange their schedules at short notice, and take their weekend breaks mid-week. Tom met John at the ferry port in the middle of the afternoon. John's ship was the Horsa, Tom noticed. It always was these days: the Hengist was still out of action, undergoing major repairs to her hull, following her grounding at Folkestone during the hurricane night.

'We've been invited to dinner with Michel and Armand this evening,' Tom told John at once. 'I know you haven't met them…'

'I know exactly who they are,' John said. 'What you used to call the big boyfriend swap.'

'Anyway,' Tom moved the conversation along a bit, 'that's not till later. We've got all afternoon to talk. Chris is at the yard still. We can go there first. There's beer and coffee on the premises…'

'There was beer and coffee on the boat,' John said. 'And I have had lunch.'

Although the Bassin Napoléon was visible from the ferry port, just a stone's throw across the docks, it wasn't so easy to get to unless you'd brought a boat. Which Tom had not. He'd brought the car instead, and they drove the long way round, circuiting the container docks and the fishing port.

The three of them sat in the little office. Luc was clattering around in the shed beyond the door, doing some metalwork. Luc didn't understand much English and probably wouldn't have listened in even if he had.

Only the buzz of an electric grindstone from time to time reminded them of his presence.

Christopher opened the subject up. 'He died in your arms, you said.'

'Quite by chance. I don't think he knew he was going to die just then. Not until the last few seconds, perhaps. He ate something at lunchtime. Not much, but something. Then we sat together on a sofa…'

'The one by the big windows…' Christopher interrupted, as though he hoped it was.

'Yes.'

'We know it,' Christopher said. 'We sat on it with him…'

'We were talking,' John went on. 'Just ordinarily, about this and that. Then he suddenly said, "Oh dear. I don't feel well. I think I'm going to faint." I wasn't sure what you did when people felt faint. I vaguely remembered you laid them flat. I looked around for a nurse or someone, but at that precise second there was no-one I could ask; no-one to help. Then Angelo said very quietly, "Put your arm round me." So of course I did. He laid his head on my chest as though he was trying to feel or hear my heartbeat. I was suddenly very conscious of it myself. In all the years I'd known him we'd never been in such an intimate embrace…' John paused for a second as though deliberating whether to add something to that or not. He compromised, and half added it. 'Well, maybe once. Anyway, I held him just like that for … perhaps a dozen seconds, though it felt like … feels like … much longer. I wasn't conscious of his breathing. At least, I thought I wasn't. But I slowly became aware that it had stopped. A nurse appeared from a doorway. I called to her. Come here, or help, or something. And then – it's funny what you do – with one arm still wrapped round him and the nurse walking towards us I started to try and take his pulse. There wasn't one in those few seconds. Not that I could find.'

'Oh wow,' said Christopher.

'I panicked at the thought that if he'd died, his bowels or bladder might suddenly open. I took my arm from round him and stood up very quickly. I'm not too proud of that. But by then the nurse was kneeling beside him and doing a proper job of taking his pulse. After a few moments she looked up at me. "I think he's gone," she said. "I'll leave him here with you while I get the doctor. He'll be all right for a few minutes."

'Well, that was really that,' John finished. 'I stood there looking at him till the doctor and the nurse came back. And I thought… Well, I'd never seen anyone die before. But I did think that, well, that was a good way to go. And, I hope when it's my turn… I hope it'll be like that. Then I remembered what you'd told me on the phone. About when you saw him, and what he'd said. That he had a strong sense of God looking after him. He quoted Thomas More, you said.'

'Methinks God maketh me a wanton, and sitteth me on his lap and dandleth me… Or something like that.' said Christopher.

'And I just thought… I just thought that maybe, maybe it was true. That all those things we were taught to believe and that now we don't… Well, supposing God had shown him mercy. Taken pity on him. Loved him, if you like. And spared him a painful death.'

'Don't,' said Tom. 'I know you're upset, but you can't start thinking like that. If there was a God – a God of mercy – why would he single out Angelo and leave other aids sufferers to die a more frightening and painful death?'

'I don't know,' said John. 'I know it makes no sense. It's just…' He didn't attempt to finish the thought but shrugged instead. 'Anyway, that's what I couldn't really say on the phone. Why I had to come here and say it face to face.'

'We're glad you did,' said Christopher.

'Anyway,' John resumed in a more businesslike tone. 'There is something else.' He looked directly at Christopher. 'An envelope with your name on it.'

Christopher was startled. 'What?'

'An envelope addressed to you, Christopher. From Angelo.' John had brought his small backpack into the office with him. Now he leaned down, unzipped a pocket and rummaged in it. He came back up with a white envelope which he handed to Christopher. 'Before I left the hospice one of the doctors told me that patients who knew they were dying often left letters for their nearest and dearest among their belongings. It would be OK, he told me, if I was to look in the drawers of his bedside table at least.

'I said I wasn't one of his nearest and dearest. The doctor gave me an odd look. He said that except for his sister he'd only had four or five visitors. I was the only one, apart from Izzy, who'd been more than once. "That must make you something to him," he said. I didn't answer that. I guessed that the doctor often had to deal with patients' former lovers and sex partners who were either not accepted by the families or else themselves uncomfortable with the fact. He probably had to read between the lines a lot. Anyway I did look in Angelo's locker. And found this. With – as you can see – your name on it.'

By now Christopher had got beyond reading his name on the envelope. He'd opened it up and was perusing the contents with an expression of the greatest concentration on his face.

The envelope contained a handwritten note or letter and some three or four slightly yellowed typewritten sheets. Christopher read the letter first.

Dear Chris

I'm still not sure if I'm allowed to call you Chris. I remember that some people were allowed to and some were not but I can't remember which one I was. Forgive me if I've got this wrong and am being presumptuous!

I found the enclosed while I was going through my papers recently. I didn't remember having written it. But it came back to me – a bit. I'm not sure who I thought I was writing it for, who I imagined might read it. But I can work out when I wrote it. It was in the weeks before I was called by God – in the bathroom of all places, you may remember that. I was looking for love at the time, I suppose, with no idea of where, and how soon, I was actually going to find it.

The enclosed essay, or autobiographical fragment, touches on the subject of love. I think I must have written it with a bottle of something in front of me, because I notice that it begins quite formally and dispassionately, then waxes sentimental and ends up rather maudlin on the subject of lost love.

I've chosen to let you have the document, Chris, because you feature in it quite a lot. Though you weren't the first person I ever 'fell for' you were the second – and I can't send it to that first person because I've no idea where he now is.

I can't remember, can't find, your address in France but no doubt John Moyse can get it to you. He visits me often and is a great support. One of the best friends I've ever had.

And although I realise that when I wrote the enclosed ten years ago I was looking for love in the wrong place (for there is no love between man and woman, man and man, or even between parent and child that approaches the greatness of the love that God has for each of us) I still think of you with love, Chris, and gratitude for the compassion you showed me that day when I was little more than a child – at great risk to yourself. You have been one of the most important people in my life.

With fondest love to Tom and yourself

Angelo

Wordlessly Christopher passed the letter over to John and Tom. Then he began to unfold and read the typewritten sheets. This was what he read.

The summer of 1962 was one in which nothing seemed to happen. Or rather, it was the summer before everything happened. The Cuban missile crisis was still three months away, the death of Kennedy a full year off. That next year would see the Beatles' first string of number one records, the first TV appearance of the Daleks, and the start of *That Was The Week That Was*. The Second Vatican Council would not publish its deliberations until three years later, and homosexuality would not be legal in Britain until two years after that. But it is not true that, as Philip Larkin famously wrote, sex only began in 1963. As far as I was concerned sex began in 1961. While in the summer of 1962 – on June 22nd to be precise – I got expelled from my prep school because of it.

I had returned to school in September 1961 to find myself a house captain. It wasn't a total surprise. The news had been given to me at the end of the previous term by a sort of committee made up of Fr Louis the headmaster, his deputy, Fr Matthew, and the head of sports, Mr Appleton. I was to be head of Fisher house, my vice-captain would be a rather serious boy called John Moyse, and my opposite number, the head of More house, would be a boy I already liked and got on with: Simon Rickman. (Fisher house was named after the bishop of Rochester martyred during the reign of Henry

VIII, and More house was named after Sir Thomas – now St Thomas – More, that king's Chancellor of England, who died a similar death around the same time.) The two house captains traditionally shared a cubicle for two in the senior dormitory. I was quite happy about that. I had no reason not to want to share my curtained-off space with Simon for that final year at school, at Our Lady Star of the Sea, on the cliffs of Kent.

The first night of term the two of us chatted matily till lights out, I don't think I thought about fancying other people, of either sex, when I was thirteen. That came a little later – two or three years along the line. So it wasn't that I actually fancied Simon. I knew I liked him – we'd been classmates and sort of friends for about three years. I was aware now that he was growing into a boy whose appearance was quite pleasing. He was beginning to show a bit of muscle development around his arms and legs, just as I was, and showed signs that he might be going to be quite tall one day. He had a mop of soft blond curls, and blue eyes with a particular shape that I won't try to describe. Enough to say that those eyes made him quite distinctive and, oh all right, attractive, if I have to use the word. But, as usual, it's the things you don't know, can't see, that entice you the most.

On the second night of term Simon asked straight out, 'Do you do it yet?'

'Do what?' I asked him, pretending not to know what he meant.

'You know what I'm talking about,' he said.

'Yeah, OK,' I said. 'And yes, I do. But I only started doing it during the hols.'

'Me too,' he admitted, and sounded a bit relieved to have got this off his chest. Then he said more earnestly, 'Is it something you feel guilty about? Tossing, I mean. Being Catholic and all?'

'I suppose I do,' I said.

Father Matthew walked past the cubicle at that moment to put the dorm lights out and our conversation had to stop for a second or two. When Father Matthew had gone I whispered across the now dark space between our beds, 'Take a leaf out of the Italian book.' (My mother was Italian; I spent part of every holiday in Umbria; I knew the culture; I was beginning to learn the sex culture too.) 'They compartment things, if that's the word. One life outside the church, another for inside it. Confession, I mean. "I've had impure thoughts. I've been impure." No priest ever questions it. You just say it. Then it's gone. You don't have to think about it till the next time.'

In the smallest and most tremulous of whispers that you could imagine, I heard Simon say, 'Come over here.'

I don't need to spell out what happened between us after I climbed into Simon's bed. We simply did to each other what we would otherwise have done to ourselves. Nothing more ambitious than that. Enough to say that it was very nice. After we'd finished we lay side by side for a minute longer, touching at the shoulder and hip, each hearing and feeling the other's warm breath, in a sort of shared wonder and almost shock. Then I knew I had to go back to my own bed. I whispered, 'Goodnight,' very softly as I made a move to leave his bed and pull my pyjamas back up. As I got out I reached down and stroked his curly blond hair, a gesture which he made no effort to resist. He reciprocated, in fact, by extending a hand and running it down my side as I moved away.

No mention of this was made by either of us when we met, as we did constantly, in the course of the next day. Everyone knew we were friends of course, but there was no room for any kind of sentimentality between us. We were house captains of the rival houses and a certain charade of friendly competitiveness was expected of us by the school at large, and not only on the football field. But our eyes met every time that our paths crossed that day, and they told their own story; Simon's china blue and my deep chestnut pair eloquently expressed approval of what had happened the previous night, and a kind of quiet delight in the new turn our friendship had taken.

That night I went to his bed again, and was as warmly received. And the next night, and then the next...

I thought occasionally of trying something with other boys, but in the end I never did – while I remained at prep-school, that is. Something nearly happened once during the summer term. With John Moyse, my vice captain, a boy of whom I found myself growing fond. But John didn't want our friendship to take that turn, as he intimated to me late one evening after we'd returned from a visit to Canterbury. Our art teacher, Miss O'Deere, had exhibited a picture of two of our youngest and newest teachers in the roles of David and Jonathan. Well, that's another story which had repercussions, and there isn't room to tell it here. John and I had drunk a glass or two of sherry each and were a bit flirtatious, both aware of hards-on in each other's shorts. But nothing happened that night and, as it turned out, even had it done, there wouldn't have been time for it to get very far. Two days later the matron discovered Simon and me together in bed, in the middle of doing "it", and all hell broke loose. We were both summarily expelled the following morning. Apart from recording the bravery of one of the teachers, Christopher McGing (one of the pair who'd sat for the David and Jonathan painting) who came and tried to help me make sense of things, and of John M., who behaved more lovingly and bravely than almost anyone in my life has ever done, before or since,

I have to confess it was an episode I don't much care to write about in more detail.: It was one of the most wounding and deeply painful experiences of my life, under which – if you don't mind – I'll now draw a line.

Despite this major upset, however, I went on to the public school I'd been put down for, and John Moyse joined me there. But we were in different houses and saw little of each other after the first few weeks. While never falling out – we always continued to respect each other – we grew apart over the years, and had different sets of friends. I can't speak for John but for my own part I was pretty active sexually throughout my remaining school-days, though always with boys; I never felt the need to experiment with the opposite sex. (Perhaps there's another story there.) I never saw or heard from Simon Rickman again. A pity that, in many ways; although I don't really think that a sexual relationship at the age of thirteen would have been likely to continue to blossom in adult life. But Simon was the precursor to everything that has happened to me, and to everyone I've met and been happy with since. Since? I'm talking about a long time. It's fourteen years, dear God!

Yet it was with Simon that I first found myself on the path in life that I now realise nature had mapped out for me, and I owe him a big thank you, I suppose, for that. I think of him, quite often, with a deep fondness. Very easily I can bring to mind his youthful smiling face, blond curls and blue eyes. To this day I treasure those memories as happy ones, and comforting.

Fondness, I've written. Dare I also think that my experience with Simon was a first rehearsal for falling in love? The second rehearsal came just a few years later when I fell in love – uselessly, pointlessly – with Christopher McGing, the teacher who had risked so much for me on the day Simon and I were expelled.

Risked so much, in fact, that he lost his job as a result. It was pointless because (a) Christopher wasn't around, he lived in France. Because (b) he was attached to someone else. Because (c) Christopher didn't feel the same towards me. Because (d) he was an adult and I was just a stupid kid; it was just a schoolboy crush.

I've been in love many times since. And other people have been in love with me. But these things have never lasted. Maybe love is overrated. Or maybe I've never really been in love. I'm twenty-seven now. Maybe life has more surprises for me yet. Perhaps I should write 'I'm only twenty-seven.' That leaves a little more room for hope.

But to get back to Simon Rickman. For the sake of argument, and rather than splitting hairs about the meaning of that big word beginning with L, I'll settle for thinking of him as my first love.

Did Simon grow up gay, as I did? That's one thing I still ask myself when I think about him. There is another question I ask myself, but to express it must resort to the words of another: they seem more apt than any that I, half Italian that I am, could possibly come up with. Please forgive my laziness, if that is what it is, in misquoting them in rounding off this narrative. You remember the tune, I hope... *I wonder if he ever thinks about me: I wonder who's kissing him now.*

'Good heavens,' said Christopher. He sat for a few seconds, shaking his head. Then, 'I don't know what to say. But you've read the letter. Now you can get your heads round this.' He looked at John, grinning mischievously for a moment. 'There's things about *you* I didn't know in it. Nice things, though.' He held out Angelo's testament towards the other two, not really caring which of them read it first.

ELEVEN

'His English was very fastidious,' said Tom. 'Pluralising hard-on as hards-on rather than hard-ons.' He looked at Christopher. 'Did we teach him that?'

'We wouldn't have taught him that particular example,' said Christopher, poker-faced. 'Courts-martial, perhaps…'

'Forgive me for being a spoilsport,' said John, 'but neither of you actually taught English to either of us. We had Mr Charteris. You taught the lower forms. 2A and 2B.'

'2B and not 2B,' said Christopher automatically. It wasn't very funny but it went back twenty-five years as, suddenly at this moment, everything did.

'I don't know,' said Tom, 'exactly what Angelo was getting at by sending us … sorry, sending Chris … that. It's mostly about Simon Rickman. Who I barely remember.'

'He was nice,' said John, and the fondness of a reawakened memory kindled a little glow on his face.

'So is Angelo trying to tell us,' Christopher asked, 'that we need to track down Simon Rickman and tell him that Angelo's dead?'

'I don't think so,' said John. 'The recent letter doesn't mention Simon by name. His presence in the older document is just by chance, I think. Angelo's main reason for sending it to you was…' John stopped for a second. '…Was because of you, I think. Just his rather garbled way of saying thank you. And he said it. You were one of the most important people in his life.'

'He said the same about you,' Tom reminded John. 'And what's this about Angelo and you anyway?' The corners of Tom's mouth risked an upward tweak. 'The night of the private view of the David and Jonathan. I didn't think you'd ever had anything to do with all that.'

'We remember the two of you very cosied up one night,' said Cristopher. 'In the Assembly hall, you playing the Moonlight sonata to an audience of one,' Then, 'Sorry. Mustn't tease you.'

'Tease me as much as you like.' Sportingly John managed to laugh. 'Nothing ever happened between me and Angelo. As you say, I was never like that. Yes, we were very close friends for a short time. In our last term at Star of the Sea. Your only term.' He raised his eyebrows meaningfully at Tom and Christopher. 'You won't remember this,' he went on, 'but after we all came back from Canterbury in the minibus there was a cold supper laid on for all of us in the staff dining room. You won't remember because you always ate there. For Angelo and me it was the first and only time we ever did.'

'Angelo was given his breakfast there on the morning he was expelled,' put in Christopher unnecessarily. 'Less than thirty-six hours after that.'

'Anyway,' John went on, 'after we'd had our cold chicken and salad or whatever it was, Angelo and I walked down the chapel cloister a little way. We had one of those talks… I don't remember what we talked about, but it was one of those talks you have as teenagers when you suddenly unbutton yourselves – so to speak – and want to tell the other person everything about yourself. Everything that's in your heart. Getting to know someone you already know, but in a completely new way.'

'Not only teenagers,' Tom said quietly.

'The only thing I remember was that Angelo suddenly said, "We could walk out into the garden. Nobody would see us." When it came to that bit, you see, I've remembered the exact words. Funny that. I said, "To do what?" Though I knew perfectly well what he was getting at. "You know what I mean," he said, with some justifiable irritation in his voice. "No," I said. "I don't want that."

'He put his hand on my shoulder then, and tried to pull my face towards him as though he wanted to kiss it. Remember, we'd both had a glass of sherry a little earlier. We were only thirteen. We were as high as kites. I jerked away from him, I'm sorry to say.' John paused for a half-second. 'I'm sorry to say ... because I'm sorry now that I disappointed him. It would only have been a kiss. What harm could it have done?'

'And yet…?' prompted Chris.

'And yet, in the end that moment did for our relationship. You're right. Even without the kiss. OK, I was his friend some thirty hours later when I went and talked to him – just as you did, Chris – while he waited with a tear-stained face and full of fear and anguish for his parents to come and collect him: for the moment when he'd have to face the music. But when we met up later, three months later, at Downside, we both saw at the instant of our meeting that it could never be the same again. We would be schoolfellows still. But never friends. I mean, friends in the real sense. Friends with a capital F.'

'Until the last few weeks perhaps?' Tom gently asked.

John's brave adult face crumpled slightly. 'I'm glad I came here,' he said.

They did go to dinner at Michel and Armand's that evening. 'I'd better tell you straight away,' Michel said as soon as they'd all greeted one another and John had been introduced. 'There's bad news from Paris. Gérard's ill.'

'He gets ill every winter when the weather turns,' said Tom.

'This time it's more serious,' said Michel. 'He's in a nursing home.'

'Merde,' said Christopher. No sooner had one friend stopped being ill in a hospice because death had taken him than someone else was moving into his place. The tears of the world were a constant quantity, as Samuel Becket had pointed out. Whenever one person stopped crying someone else started.

'He's got pneumonia,' said Armand, and everyone was gravely silent for a moment because they all knew what that meant, or thought they did.

They talked about going to visit him. Two male couples. Two visits. Tom thought he could re-allocate the time he'd planned to spend visiting Angelo again in England but he didn't voice the thought. They talked about Angelo of course, but then moved the conversation on to other things. You couldn't spend a whole dinner party talking about people who had recently died or who soon would.

'Has Tom sold the picture of the crab yet?' Armand asked Christopher in the interval between the warm salad and the Brittany monkfish.

'Almost,' Christopher said. 'His mother's thinking of buying it. To furnish her new place in the south.'

'I thought it was rather splendid,' said John, leaning into the ex-lovers' dialogue. He had seen it that afternoon, hanging on the wall of the boatyard shed but hadn't commented on it; there had been more serious things to talk about. Christopher didn't say anything about it now. He had never told Tom that since the news of Angelo's illness the crab picture had become inextricably entwined in his mind with the idea of the aids virus.

'Are you working on anything else?' Armand asked Tom. 'In the way of painting, I mean.'

'Yes,' said Tom. 'I'm doing a picture of mum's new house. In its picturesque, uninhabitable state. Before we smarten it up.' He gave a self-deprecating snicker of a laugh, in recognition of the fact that he was in the presence, in the shape of Michel, of a real artist.

Once he was dead Angelo became a friar and a priest again and was buried with all the solemnity that traditionally accompanied the funeral of someone of that rank. His sister told John who, now back in England, passed the message on to Tom and Christopher that none of them were expected to attend it. Tom and Christopher didn't go to the funeral but John did: his presence, as he kindly put it to the others, 'representing all of us.'

Instead of going to England Tom and Christopher went to Paris. They found Gérard in bed and being brave about his increasing breathlessness in a nursing home at St-Ouen, one of the capital's northern suburbs. It was one of the things that went with getting older, Tom thought. You found yourself visiting the sick and the dying with increasing frequency. You got into practice with it. With Gérard they talked about painting, about what Michel was working on at the moment, about the other people they knew in common. Gérard touched lightly on the subject of his symptoms, trying to make a joke of them. What nobody mentioned was the fact (nobody used the expression 'the elephant in the room' back then) that Gérard was dying.

Malcolm had to drop the price he was asking for the boatyard. A few people had shown an interest, had had long conversations with Tom, Christopher and Luc, but then faded from the scene. It hadn't helped that stock markets all around the world had crashed spectacularly just three days after the hurricane had hit southern England and northern France, losing a quarter of their value on average. Those with big financial decisions to make were jittery. Exceptions were the people like

Tom's mother who were buying up unwanted old houses in the Dordogne for a song.

May's house purchase and the hoped-for sale of the boatyard were tied together by the involvement of Tom and Christopher in both of them. Luc was more sympathetic to their situation than they had any right to expect. He stood to lose his job alongside the two of them should a new owner of the yard turn out to be a master shipwright himself and not need to employ another one. 'Take as much time down in the Dordogne as you need,' he told them. 'We all know how quiet it is here in the winter months. Especially while we're all in Limbo. We can keep in touch by phone.' Luc frowned for a second. 'I suppose there is a phone in this place you're doing up?'

'There is,' said Tom. 'Though it's not connected up. But we can get onto that soon. Meantime, we can give you a daily call from a call-box. Fix a regular time. Will that do?'

Not only was there a phone at May's newly acquired property, there was running water, electricity and gas. The only utility the place lacked was main drains. When Tom and Christopher went down there in late November to spend a fortnight getting work off the ground they knew they were going to have to rough it to some extent. They took sleeping-bags, torches and candles and – although the weather was mercifully mild at the beginning of that winter – all their warmest clothes.

By now plans for the new bathroom extension had been drawn up and approved. Because the intended floor area did not exceed a certain number of square metres the project did not require full-scale planning permission, *permis de construire*, but a more easily and quickly achievable *déclaration de travaux*, an acknowledgement that work was being carried out with the local authority's blessing. All this had been taken care of before Tom and Christopher arrived in the south and work was ready to start.

The extension was to be a simple brick-built structure on two floors, tacked on to the back of the house around the area of the kitchen back door. Its first floor would become a bright modern bathroom while below it the space would be divided into a back-hall area that could accommodate a washing machine and a deepfreeze, plus a small loo. But almost as major would be the task of connecting the new facilities to the main drain that ran along the riverfront road below the front of the house.

The builder they had engaged, a jovial red-faced man called Jean-Pierre, would do most of the work with the help of his apprentice Antoine. But Jean-Pierre planned to engage two extra men to do the heavy labour involved in digging up the garden to bury the sewage pipe in a deep trench that would run out into the road. Using a mechanical digger was not an option because of the cramped space at the side of the house and the steep slope at the front.

'There won't be any need for you to employ two more men,' Tom told Jean-Pierre. 'Christopher and I can do the digging ourselves.'

'And take bread from the mouths of a French family to put it in yours,' said Jean-Pierre. It was the first time he'd been less than affable towards them.

'Did you have particular guys in mind?' Tom asked him.

'No,' said Jean-Pierre, 'but I'll soon find some. There's plenty to choose from.'

'Then it's only hypothetical,' said Tom. 'Whereas I'm trying to save my mother money. She's not a wealthy lady. If I can't afford you I might have to look elsewhere.' He shrugged his shoulders in the very French, take-it-or-leave-it way that he'd learnt from Luc at the boatyard.

Jean-Pierre looked a little less adamant after the shrug. 'You probably couldn't even swing a pick-axe,' he said hopefully. He probably mentioned the pick-axe because there was one leaning up against the back door, outside which this conversation was taking place.

Tom, who up to this moment had never swung a pick-axe in his life, now picked it up, raised it high above his head and brought it down on a lump of waste concrete, which was handily lying just a metre away. Even more handily it promptly split in two. Tom didn't say anything after that. Privately he gave thanks for the heavy work he'd been doing in the boatyard for years though, remembering that he was now forty-six, he hoped that Christopher would take care of the stonier bits of the trench's course – Christopher being only forty-three.

'Bon, bien,' said Jean-Pierre. (That meant all right.) Then he added, also in French, 'You win,' and the deal was done. Tom was glad of the fluency of his French. Most of the Brits who were buying up property in the area could say little more than *bonjour*, and were at a disadvantage when it came to negotiating with the builders they employed. He wondered how his mother would manage when she finally came out here – ongoing French lessons notwithstanding.

Tom and Christopher laboured by day and camped in the house by night. Digging the sewer trench by hand turned out to be crucifyingly hard work. Had they realised the extent of the torment it would inflict on their unprepared bodies they would never have undertaken it. They learned the hard way why the people who were paid to dig holes in roads all over the world were so often spotted leaning on their shovels. Only an iron determination not to lose face prevented them from telling Jean-Pierre that they'd made a terrible mistake in deciding to do the work themselves and would he please get those two hypothetical other labourers in to finish it. With the many necessary rest breaks they took, the whole task kept them occupied for a fortnight. Mercifully Jean-Pierre and Antoine helped dig out the box junction around the main sewer in the road, and they took over completely when it came to lining the little man-hole with brick and making the connection itself with the help of an angle-grinder, its attendant dust cloud, and a lot of cement.

They had no television for the evenings. They made do with a radio and cassette player that they'd brought with them. In any case they went to bed absurdly early, usually too tired for sex either then or in the mornings. At first they laid their sleeping-bags each night on the floor of one of the bedrooms but as November became December and the weather grew colder they migrated downstairs and slept on the floor of the living room in front of the damped-down wood-burner. Tom phoned his mother and told her she would have to bite the bullet – before they could even think about decorating the place – and pay for someone to install central heating.

Getting the house phone connected was proving more complicated than they had expected. But using a call-box for a fortnight was just another of those things they were getting used to, like using the outside toilet at the end of the garden.

They made their daily call to Luc at midday precisely. As punctually as in days gone by labourers in the fields would have stopped work to say the Angelus. The day before they were due to return to Boulogne – the day the trench was finished – Luc told them that Michel had come by with a message for them. Gérard had died in Paris.

That was sad news indeed but not unexpected. What stunned Christopher, who was making that day's call, was what Luc said next.

'There's other news.' Luc's voice turned suddenly husky, almost unsure of itself. Christopher had never before heard it sound quite like this. 'I've put in an offer on the boatyard. Malcolm has accepted it.'

Christopher wasn't quite sure if he'd understood correctly. 'Sorry?' he queried. 'Did you just say you're buying the boatyard?'

'I've talked it over with my family,' Luc told him, still a little shyly. 'They're lending me the money for the deposit. I'll be running it myself, though. I've learned how to do it over the years, just by watching. Being observant. Odile will be doing the paperwork.' Odile his young wife, who at present worked at the post office.

'Mon dieu,' said Christopher, then quickly amended his reaction. 'Sorry, I should have said congratulations. I guess we'd better leave further discussion till we're back tomorrow or the next day.' He put the phone down and stood in the call-box for a few seconds. He wasn't sure if he'd be able to move from there without his legs buckling under him. Then he pulled himself together and walked back along the riverfront, wondering what sentences he was going to string together to tell Tom that, first, Gérard was dead and, second, that their former employee had just sacked them.

TWELVE

Christmas is a wonderful time for separating people from those they love. The number of people worldwide who fall in love in their first year at college or university and are then obliged to spend Christmas apart must run each year into the tens of millions. While for gay lovers down the centuries the quota must have been ninety-nine point nine percent.

Tom spent the Christmas of 1987 at the house of his brother Dominic and his wife and children near High Wycombe. May joined them for Christmas Day. That was the whole point. Christopher spent those few days with his parents and one of his sisters at Maidstone in Kent. About the same distance south-east of London – thirty miles – as High Wycombe was north-west. Both Tom and Christopher were bursting – almost physically painfully – with news that it was too soon, because it was not yet confirmed, to announce. The news was that they might both soon be rich.

They had returned to Boulogne after their two weeks of hard labour and penitential living conditions in Castillon to find a ferment of new things to deal with. Boatyards mostly close over Christmas and New Year just as work on building projects also comes to a stop. But funerals go on regardless. Undertakers are always busy, as bakers are, because the human race never stops dying or needing bread. So Tom and Christopher went to Paris just a few days before Christmas to attend Gérard's funeral in a small church that stood in the shadow, quite literally, of the basilica of the Sacré Coeur in Montmartre.

Gérard had been quite famous when a young man but in more recent years his fame had shrunk. Yet immediately following his death, when the obituary notices appeared in the national press, he became famous all over again. The art-buying public, who had omitted to buy his work for a couple of decades, now suddenly found they couldn't get enough of it. Paintings that had languished in gallery basements found a new market, and money began to pour into the dead man's bank account in a way that it hadn't done for many years since. It was fortunate for Gérard that thanks to his late partner Henri's wealth he hadn't really missed it.

The sudden upturn in his fortunes also meant that the church was packed for his funeral Mass.

This, and the reception that followed it, were organised by Michel. He was Gérard's executor and had known for some time that he would be. Tom and Christopher now realised that obviously somebody must have been appointed Gérard's executor: it was just something they'd never had any reason to think about.

Michel was not only Gérard's executor, he was among his heirs. Gérard was one of a rare breed: an unmarried man who was the only child of two parents who themselves had had no siblings. Thus he had no blood relatives closer than third cousins, with whom he had no contact. It was quite difficult in France to leave estate to anyone other than blood relations. The Code Napoléon was very hot on the matter of keeping things in the family, and long lost relatives had a period of grace of ten years in which to come forward and claim the inheritance of people they had never known or cared about. There were ways round this, though, for those who were clever enough and knew good lawyers. Henri had come into both categories. He had turned himself and his partner Gérard into a limited company. That had worked the magic when Henri had died and left everything to Gérard. It worked its magic again now. The terms of Gérard's will were made known to Tom and Christopher in stages. First in an informal way from Michel. Second in an official letter from a notaire.

Gérard's cash and investments – they were substantial – were to be divided between Michel and Armand. The house and its contents – except for the collection of pictures, which were an additional specific bequest to Michel – would go jointly to Christopher and Tom.

Neither of them had expected this, or anything like it. They had to confront the fact that they would now be joint owners of a rambling old house and a half-acre of wild garden in the middle of the Montmartre district of central Paris. It was not an unpleasing prospect. They now had to make a difficult choice, but a choice that was a luxury, given that few people in the world were ever called upon to make it: did they want to live in the huge pile they'd inherited in Paris or would they sell it? It was an exquisitely horned dilemma.

'So what do you want to do?' Tom asked Christopher on their first night back together at the flat near the fish market. 'Sell the place or live in it?'

'We already know,' said Christopher. 'We talked about it.'

'Umm?' Tom asked.

'We agreed that if we had the money we'd buy a house in the Dordogne, like your mum has, and do it up.'

'We could buy fifty houses in the Dordogne with the money the Rue St-Vincent will fetch,' said Tom. 'We can't do fifty houses up. Just remember that trench we dug.'

'Will I ever forget it?' said Christopher. 'But we wouldn't need to do fifty houses up all at once. Little by little. And we could pay other people to do them up. Then ease the properties out onto the market one by one.'

Tom looked at Christopher in surprise. He'd never heard him use expressions like that one. Neither of them had ever had any experience of business. They'd helped to manage other people's businesses, that was true, but

Tom knew well that there was a world of difference between that and going into business on your own account. 'I think we should take a few days to just think about it,' was Tom's split-infinitive verdict.

But once that had been said it became clear that they didn't need to do much thinking about it. Each of them independently knew what they wanted to do. It didn't involve moving to Paris and living in a huge house there. It did involve what they were already learning to do. Buying and improving old houses in the south of France. They would live in one, ideally, and sell the others on. They had no experience of that last part but there was nothing, surely, that you couldn't learn if you were prepared to do the practice.

There were things to do first, though. There was work to be done concerning the handover of the boatyard to Luc and his wife and there was the post-New-Year resumption of work at May's house in Castillon. They needed to be there to supervise the imminent installation of central heating and then do some of the painting and decorating of the interior that was essential before May could move in. Ideally both Tom and Christopher needed to be in both places at once. Failing that, one of them needed to be in Castillon and one in Boulogne. They tossed a coin that would decide who would do which when they had to part for a week in the middle of January. That coin decided that Christopher should take the train down to Castillon while Tom stayed in Boulogne.

That winter the weather had remained mild everywhere. Even so, Christopher found a just noticeable difference when he arrived in the south. Incautious magnolia trees and camellia bushes were already putting their big flowers out. When, at Libourne, he got off the train that had brought him from Paris he found the afternoon sun had a perceptible warmth to it.

From Libourne a small branch line ran up alongside the Dordogne, all the way to Sarlat. Its third stop was Castillon-la-Bataille, where the station was a comfortable fifteen-minute stroll from May's edge of town house.

Tom had said, 'Are you sure you'll be all right there on your own?' with concern in his voice. Christopher had said he'd be fine. He'd be busy working all day and he had his radio, a couple of books and his sleeping-bag for the nights.

But he did wonder, during his first evening alone in the little house, how May was going to cope with living here all on her own, knowing nobody and speaking very little French. Would she end up haunting the town's bars in the evening as some lonely old ladies did? Silently watching the young motor-bike boys playing table football in a cold unwelcoming room beneath a strip-light?

For there were few equivalents in provincial France of the cosy English pub. Middle-aged men didn't hang out with their mates there, chewing the fat for two hours over three pints of bitter each. Most bars closed early anyway, and the only people who would spend two hours in them were serious drinkers of the kind you wouldn't want to socialise with.

All the same, Christopher did pop into the nearest bar that first evening – the staff recognised and greeted him, which was cheering – before settling back at home in front of the log-burner with his cassette player and his book. But it was a lonely evening and night. He was glad when morning came – in January it came very late to western France – and it was time to get up and start work.

The bathroom extension had been topped out before Christmas, but it needed further work both inside and out. The plumbing still waited to be connected, and there was a small amount of structural work to be undertaken where wood had rotted in other parts of the house. In a couple of days the heating contractor would arrive with a gas boiler and radiators and fit the system up. The house would be reasonably well modernised by the time Christopher left it again at the end of the week. In the meantime he found himself plenty to do with an electric sander and tins of paint.

He wouldn't be digging any more sewer trenches, that was certain. He hoped he would never have to do that again as long as he lived. However, that experience had had one very positive outcome. It had vastly increased his standing and Tom's in the eyes of Jean-Pierre the builder, and Antoine, his apprentice. Christopher's suggestions on any subject to do with the building work were now listened to with a serious degree of respect.

Jean-Pierre was married and had two children of school age. Antoine was a youthful twenty-four-year-old with blond hair and blue eyes. Christopher thought that he looked rather the way he himself had done at that age. He knew Antoine was twenty-four because he had volunteered the information back in November and he hadn't had a birthday since. He had also volunteered the information that he had a girlfriend with whom he lived. It always amused Christopher (and Tom too) that when a straight guy met a gay one that was always one of the first things the straight guy felt he needed to point out. No matter how friendly the encounter was. In fact, in Christopher's experience, the more quickly the straight guy and the gay one took to each other the sooner the girlfriend got mentioned. In Antoine's case that had happened within five minutes of their first November handshake.

Antoine had certainly taken to Tom and Christopher. Back in November-December he would probably have been prepared to follow them around like a dog if Jean-Pierre hadn't called him to heel constantly with commands and tasks. As for Christopher and Tom, they both took pleasure in the company of the polite and intelligent young man with his trim physique (so far as you could guess at it through his winter workman's clothes) and his appealing face.

At the end of that first January day back at work on the riverside house Antoine seemed to hang about a bit before saying goodnight. Christopher was only just aware of that, though. He certainly didn't read anything into it. Once Jean-Pierre and then Antoine had departed he spent a little time deciding what he would have for supper later. He'd been to a nearby mini-market during the day and bought some supplies. Those included a sizeable stock of eggs. He thought he would probably make himself an omelette, with cheese and sliced onions in it. But that was for later. He would go out to his local bar and unwind over a beer first. Maybe two beers. You were normally served beer in a small glass in France unless you asked specifically for something bigger. Each small glass was roughly half a pint.

On the way to the bar Christopher stopped at the phone-box and made his daily call to Tom. Neither of them had any major news to impart but it was good to be able to talk. Christopher said he was just heading out for a beer, Tom said he was going to do the same thing himself, then Christopher hung up, left the kiosk and continued his walk along the street. When he walked into the bar Christopher was startled to see Antoine there, sitting at a table by himself, nursing a glass of beer. Only two other tables were occupied, and two men stood at the counter, chatting to the barman. The barman broke off his conversation to greet Christopher, and

Christopher ordered his drink. *'Un demi, s'il vous plait.'* Then he walked over to the table at which Antoine sat. *'Re-bonjour,'* he said, smiling but a little puzzled. Antoine knew that Tom and Christopher had used this bar quite regularly back in the autumn, but as far as they knew he didn't frequent the place himself.

Antoine looked up at Christopher, grinned a bit awkwardly and said, *'Re,'* the short, casual form of the hallo-again greeting that Christopher had just come out with.

Christopher checked before sitting down. 'Meeting someone, or can I join you?'

Antoine didn't say anything. He indicated with an outstretched hand that Christopher should take a seat. Then he did speak. In French, of course. 'I've had a bust-up with Elodie. She's chucked me out.'

'Oh là,' said Christopher. 'Will she let you back tonight?'

Antoine shook his head firmly. *'Non,'* he said.

'Have you got somewhere you can sleep?' Christopher asked.

'I'm just thinking about that,' Antoine said.

The barman arrived with Christopher's small glass of beer at that moment, saving Christopher from having to delve further into Antoine's plans for overnight. Christopher raised his glass towards Antoine's and said, 'Well, cheers anyway. I'm sure things will become clearer after a drink.'

'Actually,' Christopher heard Antoine say as he took his first swallow, 'I was wondering if I could stay with you tonight.'

It was one of those moments when someone says something totally surprising and unexpected and yet you realise as soon as the words are formed that you knew all along that they were going to say it. At least that was how it felt to Christopher.

'Well, of course you'd be very welcome,' said Christopher in a rather flustered voice. 'But you know what the place is like. No beds or anything. And no central heating till Thursday. I sleep downstairs in a sleeping-bag – on the floor in front of the wood-burner. You know that.'

Antoine peered into Christopher's eyes with a very serious, almost strained, look on his face. 'It would be good to have some company,' he said.

Christopher stared back at him in astonished silence for a couple of seconds. Then he said, 'Yes, you're right. It would.'

They drank three more beers together. Christopher asked Antoine if he'd eaten yet and Antoine said no, he hadn't. Christopher said that he had plenty of eggs at home and they could get a fresh baguette on the way back. Would Antoine be OK with an omelette? Antoine said that would be fine and smiled gratefully. Then a thought seemed to strike him. He said, in a wondering tone, 'I've never been cooked for by an English *mec*.'

'There's a first time for everything,' Christopher answered, poker-faced. 'And it won't be as bad as you expect.'

Although the house was still unfurnished it was not completely un-equipped. There was a gas stove for cooking on, a frying pan, a saucepan, a small selection of plates and knives and forks. And there were two plain wood kitchen chairs that were pressed into service during the daytimes for use as trestles when anyone needed to saw planks or battens to length. There were also a corkscrew and two glasses.

Antoine watched Christopher cooking the omelettes, with a glass of red wine in his hand and an approving expression on his face. He himself cut up the baguette.

They ate with their plates on their laps, sitting on the two chairs in front of the blazing log-burner, facing each other. 'You're a good cook,' Antoine said. Then he thought for a moment before asking, 'Are you always the cook? Or does Tom do some of it?'

'Fifty-fifty,' said Christopher. 'Actually Tom's the better cook.'

'You've been together a long time, haven't you?' Antoine said.

'Twenty-four years,' said Christopher. He added facetiously, 'I was a child bride.' Which made Antoine laugh. 'Though to be honest there were a few years in the middle of that time when we each went off with someone else. But somehow we got back together again.'

'Lucky for you,' said Antoine. 'With all this aids and stuff about.'

'It's made gay men more monogamous,' said Christopher. 'More careful. Cautious.'

'Though it depends what you actually do with people,' Antoine said.

'Meaning…?' Christopher asked.

'In terms of sex.' Antoine gave an audible nervous sniff. 'Isn't it only dangerous if you have anal sex? I mean, that's what I've heard. And other stuff's quite safe.'

'As far as we know,' said Christopher in a cautious voice. He changed the subject. Perhaps because he was drinking wine immediately after three beers he told Antoine about the legacy from Gérard and what he and Tom were hoping to do with it. But he didn't go as far as to suggest that Antoine might help them do it. The drink hadn't loosened his tongue to that extent.

When the meal was over, the wine was finished and the plates and frying-pan washed, there was really nothing to do except go to bed. Except there were no beds.

'Now, how are we going to manage this?' said Christopher. 'I've only got the one sleeping-bag…'

'Does it open right up?' Antoine asked a bit hesitantly.

'Yes, it does,' Christopher said.

Antoine's caution was gradually departing in the wake of Christopher's. Now he said quite boldly, 'Then we could lay the dust-sheets on the floor here – give them a good shake first – lie on those like on a groundsheet, and spread the opened-up sleeping-bag over the top of us like a duvet.' That was the first time the words *we* and *us* had been used by either of them. In French it was the same word for both. *Nous*. It had come from Antoine's lips first.

'Sounds like a good plan,' Christopher said.

They parted company for a few minutes, taking it in turn to go out into the chilly garden and use the privy at the end of it. Then they stood together in front of the log-burner, facing each other challengingly as they got undressed.

Antoine wouldn't get undressed completely, Christopher thought. He'd leave his underpants on at least. In which case Christopher would follow his example. It would be a signal from both of them that their sleeping arrangement, though of necessity very intimate, would be chaste. But Antoine did take his underpants off, without pausing for thought before doing so, and Christopher, also without pausing, followed suit. Both of them were erect; there was no hiding the fact, and they made no attempt to. They didn't get down and between the covers straight away. They moved towards each other's naked bodies, glowing in the firelight, and embraced. Deliberately they pushed their cocks against each other's, mashing their hardness for a minute. But it was cold despite the log-burner, now damped for the night. And even a mild January night on the Dordogne isn't as mild as all that. After that minute was up they disentangled themselves and climbed into their makeshift floor bed. And then re-embraced each other. And went on to do a bit more than that.

THIRTEEN

After a night of that sort the morning arrives like the bill in a restaurant where you've dined more expensively than you'd planned to. At least that was the thought that first came to Christopher's mind when he awoke. He and Antoine both woke early and had to make emergency arrangements that would prevent Jean-Pierre from realising they had spent the night together when he arrived for work at half-past eight.

'You'll have to go out and get a coffee and a croissant in some café where they don't know you,' Christopher told Antoine. 'Come back a few minutes after Jean-Pierre gets here.' He looked around him. Antoine's tool bag lay on the kitchen floor. That was all right. Back in the autumn he had regularly left his tools overnight, rather than hump them back home each evening. The two glasses and plates on the draining board were more of a giveaway. Christopher would put them back in the cupboard as soon as he was dressed.

Antoine scrambled into his clothes a little before eight o'clock. He gave Christopher a kiss just before he let himself out into the dark morning, like a husband leaving for work. Christopher remained alone in the house, almost unable to believe what had happened. He tidied away the crockery, then picked up the sleeping-bag and folded it up. Then he looked down at the heavy-duty dust-sheet on which they'd lain and had sex. It was covered with a multitude of stains and spillages anyway, and Christopher was pretty sure that a couple more would go unnoticed. But would it smell of the two of them? Christopher lugged the thing to the door and, standing on the outside step, shook it as best he could in the hope of freshening it up a bit. It was a difficult thing to do alone: the thing was as big and nearly as heavy as a carpet. He regretted that he hadn't thought to ask

Antoine to help him with the task before chivvying him out.

Then he was left with nothing else to do except make himself a cup of coffee and wait for Jean-Pierre to arrive … and then for Antoine's reappearance. To drink a coffee. To sit. To wait. To think.

Christopher hadn't slept with anyone except Tom for the last nine years. Since the big boyfriend swap had played itself out and they had got back together again they had been totally monogamous. At least Christopher knew that he had. He wouldn't be telling Tom about what had happened. Fortunately he wasn't going to have to look him in the eye until he got back to Boulogne on Saturday. That gave him five days in which to compose himself.

At least it would do if last night had been just a crazy one-off. But supposing it hadn't been? What if Antoine's girlfriend wouldn't take him back tonight? What if Antoine wanted to repeat the experiment? What if Christopher did?

Feelings of guilt and domestic complications aside, it had been a very pleasant experience. They had cuddled and kissed beneath the sleeping-bag at first, then played with each other's cocks until they came, all over each other and over the improvised groundsheet. They'd done this twice. Then Antoine started to cry quietly. So quietly that Christopher almost didn't notice. But he had noticed. He was wise enough not to ask Antoine what he was crying about. The reasons were probably multiple, interwoven and complex. Christopher didn't know if Antoine had previous experience with men or if this was his first time. Asking questions at that point would probably have opened up difficult subjects that Antoine would have been unwilling or unable to articulate. Instead, Christopher had held him tightly, stroked his hair and face in the darkness and kissed his wet cheeks.

Sitting alone now over his first coffee of the morning Christopher found to his confusion that he missed Antoine's presence in the kitchen; he was almost counting down the minutes of the half hour that was left before he would be coming back.

When Antoine did return it all played perfectly. Jean-Pierre arrived first, greeted the solitary Christopher, then Antoine came in about two minutes later. He said *bonjour* to Christopher with the practised nonchalance of an actor and then set to work. But in the course of that day, if Antoine came into close range of Christopher while temporarily out of sight of Jean-Pierre he would make some slight physical contact with him: a light ruffle of the hair, a pat on the bottom, a stroke of the elbow. And, after checking that Jean-Pierre was still not looking at them, Christopher would reciprocate. As the day wore on it began to seem more and more likely that the previous night had not been a one-off but that this evening would see a repeat performance.

When it was time to down tools as the pale afternoon darkened to evening blackness Jean-Pierre left first. Antoine put his coat on and told his departing boss that he was going down the garden to the toilet and that he'd see him in the morning. He said nothing to Christopher at that point and made no eye contact with him. But when he returned through the new back door a minute later he immediately grinned at Christopher – who was standing in the kitchen doing nothing but thinking about quite a few things that all seemed rather difficult – and took his coat off. A few minutes later the two of them were naked beneath the opened-out sleeping-bag with the dust-sheet under them to mitigate ever so slightly the bare floor's hardness.

After an hour or two had passed extremely quickly Christopher asked Antoine, 'What would you like to do this evening?' But he didn't wait for Antoine to answer.

He went on at once. 'I'd like to take you out and buy us dinner.'

Antoine looked uncertain. He said, 'What, in Castillon?'

'Where everyone knows you.' Christopher nodded his understanding. 'We could get the train to Ste-Foy or Libourne. Or even Bordeaux if your fame extends to those two places.'

Antoine grinned into Christopher's face and squeezed him. They were still snuggled together beneath the sleeping-bag. 'Nobody knows me in Libourne,' he said. 'In fact I don't know myself in Libourne. Except for changing trains at the station I've hardly been there a dozen times in my life.'

'In which case,' said Christopher, 'that's where we'll go.' He returned Antoine's squeeze. 'Now get up and put some clothes on.'

They walked to the station on opposite sides of the street, pretending not to know each other. When Christopher stopped on the way to phone Tom from a call-box Antoine loitered fifty yards away, pretending to be very interested in the contents of a shop window full of teddy-bears. At the station Christopher bought both their tickets while Antoine walked straight onto the platform. Only when the train came in and it was clear that no-one Antoine knew was getting on or off it did they move towards each other and board and take their seats side by side.

In Libourne they walked through handsome streets towards the ancient centre, a colonnaded square near the river. There was an imposing hotel in the square, which had a restaurant. They went in and, not least because it was a quiet Tuesday night in January, were given a great welcome. As they sat, drinking a kir aperitif and waiting for their starter of crab mousse, they talked banally about cement render, planning regulations and stone-cladding.

About anything in the world actually, except about the sex they'd had together and wanted to have more of. And as they talked an idea came timidly to Christopher. Though as he studied the waiters around them and formed a certain impression about one of them the idea grew bolder. He shared it with Antoine. 'We could stay the night here. What do you think? I'd be paying.'

There were still hotels in France and England where the idea of two men who fancied each other wanting to share a room in order to have sex together was considered shocking. 'Are you sure?' Antoine asked doubtfully, looking around him. 'We'd have to get up very early.'

'We'll get a wake-up call,' Christopher said confidently. 'I'll have a word with that waiter when he comes back.' Christopher noticed that Antoine didn't ask which waiter he was talking about. He added, 'I mean, if you'd like to…'

'I'd like to,' said Antoine. 'I just wasn't sure… I mean, we've got no luggage.'

'I'll talk to the waiter,' said Christopher. 'I think he'll be understanding.'

Christopher chose his moment and put his question. He explained that their wanting to stay the night was a sudden decision. That was why they had no luggage. If a room could be found for them he would pay with his credit card this evening. The waiter said he would ask at reception. He came back a few minutes later, cheerfully smiling, and by the time Antoine and Christopher were tucking into their darnes of salmon the deal was done, the room was booked, and even the wake-up call was sorted.

So Christopher spent the night in a double bed in a plush hotel room with a handsome man nearly twenty years younger than himself. Before climbing in for the night they showered together. As they grappled with each other under the running hot water, and then snuggled beneath the cosy covers happily masturbating each other to climax after climax, one part of Christopher could hardly believe his luck; while another part was aghast, wondering what unpredictable new world was going to be created out of this big-bang chaos.

The wake-up call came all too early. But there was nothing to be done except obey it. The darkness of the countryside their train clattered through was eerie and deathly quiet. The wintry wastes of dormant vineyards were lit only by pin-pricks of light from Pomerol and St-Emilion. The train at last drew into Castillon and there, for tactical reasons, Christopher and Antoine briefly parted. Christopher hurried through the streets in order to arrive home before Jean-Pierre got there, while Antoine sauntered off to kill a few minutes in a café.

Their deception went un-spotted by Jean-Pierre or, as far as they knew, by anyone else and most of that morning was a repeat of the previous one; again the two of them fondled each other or exchanged significant glances whenever Jean-Pierre wasn't looking. But then, a little before eleven o'clock, someone rang the front doorbell.

Christopher answered it and found himself looking into the very challenging eyes of a pretty young woman. 'Yes?' he said.

'I'm looking for Antoine. He works here.'

'That's right,' Christopher said. 'Hold on a second.' He left the visitor outside on the doorstep and found Antoine. In a flat voice he told him, 'It's your girlfriend.'

Antoine didn't say anything. His face had gone the colour of uncooked pastry. He nodded to Christopher, then walked out onto the front step, pulling the door shut behind him.

For several minutes Christopher could hear the sounds of their two voices in continuous conversation. He could distinguish none of the words, but was aware that neither of the young pair was shouting. Nor were they interrupting or talking over each other. Elodie said approximately twice as much as Antoine. Jean-Pierre grinned at Christopher across the kitchen. 'Young love,' he said with a knowing chuckle.

'Yes,' agreed Christopher, but without the chuckle.

Then the voices stopped. Antoine came back into the house. His face was expressionless. So was his voice when he said to Christopher, 'Looks like I'll be going home tonight.' He didn't attempt to touch Christopher and Christopher didn't reach out to him. 'OK,' Christopher said.

There was a lot going on that day. The contractors arrived with the central heating parts and began to install them. The bathroom plumbing was finally connected, and you could at last relieve yourself without leaving the house. But when it came to going-home time Antoine made a point of putting his coat on a minute before Jean-Pierre did. 'Till tomorrow,' he said to Jean-Pierre. Then he turned towards Christopher and mouthed, 'Sorry,' to him, before turning and leaving the house.

They had only spent two nights together. Yet even so Christopher felt a deep sense of loss. He went out to his local bar and drank a *demi* by himself. Antoine wasn't there. Christopher hadn't remotely expected him to show up. But something in him had hoped he would. He drank two more half-pints.

Back at the house he cooked toad-in-the-hole for himself and ate it with some lettuce from the mini-market, washing it down with a glass or two of red plonk. Later he laid his sleeping-bag down in front of the log-burner and zipped himself up in it. Although there were radiators on the walls tonight they weren't working yet. As he curled up by himself inside the sleeping-bag he felt very alone in it. And chilly. At least he'd had the forethought to retrieve the toilet-rolls from the privy at the bottom of the garden and place them in the two new indoor toilets. He tried to console himself with that thought as he sank into sleep.

Back in a bracingly breezy Boulogne on Saturday afternoon Christopher was able to report to Tom that his mother's heating was up and running; the bath, shower and toilets were working perfectly. Future visits to the property would involve interior painting and decorating only. They would need to call on Jean-Pierre and Antoine only for a few odd jobs.

Tom had been spending his handful of solitary evenings painting a still life by candle-light. Christopher inspected the results. The painting, which featured a basket of fruit with a wine bottle in front of it appeared very accomplished to Christopher, but it did look much like any other still life.

'Have you noticed,' said Tom, 'how in old master paintings, when a wine bottle appears it always seems to be giving a Gallic shrug? How one shoulder seems higher than the other? The shoulder that holds the seat of light.'

'The seat of light?' asked Christopher. He hadn't lived for years with a partner who was also a professional painter – unlike Tom, who had.

'The seat of light is the point on any object in a painting where the light falls and is reflected back to the viewer. You must remember the cricket ball in the David and Jonathan picture…'

Christopher nodded. 'Yes, of course.'

'It's easiest to deal with in the open air, in sunshine, or in a studio with a single source of light.'

'Because?'

'Because in a modern room with electric lights bouncing off the walls in all directions it's…'

'Hmm,' said Christopher.

'I'll show you,' Tom said. He got up from his chair and switched off all the lights in the room except one. There was a bottle of claret on the table between them. It was nearly empty, but that was not the point. As soon as Tom changed the lighting state Christopher was astonished to see the bottle give a very sudden, unmistakeably Gallic, shrug, and hoist its nearer shoulder towards the light.

'You're absolutely right,' said Christopher. 'I'd never noticed that.' He looked back at Tom's painting as soon as he'd put the main lights back on and saw that Tom had captured exactly that optical effect. 'Well done,' he said. 'You've got it absolutely right.'

'That is what art teaches us,' Tom said gravely. 'That is the point of art.'

When they went to bed together that night Christopher burrowed very deeply into Tom with head and shoulders, knees and elbows, as well as cock. 'Do you love me, little one?' Tom whispered in the darkness.

'Never more so,' Christopher whispered back, a hint of tears in his voice. And Tom realised with an aching gratitude that he'd been deeply missed.

Michel approved of the still life with the wine bottle. He saw it the evening after Christopher's return to Boulogne, when he and Armand came round to dinner at Tom and Christopher's flat. 'You're turning into quite a pro,' he told Tom. 'Trouble is with paintings, they're like kids. Either they leave home and you never see them again, or you have them forever cluttering up the house.'

'Right,' said Tom. 'I mean you're right when it comes to paintings. They get sold and that's goodbye for ever. Or else… But that's not quite so true of kids. Kids do come home on visits. Or visit their parents. We still all go to your mother's on Sundays quite often. And there's my mum moving to France now…'

'Mmm,' said Christopher in a non-committal voice. He was the one among them who had a difficult relationship with his parents, usually seeing them only at Christmas.

'Going back to the subject of pictures, though,' Michel said – he sounded quite keen to do this, 'they may make lovely offspring but they do take up space.'

'Better to have gone in for painting fans,' said Armand mischievously. 'Easier to house a collection of them. Or cameo brooches.'

'Portraits on grains of rice,' Christopher suggested, glad to have escaped the uncomfortable area of relations with parents.

Michel did grin at him and chuckle, but he hadn't made his point yet; he'd only introduced it. Now he came to the heart of it. 'There's all Gérard's collection now…'

'Of course,' said Christopher, at last seeing where Michel had been going with his analogy with grown-up kids. 'What's going to happen to that?'

'I don't know yet,' said Michel. 'It depends. One of the things it depends on is what you two decide to do with Gérard's house.'

Tom said levelly, 'We haven't quite decided yet.'

Michel went on, trying not to sound too eager about this, 'Because if you decided to live at Rue St-Vincent the pictures could stay there and furnish the place like they do now.' He smiled wryly. 'Until I run out of money, that is…'

Tom and Christopher looked at each other. They still hadn't talked about this properly, shying away from the tricky subject in case they found they couldn't agree about it. Now Christopher said suddenly, 'We won't be living there. We'll sell it once the lawyers have tied things up.' He looked at Tom almost challengingly. 'Isn't that right?'

Tom thought for a split second, then made his decision. 'Yes.' Now he wondered whether in agreeing with his lover he had also agreed with the idea of buying houses in the Dordogne and renovating them. But that was a discussion for another time, he thought. There was already quite enough on this evening's agenda – this conversation over a pasta supper. He looked back at Michel, who for eight years in his past had been his partner, and asked, 'Is that a disappointment to you? I mean when it comes to having a place to keep Gérard's paintings.'

'No,' said Michel generously. 'It just would have been one option. Obviously it's your decision about the house. It's good to know what it is.' He stopped and looked down for a moment. Then he looked back up again at Tom and Christopher with a difficult to read expression on his face. 'I think it means I'll have to sell the collection, though. There's no way we could find room for them at Wimereux.'

'What about the David and Jonathan?' Armand asked suddenly. The others all looked at the thrower of this spanner into the works. They hadn't given that particular picture any recent thought.

Tom looked at Armand sharply. Was the David and Jonathan going to work yet another lot of mischief? Would they end up arguing over it?

While Michel suddenly found himself wondering, would Tom and Christopher like it if he were to make them a present of it? Would they perhaps expect him to do that? And then there were pictures of themselves – their younger selves naked – scattered among the works that Gérard had left him. Would they want those too, perhaps? Either to buy them or … again, would they expect them as gifts…? Where would they put them if they had them? He found himself looking round their smallish apartment. That brought him to yet another tangle of thought. He said, 'If you don't live in the house in Paris … would you go on living here…? I mean, without the boatyard…'

'We had an idea,' Tom said a bit diffidently. 'At least Christopher has.' Christopher looked at Tom, wondering what he was going to say about this. Tom went on, 'It's still just a thought. But with the experience we're getting with my mother's house down in Castillon, we thought we might get a couple of houses down there with the money from Rue St-Vincent, do them up, sell them on… Maybe.'

Tom saw a sudden change in the expressions on Armand's and Michel's faces. It was a tiny change, like the change that happens when the person you are talking to has seen someone else come into the room behind your shoulder. Michel spoke. 'Would you go and live down there?'

Armand added, 'Leave us?' He said it in a bantering way. But there was no doubt about it. Neither Michel nor Armand was happy at the thought that Tom and Christopher might move away from them. They were both actually upset.

'If we did move down south,' said Christopher carefully, 'we'd come back often. And you'd come down to us. There'd be as much to paint in the Dordogne, I imagine, as there is up here on the coast.'

'That's true, of course,' Michel said. 'But life would be very different.'

'Down in the Dordogne?' Christopher checked.

'I meant up here without you,' Michel said.

Tom put down his fork and got up from his chair. He went round to where Michel sat and, grinning, wrapped his arm around Michel's neck, boisterously giving him a little shake. Not wanting to leave Armand short of attention Christopher got up and did exactly the same to him, so that all four of them laughed. When they were all back in their seats again Tom said to the French pair, 'To be honest, Chris and I hadn't discussed any of this very much. So you had the privilege of seeing us come to our decision right in front of your eyes. But if we do go ahead with it, come down and stay with us. Come and be our neighbours. We'll find you a cottage, do it up, and sell it to you at an interesting price.' He was only half joking.

Michel knew he was half serious. 'So you'll do up these old wrecks of houses all by yourselves?'

'The guys who're working for us at mum's place are very good,' said Tom. 'We might be able to rope them in. Give them a bit more work. Jean-Pierre and Antoine.' Tom looked at his partner. 'Chris? What do you think?'

Christopher was startled. The possibility of employing Jean-Pierre and Antoine on a longer-term basis hadn't occurred to him. Even if it had he probably wouldn't have mentioned it. Now that Tom had he wasn't at all sure about it. Antoine had hardly spoken to him during the second half of their eventful week in Castillon. Christopher still liked Antoine and guessed that Antoine still liked him at some level. But continuing to work together… Now Tom had introduced the idea Christopher found it an attractive one to toy with. But the reality? He feared that working closely with Antoine for the indefinite future could be an uncomfortable experience. Not to say dangerous for his relationship with Tom. 'Um… Yes, maybe,' he said brightly, and hoped he'd sounded non-committal enough.

'Going back to your painting, Tom,' said Michel, thinking they'd gone as far with talk of major changes as any of them could manage for the moment, 'It's time you grasped the nettle and had another go at the human face.'

'It's just not my thing,' said Tom, shaking his head. 'I don't have a talent for it.'

'That's what people say when they haven't practised enough,' said Michel. 'When you're down in the Dordogne get cracking with it. Make a start with Christopher. Start sketching him. He won't mind if you make a few balls-ups at first.' His tone grew mischievous. 'Or get your two builder friends to sit for you. Jean-Pierre and … who did you say?'

'Antoine,' said Christopher.

FOURTEEN

It was an afternoon in late March, and warm enough for people to be sitting outside all the pavement cafés in Boulogne. Christopher and Armand were drinking an espresso together in the sunshine at one of the tables in front of La Chope, the café they had once managed together in what now felt like another life. 'How are things with Luc?' Armand asked.

'Absolutely fine,' said Christopher. 'He felt a bit awkward at first, buying the place out from underneath us as you might say. Just as Malcolm did about selling it over our heads. But we made it clear to them both that we had no hard feelings towards either of them. After all, we'd been given first refusal on the place and had said no.'

'But you didn't have the funds to buy it at that time,' said Armand. 'Would you have answered differently if you'd known you'd inherit Rue St-Vincent?'

Christopher thought for a moment. 'No, I don't think so,' he said. 'It was time for a change, we both thought. And then this Dordogne idea somehow came to us…'

'Not that you can put that into action yet,' Armand said. 'You won't be able even to put Gérard's place on the market till June at least. But I know what you mean by having a change.' Armand jerked his head round towards the café's plate-glass window. 'It was fun running this place with you for a time. And it was fun running the boatyard with you. But I didn't miss it when I got back with Michel.' He stopped and looked at Christopher. 'That doesn't mean I didn't miss you. But you can't have everyone.'

'No,' said Christopher, looking down at his small white cup and saucer. 'And just for the record, I missed you too. But I wanted to get back with Tom. We'd been through so much together…'

'Sometimes,' said Armand, 'I think that most of life is about missing people. That emotion seems to govern so much of what we do.'

'That's a very deep thought for a sunny afternoon,' said Christopher.

Armand smiled. 'Well, Tom isn't here to provide the thoughtful stuff. I guessed I had to step into the breach.'

Tom wasn't there because he was down in Castillon, putting in a final week of fitting out and decorating with Jean-Pierre and Antoine, while Christopher tied up the very last loose ends at the boatyard. Having mentioned Tom Armand now asked how he was getting on.

'Fine,' Christopher said. He'd spoken to him on the phone the night before. 'It isn't quite as uncomfortable for him as it was for me in January. Central heating's up and running. Phone's connected at last. And the weather's seriously good, he says.'

'There's no furniture yet, though, is there?' Armand asked. 'Is he still having to sleep in a sack on the floor?'

'Yes,' Christopher said. An image came into his mind of Tom curled up under the sleeping-bag with Antoine, in the way that he himself had been a couple of months before. He guessed that guilt had conjured the image there. He'd tried to suppress the memory; he hadn't told a soul about what had happened between himself and Antoine; now he felt a great urge suddenly to unburden himself to his old friend. Perhaps it was an effect of the sunshine. Sunshine in March is something that northern Europeans were almost pathetically grateful for. 'Armand, can I tell you something?' Christopher asked.

Armand was hardly going to say no.

'So,' said Armand when Christopher had finished telling his tale, 'how much further do you want it to go?'

'Not quite sure what you mean,' said Christopher.

'Your adventure with Antoine.'

'I want to draw a line under it,' said Christopher. 'Of course I didn't at first. After those two nights together I wanted there to be a third. But that wasn't to be and that was just as well.'

'You left Tom for me once,' said Armand. 'I just wondered if you were going to do the same thing with Antoine. Leave Tom, I mean.'

'No,' said Christopher thoughtfully. 'When all that happened … we were all very young. And it worked out as it did – almost miraculously – because Tom and Michel fell for each other at the same time as you and I did. And equally miraculously we all wanted to return to our previous pairings at the same time. None of that could conceivably happen a second time. Tom isn't going to want to pair off with Elodie.' A thought struck him and made him laugh. 'Or with Jean-Pierre.'

'No, of course,' said Armand and smiled. 'I know that with Michel and me there's a feeling that the music's stopped now and we're relieved to find ourselves sitting together in the same chair. We don't want to get out of it now. I don't know if…'

'It's exactly the same for Tom and me. In for the long haul and happy that way. It was just for those few days that I found myself thinking differently. Those days with Antoine…'

'Lust's like that,' said Armand.

'So I'm glad, now time has passed, that I can put it in perspective and see it as just a lustful one-night stand … or two-night stand. And I'm sure the same goes for Antoine. I'm also glad that Tom didn't find out about it…'

'Or hasn't done yet,' corrected Armand warningly. 'I'm remembering that evening when you and Tom told us about your Dordogne plans. The look on your face when Tom talked about employing Antoine and his boss in a long-term way… It went beyond surprise … and I couldn't imagine why. Well, now I can.'

'It would add a little complication to my life that I could do without,' said Christopher. 'Only a potential complication, but all the same…'

'Leaving the future aside,' said Armand, 'there's the present situation: Tom and Antoine down there together without you around. You think Antoine might fall out with Elodie again and this time come on to Tom?' Armand's tone struggled between incredulity and prurience.

'No,' said Christopher, 'I don't think that. I hadn't got quite as far as imagining that. I was thinking more that Antoine might accidentally let something slip…'

'Like by demonstrating a familiarity with the workings of the sleeping-bag that would otherwise be difficult to explain?' suggested Armand facetiously. They both laughed.

'No, but you know what I mean. I've no idea how good Antoine might be at deception. He might be the sort of person who'd suddenly confess it all to Tom because he wanted to get it off his chest.'

'Like you've just done with me.'

'Exactly,' said Christopher. 'People generally aren't good at keeping things to themselves. It doesn't come easily. For some reason blurting things out to the most inappropriate people seems to come more naturally.'

'There's nothing you can do about that,' said Armand. 'I mean as far as this week's concerned. You just have to hope that Antoine is clever enough not to give himself away to his girlfriend or to Tom. Hope he's got a discreet friend he can confide in – if he feels compelled to unburden himself.'

'Lucky man if he has,' said Christopher.

When Tom phoned Christopher that evening it was not to tell him that his moment of infidelity had been discovered, but that he'd had a surprising and rather wonderful conversation with his mother on the phone. By now May knew that Tom and Christopher had plans to set up in the Dordogne. She knew they had come into a valuable property in Paris that they wanted to sell. She knew that a few months would pass – a few months at the very least – before they could turn the legacy into cash. She'd been thinking about all this and come to a decision, she'd told Tom.

'I'm going to lend the pair of you ten thousand pounds,' she'd announced down the phone to her astonished son. 'For a year. Interest-free.'

'Good God,' said Christopher when this was relayed to him. 'You said yes, I hope?'

'I said yes. Of course I did,' said Tom. 'I said yes, and thank you very much indeed.'

The weekend of Tom's return to Boulogne was a moment of excitement and jubilation. There was not only the news of May's generous offer to celebrate; it was also the date of the final handover to Luc and his wife of the boatyard. Roger and Malcolm travelled over from England for the occasion. There was a dinner at the restaurant Chez Alfred in the Place Dalton. Michel and Armand were there, and Michel's mother Sabine, as well as Luc and his wife Odile.

Over the mussels starter (it was a tradition for them to have mussels Chez Alfred: a tradition that went way back) Sabine asked Christopher what they were planning to do in the immediate aftermath of the boatyard handover. 'Have a holiday,' Christopher said.

'I've heard about your plans to move to the Dordogne,' she said. 'Do up houses. In the wake of … well, you know.' She meant the Gérard inheritance.

'Eventually,' said Christopher. 'And the holiday will have something to do with that. We'll go down there and look at property in a general sort of way.' He told Sabine about Tom's mother's loan of ten thousand pounds. 'Tide us over till the sale of Rue St-Vincent.'

Sabine made noises of surprise and appreciation, managing quite commendably to hide the fact that her son had already told her about May's subvention.

'We haven't decided how we're going to spend it yet,' Christopher said. 'We could buy one nice cottage like May's, or try and get two absolute ruins for the same price. But do we want to begin with a place to buy and do up in order to sell it on at a profit? Or begin by buying a place to restore and then live in ourselves?'

'When you see a place you like, then you'll find that decision will make itself,' said Sabine. A Mona-Lisa-esque smile crossed her face.

Malcolm heard the same story, told by Tom. 'Brilliant news,' Malcolm said. 'To tell the truth, Luc was a bit worried about you. He's just been asking, should he offer to keep you on for a bit at the boatyard doing odd jobs? He wanted to know if I thought you'd appreciate the offer or consider it an insult.'

'That was very sensitive of him,' said Tom, surprised. He'd known Luc for years but was only now beginning to see sides of the man he'd never before bothered to think about. 'He'll be pleased to know – you can tell him, or I'll tell him myself – that he won't have to worry. He'll never need to find out if his proposal would have been seen as a lifeline or an insult.'

'But would you have seen it as in insult?' Malcolm asked with concern in his voice.

Tom laughed. 'Of course not.' He nodded towards Luc, who was now talking to Sabine and hadn't heard that little conversation between himself and Malcolm. 'And you can tell him that.'

The big bowls of empty mussel shells were cleared away and the group around the table prepared their minds and stomachs for the arrival of sizzling steaks. Armand, sitting the other side of Christopher from Sabine now had a question for his ex-partner. He put his head close to Christopher's and spoke very quietly. He didn't particularly want Tom, Michel or Sabine to hear this. 'How near do you both want to be to Tom's mother when you get down there eventually? I mean some people do, and some don't…'

'I haven't expressed an opinion on the matter,' Christopher said, equally quietly. 'I think that question needs to be decided by Tom. Unless he asks for my thoughts, of course. Though he hasn't yet.' They shared a collusive smile over that.

Their steaks arrived. Christopher felt comfortable and at ease with life. There was no urgency attached to any of these questions anyway. They had their ten thousand pounds from May; they had their redundancy money: they were cushioned against the sharp-cornered world for now. They were ready for a holiday; let them simply enjoy it. Meanwhile he was celebrating one of the milestones of his life – his and Tom's – in a cosy restaurant surrounded by most of the best friends he'd ever had. Eating steak and frites. Life could seem quite perfect sometimes, provided you didn't have absurdly unrealistic expectations of it.

They drove down. Down the motorway to Paris, skirting the city centre by means of the *périphérique*, the inner ring-road on which frightening foreigners is the principal sport of regular users. Tom and Christopher had only driven round it a couple of times in all their years of living in France and they approached it now with no less trepidation than they had on those previous trips. But they came through the experience without harm and headed south. In no hurry, they made an overnight stop at Gien, a pretty town enhanced by its pinnacled castle on the fast flowing, youthful River Loire, before their road took them up into the Massif Central, the granite heart of France.

They had decided to begin at the beginning, following the Dordogne from its source in the mountains, downhill towards the western sea rather than – as Tom had done with May – travelling inland from Bordeaux. The Massif appeared ahead of them initially and then encircled them with gaunt volcanic peaks. At first sight it seemed that nobody could live in this lunar mountainscape, but then it became clear that people did. Three or four big industrial cities hid among the region's valleys. The biggest of them, Clermont-Ferrand, grown big on the fortunes of the Michelin tyre company, lay along their route. Beyond the sprawl of its suburbs, though, lay the highest and loneliest part of the Massif.

Here the big rivers of France began as tiny streams among the old volcanic peaks. The Loire now lay towards the distant west; nearer at hand two streams united in the shadow of the region's highest summit, the Puy de Sancy. Those two streams were named the Dore and the Dogne above their meeting point. Following their union …

'Do we need to actually…?' asked Christopher, who was driving as they approached the peak.

'No,' said Tom. 'Sources of rivers are better imagined than traced right back to the boggy patch of grass. I did that with the Exe once, as a child on holiday. Deeply disappointing.' He might have gone on to say the same about mountain tops but he didn't. So they parked their car at the cable car station and ascended the Puy de Sancy above a roofscape of trees and rocky outcrops.

The Puy de Sancy was far from being the highest point in France – the country had a toehold in both the Alps and the Pyrenees after all – but outside of those two snow-crowned ranges it was the highest peak. Standing on it, his feet planted on the Puy de Sancy's topmost floor of rock, viewing nothing but crests of misted mountains in all directions beneath the clear sky, Christopher felt his chest ache with the wonder of it. He felt a strange mixed emotion: a feeling of power combined with insignificance. I am at the centre of my world, he thought. At forty-three I am at the centre of my life. Standing next to Tom he clasped his partner's fingers quietly and had the luxury of knowing that Tom, his fellow traveller along life's road for half of both their lifetimes, knew his thoughts.

They followed the young Dordogne through the high un-peopled region. They followed the stream as best they could; sometimes up close to it, sometimes thrown away from it by the road's course. This was the Auvergne, land of aching songs and wild-flower meadows – those fields pale yellow at this time in early upland spring. This was the Cantal département, home of distant shepherds – and artisanal cheeses that were pale yellow like the flowers. Ravines and gorges cut the landscape and in their depths the Dordogne coiled and shimmered, dam-swollen and harnessed to hydro-electric plants. They glimpsed the river at intervals where roads crossed it; no road followed it along its wanderings in this wilderness.

Even up here houses were for sale. From time to time Tom and Christopher stopped and looked. The equivalent of two thousand pounds, no more than that, would have secured a small half-ruined farmhouse in this beautiful, remote, unliveable-in place.

They descended imperceptibly from the heights of the Massif. Almost as imperceptibly the pale yellow flower meadows gave way to blue ones as they reached an altitude at which the spring was more advanced. Farmhouses built of honey-coloured limestone replaced forbidding piles of black volcanic rock as the geology of France changed beneath them, the igneous outcrop that was the core of France now overlaid by the limestone *causses* – deposits laid undersea an aeon or two ago and still full of seashell fossils though now two hundred miles from the Atlantic and a thousand feet above it.

Evening brought them down at last to an inhabited place. Martel, bristling with fortifications in medieval times and with an impressive history of bloodshed, now had the appearance of a fairy-tale village, preserved as if by a spell, all energy spent and violence dissipated. They took a hotel room there for the night.

For a decade or more before the advent of the euro the French franc stood at a convenient ten to each British pound, give or take a cent or two of fluctuation as the years passed. This meant that, standing outside an estate agent's window, you could place your hand over the final nought of an asking price and read the figure in sterling without any mental effort. (If you were reading prices in a newspaper you simply used a finger-tip.) Tom and Christopher spent an enjoyable morning in the beautiful streets of Martel doing exactly this.

They wondered whether this might be a good place to live in and make a base for their house renovation business. It was certainly an attractive place, with its seven medieval church towers, town walls and ancient market. White stone walls and chocolate roof-tiles were its pleasing leitmotifs. There were few British tourists in the little town, though. And, a hundred and forty miles upstream from Castillon, it still had an upland feel about it. Its winters would be bitter.

A hundred and forty miles from where his mother was going to live, pondered Tom inwardly. A hundred and forty miles from where Antoine was, Christopher meditated equally privately, still unsure whether he thought that a good thing or not.

Over the next few days they meandered down the river, sometimes heading dozens of miles away from it. They saw the bastide towns of Monpazier and Beaumont, all golden stone in sunshine, with deep shadows in their old arcaded squares. They drove into Sarlat, to find yet another fairytale place: an ancient huddle of stone houses crowned by pepper-pot towers and buttressed by turret-staircases. Those houses had slept for centuries in the depths of the oak and chestnut woods, their owners living on chestnut flour and truffles, distilling walnuts, and fattening the livers of geese, till the nineteenth-century railway line opened Sarlat up to the delight of Parisian seekers after the picturesque. Two generations after that the car had prised the secretive oyster even further open and now, thanks to the writings of Freda White and others, its streets were full of English visitors buying tinned foie gras.

Sarlat was certainly a good place in which to eat. Tom and Christopher's restaurant dinner of confit duck was accompanied by a hill of Sarlat potatoes (diced, sautéed in goose fat, tossed with bacon lardons, parsley and garlic) and a tureen of early peas topped with last year's dried ceps. The dinner was substantial enough to keep them groaningly awake in their hotel bed for half the night.

They followed the river through La Roque Gageac, where the houses perched on a ledge beneath a cliff, so close beside the river that they looked, like nestling seabirds on a rock-face, as though they might lose their balance and tumble into the water beneath. They came to Beynac, where Freda White had stayed in the Hotel Bonnet and written memorably about the view from it of the local population doing its washing in the spring, and the young people sitting chatting on the wall beside the river until their voices subsided in the evening dusk.

'We may as well base ourselves at mum's place for the last couple of nights,' Tom said, as Beynac's romantic skyline of cliff and castle disappeared from the rear-view mirror. 'Save on hotels.'

'I agree,' said Christopher in the old-mannish way he sometimes had. 'Makes sense.'

They by-passed Trémolat where May's mother's friends the Pattersons lived, and went on towards Bergerac and Ste-Foy, places they knew by now a little. For they were getting close to Castillon. Christopher wondered if they would bump into Antoine when they got there. He had deliberately not asked Tom if he still intended to seek him and Jean-Pierre out in order to talk about future work. Christopher thought about that possible encounter and braced his mind and heart in readiness.

FIFTEEN

There was an oddness about arriving at May's house, not from the train, coming up the lower Dordogne from Bordeaux or Libourne, but taking it from the rear, descending on it from the uplands of central France, following the stream that combined Dore and Dogne until it became the grand and placid waterway with mirrored surface that glided past the quays of Castillon.

It was late afternoon. Tom took his key from his pocket and turned the lock of his mother's new front door.

They hadn't stood here together since the back end of the last year. It had been transformed since then. Tom had overseen some of the improvements, Christopher others. 'It looks great,' said Christopher, who hadn't inspected the most recent work, carried out during Tom's last visit a fortnight back.

It did look great, but there was still no furniture in it. No beds, carpets or comfy chairs. True, there was central heating now and it would be warm enough to sleep upstairs. But still they would need to spread sleeping-bags on the floor. Tom turned to Christopher. 'You know what?' he said. 'I know we agreed to sleep here and save a bit of money on hotels, but…'

'I know what you're going to say,' said Christopher, 'and I agree. We're not paupers any more. Perhaps it's time we got out of the habit of behaving as if we were.'

'Good,' said Tom. 'We've seen the place and all's in order. Now let's drive out somewhere and find ourselves a hotel.'

'Not in Castillon, perhaps,' said Christopher. 'Somewhere near, but where we haven't been.'

'We've stayed in St-Emilion,' said Tom, 'and we know Ste-Foy-la-Grande very well. What about trying

Libourne? We've never been there except to change trains. Unless you want to go further afield?'

'No,' said Christopher very quickly. 'Libourne's fine.' He wasn't going to add that unlike Tom he had been there, had had dinner there, and had shared a hotel bed there with a man who wasn't Tom.

They got back in the car. Tom drove. It took no time at all to get to Libourne, skirting the vines and spires of St-Emilion, when you didn't have to wait on a station platform for a train. But Christopher had no control over where they ended up. Tom drove them into the market square with all the inevitability of a Greek tragedy and, in the same vein, pointed at once to the imposing hotel where Christopher had spent the night with Antoine and said, 'That looks OK.'

Hotel staff were trained to be discreet and tactful, Christopher knew. But he was grateful that the pretty young man who had arranged a room for himself and Antoine two months before, and who now carried his and Tom's bags up to the room they'd taken, had mastered the art to a wonderful degree. With a single nod and smile that Tom could only see the outside of, the lad conveyed to Christopher the twin messages that he hadn't forgotten him and that his secret was as safe as a pearl inside an oyster.

After they'd unpacked they went out for a stroll around the old walled town, its cobbled streets and its quays. The town's centre lay at a point where two rivers met; the River Isle picturesquely flowing out into the Dordogne. Christopher hadn't walked these particular streets with Antoine; it had been late and January dark, and they'd had other things on their minds. So he was able to enjoy the spring evening walk, a beer by the watersmeet at the Quai Souchet, and the return to their nearby hotel with a first-time visitor's delight that he didn't need to feign.

Tom thought the hotel's menu looked good. He suggested to Christopher that they didn't need to go out again: they could get a perfectly good meal where they were. Christopher didn't attempt to disagree.

But when they came down to dinner a little later Tom was surprised, and Christopher startled out of his wits, to see Antoine, dressed up for an evening out, sitting dining at a table for two with his girlfriend Elodie.

They acknowledged one another with cautious smiles. Except for Elodie, who had only ever seen Christopher once on a doorstep and had never seen Tom at all. Tom and Christopher walked a little way towards their table, Christopher hanging back a foot or two. He would let Tom do the talking, if there was to be any: it was easier that way.

'Nice to see you,' said Tom, and was rather mumblingly introduced to Elodie. 'Actually, Antoine,' Tom went on, 'I might want to talk to you sometime. About building work. You and Jean-Pierre. But it's only maybe. And not now, obviously.' He inclined his head towards Elodie. 'Catch you some other time. Enjoy your meal.' With a tiny nod of his head he dismissed himself; Christopher followed suit, with a relieved *'Bon appétit.'*

Christopher and Tom just about managed not to look in the direction of Antoine's table while they all ate. But eventually Antoine and Elodie came to the end of their meal and got up to leave the restaurant. They seemed to be making for the interior of the hotel. Christopher realised with something like horror that the young couple were going to spend the night here. He wondered for an awful second if they'd got married suddenly without his knowledge and were on their honeymoon. To get to the main reception area they had to pass right by Tom and Christopher. As they did so Antoine turned towards them and, stopping just for a second, said, 'If you're still looking for a house to buy round here I think

I've found just the place for you.' He took a step and paused again. 'Also to be discussed another time. *Bonne nuit.'*

'Bonne nuit à vous,' said Tom, astonished, while Christopher was barely able to utter the polite formula at all.

'How did he know we were looking for a place to buy?' Tom asked when the younger couple had gone.

'I think I may have mentioned it,' said Christopher, trying to sound vague about it.

'And she? Is she the famous girlfriend we've never met? She seemed to recognise you, though.'

'We met once on the doorstep,' Christopher explained awkwardly. 'She came to see Antoine about something. I wasn't sure she'd remembered seeing me.'

'And odd to go out and spend the night in a nearby hotel with your own girlfriend. I mean, it's more usual to spend a night in a hotel with someone who isn't your girlfriend.' Tom snickered.

Christopher felt himself go hot and cold.

'They might be making up after a row,' Christopher suggested, then worried that he was getting even closer to dangerous territory.

'I suppose so,' Tom conceded, then to Christopher's relief changed the subject. 'But if he's been interested enough in our affairs to find a house to recommend to us, that gives an easy intro to the subject of whether he'd like to get involved in doing it up for us.'

'I guess it does,' said Christopher, and he picked up a forkful of apple *tarte tatin* to chew on.

The two couples met again at breakfast, greeting each other from a polite distance. When the small meal was finished Tom went over to the others' table and, with a polite nod and an *excusez-moi* to Elodie, asked when and where it might be convenient to have a chat with her boyfriend. Antoine suggested the familiar bar in Castillon – the one in which he and Christopher had picked each other up – after he'd finished work that evening. Then Tom returned to his own table and reported the arrangement back to a Christopher who was doing his best not to look flustered.

They spent the day exploring the area south of the river, the Entre Deux Mers between the Dordogne and the Garonne. On the banks of that second river they found the wine towns of Sauternes, Barsac and Cadillac, Ste-Croix-du-Mont and Cérons. All were picturesque, built of cream and honey coloured limestone. They were also wonderfully manicured. Properties for sale there were unsurprisingly expensive. Which prompted Tom to say to Christopher, 'I wonder what Antoine imagines our budget is.' Christopher decided not to mention the fact that he'd already told him.

They made their way back to Castillon in the late afternoon and entered the small bar on the stroke of six. Antoine came in less than a minute later, back in the working clothes in which they were more used to seeing him, and they all ordered a beer together and sat at a table with them.

'It's eleven kilometres away.' Antoine came to the point directly. 'A little way north. In among the Côtes de Castillon vineyards. It's on the edge of a village. St-Philippe-d'Aiguille.' He took a slurp of beer. 'The thing is that it's not a house exactly. It's a disused winery building. You'd need to put in windows.'

'Really?' queried Tom. 'That might be a bit beyond us…'

'No, wait,' said Antoine. 'They only want thirty thousand francs for it.'

Tom and Christopher each mentally put a thumb over the last nought and saw a ridiculously attractive three thousand pounds in the remainder of the figure.

'And it's got a brand new roof on it,' Antoine went on. 'There were some EU grants floating around and there seemed no reason to miss out on one.'

'How do you know all this?' asked Christopher, who until then had sat sipping his beer in rather uncomfortable silence. 'Who owns it?'

Somehow, even before he uttered the words Christopher knew exactly what was coming. 'My uncle.'

Tom and Christopher both found their thoughts in a whirl. They had agreed before the meeting that they would ask Antoine whether Jean-Pierre and he – or just he, Antoine – would be interested in working with them on new projects. But if the answer was yes, they would have to explain that money would be tight until at least midsummer. But with this new information… If they only had to spend three thousand pounds of May's ten thousand then things could move ahead more quickly. 'When can we have a look at the place?' asked Tom.

'Now would be quite a good time,' said Antoine.

Christopher drove. He'd only had the one beer. Although they had just explored the wine towns of Sauternes, Barsac and Cadillac, Ste-Croix-du-Mont and Cérons, the streets of those places were not lined with dinky wine bars selling their world famous products to casual tourists (it seemed that nobody had thought that particular idea worth trying) so they had spent the day drinking nothing stronger than fizzy orange and coffee. Antoine sat in the front passenger seat because he was showing the way, while Tom reclined in the back.

The village of St-Philippe-d'Aiguille was tiny, clustered around a green. It boasted a baker's shop and a bar. But with the big supermarket at St-Magne just six miles away, that was all anyone would need. Anyone who had a car. Antoine directed them out of the village a little way, along a narrow lane that ran between green seas of vineyard on both sides. A small dip in the land contained a scatter of buildings, half screened by trees, that looked like a wine château that no longer functioned as such. A hundred metres from the main cluster was an abandoned storehouse. It looked something like a Victorian engine shed, big enough to contain two medium sized locomotives. Its main entrance was an arched doorway high enough to drive an engine through. In reality it would have been a tractor and trailer, loaded high.

The building appeared to be in good condition. Its stone walls were clean and honey-coloured, the pointing showing no signs of crumbling or falling out. Its shallow-pitched roof was of bright red canal-tiles, very pretty and, as Antoine had said, spanking new. What Antoine had said about the windows, though, was not quite true. The building did have windows; they were just rather small and rather few.

It seemed that Antoine didn't need permission from anyone to take them inside, nor did he need a key to open the enormous door. Though all three of them helped to push it open: it was that big. The windows, though glazed, were still shuttered, so the only light that entered had streamed in alongside them as they came through the door. It showed that half the building was open to the rafters – the half you'd have driven the tractor and trailer into – while the other half had a solid beamed storage floor at exactly the height where a house would have its ground-floor ceiling.

'There's no chimney,' said Tom.

'No plumbing,' said Christopher.

'No heating source of any kind,' said Tom, shaking his head.

'It's exactly what we're looking for,' said Christopher suddenly, surprising himself as well as Tom. He hadn't known what they were looking for until this moment but now he did know. Tom hadn't known what they were looking for either. But he didn't show signs of disagreement with Christopher. Instead he began to nod his head slowly, in a positive if thoughtful way. Antoine was the only one of them who didn't seem surprised by Christopher's reaction. It was as if he'd known all along what it would be.

'It'd need an awful lot of work to make it habitable,' said Tom. 'Chimney, a bit more first floor... Partition walling, bigger windows pierced through the stone. Kitchen and bathroom. Drains...' He looked at Antoine carefully. 'Would you be able to do all that for us? I mean with us? You and Jean-Pierre?' This wasn't the way he'd expected to sound Antoine out; it had just happened that way.

Antoine didn't even bother to answer the question. 'We'd get planning permission easily enough,' he said. 'My uncle's the mayor.'

They hardly needed to ask each other whether they shared the same opinion, had made the same decision. That the old storehouse outside St-Philippe-d'Aiguille would not be a restoration project they would sell on to other people. Other properties would serve that purpose in the future. This place, partly – enticingly – screened by trees from the emerald sea of vines around it, notwithstanding the proximity of Antoine's mayoral uncle and the fact that Tom's mother would be living just eight miles down the road, was going to be the place in which they'd live.

Back on the Channel coast a few days later they shared this news with Michel and Armand, sitting on their balcony at Wimereux. Jean-Pierre and Antoine had agreed to do the skilled work involved in the building's conversion to a dwelling, they explained, while they themselves would do the unskilled stuff. Even so the project would cost a great deal more than May's loan of ten thousand pounds.

'Hope and pray the title to Gérard's estate comes through soon, then,' said Michel.

'And that we then manage to sell the Rue St-Vincent,' said Tom. Michel and Armand too were still waiting for their part of the inheritance, but their share lay in investments that could be liquidated within a week or two and the money effortlessly transferred to their bank accounts; they didn't need to wait on the mood swings of the real estate market.

'There are some good things,' said Christopher, wanting to brighten the moment a bit. 'Things we might not have expected at first. The place has mains electricity. It was just that when we first walked in there Antoine didn't know where the switch box was. It has mains water, just no sewerage. And there's a fallen-down outbuilding from which we can get enough good stone to build the chimney, saving one big expense...'

'Another plus is that it's got long straight walls right down it,' said Tom. He looked at Michel. 'If you wanted space to hang Gérard's picture collection while you decided what to do with it...'

'Including the David and Jonathan,' said Michel. 'Which is interesting, because I had actually been giving some thought to that. I've decided to make you a present of it. At least I know now you'll have space to hang it.' He smiled teasingly. 'And I may well take you up on your offer to house the other stuff.'

'So it's not just interesting but fortuitous,' said Armand. Tom and Christopher both made polite noises of gratitude for Michel's generosity in giving them the David and Jonathan. All of them thought that actually, if a picture collection was housed in a house that was part of the lives of a group of four friends who were lovers and ex-lovers, it was rather irrelevant who owned the pictures provided they all had access to them. But nobody gave any thought to the question of whether the David and Jonathan was something that Tom and Christopher wanted to share their living-space with.

'You'd see the paintings often,' said Christopher. 'We'll expect you to spend lots of time down there with us. There'll be four bedrooms, and loads of ground-floor space. We're having a couple of huge windows, and most of the ground floor will be open-plan, part of it still open to the rafters...'

Michel brought him gently down to earth. 'Where will you live while you're converting it?'

'Sleeping-bags on the floor again,' said Tom. 'Like at mum's place. At least it'll be summer by the time we get started. We may need to hire a portable toilet at first. But Antoine knows where we can get one cheaply.'

SIXTEEN

May moved from High Wycombe to Castillon-la-Bataille, with a stop-off at Boulogne, as easily, calmly and serenely as a swan gliding down a stream. If there was much mental paddling going on beneath the surface it was well hidden from anyone observing the process from the riverbanks. Tom's brother Dominic drove her – with a suitcase-full of valuables and an overnight bag – to the ferry at Folkestone. Tom and Christopher met her off it at the Boulogne end. They would drive her down to Castillon the following day.

The evening of May's one-night stay in Boulogne was spent over dinner in Michel's mother's house at the top end of the town, where the cathedral and the castle were, along with some of Boulogne's best houses. Michel's mother, Sabine, lived in one of them, in Boulevard Auguste Marlette. Sabine's generation of French mothers were excellent cooks for the most part and Sabine, happily, was not among the exceptions. Unfazed by cooking for six she provided – for May and herself, her son and Armand, and Christopher and Tom – a cheese soufflé starter, the stew of lamb and early baby vegetables that the French call *navarin printanier*, a selection of cheeses and, to finish, a bowl of early raspberries and cream.

'I worry about mum being lonely in Castillon,' Tom told Sabine across the table. May was only two places away; Tom had intended her to hear.

Sabine answered Tom, 'But you'll only be a few miles away, working on your new property. You'll be close.'

Tom nodded. 'Eleven kilometres. It's not far, it's true. But it's not like being in the next street. I mean, Michel's only five kilometres away at Wimereux but you don't see him every day.'

Sabine turned to May. The two women had met several times over the years. 'Do you go to church still?'

'Of course I do,' said May, sounding almost as affronted as if Sabine had asked if she still wore underwear.

'Then you'll find it relatively easy to make friends,' Sabine said. 'At any rate you'll meet a lot of new people. Among the many you can't help but make a few friends.' She smiled thoughtfully. 'And if they're good friends, who needs more than a few?' She went on. 'Most of the British who are buying up the Dordogne don't integrate. They aren't Catholic, they don't go to church, they don't speak French…'

'Mummy doesn't speak French,' said Tom. 'Not to any extent.'

'Mais si,' objected May. *'Je parle francais,'* and she demonstrated the fact, and startled her son, by adding a few further sentences in that language, describing the course she'd just completed in High Wycombe. Even Tom admitted that the results weren't that bad.

Sabine laughed, probably out of relief as much as anything else. 'That's a very good start,' she said. 'But the other thing you must remember is how to talk to people without accidentally giving offence. Say *Madame* and *Monsieur* every time you address someone. Never leave it out. And if it's the mayor you're talking to, then it's *Monsieur le Maire* every single time. Never be tempted to say *tu* and *toi* to anyone older than about six – unless it's a cat or a dog – and never invite anyone else to say *tu* and *toi* to you however obvious it may seem that they should. You'll have to go on being Madame Sanders to everyone for a long, long time. If there is an invitation to say *tu* and *toi* it must come from the other person. But once the invitation is made you must never forget it. Don't go back and call them *Monsieur* or *Madame* or *vous* or you'll give grave insult.' Sabine smiled. 'I know. It all seems a bit rigid. But all the inviting has to come from them at first. They'll see themselves as representing France as your host country. You'll always be the Englishwoman in their eyes. Though you may forget the fact over time, they won't.'

'Irishwoman,' May corrected.

'Sorry,' said Sabine. 'I meant to say Irish. But a foreigner is a foreigner down there, wherever they may have come from. They won't really understand the difference.'

Michel intervened. 'Don't take my mother too seriously,' he told May. 'She's very hard on the people in the south. They're not as bad as all that. She's remembering how it was down there when she was a child.'

Sabine challenged her son. 'And when have you been down there recently?' she asked.

That shut Michel up. But Christopher said brightly, 'He'll be coming down very soon, though. To see us. As soon as we're halfway shipshape.'

And Tom added, looking at Sabine, 'And you too, of course.' He called Sabine *tu* and *toi*, and she smiled at him. After all, as Michel's sometime partner, he'd been her sort-of son-in-law once.

They headed south the next morning, Tom driving, his mother next to him, and Christopher in the back. Tackling the ferocious Parisian *périphérique* by the east this time, they made their way down the Aquitaine motorway, past Orléans and Chateauroux. They stayed the night in Périgueux, principal town of the Dordogne department. Seeing the sign that announced this fact on the edge of the town as they drove into it Tom had a feeling of coming home. Admittedly, Castillon and St-Philippe-d'Aiguille lay just outside the Dordogne department, in the Gironde. But that was splitting hairs.

The region as a whole was home now. It was the region in which Christopher and he had bought a house. Or at any rate a barn that was going to be a house.

But it was May's house that they drove to early the next morning, to rendezvous with the Pickford's lorry that had trundled all the way from England with May's furniture and other worldly goods. As he helped with all the small tasks that created order out of moving-day chaos Christopher, looking around him at the garden and the fast flowing river at the front, was more and more aware that early summer had come galloping northwards to meet them as they had headed south. From the car this morning they had seen hay being cut in the meadows. That wouldn't be happening on France's northern coast for another three weeks. Across the river from the house the elder trees were white as brides, covered from top to bottom with creamy flower-heads as big as soup plates. Their bright reflections shone and rippled in the water slipping beneath. An unseen cuckoo called from across the fields beyond them and a redstart twittered rustily from the ridge of May's roof.

Towards the end of the afternoon a visitor arrived. It was Antoine. Christopher found that he'd rather expected this – without expecting it. Antoine asked if they needed any immediate help. They didn't in fact. The day's work was nearly done. But Antoine took advantage of his introduction to May to offer his services, and Jean-Pierre's, for the future. Building work, odd jobs, anything at all, really, that May needed. May was visibly impressed by the handsome twenty-four-year-old, accepted his business card and told him that as soon as she found she needed anything doing she would be in touch. She made him drink a cup of tea before he left.

They dined in a nearby restaurant that evening and Tom and Christopher stayed the night in May's spare room. The following day was Saturday and Tom's work was already cut out. He had to find a second-hand car for his mother at a reasonable price. But May had another request to make. She made it over dinner. 'Would the two of you mind staying on till Sunday, and coming with me to church?'

Tom and Christopher knew the church of St Symphorien in the Rue des Remparts, but they knew it from the outside only. Their Sunday morning visit there (although it was only a ten-minute walk away May insisted on driving them there in the car she'd acquired with Tom's help the previous day) was the first time they'd been inside it. Like most French churches it was named after a saint of whom most foreigners had never heard. More unusually, the Mass they attended was said in Latin, a rare event since the Second Vatican Council's rulings were implemented in 1965.

This meant that May knew the words – which she wouldn't have done had the Mass been in French – and, because the musical setting was the universal Missa de Angelis, she could join in the singing. Which she did, in her comfortable, pitch-secure mezzo voice. To great effect. Tom hadn't heard his mother sing since the death of his father and was moved almost to tears. Once he'd got over the shock of that and was in control of his own voice again he joined in too, and then Christopher followed suit, to give moral support.

A few heads turned in their direction. Reassuring smiles followed. Tom thought it was as though the Von Trapp family had turned up at the church. After the Mass was finished a little knot of people formed around them on the pavement outside the church.

'You're new,' a woman said. Another asked if May was English.

'Non, madame. Irlandaise,' she answered at once, but smiled graciously as she said it. Then she went on, still in French, 'These are two of my boys,' introducing Tom and Christopher. Carefully she chose the word *garçons*, not *fils*. She didn't brazenly lie by saying the two men were both her sons, but was clearly happy to let the people around her assume it.

Had they all come to live in Castillon? someone asked. 'No, only me,' May said. 'I moved in two days ago. The boys live at St-Philippe-d'Aiguille.' She added for good measure, 'They're friends of *Monsieur le Maire.'*

'Monsieur le Maire de St-Philippe-d'Aiguille?' an older lady queried, *'Ou Monsieur le Maire de Castillon-la-Bataille?'* She sounded as though she would be impressed in either event.

'Tous les deux,' said May blithely. Both. Then she took a little bundle of address cards that she'd had the forethought to have printed in advance of her move and handed them out.

It took Tom and Christopher a few days to break free from May's powerful gravitational pull but they eventually managed it, with a little help from Jean-Pierre, who announced that he and Antoine were ready to start work at St-Philippe-d'Aiguille, and from Antoine himself, who came round to say that he'd found them a portable toilet and had already taken it up there in the back of a pick-up truck.

By now May had received several visits from churchgoing women of her own age, and had been out to coffee with two of them. All had been charmed by her 'two boys' and had praised their good looks, their goodness of heart in helping their mother with her move and settling in, and had complimented them on the quality of their French. One of them expressed the hope that Tom and Christopher would join the small band of laypeople who read the lessons at Sunday Mass. 'We have too few young men in the congregation. Though it's the same everywhere. So sad, so sad.' The lady shook her head. Tom and Christopher shook theirs' too, in polite sympathy, but carefully kept their mouths shut.

It was good to have a place to escape to. A place of their own eight miles away at St-Philippe. Even though it was a barn that would soon be a building site. Even though it meant sleeping-bags on the floor again, and a portaloo for a toilet.

But those details scarcely mattered when they had a place that they owned, for the first time in their lives. They'd called other places home before now. But nothing else in their lives had been anything like this experience. Returning here, to this empty barn, after dining in a small restaurant beneath the ramparts of St-Emilion, they looked around them in the glare of the as yet un-shaded light bulbs. In their imaginations it was already furnished. Carpeted. With Gérard's paintings on the walls. With Tom's as yet unpainted paintings in amongst them. 'Come to bed,' said Tom. He led Christopher up the rickety wooden steps to where their two sleeping-bags lay on the bare plank floor. They opened them out and laid them one on top of the other. By the time they'd got undressed and had sandwiched themselves between the upper and the lower sleeping-bag they both had sturdy erections. They made the most of them in the course of that night.

Opening the shutters in the early morning they realised that they'd never before lived in such deep countryside. Their new home was surrounded by a garden-sized area of bare stony earth and weeds. It would be a real garden one day, they'd promised each other already. A garden they would create themselves from out of the rock and the bare earth. Beyond their immediate surroundings waved the fresh green sea of the Côtes de Castillon vineyard on all sides. The vines were in small early leaf still, and the dew-drops that coated them sparkled in the sun. Birds had flown up from the ground around the house when they flung the shutters open. Between them they managed to work out what they were. A green woodpecker. A hoopoe, pink, white and black. A golden oriole. 'A beautiful beginning,' Tom said.

But it was very much a beginning. Before the place could be lived in easily a lot needed to be done. At least they weren't going to dig the sewage trench by hand this time. The ground was fairly level and Jean-Pierre would be bringing a mechanical digger to do it. But it still needed doing. A damp-proof floor would be laid. A new staircase would be installed alongside the new chimney. The chimney would be in the centre of the house, in the middle of the big open-plan area. A small section of the roof would need to be cut out for it. While its big fireplace would be open on two sides, to send heat and cosiness radiating out in both directions. The massive barn door would be replaced by a great window, with a smaller, person-sized door below it. But already they could imagine it: the incoming light brightening both storeys.

Among the many comforts that were missing from their new residence was a telephone line. Mobile phones hardly existed in the public consciousness in 1988, and it would be another three or four years before they became a common item in people's pockets. One of the first tasks that Tom and Christopher had to deal with was to apply to the telephone company to be connected to the system. This might have taken a long time, but a well-judged call from Antoine's uncle the mayor to the right person brought the wait down to a mere couple of weeks. In the meantime they made outgoing calls from the phone-box in the village. If anyone among their friends needed to contact them urgently… Monsieur le

Maire, whose own house was just half a vine-field away, had allowed them to give his number for emergency use. So had the village bar, a pleasant ten-minute walk away through the vineyards and a place they visited briefly most evenings.

It was to the bar that Michel's call came. 'Your friend left no message,' the bar's *patron* told them. 'Except to say could you call him back. But he said not to worry. The news was good. He even said very good.' The *patron* looked at Tom and Christopher narrowly. 'Your friend is French, is he not?' They told him yes. The *patron* nodded, pleased to be told that. Tom and Christopher felt they had suddenly gone way up in his estimation. 'I thought so,' he said knowledgeably. 'He has the accent of the north.'

The patron offered them the use of his phone to call Michel back but they declined politely. A village bar was a very public place to receive major news, of whatever sort. Tom called Michel from the public call-box a little way up the village street.

'Gérard's estate has been settled,' Michel told him. 'You'll get a lawyer's letter in the post, along with the title deeds to the Rue St-Vincent house.'

'And you?' Tom asked. He didn't need to relay the news to Christopher: his partner's head was pressed against his own; he could hear everything that was being said.

'It's in the pipeline,' Michel said. 'Money almost in the bank.'

'We'll come to Boulogne and see you,' Tom said. 'We'll need to sort our old flat out. Give notice. Get our stuff out…' He thought for a second. 'Once we've been to Paris.'

The estate agent in the Rue Lepic didn't believe them at first. They didn't blame him. Two men with English accents had walked in off the street and said they wanted to sell a six-bedroom house with two thousand square metres of garden, situated near the top of the Butte de Montmartre, a three-minute walk from the Sacré Coeur basilica and just six minutes' walk from the nearest metro stop. They had to show him their newly acquired title documents. At that point he agreed to come and value it. There and then. It was only a ten-minute walk, though up an extremely steep slope, from his office in the Rue Lepic. He left his assistant in charge of his office.

He proposed an asking price of just under ten million francs. Tom and Christopher each mentally covered up the final nought to see the sterling price. 'It needs some renovation,' the agent told them. 'And complete redecoration. That's why I'm not recommending a higher price.'

'How long do you think it'll take to sell it?' Christopher asked anxiously. He hadn't the remotest idea himself. He'd never before sold a big house in Paris. Or any house.

'At that asking price it'll be snapped up within a fortnight,' the agent told him confidently. And so it was.

A million pounds in 1988… Invested carefully in bonds and unit trusts it could have provided a modest income for the two of them for the rest of their lives. Except that it couldn't. Following the crash of the previous autumn the financial markets were lying prostrate. Tom and Christopher's plan to invest in run-down property and do it up for resale at a profit still looked like the most sensible decision they could have made.

They discussed this with Michel and Armand when they were back in Boulogne and Wimereux. They were in buoyant mood. They'd just heard from the estate agent that an offer of the full asking price had been made for the Montmartre house, and were celebrating with a dinner at the Hotel Atlantic in Wimereux.

If the deal went through soon they would have to move quickly to get the Montmartre house cleared. And the estate agent had told them there was no reason not to expect a rapid completion. 'Buyers of that scale of property are usually not waiting in a chain,' he'd said on the telephone.

'How much of the old furniture will you want to take to the Dordogne?' Michel asked them.

'Probably not six old beds,' said Tom. 'But wardrobes and stuff...'

'If you're paying for a lorry to take stuff down you may as well fill it up,' Michel advised. 'Chuck things out at your leisure when you're down there. You don't want to be forking out for four new beds all in one go.'

'The pictures, of course,' said Christopher. 'They'll be first in the queue to get in the van. The rest, well, we'll see. We'll get a house clearance firm to get rid of the junk.'

That sounded easy but of course was not. It took all four of them, on a two-night visit to Paris, to go through all the contents of Gérard's labyrinthine house, deciding what was valuable and what was junk. Big items of furniture were the easy bits. Trinkets and knick-knacks were not. They were sent away to be valued. Worst of all was the paper – and the books. There were letters, there were sales records for paintings from a lifetime ago, there were financial documents, there were photograph albums dating from before the First World War... They did it in two long days, though a fortnight was what it felt like.

'We've been thinking,' said Armand out of the blue during the second afternoon in the Rue St-Vincent's now gloomy rooms. 'It's about what we do with our portions of Gérard's property. His bonds and shares.'

'Mmm?' said Christopher. Tom said, 'Go on.'

Michel took over. 'We thought we might take a leaf out of the British book. Invest in some property in the Dordogne. For use as a second home.'

'Down near us?' said Tom.

'Not necessarily slap-bang on top of you two,' Armand said quickly. 'But somewhere near.'

'We thought about this because of you, to be honest,' said Michel. 'Your plan is to buy up places going cheap and do them up with the help of … what are their names? Yes, Antoine and Jean-Pierre. Then sell them to people who don't want to do all that work themselves. So we thought that we could become your first clients.'

'You'd want us to find a house down there for you?' Christopher asked.

'We'd want you to do it up for us, certainly,' Michel said. 'Though I think we'd want to get involved in the process of choosing which actual wreck to go for, and where.'

Tom smiled. 'Sounds an interesting plan. You come and stay with us and we can all go house-hunting together.' He paused for a second. 'Once we've sold this place and have some cash available.' He paused again. 'Plenty of room for you both to stay if you don't mind roughing it. Now I see why you were so keen for us to take the beds down there.'

The chimney grew slowly: it couldn't climb faster because of the setting time required for the mortar. But the new staircase was built in almost no time, and the small extension of the first floor around it followed suit. A quarter of the whole building would remain, in memory of its days as a storehouse, open to the rafters. That area would be lit, as would the gallery landing of the bedroom floor, by the big high window in the old barn-doorway. New partition walls also went up quickly.

Enlarging the smaller window apertures was a trickier task, yet gradually it happened. Jean-Pierre carefully supervised the chiselling out of the stonework. Fortunately the weather was quite hot during the few days during which tarpaulins hung over the empty holes before they could be filled with window-frames and glass. But by the time the central heating people arrived at the end of June there were walls to fix the radiators to, and when the beds and other furniture arrived from Paris there were the rudimentary shells of bedrooms into which they could be put.

At the beginning of the conversion process Tom and Christopher had returned every few nights to stay in a comfortable bed at May's. May's house was decorated now with paintings by her son, which she had proudly placed on the walls. They included the one he'd done of the rearing crab with pincers agape. Christopher still felt uncomfortable in its presence. He could never look at it without thinking about Angelo's death, and about aids. But he'd never told Tom this, and he didn't tell him now. At least they could shower and bath when they were here, and do their laundry. Their visits suited May too. They gave her a bit of company to tide her over while she continued to work at befriending the natives. Tom and Christopher always made sure, though, not to arrive at a weekend. They wouldn't be going to Mass again with May in a hurry. Not if it meant having to pretend to be brothers. Or having to read the lessons. Some areas of May's new life had to remain her own province.

Little by little the overnight stays at May's house tailed off. Not that 'her boys' left her unvisited. They just no longer needed to stay the night. Their own place had a plumbed-in toilet at last, and a working bathroom. A bed, and three spare ones. Tea-chests full of bed linen, books, plates, and other everyday items – from Boulogne as well as Paris.

Along with all this came the pictures. The one that belonged to Tom and Christopher – the David and Jonathan – and the others that were now Michel's. Not that the details of ownership would matter very much. Unless Michel wanted to sell them, or there was a fire, or the two couples fell out. But the walls weren't ready to receive them yet. Some areas would be plastered, in others the bare gold stonework would be exposed. But even that would need some cleaning and re-pointing to a standard worthy of the interior of a house. So for the moment the pictures leaned against the walls in the big living space, in two stacks, beneath heavy-duty dust-sheets.

The place had a phone in it by now. And a postal address. You couldn't have a telephone line without that. After a quick discussion they had decided to call their property Le Vieux Chai, which meant the old wine store. It wasn't very original or even unusual in this part of France, but it had the merit of spade's-a-spade truthfulness and was not remotely camp.

SEVENTEEN

The Montmartre estate agent had been right. Less than a month after Tom and Christopher had accepted the offer for the Rue St-Vincent house the funds for the purchase had been lodged with a notaire in Paris. It only remained for both parties to sign the completion documents and the money would be released, in two equal portions, to Tom's and Christopher's bank accounts. Because a lot was going on at Le Vieux Chai, and it was the height of summer, Tom and Christopher decided they didn't both need to go to Paris for the signing. Tom went on his own, carrying a letter from Christopher that gave Tom authority to sign the sale deed on his behalf as well as his own. Christopher drove Tom to the mainline station at Libourne early on a Monday morning. The exchange of signatures and funds was scheduled for four o'clock that afternoon. Afterwards Tom would spend a night in a hotel near Montmartre and would be back at Libourne the following evening. The TGV-Atlantique high speed line was still being built, and the journey from Libourne to Paris still took five hours to complete – plus five to come back.

Christopher returned to Le Vieux Chai at about nine o'clock to find Jean-Pierre and Antoine already arrived and hard at work. As the morning went on Christopher began to be aware that something about Antoine was different. He seemed agitated, and at the same time distracted, like someone whose mind is somewhere else or is dealing with a problem inside his head. But it wasn't something Antoine was going to share with Christopher, evidently, as his communications with him were restricted to the necessary practical exchanges between people working together to build a house. Though Christopher found an oddness also in that.

But things changed abruptly at midday. Jean-Pierre walked off towards the village to get something from the shop. As soon as Antoine had Christopher to himself – they were standing idly outside the front door in the sunshine, watching Jean-Pierre's disappearing back – Antoine came to the point at once. 'I've split up with Elodie,' he said. 'Would it be all right if I stayed here for a bit?'

Christopher felt as if he'd been whacked with a piece of wood. 'What?'

Antoine gave him a look that Christopher would never be able to describe, but that was easy to interpret. He said in a quiet voice, 'I haven't got anywhere else.'

There are your parents, Christopher thought. Your uncle lives just a field away. And anyway, it was suspiciously coincidental that this should happen when Tom was going to be away for the night. But he didn't say any of this. With Antoine gazing at him with that look in his blue eyes he couldn't. Instead he said, 'Well, you can stay tonight.' And as Antoine smiled his relief – his whole body joined in, and he seemed to be wagging a non-existent tail – he added, 'But I can't promise after that. It would be up to Tom. And I'm not even sure it's something we could ask him about.' He paused a split second. 'You know why. You know what I'm talking about.'

Antoine nodded slowly to show that he did know what Christopher was talking about. 'Even just for tonight would be good,' Antoine said. And Christopher's heart told him that it felt the same way. That whatever his head and conscience might say to the contrary, his heart was over the moon at the prospect of Antoine's staying the night.

They didn't touch each other at that moment. They were standing outside the front of the house. Though the nearest other dwelling was over a hundred yards away, the countryside was never unwatched. Everybody knew your business, even if they had to squint across half a mile of vines at you from the vantage point of a tractor seat to discover what it was. Nor did either of them refer to their conversation during the afternoon. But when it was time to down tools and for Jean-Pierre to head back to Castillon, and when Jean-Pierre made ready to depart and looked at Antoine expecting him to do the same, Antoine surprised Christopher by saying to Jean-Pierre, 'Elodie and me have had a bit of a falling-out. Christopher's letting me stay here for the night.'

The look that appeared on Jean-Pierre's face was more eloquent than anything he might have said in response. But he did manage to say, 'Well, good luck,' as he turned and departed. Though whether he meant good luck with Elodie or good luck with Christopher was anybody's guess.

Practicalities first, Christopher thought. He said, 'Better sort you a bed out.'

'Mmm?' queried Antoine and, because they were indoors at that moment, hugged Christopher and gave him a kiss.

Christopher accepted the hug and returned the kiss. But then he extricated himself. 'We can't sleep together,' he said. 'Not this time… I mean we shouldn't.'

'I've brought some *capotes*,' said Antoine and Christopher had to think for a second what he meant. But only for a second. He remembered the word, though he rarely used it. And because he'd not had penetrative sex with anyone except Tom since before the start of the aids epidemic he'd never had to use a *capote*.

'Well, whatever,' said Christopher, weakening. 'But for obvious reasons we still need to make up a second bed.'

Domestic arrangements were still in their infancy. Spare bed linen lived in a tea-chest. As they fished in the chest for sheet and duvet together, then made up a bed in one of the spare rooms, Antoine smoothing the bottom sheet with a tender finesse that took Christopher by surprise, Christopher thought for the first time what an intimate thing this was. Making a bed with someone else. He tried not to remember the proverb about making your bed and lying on it.

Before Christopher had time to wonder what they were going to do with the rest of the day if they were not going to go to bed together immediately, Antoine said, 'Will you show me the paintings? I only got a glimpse of them as the removal men were stacking them.' He grinned shyly. 'They looked interesting, I thought.'

Christopher found that he had no objection to showing to a man nearly twenty years younger than he was paintings of himself aged five years younger even than that. They went downstairs and Christopher unwrapped the leaning stacks.

'These were painted at Audresselles, near Boulogne,' Christopher introduced one group. Four young men were playing naked in the sea, climbing around a boat. 'There's Tom and me and our friends Michel and Armand.' He then had to explain that the picture had been painted by the famous Gérard de Martinville: the man who, as Antoine sort of knew, had left them the house in Paris that had given them the money to do up Le Vieux Chai and pay Antoine's wages.

Antoine peered at the pictures very intently. 'Tom's cock looks nice,' he said.

'It is,' said Christopher.

'Yours too, of course,' said Antoine and – as he was conveniently situated, sitting on his haunches next to Christopher as they went through the stack – made a playful grab for it through Christopher's shorts.

They didn't go further just then. The paintings were intriguing Antoine and he made sure that he saw all of them. 'This one's a bit different,' he said. 'And you both look very young in it. You also look very much in love. What's that game going on in the background? Is that cricket?'

'Yes,' said Christopher. Antoine was looking at the picture of the two of them in, and not quite in, cricket whites. 'It was painted by a dear lady called Molly O'Deere. We were all teaching in the same school. Though I had only just left school myself. I was eighteen, Tom twenty-one. The subject was David and Jonathan.'

'Yes,' said Antoine thoughtfully. 'You can sort of see that. That shiny red ball Tom's holding...Is that what a cricket ball looks like?'

'Yes,' said Christopher.

Antoine turned his head sideways and looked searchingly into Christopher's face. Christopher did likewise. They were still squatting side by side on the floor and it was beginning to be uncomfortable. 'Do you want to go upstairs for a bit?' Antoine asked.

Later they walked along the lane through the vineyards that led to the little village. The narrow lane could have been purpose-built for romance. Only a tiny ditch in the grass verges separated it from the head-high vines on either side of it. At intervals flowering rose bushes grew among them. (Though Christopher had learnt they were not there for decoration. Arriving swarms of greenfly would attack the roses before moving on to the tougher vine-stocks. Inspection of the roses would tell the vine-grower that it was time to spray the vineyard with insecticide. The roses were like canaries in a coal-mine.) Birds popped their heads out from the tops of the vine hedges: wheatears, robins and stone-chats. At one moment they saw a stoat hurrying across the lane just in front of them with one of its babies in its mouth, the way a cat carries a kitten. The temptation to touch each other, to fondle and kiss each other as they walked was powerful but they resisted it. They didn't need to voice the reason. Anyone could walk around a corner; there could be people in among the vines, working, lurking. Anything that anyone saw in such a place as this would not long remain a secret.

Arriving in amongst the cluster of houses that formed the village they went into the bar, ordered a beer each and sat outside in the little walled garden to drink it. The *patron* and his wife, and their occasional other staff, knew Tom and Christopher well by now. They knew Antoine and Jean-Pierre too, a little bit. Occasionally all four had gone in together for a lunchtime or early evening drink. Everyone in the bar knew where they were working; they knew that Tom and Christopher had bought the old wine store and that the other two were helping them to convert it. They seemed very accepting of Tom and Christopher as a gay couple. There was an agreement so obvious that it didn't need to be thought about, let alone spoken of. It was that if Tom and Christopher didn't hold hands in the bar or kiss each other as they walked back through the vines, no questions would be asked.

But this evening there was a difference. Not that anyone said anything. Yet somehow surprise and disapproval hung over the place like a light mist. Antoine and Christopher both sensed its chilly dampness and exchanged a glance as they carried their glasses out into the garden that told each other they could feel it. It was clear that though Tom and Christopher being discreetly gay and faithful to each other was not merely tolerated but also accepted, Christopher and Antoine playing around together in Tom's absence was not.

When it was time to eat they drove to a little town called Montpon-Ménestérol. It was some thirteen miles away, going north, so in the opposite direction from Castillon. Neither of them would have considered driving so far for dinner but their experience in the bar had made them think. They chose their unlikely destination after careful discussion. Christopher had never been near Montpon-Ménestérol while Antoine had only ever driven through it. It seemed fairly safe. They both realised independently, and without commenting, that when it came to clandestine liaisons they were a pair of unschooled innocents.

Back at Le Vieux Chai, now rendered a little less cautious by what they'd already drunk, they sat out in the dusk, outside the back door, with a glass of something local and red. (Everything local, at least everything within a five-mile radius, was red.)

'So you and Tom were teachers,' Antoine said, sounding interested and meaning, tell me about that.

So Christopher did. 'Teacher in a Benedictine prep school. That was my first job. My main subject was history. Tom's likewise. Then I was a waiter. Became co-manager of a café. Then joint manager of a boatyard. Now this.' He looked down at his glass. 'Is that a downward spiral, do you think?'

'No,' said Antoine quite firmly. 'It's almost the opposite. Most people limit their experience of life by thinking you can only do things in a certain order. You know. Like in the army. Corporal, sergeant, major, captain…But life doesn't have to be like that.'

'It's a good thought,' said Christopher. 'Actually quite cheering.'

'Not that it can matter much now,' said Antoine. 'You and Tom must be pretty rich. I mean, since the death of Gérard whatsit.'

Christopher's spirits sank. Was that what this was all about? 'Not that rich,' he said defensively. 'Anyway, no-one's ever rich until they're dead.'

'Merde,' said Antoine, sounding annoyed with himself. 'That sounded…' He put a firm hand on Christopher's bare forearm. 'I'm sorry. I didn't mean it like that.'

Christopher felt his spirits soar again. 'I know you didn't,' he said, for by now that was the truth.

Antoine changed the subject. 'You went to a religious school, you said. Me too. I was an altar server. Sang in the choir. Went to Mass…'

'Do you still believe?' Christopher asked him gently.

'No,' said Antoine. 'I mean, these days…'

'Yes,' said Christopher. 'I mean, it's the same with me. My mother…'

'Do your parents know you're gay?' Antoine asked.

'Yes, but they're not happy with it. I mean my mother isn't. That's partly why I'm not a believer. No God could create you in a certain way and then encourage a religion that forced your parents to reject you…'

'I've never talked about the subject with my own parents,' said Antoine.

'You might be lucky,' said Christopher. 'I mean, when they do find out. Tom's mother's fine with it.' Only after the words were out did he realise what he'd just said. 'Oh *merde*, I'm sorry. That sounded like I think you're as gay as I am. As Tom is.'

'Elodie thinks I am,' said Antoine quietly. 'I think she guessed that might be the case before I did. That's what our rows have been about.' He looked up at the sky. 'But, to be honest, I'm still not sure yet.'

Dusk had given way to a star-canopied night. An owl startled them by hooting suddenly in a cedar tree almost over their heads. 'Time to go in, is it?' said Christopher.

'It seems a shame to leave the owls and stars,' said Antoine. 'But yes, it's time you took me to bed.'

They went in, and then upstairs, but they left the bedroom window open, so the owls and stars shouldn't feel shut out.

Christopher had a lot of sorting out to do the next day before Tom got back. He wasn't going to allow himself to fall in love with Antoine: that was the first thing he sternly told himself. He loved Tom and he always would do. On the other hand Antoine was young and very attractive; he'd also proved himself in the course of last night's rambling conversations to be sensitive and intelligent. It would be very nice to have him around the house for a while, if Tom would wear that. *En plus*, Antoine was a very nice person to have sex with: Christopher had discovered that back in January. But Tom was hardly likely to allow that to continue. They had enjoyed an open relationship for a time when they were in their twenties; they had experienced the big boyfriend swap. It had all been even riskier than they'd imagined at the time, with the aids virus running amok. Yet somehow they'd come through it. But like speculators who'd risked their capital in younger days but grown ultra-cautious as middle age approached, they weren't going to hazard their precious, hard-won relationship at this point in their shared life.

Or had Christopher done that already by having sex with Antoine? By allowing him to stay the night in the first place? Christopher was giving some thought to that. He wondered if Antoine was having the same thought.

It had been a lovely night for both of them. Looking into each other's faces as they drank their morning coffee and ate their jam-spread *biscottes*, each could see that the other felt the same about that. Antoine had confessed that, though he'd been fucked by a couple of boys in the past, he'd never fucked another bloke. And Christopher had admitted that he'd never rolled a *capote* onto his cock before and had asked if Antoine would show him how by doing it for him, which Antoine laughingly did. It seemed natural to both of them that Christopher should roger Antoine first. That had happened on their first visit to Antoine's bedroom, after they'd looked at the paintings and before they'd gone out, walking through the vines to the village bar. While Antoine's turn had come when they finally went to bed at eleven o'clock. Christopher was glad now of the fact that, although they were both attractively equipped in the genital department, neither of their cocks was particularly big. There would be quite enough difficult stuff to explain to Tom, and plenty of things to try to cover up, without having to come up with a believable reason why one or both of them was walking awkwardly, or unable to sit in a chair with any semblance of comfort.

All this was going through Christopher's mind, revolving as if on a tape-loop, as he drove along the pretty back road through St-Genès and St-Emilion to Libourne station at the end of the afternoon. Antoine would be waiting for them at Le Vieux Chai when they got back. There could be no hiding that.

Christopher heard Tom's news first as they drove away from the station car-park. The signing ritual had gone smoothly. The new owner of Gérard's house seemed a very nice chap, Tom said. He was an investment banker who had a wife and six children. His name was Dumont. Tom hadn't expected him to be black, he told Christopher. When he'd come face to face with him that detail had surprised him. It would have been putting it too strongly to say he felt ashamed of being surprised by this, but he'd felt caught out by it. As a gay man he was impatient of other people's preconceptions and misplaced assumptions. He'd discovered in the course of his encounter with Monsieur Dumont that he wasn't free of preconceptions and assumptions himself. He didn't share all this with Christopher.

There had been a polite small drink in the notaire's office to celebrate the completion. Then Monsieur Dumont asked Tom if he would join him and his wife for dinner at the Tour D'Argent. He would be paying, he added smoothly. For though Tom had just come into half of the million pounds Monsieur Dumont had forked out for the house in the Rue St-Vincent, it was obvious to the investment banker that Tom didn't have a penny to his name apart from that. He could tell a person's wealth just by looking at him: that was his job. The dinner had been spectacular, Tom told Christopher – he listed the magical dishes – and Tom and the Dumonts had parted for the night afterwards with promises to keep in touch that they all knew were not binding. 'Well, that's all my news,' Tom finished. 'How are things on the home front?'

'Ah,' said Christopher. He found that, despite all his careful rehearsal of what he was about to say, his heart was starting to pound in his chest. 'There's been a bit of a development.'

'With the building work?'

'Domestically,' said Christopher, trying hard to focus on the road ahead and not to run through any red traffic lights. 'Antoine's had a bit of a row with his girlfriend. He's asked if he can stay with us for a night or two while he sorts himself out. I've had to say yes. He's got nowhere else.'

'Good God!' said Tom. Then, 'He hasn't got anywhere else? Everyone of his age has got somewhere else. He must have parents… Brothers or sisters in Castillon. We could put him up at my mum's if push comes to shove.

That would be more comfortable for him than sharing a half-built house with two forty-year-old poofs. We must suggest that.'

'Well, we could, I suppose,' said Christopher uncomfortably. 'But you'll find him at home when we get back there in a minute. He actually stayed last night.'

Tom's breath came out loudly, as if from a woodwind instrument. 'Jesus, Chris! You take the bloody biscuit!' There was another loud expulsion of breath. 'So he's installed already… And if I don't want him to stay with us I've now got to try and get him out. Darling … you do sometimes make life hard work.'

'Sorry, darling.' They were out in the country now, speeding along the road between the Pomerol and St-Emilion; grand châteaux loomed up like islands in the vineyards to left and right. 'I didn't have a chance to ask you. I didn't think you'd mind. He's a very nice chap.'

Actually Tom did think Antoine a very nice chap and, just as had been Christopher's case the day before, a large part of him was inappropriately pleased at the thought of having him as a house guest. That softened his reaction quite a lot. All the same he said, 'But what on earth will we do with him in the evenings? Three of us living on a building site…' A thought struck Tom. 'What did you do with him last night?'

'We had a beer at the village bar. Then we went to Montpon for dinner…'

'You went to Montpon? It's miles!'

'I know,' said Christopher. 'We were afraid that if we went anywhere closer to home we'd run into people we knew – or that he knew – and there'd be talk.' At least that part of the story was the honest truth.

'There'll be talk anyway!' said Tom. 'You should have thought of that before you invited him to stay in the first place. And so should he have done – before he asked. Hey, ease up!' His reminder was timely. Christopher managed to brake just in time as a lorry pulled out ahead of them into St-Emilion's singular little edge-of-town roundabout.

'I suppose you paid for dinner,' said Tom, knowing full well that the answer would be yes.

'Of course,' said Christopher bravely, heading into one of the two parallel roads to St-Christophe-des-Bardes; they chose between them each time indiscriminately. 'I'm the one that's inherited half of a big house in Paris; he isn't. It's just the same as you being taken to dinner by our Monsieur Dumont.' He only heard a snort from Tom in response to that.

'Don't worry,' said Christopher. 'I hadn't imagined either that he'd be black.'

Ten minutes later they turned into what would one day be the driveway and garden of Le Vieux Chai. For the moment they called it the yard. Christopher was more aware than Tom was of the fact that Antoine's pick-up truck, the one he always arrived at work in, was gone. It had been there when he'd set out for Libourne fifty minutes earlier. For the moment he didn't say anything about this. They both got out of the car. Tom looked around him, realised after a second that he'd been expecting to see the pick-up and said, 'No sign of your house-guest.'

'No,' said Christopher. Privately he was puzzled at Antoine's disappearance, and disappointed by it. He was also deeply annoyed. If Antoine had decided not to stay but to go back to Elodie, or go to stay with other friends, then Christopher had gone out on a limb for him for nothing. Christopher could easily have removed all traces of Antoine's overnight visit and said nothing to Tom about it.

Inside the house there was no sign of Antoine either. Not even a note on the kitchen table, which was where Christopher instinctively looked for it. A sense of anticlimax pervaded the house and was felt by both of them. Tom climbed the stairs to deposit his overnight things in the bedroom. He stared rather hard at the bed he shared with Christopher and Christopher felt that Tom's fingers itched to pull back the duvet and inspect the sheet beneath it: that only good manners stopped Tom from doing this. Tom then looked through the door of the room that Antoine (and Christopher too) had slept in. The bed was made, but it did look vaguely slept in. Grudgingly satisfied, Tom nodded his head involuntarily. 'Looks like the bird has flown,' he said. 'He'll be back with his girlfriend, putting on his best suit and wining and dining her in Libourne. You said they were always having rows and getting back together again. What's the issue between them? I'd have thought Antoine was an easy enough chap to rub along with.'

Christopher was saved from having to invent an un-alarming answer to this question by the sound of a car being driven into the yard below them. They looked out of the window and saw Antoine's pick-up coming to a stop and Antoine getting out of it. He didn't seem to have anyone with him. 'Ah,' said Tom. 'Now what?'

They walked down the stairs together. Christopher found that he was both pleased and relieved by Antoine's reappearance – to an absurd degree of both those feelings. While Tom found to his surprise that he was also pleased by Antoine's arrival. After all, Antoine was young, handsome and personable. Tom knew then that he wasn't going to give Antoine his marching orders. What forty-something gay man would conceivably do that, in such circumstances, to a beautiful lad like Antoine?

Tom and Christopher walked out into the yard as Antoine came towards them. He was carrying a fullish bag of groceries from the Leclerc supermarket.

'I've got some things for dinner,' Antoine said, in a voice that was trying to be brisk and matter-of-fact. But his face still gave away his apprehension and nervousness.

Tom was astonished then to hear his own voice say, 'I heard you'd come to stay with us. You've very welcome.'

Antoine's face melted with relief and he beamed at them. 'I've got some beef, carrots and potatoes I can throw into a pot. Salad and cheese for after. I thought … maybe … we could walk down to the bar in the village and have a beer while it's cooking?'

EIGHTEEN

Christopher didn't paint. But he'd painted the hulls of boats and their cabins and their fittings when they'd worked in the boatyard, and now he painted the interior of Le Vieux Chai. Alongside Tom. Alongside Antoine. All the building work had now been done. Jean-Pierre had gone off to do another job elsewhere, and Antoine left early each morning to go and join him. He helped with the painting of Le Vieux Chai in the evenings because he lived there.

Carpets had arrived. They lay still rolled up, waiting for the painting of the walls and ceilings to be finished before they could be laid. And the pictures were still waiting to be hung on the walls. It was just a matter of living a final few days, working away in a state of excited, happy impatience.

At last the day came when the carpets went down and the pictures went up. There was a house-warming dinner that evening at which the guests were May, Jean-Pierre and his wife, and Antoine's uncle Monsieur le Maire (though these days they called him by his first name, François). François also brought his wife. The dinner was cooked proficiently by Antoine. If François and his wife were puzzled by Antoine's being a part of the household that welcomed them, or even dismayed by it, they did a very good job of not showing it. Jean-Pierre was indeed puzzled by it and had occasionally made puzzled remarks out of the corner of his mouth while turning away from whichever of the three he happened to be talking to – it was a tactic that guarded against the possibility of a reply – but he didn't bring his puzzlement or any disapproval to the dinner table that evening: he would be working with Antoine in the days and months that followed. As for May, she had always chosen to stay out of any areas of Tom's life that he didn't want or need to share with her. She seemed delighted that her 'two boys' had found another friend, and asked no questions. She had asked no questions when her son had left Christopher for Michel, while Christopher had gone off with Armand for eight years. And this evening she found herself appreciating Antoine's cooking too.

The day after the housewarming Michel and Armand arrived and there was a second one … which lasted a week. It was the height of summer and all around the Vieux Chai the grapes were visible and growing, on rows of vines that were now thick deep hedges. The cuckoo had stopped calling and few birds sang in the midday heat. Instead the bees and the grasshoppers created the soundtrack.

Antoine at first seemed overawed in the company of the two visitors from the Channel coast, who were Tom's and Christopher's age respectively, and had known the English pair since about the time he was born. At the same time he found it amusing to be sitting at dinner with these forty-somethings while paintings of their naked selves aged nineteen or twenty hung on the walls around them. Though not until the second evening of Michel and Armand's visit did he mention it. They were eating pork chops that had been slowly oven-cooked in white wine that Antoine's Uncle François had given them.

'I've got used to seeing Tom and Christopher's cocks on the wall,' he said to Armand conversationally. 'Yours too, and Michel's. But now you're here – in the flesh, so to speak…' Hearing his own words he broke off with a giggle.

'I can imagine,' said Armand. He stopped too. Antoine's giggle was catching. In fact only five of the sixteen paintings that hung in the open-plan living space were of youths frolicking naked, but they did draw the attention rather. Armand recovered himself. 'But there's two more up there you probably won't get to meet.' He pointed to the one canvas in which a naked Benoît and René were depicted. 'Do you know who those two are?'

'Two more friends from the north, I think,' said Antoine. 'Benoît and René, who you've all lost touch with?' He looked at Christopher for a split second to see if he'd got this right. At the same moment Tom looked at Antoine, and then at Christopher for an even shorter moment. 'They certainly looked handsome at nineteen or whatever,' Antoine said.

Michel and Armand had not simply come south for a holiday. As they had planned months ago they were going to join Tom and Christopher in the search for a place to buy for themselves. They began, as Tom and Christopher had done in the spring, as Tom and May had done the autumn before, by driving round the countryside, to get the feel of the region, look at prices, and let the eureka moment of learning what it was they were looking for come in its own time.

They looked at a charming wreck of a cottage higher up the Dordogne, halfway to Sarlat. Its roof was sagging badly for lack of care. Tiles had gone and the rafters below them were rotting away. Armand was very taken with it. 'You'd need to buy it quickly and get the roof done before the autumn rains,' said Tom. 'Otherwise we couldn't do any interior work over the winter. We'd have to wait till spring.'

Michel took the point and finished it to save Tom having to do so. 'And spend the winter twiddling your thumbs,' he said.

That experience helped to narrow down the search a bit. They would try to find a property whose roof was in good repair at least. In the Upper Dordogne, and in the town of Sarlat itself, the roofs were made of thick stone tiles called *lauzes*. Usually hundreds of years old they were weather-sealed by time and the lichens that grew on them. These beautiful roofs could weigh a hundred and fifty pounds per square foot, Tom said. That was a fact he'd learned from Jean-Pierre. A broken roof of *lauzes* would be massively expensive to repair. Though they were one of the attractions of the Périgord Noir the house-hunters decided to leave them well alone. Easier to deal with would be the red canal-tiled roofs of the lower Dordogne, such as crowned the Vieux Chai.

'We don't want anything quite as big as yours,' Michel admitted at last. 'It'll be our second home, not our first.' That usefully narrowed the field a little further.

Périgord Noir and Périgord Blanc had been the names of the old provinces that were replaced by the modern department of Dordogne at the end of the eighteenth century. In 'White Périgord' the landscape was open and pastoral, full of vineyards, the way it was around the Vieux Chai and Castillon. 'Black Périgord,' upstream, around Sarlat, had taken its name from the darkness of its deep forests, where chestnuts and walnuts grew and – if you were lucky – dark truffles lurked beneath your feet. 'It's almost too beautiful' said Armand, when confronted for the first time by the fairytale turrets of Sarlat.

'Too beautiful to be lived in, do you mean?' asked Michel.

Armand said, 'Maybe.'

Tom and Christopher said nothing. They had made the same journey of the mind, the decision-making process of house-hunting, just a few months earlier.

It was not until day three that Armand found a chance for a private word with Christopher. He seized a moment when Michel and Tom were walking round a property, engrossed in discussion about its possibilities. As Michel and Tom walked upstairs he pulled Christopher back. As soon as the other two were out of earshot he said boldly,

'Tell me the latest about Antoine. Him actually living with you. After what you told me back in the winter...'

Christopher told the story of Antoine's moving into the Vieux Chai while Tom was away in Paris and of what had happened that first night. 'But do you still…?' Armand began to ask.

Christopher stopped him short. 'No. Since what happened in January there's just been that one night. Now that he's living with us, well, I sleep with Tom, and Antoine's out at work all day. There isn't the opportunity.' He paused for a second. Then, 'And it probably wouldn't feel right anyway. Taking advantage of Tom's hospitality…'

Armand didn't say, that's never stopped you before. It wouldn't have been true. He did say, 'You took advantage of Tom's absence, though.' That was true, and Christopher had nothing to say in answer, although his face told Armand everything he needed to know. 'Does Tom know?' Armand went on. He clarified. 'I mean, does he know that Antoine's gay?'

'No, he doesn't,' said Christopher. 'And if he guesses it he hasn't said so. Anyway, not even Antoine seems quite sure if Antoine's gay. He drives into Castillon some evenings to spend time with friends. Eats and drinks in bars. That sort of thing. If there's more to it than that…' Christopher shrugged. 'Well, we don't know.' A new thought came to him and he frowned. 'I suppose Michel knows? I mean about Antoine and me.'

'Not unless Antoine's told him,' Armand said. 'I tell Michel most things. But what you told me that day in Boulogne … what you've told me now … that stays with me. We were *copains,* partners, lovers once, remember. Some things can still be just between the two of us.' Then he said, 'It must be very difficult for you, having him living under your roof, sleeping in the room next to yours, and not being able to do anything about it. Not to be able to touch him, or talk to him about things.'

'I just have to accept it,' Christopher said. He didn't quite shrug but his eyebrows did. 'Life has a habit of throwing you into situations so crazy that no audience would believe them in a film or a play. There's not much you can do about it except get on with life and make the best of it. At least I've got Tom. He loves me and vice versa. Antoine doesn't have that at the moment.'

'You think it's even harder for him than it is for you?' Armand asked.

Christopher grimaced. 'I don't know that. I can't know that. He's younger than me by nineteen years. I can't easily imagine how different that must be from the way I feel about him. He doesn't talk abut it.'

'Because neither of you gets the chance?' Armand didn't wait for Christopher to answer. 'Are you in love with him?' he asked.

'I can't let myself fall,' said Christopher firmly. 'That would be disastrous.'

'What about Antoine? Is he in love with you?'

'I've no way of knowing that,' said Christopher.

'I've seen the way he looks at you,' Armand said. He didn't elaborate but left Christopher to make what he would of his remark. He led the way upstairs to join the others.

They went south and explored the Lot department: its hilltop towns, bastides, and its old capital, Cahors. 'Another fairytale,' said Michel, as they admired the turret-staired houses of Cahors and its medieval bridge with its three spire-capped towers.

'It's only centuries of poverty that keeps places beautiful in this sort of way, don't you think?' said Tom. 'Think of Venice. Think of Bruges.'

'Think of Sandwich in England,' said Christopher. 'And the other Cinque Port towns.'

'Like the bastides,' Armand added. 'Monpazier, Monflanquin. And Sarlat. It's like *La Belle Dormante.* Towns and villages sidelined for centuries while progress moves on elsewhere. To sleep and sleep, until the twentieth century came calling with cars and trains and hacked down the thorn forests.'

In the end it all fell into place very quickly and suddenly, just as it had done for May, and for Tom and Christopher. A pair of attached cottages did it for Michel and Armand. It was love at first sight. The pair of stone-built cottages looked as though they had been a single dwelling once. It would not be difficult to pull down dividing walls and make them one again. They were part of a small hamlet called Nastringues: a name that English tongues might have found daunting; but Michel's and Armand's tongues did not; they had been French from the outset. Nastringues was not fifty miles up-river like Sarlat, nor, like Cahors, fifty miles south. It was just outside Ste-Foy-la-Grande; it was about a ten-mile drive from Le Vieux Chai along winding lanes; slightly longer, though quicker, if you took the main road along the Dordogne flood plain. Like St-Philippe-d'Aiguille the hamlet was surrounded by a sea of vineyards. Not in claret country any more, not the Côtes de Castillon, but in an area producing a wine called Montravel, which none of them had heard of. Whatever the brew might taste like, the views across the vineyards of Montravel and those of Castillon were pretty similar. And similarly pretty.

Negotiations for the purchase of the pair of cottages went smoothly. The vendor was the owner of the surrounding wine estate. An offer was made and accepted, and a notaire engaged to do the next bit. Tom and Christopher had no involvement in the transaction.

Michel and Armand would be using their own money; they didn't need Tom and Christopher's. Nor did they need their services as translators. Michel and Armand might be incomers, just as much as Tom and Christopher were, but they were Frenchmen dealing with other Frenchmen. It seemed to help.

NINETEEN

May was invited again to eat at the Vieux Chai towards the end of Michel and Armand's visit. She had known both men for years and was comfortable chatting with them in a mixture of French and English. She now saw herself as a bit of an expert on buying property in the region and was full of advice for the two Frenchmen. And questions too. How soon did they expect completion on the purchase of their pair of tumbledown cottages at Nastringues? Michel told her about the offer they'd made and that it had been accepted. With any luck it could all go through in a couple of months, then work on the property could start. 'Good,' said May. Her son had returned her loan of ten thousand pounds over a month ago, but she still took a keen interest in his cash flow and his prospects; she was still his mother. In spite of this she was quite unfazed by the fact that pictures of him naked, with Christopher and Michel and Armand, adorned the walls around her. They all gave her full marks for that.

She turned her attention to Antoine. She had met him a dozen times now and treated him as a family member. She had asked no difficult questions about his presence in the house. 'I met your grandmother on Sunday,' she told him. 'Madame Deblouze introduced us.' Antoine gave May the look that everyone gives a person who's just told them they've met their grandmother. 'I told her you worked with my two boys and were living with them.'

'Oh bloody hell, mum,' Tom said curtly. 'Can't you see how that's going to play out among the churchgoers of Castillon? For the moment they're still under the misapprehension Chris and I are both your sons. Although they know we live together. They must find that a bit hard to swallow to start with. I don't mind them finding out that Chris and I are a couple. That's no skin off our noses. We don't know those people. But it won't do you any good with the people you're trying to cultivate if they think you've been lying to them…'

'How dare you!' May flared back. 'I've never lied to anyone about the two of you…'

'You deliberately allowed them to make a wrong assumption,' Tom countered. He lifted his hands from the table and held them up for a second. 'But that's your decision and I'm fine with it.'

'Hey, hey,' Michel interrupted. 'Family discussions over dinner… Not the best place…' Neither mother nor son took any notice.

'What does matter,' Tom went on, 'is what people in Castillon are going to think about Antoine. He doesn't want to be tarred with the gay brush. Why should he have to be? It's not fair on him. Castillon is where he comes from. Where he's going to spend the rest of his life, most probably. He could do without an incorrect label.'

'Then he should have thought about that before he moved in with you,' May said robustly. She softened suddenly and looked across the table. 'Sorry, Antoine,' she said. 'It's the Irish in me. I tend to be a bit forthright.'

Christopher translated forthright for him. Antoine sat looking a bit sheepish, but didn't attempt to say anything – which Christopher and Armand both thought very wise of him. Tom, repenting of his sudden tirade against his mother, immediately topped her glass of wine up without saying anything. It was a gesture that May decoded without difficulty. She said nothing either, but smiled back.

The next day Michel and Armand departed for the north coast, leaving the lawyers to take their time over the conveyancing of the Nastringues cottages. Tom and Christopher drove them to Libourne station to catch the Saturday midday train; they made a detour via the supermarket on the way back.

On their return to Le Vieux Chai they found Antoine with a message for them. 'Your English friend John Moyse telephoned,' Antoine said. 'He's the one who was a friend of Angelo who died, I think. He said he thought you'd like to know that, by some chance, he'd run into Angelo's other friend… Simon. Simon someone. Hang on. I've written it down…'

'Simon Rickman,' said Tom. 'Good God! But did you do all that in English?'

'No. As soon as I told him you weren't here John went into French. His French isn't fantastic but it's still not bad…'

'How did he meet Simon Rickman?' Christopher asked.

'Through Angelo's sister, he said. I'm sure he'd give you more details if you rang him back.'

'I'll ring him later,' Tom said. They'd just walked in. They hadn't got the shopping out of the car yet.

'Angelo was in love with Simon, wasn't he?' Antoine asked.

Tom looked at him in astonishment. 'How in God's name did you know that? How come you're so familiar with all this stuff? ' He only just stopped himself from saying, how come you're so familiar, full stop?

'Chris told me,' said Antoine. The 'Chris' just seemed to have popped out by accident.

'Christopher,' Tom corrected, trying hard not to sound angry about it. 'Nobody calls him Chris.'

'You do,' said Antoine.

Christopher stepped in before Tom could say anything in reply to that. 'He can call me Chris if he wants to,' he told Tom. He turned to Antoine. 'It's fine if you call me Chris.'

Tom gave a small snort of annoyance. 'You two have obviously had a lot of private conversations I know nothing about.' He turned towards the door. 'I'll get the stuff in from the car.'

'Everybody has conversations,' Christopher called after him. 'They're not necessarily private.' Then he went after Tom to help him unload the boot.

Tom did phone John Moyse later. After they'd eaten. Tom and Antoine had both made a point of being very nice towards each other during the preparations for dinner and the eating of it, and Christopher was relieved by that.

On the phone Tom listened mostly while John talked. The other two sat watching Tom listening. After he'd put the phone down Tom relayed the gist of what John had said.

'John wrote a script for a TV show, apparently, in which Angelo's sister was involved somehow. Anyway their two names appeared on the same set of credits. Simon Rickman saw it and it rang a sort of double bell for him. It was a bit of a fluke: he doesn't watch much television, John said. He decided he wanted news of Angelo and phoned the BBC on an impulse and asked to speak to Izzy.' Tom turned to Antoine. 'That's John's sister. She works there.' Then he went on. 'John said that was also surprising: Simon's not very good with telephones.'

'Oh?' said Christopher. He remembered Simon as a bright-as-a-button thirteen-year-old who had been a house captain.

'Izzy had no idea who he was. If she'd ever heard his name mentioned by Angelo she'd forgotten it. But she listened to him and got the John connection. In the end she put the two of them in touch and yesterday John went to see him.' He paused. 'This is a bit sad now. He lives alone on a caravan site near Hastings. With almost no money. Apparently he can't work much.' Tom felt uncomfortable saying this. He had only recently become rather well-off. Feeling uncomfortable about the relative poverty of people he knew went with the new territory but it was an unfamiliar experience and difficult to deal with.

'How's that come about?' asked Christopher. But he thought, it could happen to any of us.

'Ah,' Tom said. 'He had some sort of breakdown in his teens, ran away from home, got into drugs…' He broke off and shrugged.

'So he isn't fit for work,' said Christopher. 'What does he do with his time? Did John tell you that?'

'He goes fishing, he said. And spends a lot of time sitting around in libraries reading books about New Age – whatever that is. And the occult. Astrology. That kind of stuff.' Tom stopped. 'Anyway, that's all, really. John just thought we'd like to know that.'

'John told him about Angelo and how he died, I suppose?' Christopher checked.

'Of course,' said Tom. 'Sorry, I should have said that. Simon had no idea he'd become a priest.'

'It's a very sad story,' said Antoine. It was the first time he'd spoken since Tom had gone to the phone and dialled John's number up. Tom had reported the sad story in English, but had also translated the more complicated bits into French when he'd seen from Antoine's face that he'd lost him. Now suddenly Antoine surprised them both with what he said next. He looked at Christopher and said, in French of course, 'You used to be a teacher. I wish you could teach me English.'

'Tom was a teacher too, don't forget,' Christopher said.

TWENTY

August was the time when most French people took their holidays. For Parisians especially the month – from the first Saturday to the last one – was held sacred in an almost religious way; the motorways that led south were crammed with traffic on both those days – heading out of Paris on the first Saturday, heading back again on the last.

Throughout the rest of France the custom was not quite so universal; someone had to be around to welcome the invading Parisian hordes and take their money from them. Even so, for many it was still holiday time. Around Le Vieux Chai the wine growers and makers took their holidays in August; the grapes had nothing to do but steadily grow and ripen in the sun. The frenetic activity of the grape harvest would begin in mid-September. By then the purchase of Michel and Armand's property at Nastringues should be completed and work on it could start. Tom and Christopher planned to pass their August creating a garden around Le Vieux Chai. May would be returning to England for a couple of weeks to catch up with old friends. It was not yet clear what Antoine was going to do.

For the moment Antoine was enjoying learning English. Both Tom and Christopher were helping him do this. They'd started with some trepidation. They had both taught English to British seven- and eight-year-olds. That included reading works of literature and poetry and parsing an occasional sentence. But that had been more than twenty years ago and in any case it was a totally different job from teaching English to an adult for whom it was not a first language. They had to phone Michel to ask him if he'd ever been on the receiving end of such training. Michel said he hadn't. Surely they must know that. Tom had been Michel's partner for years. It wasn't something Tom would not have known about. On the other hand, Michel did know other people who'd had English lessons as adults. There was a book that they'd all talked about. It was called English Grammar in Use – written by someone called Murphy. (Tom with his Irish family background thought this hilarious, but Michel didn't see it.) The book would not only be useful when it came to giving Antoine exercises for homework. The grammar was explained so well and so simply, Michel said, that the book would actually explain to Tom and Christopher all the things they needed to teach Antoine but didn't themselves know about.

They found a copy of Murphy in the Bordeaux branch of FNAC.

Antoine was a diligent and rewarding language student. He enjoyed his lessons, asked lots of questions and did forty minutes of homework every night. It wasn't that he'd never come across the English language before, he said. He'd done it at school for years but hadn't really taken much notice of it. It hadn't seemed important before now, he said. Whatever he meant by that.

One afternoon, before Antoine returned from work his uncle François came and knocked at the door of Le Vieux Chai. Tom and Christopher didn't see François very often. He had proved a good neighbour over the months since they'd bought the Vieux Chai from him. He'd been there for them when they'd needed advice or help with anything. He'd invited them into his own house for a drink once or twice, and they had returned the compliment the same number of times, but otherwise they had left each other in peace, in the very French spirit of respect for the privacy of others. François had never commented on his nephew's joining the household at Le Vieux Chai. Not to Tom and Christopher at any rate nor, as far as they knew, to Antoine. But now

François stood at the door, with the bashful smile on his face that is commonly worn by neighbours who are about to ask a favour and said, 'May I come in?'

They sat at the table at the kitchen end of the living space. Tom poured the three of them a small glass of Monbazillac wine. 'I need to talk to you about something.' François came to the point quite quickly; almost as soon as he'd said chin-chin. 'It's about my nephew Antoine.'

'OK,' said Tom, nodding his head gently to show that that was fine by him.

'It's very good of the two of you to help him out in the way you have. Taking him into your house after he fell out with his girl. He appreciates it very much. And so do I. So does his mother. And my mother … who is Antoine's grandmother, of course.'

The mention of the grandmother set alarm bells ringing for both Christopher and Tom. The grandmother had met May at church. May had talked to her about her grandson and about Christopher and Tom…

'Of course,' said Tom.

'Now, everybody's life is private,' François went on. 'I uphold that principle most strongly. I also realise that we are living in more enlightened times than we were even ten years ago.'

'You're talking about the fact that Tom and I are gay,' said Christopher matter-of-factly.

'Gay?' François queried.

Christopher clarified. 'Gay in the Anglo-Saxon sense of the word.' The French word *gai* still also had the meaning of cheerful or bright, just as its English counterpart did. Just as in English the word enjoyed two separate meanings.

'Indeed,' said François. 'You have the right to find fulfilment in your own way. That has been the case in France – in French law at least – for centuries. In your home country only since more recently, but it's still the same. My point is…' François was clearly finding this difficult. He was about a dozen years older than Tom but looked more than that because he was nearly completely bald except for his beard. He took a sip of the clear yellow Monbazillac in his glass before going on. 'My worry is… I wonder, and so do his mother and grandmother, whether it is good for Antoine to be living here. There. Now I've said it. I'm deeply sorry if I've offended you.'

'No offence taken,' said Tom. 'But are you worried about Antoine's sexual orientation? Afraid we might influence it in some way, simply by our company? Or worried about the way he'll be regarded by other people? By people who know him in Castillon? People we meet in bars?'

'All of those things,' said François and sighed. 'And his grandmother in particular is worried about the danger of aids.'

Christopher was so astonished that he exploded into a laugh.

'Oh for heaven's sake,' said Tom. 'I thought everybody knew by now how you can and can't catch aids. You can't get it by sharing a house with someone; you can't pick it up from the toilet seat. Unless we're talking about blood transfusions or junkies sharing needles you can only get it by having sex with an infected person. And there's no question of that in this case. Because, first of all, both Christopher and I were tested last year – just as a precaution, in case of things in the distant past…' François nodded his head slightly. All men knew about things in the distant past. 'And secondly because there's no question of either of us having sex with your nephew in the past, present or future.'

François lifted one of his hands an inch from the table as if trying to ward Tom's words off or turn them back. 'Sorry,' he said. 'I only meant…'

But Tom went on, 'About the other things – about Antoine's sexual orientation and what people will say about him – those things are entirely his to deal with, not ours. Not that I've any reason to imagine he's anything other than heterosexual. And if he was worried about what people would say or think, then he wouldn't have moved in with us; or else, having done so, would have moved straight out.' Tom stopped, hearing himself getting a bit pumped up. 'Sorry,' he said. 'But you can tell his grandmother, your mother, she has nothing to worry about.' Though he wondered if his own mother did have something to worry about. He also realized that he'd just been making a point that May had made first and that, at the time, he had disagreed with her about it. He leaned across the table and fractionally topped everyone's glass up.

'I'm sorry,' said François again, this time quite meekly for a mayor. And they all drank the rest of their Monbazillac and talked about predictions for the forthcoming grape harvest.

When François had gone, leaving them with friendly handshakes, Tom and Christopher could find nothing to say for about a minute. They washed and dried the wineglasses at the kitchen sink. Then Tom said, 'I'm worried about my mum now. If people have worked out that you're not her youngest son but my partner, and they feel that she's lied to them about that…'

'She's in England for another week at least,' said Christopher comfortingly. 'It'll have blown over by the time she gets back.'

'You really think so?' said Tom. 'We're talking about the devout congregation of a Catholic church. You only have to think what your own mother's like.'

Christopher shrugged a bit uncomfortably. 'Well, anyway, I thought you were splendid just now. Talking to François the way you did.' He put the tea-towel he'd just dried the glasses with back on its hook.

'I had to,' Tom said. He was holding two of the dried glasses in his hands, on the point of returning them to their shelf. Christopher heard two of them touch with a tiny bell-like note. 'I mean, it had to be me that said it.' Tom gave Christopher a very piercing look. 'I don't think that you could have looked François in the eye and said all that.' He paused meaningfully, then finished, 'And I don't think either that Antoine could.'

Part Three

1998 – 1999

School Ties, Blood Ties

TWENTY-ONE

There were roses everywhere. It was that time of year. 'We grew them from cuttings,' Christopher said. 'You've seen the roses flowering at the ends of the rows in the vineyards. Well, we just snipped off bits. Usually with the owners' permissions – but not always, I have to admit.'

'But the little white ones clambering over the boundary fence…?' John asked.

'No,' Christopher said. 'They're just wild ones, dog roses. They turned up of their own accord, unannounced and unexpected. We can't claim the credit for those.'

'They still look nice,' said John.

'At the moment,' said Christopher. 'You came at the right time of year to see the garden at its best.'

Not only roses filled the garden that Tom, Christopher and Antoine had created around the Vieux Chai. There were lupins and columbines, yellow geums, white daisies that nodded, pale blue geraniums, and the spangling flowers of Alpine strawberry plants. Some areas were shaded by rustic wooden pergolas that Antoine had built ten years before and up which several kinds of clematis and yet more climbing roses swarmed with anarchic exuberance.

'It's very English and un-classical,' John said. 'What do your French neighbours make of it?'

'They're complimentary,' said Tom, arriving through one of the clematis arches with a bottle of champagne and three glasses. He'd just caught John's last remark. 'They allow us to be good at gardening. They expect it, even.' He made a clicking noise with his tongue. 'Cooking remains a harder nut to crack.' He set the tray he was carrying down on the garden table the other two were sitting at.

'All this in ten years,' said John, still looking round at the flowers and foliage. A little way from where they sat were sun-drenched beds of courgettes, peas and asparagus. 'I can't believe it's taken me all that time to find my way here.'

'Time plays tricks,' said Christopher. Neither of the others bothered to say they agreed with him. Tom unwired the champagne and sent the cork banging off into the sunshine by way of a riposte.

John's visit to St-Philippe-d'Aiguille was almost a spur-of-the-moment plan. His eldest daughter had recently had her first child, turning John into a grandfather literally overnight. Now, a few weeks after the event, John's wife had gone to spend a week helping her daughter cope with the enormous change that had overtaken her life. John, at a loose end, had decided to cash in the *you must come and stay some time* offer that had been made ten years earlier, and remade many times since, though until now not taken up. Now his arrival was being toasted in champagne.

'Is your mother still with us?' John asked Tom. 'Still living down here, I meant to say.'

'Yes to both,' said Tom. 'We had serious doubts at first. Whether she'd done the right thing, moving out here on her own…'

'Well, you weren't a million miles away,' said John.

'That was fortuitous. We had no idea, when she first bought her place, that we'd be living just eight miles up the road by the time she moved in. But she doesn't depend on us. She's made a crowd of good friends.'

'That can't have been easy,' said John.

'Strangely enough it was. And though I hate to admit this, it was all because she still goes to church. The parishioners of Castillon took her under their wings. Of course they're mostly elderly middle-class women like she is.'

'There was a bit of a hiccup, though,' Christopher chipped in. 'Around the time that Antoine first moved in with us…'

'You know who we mean by Antoine?' Tom checked. John nodded in reply.

'May – Tom's mum – had rather allowed the people at church to assume we were brothers. Once Antoine moved in with us … they knew about this because his grandmother went to the same church as May … it became obvious that we were a gay couple. They sort of assumed we were corrupting young Antoine. For a few weeks May lost all her new friends.'

'We worried for her,' Tom continued seamlessly. 'But she just went on going to church, going to Communion, behaving with great dignity in fact, and continuing to smile at people who no longer spoke to her. And in the end they all came back. They said things like, "What our children do in their private lives is up to them," and, "Of course we must all live in the modern world now." She didn't argue with them, or call them hypocrites or tell them they were spouting platitudes. Somehow it all got put right. She got her friends back and still has them.'

'Except for the ones who've died since,' said Christopher.

John looked around him. 'Antoine doesn't still live here, does he?'

'No,' said Tom. 'He was with us for about a year. Then miraculously he met an older man who lived near Ste-Foy-la-Grande…'

'Which is where you work now, right?'

'Where all three of us work. He and his partner have a very nice little house just outside the town. In a pretty hamlet called St-Avit-du-Tizac.'

'We call it Saint Margaret Tyzack,' said Christopher.

Tom went on. 'It's actually not far from where Michel and Armand have a place – in a village called

Nastringues. Antoine keeps an eye on their house for them when they're not around. And they're not around at the moment, I'm afraid. They're at home in Wimereux.'

'They'll be sorry they missed you,' said Christopher.

'And I'm sorry I've missed them,' John replied graciously. Everybody took a sip of champagne.

'So your mother gets on with her neighbours,' John said, looking towards Tom. 'How are you with yours?'

'Well, there are no close ones, as you can see,' said Tom. He pointed between the rose trellises across the waving vine sea to where a cluster of trees half hid a stone house and its outbuildings. 'That's our nearest. François. The village mayor… For God's sake if you meet him don't call him François just because we do. He'll be *Monsieur le Maire* to you. He's been the mayor since before the Big Bang.'

'Like God,' said John.

'Exactly,' said Tom. 'Though possibly for even longer. He's also Antoine's uncle and the man we bought this property from.'

'He once tried to read us the riot act,' said Christopher. 'When Antoine first moved in with us. He thought it was all wrong and his nephew would end up catching aids from the loo seat. But Tom stood up to him and sent him away … well, not exactly with a flea in his ear, or his tail between his legs. It was all very friendly. Antoine stayed, and François hasn't made any trouble for us in the ten years since. He's actually quite a friend.'

'A few English people live nearby,' said Tom. 'If they run into trouble with their neighbours – and it's usually no more than a question of language – we try and smooth things over if we can. That might sound like us sticking our oar in where it isn't wanted but actually it seems to be appreciated by both sides.'

John had another swallow of champagne and exhaled something like a contented sigh. Then he said, 'Simon would love it here.'

'Simon Rickman,' echoed Christopher. Though the surname was superfluous. He was the only Simon who was common to all of them.

'He's not thinking of buying a house here, is he?' asked Tom.

John laughed. Property was not as cheap along the Dordogne as it had been ten years ago. You certainly couldn't pick up a house for the value of a rusting caravan. That was the only asset that Simon possessed as far as any of them knew. John helped him out a bit financially, and in order not to feel guilty about this Tom and Christopher sent him a couple of hundred pounds each Christmas. Plus a couple more in the middle of the year. 'No, I wasn't thinking that,' said John. 'I just imagined him out here, enjoying the weather and the countryside for a bit. Fishing… I suppose there's fishing round here?'

'Plenty in the Dordogne and other rivers,' said Tom. 'The French actually eat the fish they catch, believe it or not. There's stalls full of river fish just along the quay from where my mother lives in Castillon. Perch, roach, zander… Pike and eels. There's a thing called *alose* which translates to English as shad and which is composed almost entirely of bones…'

'Don't forget the lampreys,' said Christopher. 'All the things the Brits would simply chuck back. Lampreys are a speciality in top restaurants round here.'

John wrinkled his small nose. 'I might give those a miss. Didn't Henry II die of a surfeit of them?'

'Yes,' said Christopher. 'Just up the road at Chinon.'

'And I'm not too sure about the ones you say are made entirely of bones…'

Tom said, 'I suppose we could have him down here for a holiday.' The other two looked at him.

'You might not be able to get rid of him if you did,' said John. 'We had him up to Godalming once and he stayed and stayed. In the end Maisie had to tell him it was time to go.'

It was striking, thought Tom, how much tougher wives seemed to be than their men-folk when it came to that sort of situation. He said, 'But if we clubbed together and bought him a plane ticket… One with a return date… That would reduce the risk.' Then he turned to Christopher. 'Sorry. I'm talking as if it's really going to happen, and without consulting you. I was just daydreaming, really.'

'I don't see why it shouldn't happen,' said Christopher. 'Give the poor chap a holiday fishing for bony tiddlers. It'd be something … well, it'd be like doing something for Angelo. He'd have wanted it, I'm sure.'

'Like he'd have wanted us to give Simon all those Christmas handouts,' said Tom. He grinned. 'Sorry. I wasn't really being cynical.'

'Well, if it did happen it might at least give me a break from him,' said John.

'Why?' Christopher asked. 'He doesn't keep turning up at Godalming, does he?'

'No, I didn't mean that,' said John. 'He's not forever on the doorstep. What I meant was that he might meet someone down here who takes his fancy. At the moment he's rather unfortunately in love with me.'

'I hadn't given any thought to whether he might be gay or not,' said Christopher. 'Not everyone who enjoys a fumble with his best friend in his teens grows up gay. Most don't. I'd rather assumed he hadn't.' He was in the back seat of the car, talking to the backs of Tom's and John's heads.

'I didn't give it a thought either,' said John. 'Until I'd met him for about the second or third time. And after that it gradually became more and more obvious.'

'It may be a transference thing,' said Tom. 'You were – you are – the closest he can ever get to Angelo.'

'Perhaps,' John accepted. 'His feelings towards me certainly seemed to get stronger after I gave him that document you sent back to me.'

'The one in which Angelo wrote about his love for Simon,' said Christopher. He added, 'I have to admit I kept a photocopy.'

'Strange how Angelo's influence lives on,' said Tom. 'He continues to affect all of us.'

'Isn't that as it should be?' said John. Neither of the others was going to disagree with that and they drove in silence for a minute. Tom and Christopher had decided they would take John to Ste-Foy-la-Grande by what they called the back road. It took them through vineyards most of the way, the road cresting the gentle hills one after another. The landscape appeared to move in soft undulations like a green flying carpet as they passed through it. Its landmarks were all honey-white stone buildings with red roofs; every house was a wine château. Each was impeccably kept, shaded by a couple of cedar or cypress trees; there were usually a couple of four by fours on the gravel driveways. The front lawns were immaculate. One elegant château was distinguished by the massive figure of a rearing horse made of scrap metal which stood in front of it, looking glorious.

They drove through the pretty village of Belvès, full of hanging baskets, and with pavements so clean that no-one would dare to drop a cigarette-butt on them. Through the hard-to-find hamlet of Rouye, almost hidden among deep hedges and looking as though the twentieth century, drawing to a close elsewhere, had not yet reached it. Montaigne, Moncaret, Le Breuilh, then, with the church spire of Ste-Foy already in sight, the tiny village of St-Avit-du-Tizac. 'This is where Antoine lives with his boyfriend,' Tom said, pointing to a row of quaint houses. 'You'll meet him in a minute. Antoine, that is. Not the boyfriend – well, not today. I told you he was older than Antoine, by the way. He's not that old, though. Younger than we are. Your age, I suppose. He's called Patrick. He's one of the top brass in the regional tourist authority.'

'French?' checked John. Tom had pronounced the name the French way, with the accent on the second syllable.

'As French as they come,' said Tom.

'Remind me how it came about,' said John. 'I mean you two becoming estate agents.'

Tom ran over the story for him. About how they'd been very successful with their property conversion business, selling their renovated houses through the local agencies and by word of mouth among incomers and their friends who, as they themselves had once done, simply drove around looking.

'But then Jean-Pierre retired. By then I was fifty-three, Chris fifty… There comes a time at which you fall out of love with the idea of yourself stripped to the waist digging trenches, even with a mechanical digger. We'd have needed a replacement for Jean-Pierre anyway. There just happened to be an estate agent in Ste-Foy – someone we worked a lot with – who was selling up. We talked it over with Antoine. Though he was only just over thirty he turned out to be only too happy to exchange his life as a builder for something … different.'

'So you have the best of both worlds,' said John. 'You present a French face to French customers and a British face to British ones.'

'Exactly,' said Tom. 'And we have Roger and Malcolm to handle the English end of it. As I'm sure I told you.'

'I'd forgotten,' said John, not unreasonably.

'All we needed was a British phone number. For British customers to feel safe with. People are afraid of phoning an office in France. They're afraid someone might speak French to them. Afraid that they'll get shafted. A phone number and an address in Sandwich are very reassuring.'

Christopher continued the story. By this time Tom was looking for a parking space in Ste-Foy's main street and needed his concentration. 'They'd both retired. Roger and Malcolm. They keep a list of all the property we're selling. We update it by email. Thank God for email. They handle the initial enquiry then, if the customers seem serious they hand them over to us, promising that they'll find themselves talking to someone who speaks English. Even Antoine speaks brilliant English.'

'Did you teach him?' John asked.

'We taught him everything we know,' said Tom, who had by now successfully slipped the car into a parking space and turned off the engine.

Antoine was alone in the office when they walked into it. He was not dressed like an estate agent. But neither were Christopher and Tom. There had been a major discussion about this when they'd taken on the agency. They had decided to put their builders' credentials on show by eschewing suits and ties in favour of (clean) jeans and work boots, with open-necked shirts above. Whether this novel approach increased their business it would have been hard to say. But it certainly made them look different from other estate agents.

While Antoine updated Tom and Christopher with a few bits of business John looked at the houses pictured in the windows. There were manors and barns, farms and cottages. Town-centre apartments. There was even a Sleeping-Beauty type château. 'That one's been hanging fire for ages,' Tom told John when he'd finished listening to Antoine. 'Not sure if anyone's going to buy that. You don't need a degree in economics to see the upkeep would be horrendous. But it's nice to have it in the window.'

Antoine, who had joined them, asked with a laugh in his voice, 'Are you thinking of buying it?'

'No,' John answered. 'But I'm glad Maisie's not here. She'd already have her credit card out and be asking if she could put down a deposit.'

They closed the office and walked across the little square to the café opposite. The whole square was attractively arcaded, bastide-style, full of overhanging half-timbered houses. You could sit under the arcade and sip a coffee at break time, with half an eye on the door of the office. It took less than half a minute to cross the square and catch up with anyone who looked interested. As for the phone, everybody carried a mobile these days, while the one in the office could safely be left for short periods on automatic pilot.

Antoine was given an update on the Simon Rickman story. As he was practically a family member he already knew most of it. It was only the possibility that Simon might come down to the Dordogne for a holiday that was news to him. 'Is he still into all his New-Age stuff?' Antoine asked John.

'Yes,' said John. 'An English writer called G. K. Chesterton said that, when people stop believing in God they don't believe in nothing; they believe in anything.' He looked closely at Antoine's face to see if he understood the subtlety of *nothing* versus *anything*. He saw that he did. It seemed that Tom and Christopher had done their job thoroughly.

'But none of us four believe in God,' Christopher objected. 'We haven't started believing in nonsense.'

'That's because we're not Simon Rickman,' said John.

Antoine said soberly, 'Who is to say what is and isn't nonsense?'

Antoine had earned the floor for a minute with that and he made use of it. 'You're a writer,' he said to John. 'Why don't you make a TV drama out of Simon's story? A traumatised boy has a breakdown and then lives without money in a caravan…'

'John's speciality is domestic comedy,' Christopher reminded Antoine. 'I don't think it would be…'

Antoine took no notice. 'Or they could write a book together. "By Simon Rickman, told to John Moyse." Is that the way you say it?'

Tom and Christopher chuckled but John didn't. 'It's not a totally stupid idea,' he said.

No more was said on that subject then or later. Though on the drive back to Le Vieux Chai John did say, 'Antoine's a bright chap. And very likeable. I hope his boyfriend appreciates him.'

'We think he does,' said Tom. 'We socialise with them often – as two couples. Three couples when Michel and Armand are down here. As far as we can tell things are pretty good between them.'

'Anyway, we appreciate him,' said Christopher from the back seat.

'He's like a sort of son to us,' said Tom.

'The son we never had,' said Christopher, and laughed.

TWENTY-TWO

John stayed six more days with Tom and Christopher. He went to Castillon and met Tom's mother He went to St-Avit-du-Tizac (he liked the alternative name of St Margaret Tyzack) and had dinner there with Antoine and Patrick. And in the middle of the week, Tom and Christopher drove him away from home for two nights. They stayed in simple hotels. At Beynac in the east – where Tom insisted on reading Freda White to John as the three of them sat outside the Hotel Bonnet, watching the spring splash out from its pipe by the roadside, watching the glassy evening river and the sunset. And then to Cahors in the south.

In Cahors John had a sense of being very far south indeed. In a bar they visited the local farmers and the staff were conversing in what their northern French friends would have called *Patois*. To their ears it sounded like Catalan or Spanish. The disorientation caused by the sound of a Spanish-sounding dialect in the streets of a town that was very fairytale French was compounded by the sight of huge pans of paella at fast-food stalls on the pavements. *'La France profonde,'* was Tom's comment. La France profonde was the expression that northerners and Parisians used to describe places like Cahors and their local customs and attitudes. Deep France. John loved it. But he didn't open his chequebook when they next went to the estate agency in Ste-Foy. Not that he'd been expected to.

Yet the experience that had the biggest impact on him during his visit was his re-encounter, after thirty-six years, with the David and Jonathan picture. 'It's difficult to believe I'm looking at it,' he said when he was first confronted with it. He stopped and looked at it many times during his visit. 'Yes, it is a very accomplished picture. Miss O'Deere was much more talented than any of us kids ever realised. But it was like a rock thrown into a pond. She never guessed the impact the ripples would have on everyone, on all of us, as they spread out.' Another time, as they all walked past the picture – which they did a hundred times a day – he said, 'It's difficult to reconcile myself with the idea of how young you look. In my eyes at that time you both looked so grown up. Full-grown adults. Now I see you for what you were.' He turned and looked at Tom, then Christopher. 'A couple of kids who didn't know what they were getting into.' He smiled at them rather seriously.

He commented on the other pictures of them – aged nineteen or twenty and naked. 'I saw others like these at Wimereux some years ago. But these ones are new to me.'

'They came from Gérard's house in Paris,' Tom reminded him.

'I came to your flat in Paris,' John said. 'I never went to Gérard's. Of course you look wonderfully young in these pictures too – quite apart from revealing everything about yourselves. But somehow you look a bit more knowing than you did in the David and Jonathan.'

'A couple of months had passed,' said Christopher. 'Rather crucial ones. We'd done a bit of mental growing.'

'That would figure,' said John.

'Did Simon ever see the David and Jonathan?' Tom asked John.

'Not that I remember,' John said. 'He didn't come to Canterbury that night, you might remember. Maybe he saw it before, in the art room… If he did he never said so. Not to me, anyway.'

'You will get in touch with him, won't you?' Tom prodded John before he returned to England. 'Tell him about our offer. It was meant seriously.'

'It'll be the first thing on my agenda,' said John. They drove him back across the Entre Deux Mers to Bordeaux airport.

Simon Rickman appeared through sliding doors at the same airport just two weeks later. He was quite unrecognisable as the cherubic thirteen-year-old with the mop of blond curls they remembered; he was tall, lanky, shabbily dressed and his hair was lank and iron grey, rolling down over his collar like a broken window-blind. He was also thirty-six years older than he had been then. But there was no doubt about who he was. Nobody else was peering about the place so nervily, so hungrily almost. He was dangling his backpack from one hand instead of wearing it on his back, and in his other hand he carried a scruffy thin jacket. None of the other passengers looked as alone as he did.

Tom called his name and he came towards them the way a dog would, with no particular expression on his face. 'Got to have a cigarette,' he said. He made half a move to shake hands but it wasn't easy with the coat and backpack, and the move quickly morphed into a rummage in a pocket for lighter, papers and tobacco pouch.

They stopped outside the terminal before heading towards the short-stay car park, so that Simon could have his cigarette. 'One of you is Mr McGing, the other Mr Sanders. Right?'

'You can call me Tom,' said that name's owner, trying not to show his annoyance in his voice. 'My partner's name is Christopher.' Simon had had four thousand pounds of their money in the last ten years. Not a word of thanks had been forthcoming in that time. They'd given him the benefit of the doubt over that. Mental health problems excused a lot. But now they were face to face. Tom decided not to bother with matching up surnames with Christian names and faces.

'It's forty miles in the car,' said Christopher. 'Hope you're OK with that.'

Simon nodded and hoovered up the rest of his cigarette.

Simon spent the whole of the car journey in silence in the back. He smoked incessantly but, Tom noticed in the mirror, he did look out of the window at least. In fact his gaze was fixed raptly on the unrolling countryside beyond it, and he wound it down from time to time to throw out the stub of yet another cigarette.

When the car turned into the driveway at Le Vieux Chai Christopher and Tom both discovered a clenched knot of something in their stomachs. Each independently felt that they'd been naïve and stupidly idealistic in proposing this do-good gesture. Each privately wondered how they would get through the week.

When he got out of the car Simon looked hard at his hosts through a cloud of grey smoke with a still expressionless face. 'That was beautiful,' he said.

'What was?' Christopher asked.

'The drive. The countryside.' He paused for a second. 'We used to have camping holidays in France when I was a kid. I'd forgotten what it was like.'

They showed Simon up to his room. He promptly threw himself down on the bed in there, shoes still on, and lit another cigarette. Tom pointed out the bathroom curtly. Christopher nipped downstairs and returned with an ashtray. Simon showed no sign of making any further conversational effort. 'We'll take a walk to the village bar at six,' Tom said. 'Join us if you feel like it.' Simon said nothing and they left him to vegetate.

Christopher knocked on his door at six. 'Going to the pub. You up for it?' He didn't expect an answer but then there was the door opening in front of him and the tall spare figure of Simon framed in it.

'Yes,' he said. 'I want to come. I'd like that.'

The walk through the full-leaved vineyard passed in near silence. The grapes were almost full-sized by now, though not many had yet taken colour; they hung down from the vine hedges like cows' udders.

'It's red wine, isn't it?' said Simon suddenly. 'Claret?'

'Côtes de Castillon,' said Tom. 'Red Bordeaux. Yes, claret.' He jerked a thumb behind him. 'We drove you through the St Emilion vineyards earlier.'

'Right,' said Simon, nodding slowly. 'Which is claret too. My dad used to drink that. You could merge the two areas. Côtes de Chameleon. That'd be good.'

Tom and Christopher both laughed extravagantly at the little joke. It was wonderful that, after four hours of his dead-weight company Simon had at last given them something they could laugh at.

Then when a beer was set in front of him and Simon, sitting with them in the café-bar's garden courtyard, began to drink it a further improvement came about. 'John's been good to me,' he said suddenly. 'Not that you two haven't. I mean, I really won't forget those Christmas presents. But John…' Simon tailed off and looked into space.

'You love him, I think,' said Christopher. Tom shot him a warning glance.

Simon turned to Christopher sharply and stabbed the ashtray with his cigarette. 'Who told you that?'

'You did,' said Christopher. 'The way you looked just now. You told us that.'

'You must think it weird,' said Simon. 'That I'd have romantic feelings for someone like John. We're both nearly fifty. He's not good-looking. He's married, with kids.'

'Not weird at all,' said Christopher gently.

'I find it weird,' Simon said.

'Do you find it weird that I love Christopher?' Tom asked. 'He's fifty-five or something. I lose count.'

'There's no accounting for taste,' said Simon, poker-faced. Then the poker face broke open and he laughed. And Tom and Christopher laughed.

'Of course there's nothing sexual about it,' said Simon when his second beer had begun to bite.

'About what?' Tom asked. Conversation had begun to ramble quite successfully around a trelliswork of different topics. The last subject of discussion had been trout.

'John Moyse,' said Simon. 'I never did anything with him at school. I had fun with Angelo and, for that short time, that was enough. And now…' He shook his head. 'It's the last thing I'd want.'

'Maybe the last thing he'd want,' said Tom very gently.

'Have you ever…' Christopher began diffidently. 'Have you ever … I don't mean just sex … I mean, been in a relationship?'

Simon shook his head. 'No,' he said. 'It was beaten out of me. All that.'

'Beaten out of you?' Christopher had heard from John that following Simon's disgrace at Star of the Sea he had been sent to Ireland, to a school run by an order less tolerant than the Benedictines were of human foibles and weaknesses.

'By the Christian Brothers,' said Simon nodding. 'I never got it back. No appetite for sex. Or love.'

Christopher knew the expression: though you drive out nature with a pitchfork, she will always come back. He had always assumed it to be true. He had just learned from Simon that in some cases it was not.

Simon looked around him, seeing perhaps for the first time the soft brick garden walls, clad with Russian vine and wisteria, the roughly mown grass, the other customers happy at their tables with glasses of beer or Pastis, and lemonade for their kids. 'It's lovely here,' he said. 'You've got a garden back at your place. Didn't really notice it when we arrived but I saw it from my window, looking down into it. Will it still be warm enough to eat out there when we go back?'

It was, and they dined in the garden, once they'd sprayed themselves all over to deter mosquitoes. Somehow, perhaps because a quantity of wine was involved, conversation was easy – admittedly the subjects they discussed were undemanding – and Simon had as much to say as anyone. Not until bedtime did they return indoors and only then did Simon stop and look at the paintings. 'You looked nice when you were younger,' he told Tom and Christopher, as everyone did. He was looking at the naked, Audresselles, paintings. Then he turned his attention to the David and Jonathan.

'Do you know?' he said. 'I once saw that picture. Before it went into that exhibition in Canterbury cathedral it used to lean against a wall in the art room with a cover over it. I peeled off the cover one evening and looked at it. When it caused all the fuss a few weeks later I couldn't understand it. I hadn't realised what was in the picture. I've thought about it often since. I still couldn't see it.' He paused for a second. He didn't look at Tom or Christopher; he stood looking at the picture. His head nodded slowly. 'I see it now.'

Tom had already looked into the matter of getting a fishing permit for Simon. You could pick up a special one for holidaymakers at any tobacconist's shop. And

Simon wouldn't be long in France before needing to visit a *tabac*. There was one in the village.

Fishing tackle was a different matter. Simon hadn't thought to bring rods and other kit with him but unexpectedly François helped out. They had told him a week or so before Simon's arrival that fishing was his big thing. François had said that he'd been a keen fisherman himself in earlier years and still had a garage full of stuff. 'Tell him to come round when he gets here,' he'd told Tom and Christopher. 'Let him borrow what he wants. Mind you,' he added, 'my stuff's not exactly state of the art.'

Simon didn't mind that François's fishing tackle wasn't state of the art. He spent a happy morning with the mayor of the village, some of it involving a good look at the equipment in his garage and choosing what to take, a rather longer part of it taking in a tour of François's wine cellar and tasting samples of its contents. 'Don't forget to call him *Monsieur le Maire,'* Tom had cautioned him. 'Constantly. Not just once or twice. And remember to say *merci beaucoup*, even if you come away with nothing.'

Simon did manage to call François *Monsieur le Maire* at very regular intervals and to say *merci beaucoup* a lot. He didn't come away with nothing. Tom and Christopher saw him returning up the lane from François's house laden with so much fishing equipment that he was practically staggering under its weight.

They drove to the river in the afternoon, parking outside Tom's mother's riverfront house on the edge of Castillon and walking upstream a little way. They had tried May's door before heading off, but she wasn't in. They left her a note. Neither Tom nor Christopher were fishermen; they let Simon choose his spot. Then they realised that they'd given no thought to what they might do while Simon did the next bit. They sat down with him on the river bank.

The rites of fishing seemed almost as serious and unchanging as any that might take place in a church. There was the initial ritual of Finding a Spot. After that came the ritual of Casting, which sometimes needed repeating several times, like the *Kyrie eleison*, to be sure you'd got it right. Then there was the ritual of the Long Wait.

Actually the Long Wait, a new experience for Tom and Christopher, turned out to be a time of magic. It was perhaps the main thing that made fly fishing worth doing, maybe the main point of it. At first there was nothing to see except the surface of the river, gleaming quietly past. Then a moorhen came by, paddling upstream. After that a mother mallard with a flotilla of ducklings behind her. A weasel popped its head out of a hole in the ground almost at their feet. A kingfisher landed for a second on the tip of Simon's rod, then flew off, whistling. As its flight took it into the shadows of the trees on the opposite bank it continued to gleam like a blue spark for a few seconds before the darkness swallowed it. Then Simon got a tug on his line.

He worked the unseen fish, playing it until it tired, then reeled it towards him and landed it. It was a good-sized brown trout. After the excitement had died down and Simon had re-cast his feathered hook Tom looked at his watch. Nearly an hour had passed.

During the next hour Simon caught two more trout, then a fourth one a few minutes after that. Then just as Simon was saying it was probably time to pack up a figure came walking towards them along the river bank and called to them when it was close enough. It was May.

'I saw your car outside,' she said. 'I read your note.'

'We would have called,' said Tom. 'But you were out.'

'And now I'm back.' May gave her hand to Simon who, along with the others, had just got to his feet. 'Simon, I presume,' she said. She glanced down at the four speckle-skinned fish.

'Four fish, four people,' Simon said unexpectedly. He grinned at May. 'Do you eat fish?'

They dined later that evening at May's house. May not only ate fish but could cook it. She did the trout in the oven, in a roasting pan with lots of butter in it. (She didn't own four frying pans, which she would have needed if she'd decided to cook them on the hob.) She had news for them, which she imparted while they ate.

'I've found a new church,' she said. 'It's actually in your direction so you may have driven past it. Though it's a little way off the beaten track.' She told them the name of the minuscule village in which it stood. 'Ste-Colombe,' she said. They had driven through it occasionally, Tom told her, but had never stopped.

'It's the most beautiful little church,' May said. 'Twelfth century, but the foundations are older even than that. It's built on the remains of a Roman villa. It's so sweet. The inside…' May abandoned any thought she might have had of trying to describe it. 'I'm thinking of going there on Sunday for Mass.'

'Can I come with you?' Simon asked. To the others' astonishment.

In the end they all went. May had been right. It was a charming little stone church on a lovely site. An escarpment of vineyards fell away from it and it looked across to two of the châteaux of St-Emilion on the other side of the valley. A valley of vines, dotted with comfortable houses with their attendant cedars and cypresses. The Romans had first planted the St-Emilion vineyards, the story went. And whichever of them had built his villa on this spot had clearly had a weakness for a pretty view, whether he had a commercial interest in wine or not.

The interior of the church gave an impression of height, or at least of height in relation to its small overall scale. It was very plain. Its windows were narrow and round arched. Romanesque churches in England went under the name of Norman because the Normans introduced the style; Romanesque they might have been but those English churches never looked as though they might have belonged in Ancient Rome. Yet this church did. Its architecture harked back to the first churches that were ever purpose-built, under the Emperor Constantine. Its arches bounded happily down its length with pleasing classical symmetry. Above the high altar, in the concave wall of the apse was a single window like an arrow slit, very high up and absolutely centred, lined up with the entrance door behind you.

The door remained open while the Mass began. The summer morning air came in and moved gently among the small congregation. The Mass was said in French. That was no problem for May these days; after nine years in France she knew the responses as well as she knew the English ones. But, slightly to the surprise of Tom and Christopher, Simon joined in with them too, in accurate and confident French. Tom thought back to his time at Star of the Sea. His times, rather, for he'd been a pupil there before returning as a young teacher (meeting Christopher that time) when Simon had been a pupil. French had been pretty big on the agenda, Tom remembered. They had learned the Our Father and the Hail Mary in French, he recalled. Perhaps they'd learned the words of the Mass in French too. Most of his teachers – and later his colleagues also – had been Irish.

They'd come from a Catholic background that felt closer ties with France than it ever could with England.

The Mass went quickly. When that happened everyone was happy; that had been the case down the ages, although it had never been considered proper to admit the fact. Soon the moment of Consecration arrived, the moment when, according to Catholic theology the wafer of bread would be transformed by the power of God, channelled through the priest, into the body of Jesus. The priest raised the Host above his head. A small bell sounded. The priest said the words. *'Ceçi est mon corps.'* This is my body, which shall be given up for you. And at that exact moment the sun blazed into the tiny crevice of the window above the altar like the brilliantest of all searchlights and lit the church as if it had been on fire. A loud bang sounded right next to where Christopher knelt and the pew trembled. Christopher turned. Simon had fainted and lay in a heap on the floor beside him.

It was the worst possible moment to disrupt a service by carrying a prostrate body out of the building down the central aisle but it had to be done, and done then. It took all three of them, plus another man who got out of his pew and came to their aid. Behind them they heard the priest's voice, un-distracted by the small occurrence among the pews, say, *'Ceçi est mon sang,'* as he held up the chalice full of wine. This is my blood, which shall be shed for you and for all men, so that sin may be forgiven.

An hour later Simon was fine. A woman in the church had had a bottle of water in her handbag. She'd brought it out and given it to Simon. They'd helped him to walk to the car, and they'd driven back to May's house in Castillon. Passing through the kitchen they noticed an interestingly appetising smell. But they didn't linger there. They went out into the back garden and sat Simon there, though prudently in the shade. It seemed he'd had enough sun for one day.

'This may sound strange,' Simon said when he'd begun to talk again, 'but I felt it like a sword or an arrow. Straight in the heart.'

'Felt what exactly?' asked Tom. Tom kept taking Simon's pulse from time to time. For no very good reason. He wouldn't have known what to do if he'd found it gone.

'Love,' said Simon. 'I didn't think I could feel it any more. I haven't felt it since … well, you know when.'

'Love?' queried Christopher anxiously. John had said that Simon seemed to be rather enamoured of him. Had his experience in the church somehow transferred those feelings onto Christopher, who had been kneeling next to him?

'The love of God,' said Simon in a very matter-of-fact way.

'I see,' said Tom. He turned to his mother, who in the last hour had spoken much less than she usually did. 'I think we'd better take him back to the Vieux Chai and get some lunch inside him. Then he can rest this afternoon.'

'There's no need to take him anywhere,' said May. 'I'd planned for all of us to have lunch here. There's a slow roast of lamb in the oven. I put it in before we went to church.'

That was Christopher's cue to get up and say that he would head out to a nearby shop and get a bottle of wine. Or maybe two.

They ate their meal out in the garden. So did everyone else around. Occasional wafts of breeze brought intriguing, appealing aromas from other people's barbecues. Simon had a habit, they'd noticed during his stay, of sometimes looking up and peering at everything around him with an air of great interest, even wonder, as if he'd never seen it before. He did this now. 'That little church,' he said. 'It's wonderful. I think it's where I have to be.'

'What do you mean, where you have to be?' asked Tom. 'And when did you last go into a church anyway?'

'Over thirty years ago,' Simon answered. 'But the first question's less easy. I just feel it's the place I need to be. The place that's meant for me.'

'You can't live in a church,' said Tom.

'I know,' said Simon. 'I'd need a place nearby.'

Tom and Christopher were immediately filled with feelings of horror and dismay. In a moment Simon would tell them he planned to come and live with them at Le Vieux Chai. The way Jesus used to descend on people: just turn up and then stay.

But May spoke up suddenly. 'I'm short of company here. I'm sure we could come to some arrangement. Why don't you come and live with me?'

Simon didn't seem at all surprised at receiving such an invitation out of the blue from someone he was meeting for only the second time. 'I think that would be ideal,' he said, and cracked an enormous smile. While Christopher's astonishment was surpassed only by Tom's. They heard May saying, like someone in an Alice in Wonderland sort of dream, 'Of course you'd have to get your hair cut.'

Tom saved his expression of dismay at his mother's astonishing invitation for a moment when they were alone together a little later, in her kitchen. 'You can't,' he told her. 'You just can't do that. You'll have to withdraw the invitation.'

'Will I indeed?' May faced him squarely. 'And what would have happened all those years ago if Michel's mother Sabine hadn't taken you into her house and given you shelter when you turned up on the French shore penniless? She even gave you a job a few days later if I've remembered rightly. How can you tell me not to offer something to Simon which I can give even more easily – when you've benefitted yourself from just such an offer? "I was hungry and you gave me food, thirsty and you gave me drink; I was a stranger and you brought me home…" Have you forgotten?'

Tom had no answer. In a chastened voice he said, 'Sorry Mummy.' He wondered what his brother Dominic would say when he told him.

TWENTY-THREE

As he was pretty much estranged from his family except for the annual truce of his Christmas home visits Christopher rarely found himself hearing his sister's voice at the other end of the telephone. (Though in the case of his brothers it wasn't just rarely: it was never, ever.) But since his father's death three years earlier there had been a little more contact. Widowhood suits few people and middle-aged sons and daughters find themselves caught up in the awkward coils of it when it overtakes their parents. Christopher knew that when he did hear from his sister these days, and from now on, it would always be because there was some problem concerning his mother that needed sorting.

This time, 'Our mother's losing the plot,' his sister's voice informed him.

Christopher had answered the call on the Vieux Chai's landline. He had a mobile now but he hadn't shared that news with his family.

'In the sense of…?' Christopher queried.

'Going ga-ga. The doctors won't tell me that when I ask them. They evade the issue, but it's very obvious. I think she's had a couple of small strokes when nobody's been looking.'

'Does she know she's had strokes? Have you asked her?'

'She says she hasn't. But in her state you might not always know you'd had them.'

'So why are you phoning me now particularly? Are you thinking we need to do something?'

'I think you need to go and see her.'

'You think it's that serious?' Suddenly Christopher was back in the moment when Tom and he had crossed the Channel to see Angelo before it was too late. 'You think she's…'

'I'm not saying that,' said Moira. 'But she needs sorting.'

'Aren't Jim and Brian there to help you?' Jim and Brian were their two brothers. They both lived within fifteen miles of their mother's house as against Christopher's five hundred and fifty.

'Sure, you know those two. When it's anything like that they're feckin' useless.' Christopher's sister made a very good job most of the time of being English. But she did revert to her roots when she became exasperated.

'I'm not sure I've been considered very useful myself over the years,' Christopher said wryly.

'Now don't give me that,' said Moira. 'Say you'll come over. Please, now.'

Christopher said yes at that point and they talked of dates just a few days ahead, and about possible travel arrangements.

It was September. Life had been trundling along quite uneventfully since Simon had got his hair cut and installed himself care-of Tom's mother. He had been no trouble at all to Tom or himself. Tom's mother had helped him to get a commercial fishing licence, and he was beginning to make an income – enough to pay May for the food he ate at any rate – from the fish and eel stall he'd set up outside May's front door on the quayside. May seemed happy enough with the arrangement. She said it was like having a teenage son of fifty. Though he caused her no problems. He spent the time he didn't spend fishing walking the three miles to and from the church at Ste-Colombe and praying and contemplating there. It was better, he said, than reading about the occult in Hastings public library. Tom worried occasionally about his own inheritance, but Christopher deeply envied him his gift of a mother.

Christopher thought how lovely it would be if he could take Tom across the Channel with him now that he had to go and deal with his own mother. But he couldn't. Tom had met Christopher's mother once, twenty years earlier, when, in a rare moment of trying to come to terms with her son's homosexuality she had proposed a meeting with his partner. But the encounter had not gone well. The meeting had taken place at the Challoner Club in London and though Tom had been as charming as he knew how to be (and as handsome as he couldn't help being) Mrs McGing had grown more and more uncomfortable as they sipped their sherries, while the atmosphere had grown frostier and frostier with each course of the lunch that followed, and the fixture had ended early. Discussing Mrs McGing's extraordinary change of mood during the encounter Tom and Christopher could only guess that she had found herself imagining her son and Tom copulating while she watched them sitting side by side demurely drinking sherry and had not enjoyed the thought of it. So Christopher parted from Tom at the departures gate at Bordeaux airport. It was quite a charged-up parting. Neither knew quite how many days and nights Christopher would be away for.

Christopher couldn't help noticing the younger man who sat almost opposite him in the departure lounge in the minutes before boarding. The man caught him looking and smiled cheerfully across at him. Covering his embarrassment as best he could Christopher smiled back at him.

Inside the plane Christopher took his middle-of-the-row seat and wondered for a minute or two as the crush of passengers moved up the aisle which of them would be sitting on either side of him. The young man from the departure lounge came into view, smiled again as his eyes met Christopher's, peered at the seat numbers above Christopher's head, looked back at his boarding pass, then grinned broadly as it became clear to both of them that they would be sitting together. The young man had a ticket for the window seat. Because of the press of people in the aisle Christopher couldn't climb out to let him into it; the young man had to clamber over him. It was quite an intimate experience. As soon as he'd installed himself the new arrival turned back to Christopher. 'Hi,' he said. 'Sorry if that was uncomfortable.'

'No problem,' said Christopher. They were both still smiling.

'I'm Chris,' said the younger man, who was small, trim and blond-haired.

'So am I,' said Christopher. They shook hands to celebrate the coincidence. The plane wasn't entirely full; nobody came and sat in the aisle seat next to Christopher; he was pleased about that for more than one reason.

Christopher's neighbour was cheerfully talkative. He was an airline steward. Off-duty, he added with a chuckle. He'd been in Bordeaux on a forty-eight-hour stopover due to a cancellation. He was married, he said, and had two daughters. 'You must have started very young,' said Christopher.

'I'm thirty-three,' said Chris.

'You don't look it,' said Christopher.

'You're too kind,' said Chris. 'How old are you, then?' He flashed blue eyes at Christopher.

'Fifty-five,' said Christopher truthfully.

Chris said, 'You don't look it.'

Everyone was seated now; the doors closed and the engines started. The cabin staff gave the safety demonstration as they began to taxi. Christopher took no notice of the demonstration. He was sitting next to an off-duty steward who would know the drill by heart. If it came to it Chris would help him. Chris and his young family lived in a terraced house in Hounslow, he told

Christopher. Christopher told Chris about Le Vieux Chai, where he lived with Tom, his partner. That last bit clearly interested Chris. 'Tom?' he queried. The plane was manoeuvring into position at the foot of the runway.

'He's a man,' Christopher set it out clearly.

That's nice,' said Chris. 'I guess you know Le Pollux, then.'

'In Bordeaux? We know of it.' Christopher giggled. 'We're a bit old for clubbing.'

'You're certainly not,' Chris assured him. 'I was there last night. There were plenty of people your age. Whoooo! Here we go.'

The plane sprang forward like a powerful animal, roaring. Seconds later it tilted up sharply, then rose from the runway. At once the Garonne waterway appeared, shining in front of them. It broadened as they neared it and then for a few seconds the Atlantic opened like a flower alongside them before they turned away from it to set their course for England.

They chatted happily all the way. Chris thought it brilliant that Christopher and Tom had come south to do up old cottages and sell them and had then ended up as estate agents. Christopher ventured to say that he knew that many male cabin crew were gay. Chris said that many others were bisexual. Christopher said he'd often guessed that. Chris said that quite a lot of pilots too were gay or else bisexual. Christopher said that he hadn't really known that. Before their plane had reached the Loire the younger Chris had confided that he himself was bisexual.

By the time they had crossed the Channel and were starting their descent towards Heathrow Chris had told Christopher that he and his wife occasionally had a threesome with a male neighbour, and Christopher had told Chris about the rather complex relationship that he and Tom had with Antoine. Not that either of them had ever had sex with him he added carefully, though only partly truthfully. Their elbows came in contact for several seconds when they fastened their seat-belts in readiness for landing: perhaps for a couple more seconds than was strictly necessary. Then their knees touched. Christopher twisted his foot round slightly, heel outward, and rubbed his calf up and down experimentally a couple of times against young Chris's. To Christopher's guilty delight young Chris copied the gesture exactly.

They walked together across the air bridge into the terminal, each shouldering a backpack. On the long walk between that point and passport control they passed a toilet, thoughtfully provided by the airport builders. 'I need a piss,' said Christopher, knowing exactly what would be Chris's response to that information.

'Me too,' Chris told him.

Standing side by side at the urinal neither of them could pass water. Each had a major erection. They exchanged compliments on the appearance of each other's dicks but had to tuck them away again, with some difficulty, un-emptied. Chris turned to Christopher. 'Are you in a major hurry, or could you spare an hour?'

Christopher had built in contingencies in planning his journey. A delayed flight, a missed train connection. He hadn't actually envisaged this particular contingency but now he was glad of his forethought. 'I can spare an hour,' he said. 'My mother's not expecting me till teatime.'

They took a taxi to Chris's house in Hounslow. 'There won't be anyone in,' Chris told him. 'Lisa's out working. But I have to pick the girls up from school at four.' Then he proceeded to recount the details of his first homosexual experience, when he'd been at choir school, with a fellow chorister. Presumably he imagined the taxi driver wouldn't be listening. Christopher wondered what Chris had been on during his night out at Le Pollux. Whatever it was must still be in his bloodstream.

They pulled up in a street of terraced houses. Despite Christopher's half-hearted protests Chris paid the driver. Then Chris took Christopher into his home with him.

The house was spick and span and nicely furnished. There was an upright piano in the living room with piles of music on and near it. Its keyboard lid was open: it looked like a piano that was used regularly. Christopher remembered that his new acquaintance had been a schoolboy chorister. 'We'll go upstairs,' said Chris, and kissed Christopher momentarily. Christopher was invited to inspect from the doorway the master bedroom that his host shared with his wife. They didn't go in there. He saw the daughters' room, full of toys and teddies, but they didn't go in there either. Chris took Christopher into the spare room.

Chris spread out a spare duvet on the floor there and the two of them took their clothes off. Christopher found there was something rather special about embracing the naked body of someone who was more than twenty years younger than he was. He'd found the same thing, all too many years ago, with Antoine. But they had to interrupt their embrace after a moment. They both needed to do what they hadn't been able to accomplish at the airport, and by now the need was more pressing. They journeyed together to the bathroom and this time they both managed it, crossing swords prettily, erections notwithstanding.

Back in the spare room they got down together on the duvet. Chris asked Christopher to lie on top of him. Christopher obliged willingly. After a few minutes they reversed it. Chris turned out to be an enthusiastic kisser, but eventually broke off and wriggled himself round to face in the opposite direction. He took Christopher's cock in his mouth and Christopher returned the compliment. As it was so handily placed he thought it would have been rude not to.

Feelings of ecstasy suffused Christopher. He could tell that the same went for Chris because of the way his body was behaving and from the little humming noises of satisfaction that he was making. After a while, though, he released Chris's springy cock from his mouth in order to tell him that he was on the brink of coming. Chris immediately removed his own mouth from Christopher to say, 'Ditto.' Neither of them, evidently, wanted to swallow the other's semen. They finished each other off very pleasurably by hand, without moving from their positions. It only took a second.

There wasn't quite time for a shower, Chris explained apologetically. He checked his watch quickly. He really would have to go and collect his children. They cleaned themselves up as best they could, side by side at the wash-basin, and made nice comments about how good their naked reflections looked together in the mirror. Christopher knew that for him to think so at his age was natural, but he wondered again about his younger namesake. He must have had a lot of whatever it was at Le Pollux. He wondered if his wife would notice it when she came in from work later.

When they were dressed again Chris took Christopher in his car to the nearest tube station, which was Hounslow Central. It involved making a slight detour on the way to pick up his daughters: a courtesy for which Christopher thanked him. 'It was nice meeting you,' Chris said as Christopher climbed out of the car.

'Likewise,' said Christopher. Then they shook hands with a shared smile, like two businessmen who had just concluded a successful negotiation.

On his way into central London in his tube train, Christopher found his head filling with reassuring phrases like *Carpe Diem*, and, life was full of surprises, and things about roasted chickens, and about the mouths of gift horses.

Christopher had spoken to his mother on the phone the previous evening. She had sounded normal and coherent. She'd also sounded as though she was looking forward to her son's visit, and that pleased him. She would expect him at about seven and would have a high tea waiting. Christopher's sister Moira wouldn't be able to join them this evening. She would call round in the morning.

Mrs McGing lived in a rather large semi-detached house on the edge of Maidstone. She had moved there with her husband when he had retired and sold his builders' merchant business. She was that rare thing, the daughter of Irish immigrant parents who had been both comfortably off and Catholic. When she'd married Christopher's father (who was *in trade*) her family pursed their lips and thought, though they were too well bred to say so, that she'd married beneath her. She was of a generation of the middle class who had grown up with houses full of brass and silver, of elaborate furniture and ornaments, and at least one live-in maid who was on hand to polish and dust those treasures. By the time that generation reached adulthood the maids were gone, replaced by more-or-less daily cleaning women. In time the number of hours such labour could be afforded had dwindled, and by the time they were widowed many women of Christopher's mother's age and station had been taken prisoners by their own furniture, by their endlessly tarnishing brass trays and silver spoons, and were forced to spend the days that remained to them working as their own charladies.

Those thoughts went through Christopher's mind as, for the second time in a few hours, he got into a taxi –

this time at Maidstone West station. His mother would by now have laid the table for their evening meal. He could see in his mind the white Irish linen table cloth, the pearl-handled knives and the once-lovely but now slightly foxed bone china. There would be the old familiar tea-pot and the woolly tea-cosy his sister had knitted – cheekily in Manchester United colours. For all that this home visit would be a sensitive and difficult one, he felt his spirits lifting slightly.

He paid the taxi driver and turned towards the house. To his surprise it, alone among its neighbours, was in pitch darkness. Night had fallen an hour or so earlier, while he'd been on the train from London. Christopher didn't panic as he walked towards the front door but he was worried. He came up to it and was about to ring the bell when he saw something that startled him almost enough to make his heart stop. In the window beside the door his mother's face was visible, dimly lit by the street-lamp a few yards behind him. Her eyes were wide open and watching him; her nose was pressed against the glass. The hall was in darkness around her.

Christopher pointed with a finger towards the door, indicating to his mother that she should come to it and open it for him. She frowned slightly but didn't move, so Christopher reached for the door-bell button and pressed it. His mother's face moved back from the window, disappearing into the blackness. 'Who is it?' he heard her voice call. It came from directly in front of him: she had moved to behind the door now and was talking to him through its oak panels.

'It's me. Christopher. You're expecting me, Mummy.' To his momentary relief he heard the chain being unhooked and the locks turned. Then the door was opened and his mother stood in front of him.

Christopher embraced his mother and kissed her. She felt right, she looked normal. It was just the lighting state that wasn't. 'Why aren't the lights on, Mummy?'

'No, they should be. You're right,' she said. Enough light was coming in from the street for her to see her way to the switches, and to Christopher's relief she turned the nearest lights on. Brightness flooded the hall. To Christopher it seemed as great a wonder as when God had said, 'Let there be light,' and there was light. In a perfectly normal tone his mother said, 'I'd just forgotten them.' She led the way through the house, turning on the lights as she went. Christopher dumped his backpack, for the moment, on the living-room sofa. They went into the dining room and Christopher's mother switched the light on.

Mrs McGing had laid the table before it got dark, evidently. The cloth was on the table, screwed up in a bundle on one corner of it. And on the bare polished surface had been placed, in no particular arrangement, the old black roasting pan, the rolling-pin, the carving knife and a cheese grater.

Christopher's distress was too deep for tears. He felt as though a chasm had opened up in the floor of life beneath him. He wanted Tom. He wanted Tom's arms around him. He needed Tom to hold him up, to stop him falling through the hole that gaped below him. Tom would know what to do; he'd take charge and do it. Then he'd give Christopher all the comfort he so desperately needed. But Tom was half a thousand miles away and couldn't help him. And anyway, Christopher thought, remembering with bitter remorse what he'd done that afternoon, he didn't deserve him.

TWENTY-FOUR

Christopher found bread, cut the green edges off and made toast. There were sausages that should have been in the fridge but weren't. Christopher sniffed them. They seemed all right. He put them in the frying pan. He cleaned up the broken egg that he spotted, fallen to the floor between the stove and the unit that stood next to it. He fried two fresh ones. He laid the table properly and made tea in the teapot. His mother was overjoyed by the occasion, thrilled like a child by the feast. The tea was especially welcome. At some point during the last few days she had forgotten how to make it and had drunk only water, scooping it up in her hands from under the tap. Christopher struggled to get his meal inside him. He was already too filled up with an unbearable aching.

Yet during the meal Christopher's mother chatted away cheerfully and coherently. She talked of family members to whom she'd spoken on the phone. She praised his two brothers fulsomely. How good they were to her; always popping in. That was quite the opposite of what Moira had had to say. Christopher chose to take his mother's words at face value. 'That's nice,' he said. She asked him no questions about his own life. Not even if he'd had a good flight across from France. It was as though he had life for her only while he was in her house. He had come like the sparrow that flies through the king's feasting hall in the legend. Given its form by the bright interior lights for a few seconds it has come in from an uncomprehended darkness and into the darkness it returns.

After he'd washed up he sat his mother in front of the television and phoned his sister from his bedroom. 'How could you?' he asked her. 'How could you leave her in that state?'

‘Leave her in what state?’ Moira asked. Christopher described the previous hour’s events. ‘She wasn’t like that when I saw her on Tuesday,’ Moira said.

‘That was two days ago,’ said Christopher. ‘Anything can happen in two days to someone in mum’s situation.’

‘Are you accusing me?’ Moira’s voice had picked up the knife-edge tone that Christopher knew well. ‘When you choose to live in another country, hundreds of miles away, and come home only at Christmas – grudgingly.’

‘I’m not going to argue,’ Christopher said, and heard himself adopting a steely tone too. ‘My relationship with Mummy has always been difficult. Dad didn’t want me around the place, if you remember. That’s one of the reasons I live in France.’

‘It’s not the…’

‘No, stop,’ said Christopher firmly. ‘We need to do something urgently. First thing in the morning. Get a doctor. Social services. Whatever we have to do. Come round early. I’ll get her to bed somehow. Hope she sleeps.’ Moira agreed to come early in the morning and they ended the call with a grudgingly civil goodnight.

To Christopher’s relief his mother hadn’t forgotten how to use the toilet or undress for bed. When he was sure she’d tucked herself up for the night he phoned Tom. When he heard Tom’s voice at the other end he broke down in tears.

Tom relayed Christopher’s account of things to Antoine the next morning at work. ‘I can’t get over how upset he was last night,’ he said.

‘You can’t go over and help him through it?’ Antoine asked him.

‘It was my first thought. Of course she’d freak out if she saw me, so I couldn’t actually do anything that involved being in her presence. But to be there in the background, I thought. Put up at a hotel, perhaps…’

'Yes,' said Antoine. 'You could do that.'

'Yes,' Tom agreed, 'but I know now that it's all going to be sorted quickly. Chris phoned again early this morning. Actually soon after six o'clock. He went downstairs and found his mother sitting in the living room, huddled over an electric fire in the dark. He told her she ought to be in hospital, then promptly rang some emergency number. It's all being sorted this morning. They're going to find her a place in a nursing home or a care home. Whatever the difference is…' Tom and Antoine spent a minute teasing that out and trying to agree on the closest translation of the two concepts in French. 'It'd all be over by the time I got there. He's got his sister. He's not alone in it.'

'Well, if there's anything I can do…' Antoine said. It was highly unlikely that he could do anything that Tom couldn't, but people always said that. Somehow it was nice that they said it.

Another phone call came from Christopher later in the morning. A doctor had seen his mother – Tom passed this on to Antoine – and Christopher now had a short list of care homes to visit. With any luck his mother would be installed in one by tonight. Christopher would be able to return to France tomorrow or the day after, he thought.

At midday Antoine insisted they close the office for an hour. He took Tom to the café under the arcade on the other side of the square and bought him a beer and a hot dog. A French hot dog was twice as big and, Tom thought, twice as interesting as an English one. The French word for hot dog was *hot-dog*; it was pronounced after the manner of Inspector Clouseau.

When they were locking up the premises at the end of the day, and ready to walk off to their cars, which were parked at different points along the street, Antoine said to Tom, 'I wondered if you could do with some company tonight.'

Tom shot his keys into his pocket and eyeballed Antoine. 'Meaning, I suppose, that you could.'

'Patrick's had to go to his parents' for a couple of nights. I did tell you that.'

'Yes, you did,' said Tom. 'If you want to come back to … ours … that's fine. And … er … I'll cook.'

'No need for that,' said Antoine. 'We could go out. We could drive to Monpon. To avoid comment.' They looked at each other, testing each other's knowledge of what had happened between Antoine and Christopher ten years earlier. At first their mutual glance was hard, their eyes like billiard balls, but suddenly that melted and they both laughed. Both knew, evidently. Neither was going to decide they needed to talk about it.

'You take me, then' said Tom. 'I don't know any restaurants in Monpon.'

'It is ten years since I ate there,' said Antoine, poker-faced. 'We'll need to explore the place.'

They stood for a moment in sight of both their cars, a hundred yards apart in the street. 'Do we take mine?' asked Tom. 'Or yours? Or both.'

'We take yours,' said Antoine decisively, answering a dozen questions with the three-word sentence.

They found a restaurant in Monpon that looked unpretentious and attractive. Tom didn't ask if it was the one that Antoine and Christopher had once dined in. Actually Antoine didn't remember, but he was glad not to be asked. Restaurants came and went. Things changed over a ten-year period.

They had a platter of charcuterie for starters, and slow-braised ox-tongue as a main course. Tom looked at Antoine across the cosy table. They'd dined together countless times in restaurants. But always with Christopher, and often with Patrick. Sometimes with other friends. This was the first time they'd eaten out à deux. Tom found that this was surprisingly lovely.

Tom's phone rang at the very moment they were choosing dessert. It was Christopher. 'How's things?' Tom asked him.

'It's all gone a bit pear-shaped,' Christopher said.

'Hang on,' said Tom. 'I'm in a restaurant. I'll go to the door so I can hear you better.' He got up, mouthed the word Christopher at Antoine and gestured to show where he was going. Antoine nodded his understanding.

'Which restaurant?' Christopher asked as soon as Tom had reached the less public arena of the pavement outside the door. 'I realised you weren't at home. I rang there first.'

'In Monpon,' said Tom. 'With Antoine. But never mind abut that. Pear-shaped, you said.'

'We found a care home quickly,' Christopher said. 'Moira and me, that is. We explained it all to mum and she seemed to take it in and accept it. I packed a small suitcase for her…'

Tom heard Christopher's voice begin to crack at that point. 'Go on,' he said firmly. If he let Christopher break down now they'd never get through the conversation. 'What happened?'

'We took Moira's car, obviously. On the way mum started to say that we would just look at the place, be polite about it and then come home again. Moira and I looked at each other but didn't say anything. But when we got there and we were all sitting in the office going through the formalities and paperwork all hell broke loose. Mum has a stick now – since her first stroke last week – and she started lashing out with it, hitting the staff and the manager on the legs…'

'Oh my God,' said Tom. He'd only met Christopher's mother once, twenty years ago, but he had no difficulty visualising this spectacle.

'I won't go through the awful things she said. About me. About Moira. In front of all the staff…'

'I'm sure they're used to that…'

'She told me my soul was in mortal danger. That I couldn't be saved unless I renounced "that person you live with". Then she cried and said she wanted to love me but she couldn't. She couldn't love someone who had my way of life. All this in front of total strangers. I told her she knew almost nothing about my way of life. She agreed. She said I might be a murderer for all she knew. That the path I'd chosen was as bad or worse than that.'

'My poor darling,' Tom said.

'In the end they said it would be best if Moira and I left. They'd give her tea and try to calm her, and I was to phone for news in an hour. Moira had to get home to cook for her husband, so I sat around at mum's house feeling wretched. Then I phoned up. Just twenty minutes ago. They said she was being very difficult. If they can't settle her overnight I have to go there and take her out. Bring her back here…'

'You can't do that…'

'They won't let me come back to France until she settles. They could phone me at any time during the night…'

'There's not just you,' said Tom, his voice showing his annoyance. 'There's your sister, for heaven's sake. Your two useless brothers. It shouldn't all be left to you… Look, I could fly over tomorrow…'

'Well, wait,' said Christopher. 'Wait till the morning. Then see where we're at. It may all work out.'

'Call me if anything happens in the night,' said Tom. 'Whatever time it is. And if there's trouble I'll be right there.'

'I love you,' said Christopher. 'Talk in the morning at the latest. Say *bon appétit* to Antoine.'

'I love you. Talk soon,' Tom said. He ended the call and walked back inside the restaurant. Antoine was still studying the dessert menu with intense concentration, as if it had been a book about rocket science.

Antoine looked up and studied Tom's face with almost as much concentration as he'd brought to bear on the menu. 'It hasn't gone well,' Tom said. He re-took his seat opposite him and Antoine saw tears spring to his eyes. Antoine cupped a hand over Tom's hand on the table. 'Can't do anything this minute,' he said. 'Just tell me what's happened. They've got *mousse au chocolat.'*

There were two main roads heading roughly south from Monpon. One went to Castillon (that was the direction for St-Philippe-d'Aiguille) and the other to Ste-Foy-la-Grande, passing near St-Avit-du-Tizac. 'Which way are we heading?' said Tom as he unlocked the car.

Without hesitation Antoine said, 'Your place.'

'No news is good news,' he said a bit later as they left the main road at Villefranche-de-Lonchat. 'Chris hasn't rung back. It's nearly ten o'clock.'

'Hmm. It's only nine in England,' Tom reminded him, 'but I take your point.'

Inside the Vieux Chai Tom switched on all the lights. For a few seconds you thought you'd entered an art gallery; everyone said this; but then you got used to your surroundings and they quickly became a home and a dwelling.

'Better have a drink,' said Tom. He'd driven Antoine here, and 'here' was some fifteen miles from St-Avit-du-Tizac. They didn't need to check with each other; there was no question of Tom's driving Antoine home tonight. He fetched glasses, a bottle and a corkscrew. He opened the bottle and poured from it.

'To Chris and his mother,' said Antoine, raising his wineglass. He was careful not to refer to Christopher as

Chris too often in Tom's presence. But he'd learnt over the years that at intense moments Tom was OK with it. Now Tom clinked glasses with Antoine and repeated his toast.

Antoine's gaze flicked away from Tom for a moment, towards the paintings that surrounded them at a respectful distance and whose details he knew by heart. 'You've never painted Christopher,' he said.

'You know the reason,' Tom said. 'You must have heard me say it a thousand times. I'm not good at the human face. I can do the figure, the body clothed or naked, but I'm never convinced by the likeness I get with the face. Anyway…' Tom looked at one of the pictures that showed Christopher, a lithe nineteen-year-old, cavorting with Armand and himself on a boat. 'I wouldn't be painting him looking like that these days.'

'Oh, I don't know,' said Antoine.

'He's fifty-whatever,' said Tom. Laughing, he added, 'When did you last see him naked?'

Antoine was quick enough to sidestep this. 'I've seen both of you only a month back in the most obscenely revealing shorts. You both looked fine in them.'

'Oh yes,' said Tom, casting his mind back to a still quite recent summer barbecue at Michel and Armand's. 'I seem to remember you were almost equally indecent.'

'You could have a go at painting me if you won't do Christopher,' said Antoine cheekily.

Tom spread one arm and hand out in Antoine's direction. 'Come over here,' he said.

For reasons that were so obvious that they didn't need to discuss them they chose the bedroom that had once been Antoine's. Nor did they discuss the question of condoms. (Actually Antoine hadn't brought any; he hadn't thought to take any to work with him that morning. While Tom and Christopher didn't keep a stock of them at home; they didn't expect to need them.) They were not going to do anything as adventurous as fuck each other. Not when they might be disturbed by a phone call from Christopher at any minute.

'You look very good naked,' Tom told Antoine after he'd watched him strip off and they were running hands over each other under the duvet. 'Perhaps I will try and paint you after all.' They both snickered. What would Christopher have to say about that? The thought ran through both their minds. Again it was such an obvious one that they didn't need to voice it.

'You look very good yourself,' said Antoine.

Tom didn't try to dismiss the compliment or pick it apart. That a man in his mid-thirties should even say that to a friend in his late fifties was good enough for Tom. 'Thank you,' he simply said. Then his hand moved down to Antoine's upstanding penis.

It was suddenly morning and no phone call had come from Christopher. 'No news is good news,' Tom said muzzily to Antoine's waking head. They had both come happily in each other's hands before drifting off to sleep. They didn't attempt a repeat performance now. They simply got up, showered separately, and dressed for work. Tom found Antoine an unused razor and a spare toothbrush. Then they breakfasted briefly on *biscottes*. Tom didn't want to phone Christopher yet. It was still only seven in Britain and if Christopher had been lucky enough to get a good night's sleep Tom didn't want to wake him from it.

'I'll let him phone in his own good time,' Tom told Antoine. He reminded him how early it still was across the Channel. 'He'll phone when he's awake.'

'Will you tell him I stayed the night?' Antoine asked.

Tom breathed in and out once while he thought about this. 'Only if he asks,' he said.

'And if he asks whether we slept together?' Antoine pursued.

'I think I won't be telling him that even if he does ask. I know that might mean lying to him but…'

'I understand,' said Antoine. As indeed he did. He was in the same position with regard to his own partner, Patrick. 'I was asking you simply because I thought we should both be… What is the expression you use in English when you agree to say the same story?'

'Singing from the same hymn sheet,' Tom said.

'Yes,' said Antoine. 'I like that.'

Christopher phoned while they were on the road to work. Tom managed to pull over just in time to answer before Christopher rang off. 'What news?' he asked at once.

'News is good. I just phoned up. Mum spent a peaceful night and is eating breakfast. She didn't eat much supper last night, apparently, but they think she's going to settle. They suggested I didn't visit for a few days in case that set her off again, but they thought that Moira could go today.'

'Do you still have to stay in England, though?' Tom asked. He wanted Christopher back with him desperately; he wanted to hold him in his arms and for everything to be all right for ever.

'No,' Christopher said. 'I can come back to France. I'm just going to get on the phone and check the flights. I'll try and make it today if I can. Tomorrow if not. I'll go back to England briefly next weekend if that's all right. To see how mum is.'

'Of course that's all right,' said Tom happily. Then, 'I was driving to work when you phoned. But I've managed to pull off. Antoine's in the car with me. He kept me company at the Vieux Chai last night.'

It was on the tip of Christopher's tongue to say for a joke, 'Not in the same bed I hope,' but he bit the remark back. It might not have been a joke, he thought, or not a very good one. And in any case pots had good reasons sometimes to refrain from invoking the blackness of kettles. 'Good,' he said. 'I'll call again when I know which flight.'

'Hope it can be today, darling. I'll come and meet you at the airport how ever late it is.'

'Can't wait,' said Christopher. He'd never used the expression more earnestly in his life.

TWENTY-FIVE

Michel and Armand's visits to their property in Nastringues were each year getting longer. Much as Michel loved to paint by the northern sea-light of the English Channel, he enjoyed the contrast provided by the Dordogne region: the brilliant lemon and lime colours of its trees in springtime, the bright, hot paint-box of its summer, the rippling reflections of its swallow-skimming rivers. They had been down several times that summer. By chance they'd missed John Moyse's visit and were not around when Simon had arrived a few weeks later. By the time they met him at the end of that September, when the wine harvest was going on everywhere around them, Simon was well established. He came to lunch at the Vieux Chai one day during their visit. He didn't drive – at least he said he didn't – so he caught the bus out of Castillon and walked the last bit. They all talked politely over lunch, Simon was fortunately quite communicative – he'd been improving in that area on an almost daily basis – and seemed to take to Michel and Armand. They in their turn clearly liked him. But it was after he'd gone, to catch the afternoon bus back down to Castillon, that they asked the questions that really interested them.

'You say he's got a licence to fish commercially?' Michel queried. 'How did that come about? They're like gold dust. Besides, he's English.'

Tom said, 'In the end it came down to my mother not taking no for an answer. There was also some doubt about who the riverfront promenade in front of her house belonged to and whether someone living at her address was entitled to set up a fish stall on it. Of course, it's always who you know, not what you know, in these cases.'

Michel nodded.

Tom continued. 'My mother thought she remembered that we used to know the mayor of Castillon. We told her that we didn't. It was Jean-Pierre the builder who knew him. Jean-Pierre's retired by now but Antoine phoned him for us. No, he didn't know the current mayor, he said; he knew the previous one. But Antoine thought that his uncle François – who's still mayor here, by the way – got on well with the new one. Antoine spoke to François … it's always better when it comes from a fellow Frenchman, as I hardly need to tell you … '

'Yes,' said Michel, cutting short Tom's long story, 'I understand now.'

'He's got this net contraption, like a giant upside-down umbrella, that he lowers into the water overnight on a sort of crane thing and hoists up in the morning. It's brilliant for catching eels and lampreys – as well as other things.'

'But he still does fly-fishing,' Christopher added. 'Sits beside the stall outside Tom's mother's with his rod out over the water. Nothing attracts customers' attention better than actually seeing the guy catching the fish he's selling – right there in front of them.'

'And this religious thing,' Armand said. 'His re-conversion after he saw the sun shining through the church window. How's that going?'

'Well, they noticed him at the church, as you can imagine,' said Christopher. 'Walking around the village, sitting in the church for hours at a time, meditating. But once they realised that he wasn't a vagrant but an educated man who spoke French and was just a bit peculiar, they welcomed him as one of their own. He's already a sidesman – takes the collection plate around. May says they're thinking of letting him loose on reading the Epistles.'

'In an English accent?' said Michel.

'And what's wrong with that?' said Tom, mock indignant. 'My father's house has many mansions.' He chuckled.

A few days later Michel and Armand invited Simon up to their place at Nastringues, along with Tom and Christopher (for someone had to drive him) and Antoine and his partner Patrick. Antoine and Patrick knew the house well: they kept an eye on it from two villages away when Michel and Armand weren't in residence. But it was new to Simon.

Simon was easily impressed by new places and new experiences, they had learnt quite early on; he thought this old stone house re-created out of two cottages was a wonder. 'It was only the third property we ever did,' Tom told him as they walked round it. 'After our own, and the house you're living in. We were still learning.'

'*We* were,' said Christopher, 'but Antoine and Jean-Pierre weren't, remember. They'd done it all before and taught us how to do it.' This was diplomatic: Antoine was walking right beside him.

The house had a hilltop situation among the ubiquitous green vineyards. From the garden and the ground floor those made up most of the view. But from the upstairs windows the Dordogne could be seen below them and a couple of miles away, meandering along its flood plain; if you let your eye follow its course upstream you would see the outskirts and church spire of Ste-Foy-la-Grande in the distance.

'We live down there,' Patrick told Simon. He pointed to an area just before Ste-Foy began, that was covered with agri-business-size greenhouses.

'What, among the glass-houses?' queried Simon.

Patrick laughed. 'We don't live in one. Though we live quite near them. But you hardly notice them when you're actually down there. You must come and see us some time.' He turned to his younger partner. *'N'est-ce pas, Antoine?'*

Christopher did a quick mental calculation. He knew the age of everybody present. Patrick was the same age as Simon. Christopher wasn't quite sure why he'd thought to do the calculation.

'You'd never know it had once been two cottages,' Simon said as the tour continued. 'You guys did a splendid job on the conversion.'

'Ours is also two cottages knocked together,' Patrick put in. 'Though it was done before I moved into it. And long before I met Antoine. Or these guys…' He indicated Tom and Christopher.

'It wasn't a *bad* conversion,' said Antoine, his voice showing that he thought that if he'd been involved it would have been a much better one. 'Anyway, you'll see it.'

'Time for a drink,' said Michel. 'Let's head back out to the garden.' The weather was still lovely, and the *vendange*, the annual backbreaking fortnight of tractors and trailers and grape-picking machines was still going on all around them.

Christopher's mobile phone went off in his pocket just as they were choosing which chairs to sit in at the garden table. To his surprise John Moyse's voice spoke when he answered it.

'I thought you might like to know,' said John, 'and you can pass this on to Simon, that I've done a pitch for a drama-documentary based on Simon's story. I've had quite a few ideas about how it might work and sent it to a few people. People I already know, obviously. Otherwise it would hardly be worth trying.'

'Wow,' said Christopher. 'That sounds very positive. Wow again… I didn't know you were even thinking of trying. Look, Simon's here himself. We're all up at Nastringues with Michel and Armand. I'll hand you over to Simon.' He did so, and Simon, who still wasn't all that good with telephones, got given the so-far-so-good news directly.

The others had their ears on stalks, understandably, wondering what could be the subject of this three-way conversation. After it was finished, after Simon had returned the phone to Christopher and Christopher had exchanged a few final words with John, Simon and Christopher explained it all between them.

'It sounds good,' Simon finished. 'I mean, if it comes off. Trouble is, I'm not sure how well I could handle being famous.'

'Don't worry, you won't be,' Michel reassured him. 'Well, you might be for five minutes, but that's as long as fame ever lasts these days. Unless you go on making programme after programme.' Like Michel, who went on painting picture after picture. 'Otherwise, once it's over it's over. On the other hand,' he smiled at Simon, 'you might make a little money out of it.'

Each month throughout that autumn and winter Christopher made the trip back to England to spend a long weekend visiting his mother and helping Moira to manage her life. Moira had eventually tongue-lashed their elder brother Jim to get involved. They had all forgotten this but in the aftermath of their father's death the family solicitor had advised their mother to give Enduring Power of Attorney to her first-born. This piece of forward planning now proved a godsend. Jim might do nothing else but at least he could move their mother's funds around when necessary and sign her cheques. There weren't many to write. Small bills for utilities at her house, a large one each month for council tax, and a truly staggering one for care home fees. You weren't supposed to allow yourself to wonder how long this would have to go on for, this haemorrhaging of family fortune, but everybody did, naturally.

Each month Christopher flew back to England, bracing himself. Wondering if his mother would still recognise him when he turned up in the residents' lounge. But she always did. To spend a long time sitting with her was difficult. She might know who he was but she was pretty uncertain about everything else in life. Cheerful conversations in which two parties could catch up on what life had done with them both since they'd last met were things of the past. But Christopher wanted his mother to have some quality time when he was there; his solution was to turn up in the car she'd driven until quite recently and take her out in it.

He was careful not to drive near, or even in the direction of, her house. During her first week in the care home she had one night raved about being held against her will and demanded that the police be called, to take her back home in a police car. Christopher didn't want to risk a repeat of that, alone with her in a car in the vicinity of her house. Instead he drove her out into the Kent countryside, weaving a meandering way through pretty villages – Boughton Malherbe, Headcorn, Sutton Valence. Occasionally, if the winter day was bright and sparkling, he would take her all the way to Whitstable and give her a sight of the sea. He could tell that she appreciated that. He didn't do that in poor weather, though, afraid the sight of a grey and wind-stoked ocean would depress her. Then he would take her back to the care home in time for teatime.

He ate a midday meal with her whenever he was on a visit. With her and the other slowly dementing residents. Each time he dreaded the moment of parting, fearing she would make it difficult, but amazingly she never did. Provided he left her with a cup of tea in front of her, with people around her – not alone in her bedroom – she seemed to be all right. He left her each time with the same words of comfort. 'See you in a couple of weeks.' It would actually be four or more, but he reckoned the meaning of the word couple was elastic. After his experiments in living, all those years ago, with Tom, Michel and Armand, he was probably entitled to think that.

'Where do you go when you're not here?' his mother once asked him. 'I've looked for your room here but I can't find it.' Sometimes she believed she was in a hotel, on holiday, and Christopher felt happy when she was thinking that way. But he could imagine only too easily how she had gone looking for him, walking into other residents' bedrooms without knocking, and causing general havoc.

'I go back to France.'

'To France?!' she exclaimed incredulously, like Edith Evans crying, 'A handbag?!' when John Worthing explained his birth circumstances.

'It's where I live.'

His mother sat and pondered that a moment. Then she said, 'Were you living there last year?'

'I've lived there for over thirty years,' Christopher said.

'How peculiar,' his mother said, sounding very puzzled. 'I never knew that.'

As the months passed his mother seemed to know less and less about what was going on in the world outside her immediate field of vision and she sometimes got confused even about that. She saw a woman, a fellow resident, sitting in an armchair and said how odd it was that she should be hanging suspended from the ceiling like that. Christopher was reminded of the time, at Star of the Sea, when Father Louis had mistaken Molly O'Deere for a dog in the chapel.

Yet there was a plus side to this. As time went on Christopher's mother grew more accepting of her circumstances and became almost cheerful about life. She also seemed to enjoy Christopher's company more and more with each succeeding visit. It was as though she was learning to like him again. Many, many years had passed since that had been the case.

Christopher wasn't her only visitor. Moira came twice weekly, sometimes more often than that, bringing her own children sometimes, and even Jim and Brian had come occasionally. Christopher was more than glad about that. It made him feel less guilty about returning home to France at the end of each visit.

Christopher's mother didn't really know that it was Christmas. Moira spent most of the day with her while Christopher was able to spend the holiday with Tom for once. He couldn't remember the last time that he'd been able to do that. They had a celebration meal at Le Vieux Chai. Antoine and his partner Patrick came and so did May, bringing Simon with her. As a contribution to the festivities Simon brought a box of writhing lampreys, of which he'd caught a surfeit. They weren't going to be eaten on Christmas Day, Tom and Christopher were certain. Leaving the decision as to what to do with them for another time they put them in the fridge.

Two days after Christmas they got a phone call from John Moyse. Tom answered it. John's news was disappointing. He'd had replies from all the people he'd pitched his idea to – or Antoine's idea, rather: the idea of making a drama-documentary about Simon and his history. The last one had arrived that morning. 'They don't want it because it's too sad, in the end,' John said. 'A kid gets chucked out of one school, has his spirit broken in another one, becomes a drop-out. There's no happy ending…'

'Sorry,' Tom cut him off, 'but there certainly is. Simon has a small fishing business. He makes enough to pay mum for his board and lodging and has pocket money over. He's a bit of a cult figure in the church-going community. We actually went along to midnight Mass on Christmas Day – Christmas Eve or whatever – and there he was reading the lesson. You know, the one from Isaiah. *The people who walked in darkness have seen a great light; Upon those who dwelt in the land of shadows a light has shone.'*

'Wow,' said John. 'And he did it in French?'

'No. Amazingly they let him do it in English. Though it's not as if they didn't all know it anyway.'

'No, of course,' said John. 'But it's still amazing.'

Tom went on, a bit more cautiously, 'I mean, that may not be the ending, but it's pretty happy for the moment. Pretty upbeat. I mean, thanks to Simon we now have a fridge full of lampreys…'

'Oh,' said John, taken aback slightly. 'I don't think I'd quite realised… I don't just mean the lampreys…'

'You weren't to know,' said Tom. 'It's all happened rather since we last saw you. We should have kept you updated. It's our fault we didn't.' He paused for a second. 'Look, phone that last person who turned you down and tell them what I've just told you. Egg the pudding a bit if you have to.'

'Well… I guess I'll have to wait for the New Year now,' said John doubtfully. 'You know what Christmas is like in England…'

Tom carried on regardless. 'This guy… Do you have his home phone number?'

'Er … yes,' said John.

'Phone him now and tell him. Everybody in England just sits around after Christmas Day doing nothing and getting bored out of their skins. He'll be delighted to get a phone call about a future work project – it's just about the right length of time after Christmas. You'll be in with a good chance, I promise.'

Something that sounded a bit like a sigh could be heard at the other end. But then John said, 'OK. Yep. You're right. I'll have a go and get back to you.'

John did phone back an hour later. His voice was transformed by good news. 'You were right. It worked. I have to say thank you. Now I'll need contact details for Simon...' Tom congratulated John and gave him his mother's – and thus Simon's – home phone number. They talked a minute or two more, then John rang off. Before saying good-bye his final words were, 'I almost think it was your story about the lampreys in the fridge that clinched it.'

Tom didn't have the heart to tell John that he'd forgotten all about the lampreys until he'd mentioned them to him earlier. Or that in the interval between the two phone calls he and Christopher had located them in the fridge bottom, found them all dead and wasted, and taken them out into the garden where they'd buried them decently beneath a rose bush.

TWENTY-SIX

In February John Moyse arrived with the producer he'd collared over Christmas to interview Simon Rickman, and to walk around the locations offered by the village of Ste-Colombe and the river banks around Castillon. The producer liked what he saw and heard. It looked as though the project would be going ahead. If it did, then he hoped they would be able to come down in the spring when the weather was better and the countryside a bit greener, to film Simon going about his daily routines. 'It fits so well,' the producer said. 'Fish and the Christian religion. The miraculous draught of fishes. The feeding of the five thousand…' They would be dramatising the events of Simon's earlier life, with a child actor playing the role of Simon. Then the producer returned to England and there was nothing to do but wait.

In the middle of March Christopher got a phone call from Moira. 'There's a big change in mother,' she said. 'I think you ought to get over here pronto.'

'How do you mean, a big change?' asked Christopher.

'They phoned up this morning to say that something had happened in the night. That she'd gone sort of vacant. I've been to see her, but she was asleep in bed. We didn't wake her and I had to go to work. That's where I am. But I think you should get over.'

Christopher had heard that you could now book airline tickets using the computer; that you could pay by typing in your credit or debit card details and get going quickly. It sounded frightening. He had a stab at it but it quickly became clear that it wasn't terribly easy. It looked like taking all morning. He gave up and walked across the square to the travel agent he used normally.

He was in Maidstone by early evening. He took a taxi from the station, not to his mother's house where he would be sleeping that night, but directly to the care home. His mother was not in bed but sitting in an armchair in her bedroom, fully dressed, which surprised him. She peered forward at him, frowning, as though she knew she ought to be making sense of who he was and where she was, and what was happening, but somehow couldn't. He touched her hands and kissed her cheek but she made no movement in response. 'Can she speak?' he asked a senior staff member.

'That I don't know,' was the answer. 'She was talking yesterday but since she woke up this morning she hasn't spoken.'

Christopher phoned his sister. 'I think we need to get a priest for her. Do we know one?'

'Of course,' said Moira. Christopher knew that in the first months of her stay in the care home Moira had taken their mother out to church on the Sundays between his visits. More recently she had arranged for a priest to visit her in the home and give her communion. 'Father Flannery heard her confession only last Saturday. But he's away in Ireland. There's a church just a block away from where mum is. Maybe you should try them. I'll come over later.'

'Heard her confession?' Christopher was astounded. 'What on earth would she have to confess now?' But he couldn't disagree with the principle. He thanked his sister and set off to walk the hundred yards to the Catholic church on the corner. He didn't believe in the sacraments. He didn't believe that having a priest read the last rites over her would make any difference to his mother's future. And yet he knew that to withhold from her this final comfort for someone who still believed (maybe) in things that he now didn't would have been an enormity, something unfathomably wicked. At the back of his mind lay the thought that is the property of every lapsed Catholic. Suppose I'm wrong? Supposing there is an eternal Hell and an eternal Heaven? And suppose that on that set of scales with which God was believed to weigh the good and evil that men and women had enacted over their long lifetimes the receiving of the Sacrament of the Dying might tip the balance?

The church was shut, of course; it was evening. But lights were on in the presbytery. Christopher banged on the door. It was opened almost immediately by a man in jeans and a cardigan, who looked about the same age as Christopher. But he was wearing a black 'stock' with round white collar attached to it poking up above the cardigan. Christopher didn't need to ask him if he was the person he needed to speak to. Christopher told him what he'd come about while, glimpsed through an open door beyond the hallway a TV set flickered and chattered.

'I'll get my things,' the priest said. 'If you'll wait here I won't be a minute.' He disappeared and then appeared again, clad in a puffer jacket and with a bag in his hand that was like the ones that doctors on house calls carry. Christopher walked with him to the care home.

Inside his mother's room Christopher watched the priest remove his jacket and take from his bag a purple silk stole, which he placed around his neck, two cards with printing on them, a small phial of holy water and another one of the greasy white ointment that Christopher remembered learning was called chrism.

'She won't go tonight,' the priest told him. 'I was a nurse before becoming a priest. I know the signs. She has three or four days left in her.' Then he gave Christopher one of the cards to read, while he read aloud from the other. He said the prayers and then the words of ultimate forgiveness. Christopher tried to say the responses but could barely whisper them as the tears rolled down his cheeks like rainwater. His mother's face remained impassive, mask-like, even when her forehead, wrists and ankles were anointed by the kneeling priest with the chrism. Moira arrived just as the priest was leaving.

The next day Christopher went to the care home in the morning. No phone call had come overnight so he was not surprised to see his mother in the same condition as she had been the previous day. He didn't stay long. There was nothing to be done, nothing to be said really, although he did talk to her, giving ordinary information about ordinary things – that he'd eaten breakfast, that the weather was cold but sunny. He kissed her before he left and suddenly she raised her hand and touched the back of his head with it. Then the hand fell back. But when Christopher then took it and squeezed it he felt her squeeze his back in answer. Though that was all there was to it.

Tom arrived the day after that. He stayed with Christopher at his mother's house. He brought news with him. The drama-documentary about Simon that John Moyse was writing had been given the go-ahead by the television company. It was definitely going to happen. What's more, John had secured a deal with a publishing company for a book on Simon's story, of which he and Simon would be co-authors. In the middle of all his turmoil and heartache Christopher still managed to find this news cheering.

Tom went with Christopher to the care home but stayed downstairs while Christopher went up to his mother. That day she didn't know him, and there was no response when he touched and kissed her. The care home staff again confirmed that she hadn't spoken.

Two more days passed in this twilight state of half living yet half not living. The state was shared, in an odd way, by Christopher and Tom. Christopher's mother no longer sat out in an armchair. She lay in bed. She was beyond eating. They were giving her carefully measured, carefully timed, drops of water.

Then came a day on which her lips disappeared, withdrawn somehow inside her. Christopher saw there was nothing left to kiss except her open mouth, yet all the same he leaned over her bed and kissed it. And then the extraordinary thing happened. His mother, who was officially in a coma, raised her arms slowly and wrapped them round his back. They were thin now as angle-poise lamps. Then he felt her stroking his hair with her fingers. A sound came from her mouth. It seemed dredged up from depths that were older and deeper than either he or she was. She uttered three syllables. Three vowels. No consonants, of course. No lips, no consonants. 'Aih – aah – oo.'

Christopher could only think of one three-syllable sentence that ran to that pattern and that someone might want to utter on their deathbed. Syllables. Christopher remembered the definition he'd taught to Form 2B all those years ago and that he'd learned years before that from his own teachers. 'A syllable is a sound produced by a single effort of the voice.' And what efforts his mother had just now made. They'd seemed almost superhuman. Something in whatever remained in the mind that produced them, however much of it was left, however little, clearly thought those efforts worth the making, those syllables worth the speaking.

'She didn't do or say the same thing to the others,' Tom told friends when they were back in France a fortnight later, a few days after the funeral. 'Not to his sister or his brothers. It was like the prodigal son returning.' He would tell the story often, and make the same point in the years that followed. Then he'd add, because he couldn't help making this point too, 'Though it's a pity she didn't change her mind soon enough to change her will and leave something for Christopher.'

For Christopher had been left nothing. 'It doesn't matter,' Christopher would say. 'We've been very lucky. Gérard, from whom we'd no reason to expect anything, left us what amounted to a fortune. And we've done well in increasing it. But to have the love of a mother, and to be told you have it in the last words she ever uttered, is worth more than all the wealth of all the world. You'll remember that when you have to deal with the death of your own mother – even though in her case there was never a wilderness of years in which she didn't love you.'

And Tom would agree. How could he not do? But if no-one else was listening too closely by that stage of the story he would say to Christopher, 'But all the same, my mother had better not go and leave the lot to Simon.'

Part Four

2003 – 2004

A Likeness

TWENTY-SEVEN

On the twenty-first of June 2003 Tom celebrated his sixty-third birthday and Christopher his sixtieth. There was nothing new about their birthdays occurring on the same date. It had happened every year since they had first known each other and, obviously, even before that. In fact, the discovery that they shared a birthday, made within an hour of their first meeting, had been one of the first bonding moments between them. Though there had been more important ones in the forty-one years since.

Usually their joint birthday was a private affair, involving dinner for two in a restaurant in Ste-Foy or St-Emilion. But this year, in view of Christopher's three-score milestone, they turned it into something a bit more public. The date was traditionally the start of summer, whatever the weather was like, and also the summer solstice: the day was long, the night was short. They had a barbecue in the garden of Le Vieux Chai.

They lit the charcoal at about five o'clock and waited for the guest list to turn up. Some were already on the premises. Roger and Malcolm had arrived the previous day. They'd taken advantage of new air routes opening up and had flown direct to Bergerac, a much nearer airport than Bordeaux. They had hired a car there, as they usually did when they visited Le Vieux Chai. Malcolm was in his early seventies now, and Roger ten years older, but they were still both in good health, looking fit, and slimmish.

The other pair of house guests were John Moyse and his wife Maisie; they'd come the slightly slower way: by Eurostar from London to Paris, then TGV to Libourne, where Christopher had met them at the station.

Half a dozen neighbours from St-Philippe and Castillon had been invited – including François, still mayor of St-Philippe-d'Aiguille after all these years.

There were Tom's mother and her eternal lodger Simon. May still did the driving for the two of them despite being well into her eighties: Simon had still not mastered the knack. Then there were Antoine and Patrick, coming over from St Margaret Tyzack, and picking up Michel and Armand en route. This was an arrangement that suited everyone most happily: Patrick did the driving; he was someone who drank very little, unlike the rest of them.

Most guests brought some sort of a contribution in the way of drink or food. Antoine and Armand oversaw the cooking of meat items over the hot glowing charcoal. This was a shrewd piece of thinking on the part of the two hosts. French guests might be just about OK with a steak or a sausage that happened to be cooked by Tom or Christopher or one of their English guests, but were much happier if they knew that it was being done under the watchful eyes of a French person. Tom and Christopher might have lived and cooked in France for forty-one years but that still wasn't thought to be quite good enough. Whereas Antoine was a highly trusted local boy and Armand, although he came from the distant north of the country, had at least been born on the correct landmass.

Tom and Christopher had an announcement to make. But they didn't actually make an announcement. There was no ringing of a bell or clapping of hands to bring the assembly to silence, glasses frozen in hands, plates of food growing cold. They simply slipped the news into the conversations they had with individual guests, going into as much or as little detail as they felt appropriate in each case, depending on how close the friendship was. The principal piece of news was that Tom was going to retire from the estate agency business.

The numbers of British people and other foreigners, mainly Dutch and German, rushing to buy property in the Dordogne had dwindled. The market was still steady, but the torrent of arrivals from outside France that had been such a feature of the eighties and early nineties had slowed. The estate agency's turnover was beginning to struggle to meet the three salaries of Tom, Christopher and Antoine. And for the same reason there was no longer quite enough work to keep three people occupied all day. The plan was for Tom to withdraw from the day-to-day running of the office in Ste-Foy-la-Grande and spend his time – and with luck earn his money – by painting and selling pictures, as Michel did.

That was about as much as Tom and Christopher were telling those of their guests who were not their intimate friends. But those who were close to them already knew a little more. Taking a leaf out of Gérard's book (or rather his banker partner Henri's book) Tom and Christopher had turned themselves into a limited company some years earlier. More recently, and after a lot of thought and discussion, they had invited Antoine to become the third member of the company. They didn't ask him to buy his way in – he had no money of his own, except the salary that Tom and Christopher had been paying him for twenty-four years. He had to pay a nominal sum to comply with the requirements of company law, but that was it. To all intents and purposes Tom and Christopher gave him his one-third share, schooled by the example of Gérard in providing, years ago, for their own future.

This had several implications. Antoine was now entitled to a third of the profits from the estate agency, was entitled to discuss and agree with them how much should be ploughed back into the business and how much could be divvied up between them. The whole company would be his to do as he liked with after Tom and Christopher were both dead. And that included Le Vieux Chai.

Tom and Christopher had felt obliged to come clean about the arrangement with their respective families. Christopher had done this by phone, talking to his sister and both his brothers separately. He told them politely that, since his mother had left all the family's money to them and none of it to him, they would surely not be surprised to learn that Tom and he had made plans to dispose of their estate after their deaths in a way that did not involve them or their children.

Tom had had a similar conversation with his brother Dominic, though in that case it had been face to face. Dominic and Tom got on well at a distance. They also got on well when they were together, though that didn't happen very often. But Dominic came down to visit his mother – their mother – every year (in the year in which Simon moved in with May that visit had been made with some urgency) and on his most recent visit Tom had broken this news to him. Dominic took it with a shrug. He might have been less sanguine about it if his mother hadn't already assured him that her own estate would be left jointly to her two sons. That was good as far as it went. She did not say what provisions, if any, she had made for Simon, if he was still calling her house his home on the day she died.

Armand, and obviously Antoine, knew all this already. From their watching post at the barbecue – occasionally intervening to turn over a chop that someone had forgotten – they were able to see the news of Tom's retirement circulating among the party guests, and could try and gauge how it was going down. The company was mixed. Old and young, adults and children (just one or two of those), gay and straight, male and female. For most of the locals the three gay couples present were the only gay people they knew … or at any rate the only people they knew whose gayness they were aware of. Not all of them knew the details of the arrangements

Tom and Christopher had made for themselves and Antoine: they were only learning that Tom intended to retire. They had probably never given any thought to the matter of how gay couples who had no children disposed of any property they might leave behind when they died. But you could somehow see from their faces that right now they were thinking about it.

'Do all these people know that you're part of the company these days?' Armand asked Antoine.

'It's not something we've shouted from the rooftops,' Antoine answered. 'Of course my mother knows.' Armand gave him a look that caused him to add, 'She's very discreet. Not like most people's mothers. She doesn't even go around announcing to everyone that I'm gay. Unless they ask her.'

'And do they?' asked Armand.

'A few over the years,' Antoine said.

There was a bond between Antoine and Armand. Both of them had slept with both Tom and Christopher, at different times during the last forty years. Both of them knew that, and both knew that the other knew. They'd spoken of it occasionally. It didn't come up in the conversation now.

Someone walked over to them with an opened bottle of Château Jouanin from just up the road. The bottle was being held towards them at an inviting angle and they held their empty glasses out towards it to be refilled. They said their polite *mercis*. 'What do you think of Tom's painting?' Antoine asked suddenly.

Armand thought for a moment. The question could mean a number of different things. 'Do you mean the idea of his spending all his days doing it? Or whether he'll make money out of it? Or if his work is any good?'

'All of those, I think,' said Antoine.

If anyone was qualified to answer those questions it was Armand. He'd not only lived with Michel for most of the past forty-five years, and seen him at work and been his agent, secretary and salesman during most of that time; he'd also watched Tom, painfully slowly, learning the job from Michel.

'I think his paintings are excellent,' Armand said. 'But unlike Michel he's not a famous name. Fame in the arts world happens by fluke, usually. It has something to do with the quality of people's work of course, but not everything: it's not a one to one ratio.' Antoine nodded his head: that was something everybody knew. 'He's not going to make as much money out of it as Michel does, I would imagine. But the pictures he paints do sell…' He paused and took a sip of wine. 'It stands to reason that the more he paints the more he'll sell. At the right price. To the right person. And it's not as if he's in desperate financial straits.'

'No,' Antoine agreed. 'It's not as if any of us are.'

'As for whether I think it's a good thing for him to spend all his time on it… Well, yes. If that's what he wants to do, that's great. Though don't be surprised if he comes creeping back into the office to keep warm during the winter months.'

Antoine chuckled. 'I'm sure you're right about that,' he said. 'Perhaps we can free up a second wall.'

'A second wall?' queried Armand.

'Sorry. I meant in the office.' One of the office's inside walls was already a dedicated display area for Tom's work. It was from there that most of it was sold. 'Turn it into a bit more of a gallery.'

'Turn it all into a gallery,' said Armand mischievously, 'and you could hang Michel's work there as well.'

'I'll bring that up at the next company meeting,' said Antoine in the same esprit.

'Mind you,' said Armand, 'I'm a little surprised at Tom letting you and Christopher spend your days together – all day every day – just the two of you at the office.'

'Now, now,' said Antoine. 'That was all years ago. Water under the bridge.' He gave Armand a very special look.

John Moyse hadn't crossed paths with Simon Rickman for over a year. Though in the two years before that they had spent a good deal of time together, working first on the TV programme and then on the book. The TV programme had made Simon famous for five minutes, as had been predicted. He had done interviews with several British magazines and newspapers and even one or two in France. It had made him a bit of money, but not a fortune. Not enough to buy a spanking new car (not that he wanted one) or put down a deposit on a house. He wouldn't have wanted that either – though Tom and his brother would have liked it.

The book had had similar financial results. John and Simon were its joint authors and shared the royalties in a fifty-fifty split. It had created a lot of interest when it first came out; reviews had been very favourable and Simon benefitted from a few more press interviews. But then things had gone quiet again. Royalties continued to come in, but at the rate of only a few hundred pounds a year for each of them. John Moyse continued to write comedy scripts to earn his bread and butter and Simon continued to fish.

'Have you ever thought of becoming a priest?' Simon asked John suddenly while they were catching up on things in general over what might have been a third glass of wine – or a fourth.

'Not recently,' said John. Instinctively he turned his head towards Maisie, in conversation just two metres away with François's wife. 'When I was a very earnest kid, perhaps. In my first couple of years at Star of the Sea, I seem to remember, but it faded after that.'

'I don't think I did,' said Simon. 'Not back then. But these days I'm thinking about it.'

'Oh right,' said John, trying not to sound surprised at hearing a fifty-five-year-old come out with that. Then he peered closely at Simon. 'Have you had another religious experience?'

'No,' said Simon. 'Well, not as such. Not since the first one. Nothing like what you told me happened to Angelo. Hearing God's voice in the bathroom with his mouth full of toothpaste.'

'He might have been exaggerating when he talked about the toothpaste,' John said. 'But seriously, becoming a priest would be awfully hard work. Years of study of very abstract subjects. Then, if you made it through to the end and got ordained … well, it's a pretty demanding job.'

'I guess you're right,' said Simon and took a sip from his wineglass. 'It was just a thought I had.'

At that point John had a thought, if a rather unworthy one. If Simon did become a priest, or even went away to study towards becoming one, it would at least get him out of Tom's mother's house.

When the sun went down, turning the vineyards into lattices of yellow light for a few minutes just before it set, first the garden lights came on and then the stars came out. The air filled gradually with the scents of honeysuckle and roses and the party continued in the lamp-lit dark.

It began to break up politely between eleven o'clock and midnight. Tom became concerned about his mother: that she would be driving home, with Simon as her passenger, late at night and after a couple of drinks. She was eighty-seven now. Because she remained fit and sprightly and had all her wits about her people tended to forget that. 'Leave the car. We'll get you a taxi,' Tom said.

He said it in the hearing of Patrick, the light drinker, who was already earmarked to drive Michel and Armand home on his way back with Antoine to St-Avit-du-Tizac. 'No need for that,' Patrick told him. 'I'll take your mother – and Simon – and then come back for the others.'

Tom told Patrick he shouldn't put himself out in this way and made all the appropriate noises but was actually relieved that he had offered. He didn't think it would be easy to find a willing taxi at this time of night. So he gave way and let Patrick take his mother away with him along with her long-time house guest. Anyway, he thought, it would be an opportunity for Patrick to spend a little time in Simon's company. The two of them liked each other a lot and seemed to enjoy each other's conversation more and more as the years passed. He couldn't help noticing that.

TWENTY-EIGHT

Tom's retirement began the next morning. He spent the first few hours of it clearing up the debris of the night before, with Christopher and their four house guests. Then the four guests left. Roger and Malcolm drove off in their hire car – they were going to spend a few days travelling around the Dordogne before flying back to England from Bergerac – while Tom and Christopher drove John and Maisie to Libourne and saw them onto the train to Paris. After they'd watched the twenty carriages of the TGV pull smoothly out, accelerating into the long run northwards, Christopher turned to Tom. 'And then there were two,' he said.

'Yes,' said Tom. 'Good, isn't it?' He grinned at Christopher and Christopher grinned back.

That day was a Sunday, so Tom's retirement hadn't really kicked in yet. It was on Monday that he noticed it. And Monday reminded him – and Christopher – yet again that they didn't actually live in a world that contained only the two of them. Christopher went off to spend the day with Antoine in the office at Ste-Foy, while Tom awaited the arrival of Michel at Le Vieux Chai. They were driving out together with easels, palettes and stretched canvasses. For Michel was not only Tom's friend and ex-lover. He was also the patient teacher who, for half a lifetime, had been helping him learn to paint.

They drove just a few miles along the St-Emilion road. Halfway between St-Genès and St-Christophe-des-Bardes they stopped at the top of an escarpment. A track ran down the hill between the rows of vines. It led, according to the rough sign beside it, to a little wine château called Moulin de Pressac. The huddle of its roofs and outbuildings could be seen at the bottom of the slope. But they had come here to paint what lay beyond it, across the valley: the landscape of the opposite slope.

The centrepiece of the view, the element that would hold together their paintings of it, was the wonderful little Roman church of Ste-Colombe, the place where Simon hung out when he wasn't engrossed in fishing. 'I can't believe I've never painted from here before,' said Tom as they set up their easels.

Tom loved to paint with Michel. He had no feelings of wanting to outclass him or compete with him. Playing a duet with someone on musical instruments must be something like this, he thought. Not that he had ever done that. Michel and he would begin their pictures separately, unwatched by each other. But after ten minutes or so, by which time a rough idea of what each of them intended could already be made out, they would stop and look at each other's work. Michel was quicker, because more assured. He knew what he wanted and knew how to achieve it; Tom was more plodding, more tentative. He learnt something from Michel at every step, found a lesson in every brushstroke. While Michel was the most encouraging teacher Tom could imagine. 'That's going great,' he'd say. And then, in a little aside that he'd manage to make sound completely inconsequential, would deliver a piece of advice that would improve things tenfold. He'd been helping Tom in this way for years. Sometimes Tom smiled at the memory that, bizarrely, Michel had once also taught him how to keep the account books of an ironmonger's shop. Another life that seemed now.

'Do you think Simon might be over there?' Michel asked.

'What, sitting in the churchyard meditating? Looking back towards us?' Tom laughed. 'You think he might turn up in our pictures as an unidentifiable dot?' The distance across the valley to the church was about a mile. You might just about spot a human figure, but you wouldn't see who it was.

'He might be watching us,' said Michel. 'Wondering who we are.'

Tom thought he remembered telling Simon he was going to spend Monday painting with Michel. He hadn't told him where they were going to do it. That hadn't been decided until this morning.

'I suppose you've noticed,' said Michel as he dabbed carefully at a tiny spot of bare canvas, 'how close Simon and Patrick are becoming. They spent most of the party talking together…'

'Perhaps because Antoine was busy being in charge of the barbecue,' said Tom, 'but yes, I have noticed.'

'Is Patrick a particularly religious person?' Michel wondered aloud. 'I hadn't thought so.'

'Neither had I,' said Tom. 'But he does like to fish.'

'That's true,' said Michel. 'But he doesn't go fishing with Simon.'

'No,' said Tom. 'I think Antoine might have something to say about that.'

'Of course it could just be good old sexual attraction,' said Michel.

'They're fifty-five,' said Tom.

'So?' said Michel. He stopped what he was doing for a second and looked at Tom. 'We're sixty-three.' There was a half second's silence, then they both laughed.

'It's usually the younger one of a gay couple who strays,' said Tom. Quickly he added, 'I mean when there's a big age difference.'

'Hmm,' said Michel. They went on painting in silence for a few minutes. Then Michel said, 'I probably shouldn't be asking you this but…'

'You can always ask,' Tom said.

'Did Christopher and Antoine ever…?'

'A very long time ago, yes,' said Tom. 'A couple of times in the early years. But nothing recent. I'm pretty sure I'd know if there was anything…' He stopped. 'Unless you're going to tell me differently?'

'No, no,' Michel quickly assured him. 'Absolutely not.'

They painted mutely for another minute. Then Tom said suddenly, 'There was one time when Antoine and I… A few years ago now. And only once.'

'I'd somehow guessed that,' said Michel. 'Don't know how but I somehow guessed it.'

'That's because you read me like a book,' said Tom. 'Eight years we lived together. One learns to do that.'

Michel chuckled. 'Fair enough.' A moment later, 'It was good though, wasn't it?'

'What was?'

'The time we had.'

Tom went on painting carefully but a smile spread slowly across his face. 'Yes,' he said slowly. 'It was good.'

'No regrets?' said Michel.

'Not about our time together; certainly not. Not about what's happened since, either.'

'Ditto,' said Michel.

Tom was just a fortnight into his retirement when his mother died. On the morning of Sunday the sixth of July. To his astonishment the news came in a phone call from Patrick.

'How come from Patrick?' Michel asked Tom when he arrived at the Vieux Chai later that day. They sat in the garden with Christopher while Tom elaborated on the sad news.

'She collapsed while repairing a kitchen cupboard,' Tom told Michel. 'Simon panicked and phoned Patrick…'

'Before calling an ambulance? Or you?'

'He seems to be becoming a bit dependent on Patrick. Patrick told him to call the ambulance at once and that he would phone me.'

'Repairing a kitchen cupboard, though…?'

'Mum and Simon had been to early Mass in Castillon – and were back home having breakfast. There was a loud cracking noise in the kitchen and they both got up from the table to go and see. The cupboard on the wall was breaking free from its fastenings quite suddenly. Even before they got to it it had moved a bit more. Simon ran to it and pressed himself against it. He asked mum to find a screwdriver…'

'Sorry,' said Michel. 'If you don't want to…'

'It's fine,' said Tom. 'I'm OK.'

Christopher, sitting right beside Tom, laid a hand on his shoulder for a moment. The gesture reminded Michel forcibly of the David and Jonathan picture that hung indoors.

Tom went on. 'She got a screwdriver from the drawer but fumbled with it, trying to get it into the slot of one of the screws. After a moment they swapped roles. Simon took the screwdriver and mum pushed herself against the cupboard to stop it falling off the wall. She suddenly said – apparently, "I've got such a pain." Then she stopped pushing and a second later fell to the floor. Simon let go and knelt down with her while the cupboard inevitably came crashing down beside them. Luckily Simon wasn't hurt. My mother was already dead.'

'Heart attack?' Michel asked.

'That's what they said at the hospital.'

'I'm sorry,' said Michel.

Tom sighed. 'So am I. I miss her already. But she was eighty-seven. She had all her faculties. Unlike Chris's mum when she died. There are worse ways to go.'

'And where's Simon now?' Michel glanced quickly towards the house. It wasn't improbable that he was somewhere indoors.

Christopher said, 'After we'd done at the hospital, Patrick took him back to St-Avit. He's spending the rest of the day with him and Antoine.'

'And tonight?'

Tom said, 'We'll see.'

As it was Sunday Tom couldn't start making funeral or other arrangements until the following morning. He sent emails to everyone he could think of, to let them know what had happened. But before doing that, before even setting out for the hospital in Castillon, he had phoned his brother with the news. And Dominic, with Simon's residency at his late mother's house among the many thoughts that now tumbled in his mind, was already on his way.

When Michel had spent a little more time with Tom and had assured himself that Christopher was looking after him properly and that he was going to be OK he went away, back to Nastringues and Armand and the rest of their Sunday. Tom and Christopher had just time to prepare and eat a scratch meal when another car pulled into their drive. It was driven by Patrick. Antoine was with him.

'No Simon?' Tom asked, greeting them as they got out.

'He's walked into Ste-Foy,' said Patrick. 'To the church. He wanted to light a candle for your mother and say prayers for her.' Patrick said this quite earnestly, looking into Tom's eyes, and Tom had no inclination to smile at it.

'That's very lovely of him,' he said. 'I'll thank him when I see him.'

'I'll thank him for you even before you do,' said Patrick.

Christopher had joined them by now. They walked the dozen yards towards the garden chairs. Even before they got there Antoine spoke. He had looked like someone with something on his mind even as he was getting out of the car. 'There's something I need to say, Tom. That cupboard… The one between the window and the door, right? I put that cupboard up. You won't have forgotten it was me…'

Tom stopped him. 'You fitted it perfectly. Brackets, wall-plugs, screws…' He smiled. 'Antoine… It was fifteen years ago. A crumbly old wall… And the stuff my mother used to keep in there. Three litre-bottles of different olive oils. Tins of tomatoes, big jars of cassoulet. Rice jars, sugar jars, assorted jams. She had provisions enough to see her through World War Three.' Tom clapped an arm around his younger friend. 'I could have told her she had too much in there. I could have just occasionally checked the fixings. I didn't.' He smiled into Antoine's troubled eyes. 'Antoine, it wasn't you.'

'Hmm,' said Antoine. 'OK.' What he meant was, thank you for saying that. (He actually did say that the following day.)

'And do you know what?' Tom went on. 'When the cupboard came down and everything spilt out of it, nothing broke, except one single jar of strawberry jam. And some sugar and rice went over the floor.'

'I told him,' said Patrick gently. 'Told him he was worrying for nothing. So did Simon.'

'Oh dear,' said Christopher. 'Simon. It keeps coming back to Simon.'

'You mean, what's going to happen to him?' said Patrick.

'He told John he was thinking of becoming a priest,' said Christopher, sounding quite optimistic about it. 'At the party. He'd had a few drinks, though.'

'Oh?' said Patrick, frowning. 'He's never said anything about that to me.'

'It would save a lot of trouble if that happened,' said Tom. 'It would certainly cheer Dominic.'

'I think it was just party talk,' said Christopher, now sounding less optimistic. 'Something you say when you've been drinking.'

'It's not the sort of thing I say when I've been drinking,' said Tom. 'But I do see…'

'Anyway,' said Patrick, 'leaving aside the longer term, you won't have to worry about Simon for the immediate future. He's going to be staying with us for the next couple of weeks.' Tom and Christopher both glanced quickly at Antoine's face when Patrick said this but it wasn't giving away anything.

Dominic flew into Bergerac airport late that evening. Tom and Christopher drove to meet him. The late sunset of high summer was in progress as they drove back from the airport. They were heading into it. It lit the high radio mast on its crag at Le Fleix, and from time to time created chasms of darkness among the double rows of poplar trees, through which Christopher, the driver, had to plough hopefully, trying to remember the layout of the road and the disposition of traffic upon it before he'd been temporarily blinded. 'It's a beautiful sunset,' said Dominic looking out at the flame-laced sky before them. 'The end of an era.'

Later Dominic was more practical, more prosaic. 'Does Simon know how the property's been left? That he won't be able to stay there for ever?'

'Mum told him,' Tom reassured him. 'I was there when she did it. If we have to remind him and he says he doesn't remember, well, I'm a witness.'

'As is her will, presumably,' said Dominic. 'Have you seen it?'

'I've actually got it,' said Tom. 'It looks quite clear and self-explanatory. I doubt that any lawyer could make it read differently.'

They saw a lawyer in the morning. The death certificate would be available the next day. They made a provisional arrangement with a funeral director.

'Did anyone say the Last Rites over Mummy?' Dominic asked his brother when a brief moment found them alone together. 'I know we're not believers but she was.'

'It's OK,' said Tom. 'Christopher had the same thing with his mother. He called a priest in. But in our mother's case Simon read the prayers. There wasn't time to get a priest. He had the book with all the rites in, all the liturgy, and he read from it. It was the first thing he did after phoning Patrick and the ambulance. Apparently, if there isn't time to call a priest then a layman can do it. It's considered efficacious in such circumstances. But if there isn't anyone – well, a repentant sinner goes to Heaven anyway… Come on. We were both taught this.'

'Efficacious,' muttered Dominic contemptuously, suddenly cross with himself for bringing up the subject. 'I don't know why we're even discussing it.'

'Yes you do,' said Tom.

Dominic was silent for a second while he considered this. Then he said, 'Well, thanks anyway to Simon I suppose. I suppose we could let him live in the house till we sell it. Which will be months off. Providing we make it clear to him that he…'

'He knows,' said Tom. 'I keep telling you.'

'But he'll have to move the fish stall. No-one's going to buy a house with a fish stall right in front of it.'

'I don't know,' said Tom. 'Some people might think it quite a feature.'

'I meant normal people,' said Dominic.

May's funeral Mass was held in the church in Castillon. Michel read one of the lessons and Simon read the other. (Simon read regularly these days in both his churches, in a French that was impeccably pronounced as well as fluent.) Tom had written a couple of paragraphs about his mother's life and he read those, both in French and English. He had Christopher standing by as an understudy in case his emotions caught him out and he was unable to speak easily or, having started, found himself unable to finish. But Christopher's services were not called on. Tom managed it. Many of the congregation – some had travelled all the way from England specially – returned to May's house on the quayside for refreshments.

'I don't suppose you'd like to live here yourself?' Tom asked his brother – by now accompanied by his wife and one of their two daughters – as they made small talk in the kitchen.

'With retirement coming up, you're thinking?' Dominic looked at his wife and she shook her head with a bit of a giggle. Dominic looked back at Tom and shook his head more forcefully. 'No, I don't think so. Nice climate mind but … there's the question of the lingo.'

'Thousands of Brits live out here without speaking the lingo,' Tom reminded him. 'They manage.'

'And are they popular with the natives?' Dominic asked him.

'Not especially,' said Tom. 'Mum was lucky.'

Patrick came into the kitchen at that moment and joined them. Antoine followed, a foot or two behind him. They both glanced automatically at the whiter than white rectangle on the wall beside the door, and the jagged holes in the plaster through which the overloaded screws had yanked their wall-plugs.

Tom took the opportunity of their arrival to tell them, 'We've just been talking about Simon. You can tell him – if you see him before we do – that he's welcome to stay on here till we sell the place. That could be six months or a year away. But we will sell it. We have to. Tell him, sorry. If he needs help finding somewhere else to live … well, I promise we'll help him.'

'I don't think that will be necessary,' said Patrick. He was a sleek, well-rounded character with the figure that went with it. He was just on the cusp of becoming chubby. He had a look on his face at that precise moment that looked like ill-concealed satisfaction. 'He wants to come and live with us indefinitely.'

Tom was startled. But you can be startled without necessarily being surprised and Tom found that he wasn't entirely surprised by Patrick's announcement. 'And that's what you'd like…?' he said.

'Oh yes,' said Patrick. 'It's lovely to know that's how he wants things to resolve themselves. *N'est-ce pas, Antoine?'*

Antoine nodded quite energetically and smiled. But he didn't actually say anything.

Tom tried not to focus on the huge relief he felt at the sudden disappearance of his and his brother's problem. 'But how will that fit in with his routines? Living with you at St-Avit-du-Tizac. It's a long way from the church at Ste-Colombe. It's a long way from here. Without a car, I mean.'

'We've looked into the bus routes and timetables,' said Patrick smoothly. 'It's easily doable. I mean both Ste-Colombe and Castillon.'

'Yes,' said Tom, 'but the fishing… That was all arranged for him by my dear mother … with a little help from François and the mayor of Castillon. He won't be able to have a stall outside the front door when it's someone else's…'

'Don't worry,' said Patrick. 'It's all taken care of. The same old Dordogne flows through Ste-Foy as through Castillon, with the same fish in it. We're less than a mile from the Ste-Foy quaysides. Simon can fish there and set up his stall there.'

Tom looked doubtful. 'Will he get a permit?'

'You know the mayor of Ste-Foy,' Patrick reminded him. And of course, as the owner of premises in the town's main square, Tom did know the mayor; he came across him regularly in the course of business. 'Well, like me, he's a keen fellow-fisherman.' Patrick racked his smile up an extra notch at the corners. 'It's all been sorted. We went to school together.'

TWENTY-NINE

Not until a few weeks had passed did Antoine remember a conversation he'd had with Armand over the birthday barbecue back in June. It came back to him as he was absently gazing at the wall of the office on which Tom's for-sale canvasses were displayed. He told Christopher about it. 'What about clearing another wall of property photographs and extending Tom's exhibition space?'

'Oh,' said Christopher. 'Has Tom mentioned this?'

'Not to me,' said Antoine. 'But I suggested it light-heartedly to Armand and he said, why not hang Michel's work in here too – alongside Tom's?'

Christopher shot a frown at Antoine. 'Really? Michel exhibits in Paris. I'm not sure he'd want his work hung next to an amateur's … down here in the provinces.'

'Oh come on,' said Antoine. 'Tom's hardly an amateur these days.' He gestured towards the paintings of Tom's that hung just a few feet from where they sat at their two desks. There were Dordogne river landscapes, the twisting steps and ancient cobbles of St-Emilion's streets. The latest canvas depicted Simon's new fish stall, down by the river in Ste-Foy, just a couple of hundred yards through a zigzag of old lanes, behind the office. The table was furnished with small boxes containing zander, pike, trout and bony shad. Because the stall was devoted to the local supply of river fish there was not a crab in sight, and Christopher was fine with that. Simon himself did not appear in the painting. Just his fish.

'Also,' Christopher went on, 'Tom might not want his work hanging next to Michel's. In Michel's shadow, so to speak.'

Antoine looked a bit crestfallen. 'I suppose Armand might have been joking,' he said.

But then, to his own surprise as well as Antoine's, Christopher picked up the baton that Antoine had let drop. 'Who are we to know what they both think, though? We could at least ask them both. I'm happy to let another wall go – if you are. Actually I don't think I'd mind if we stopped selling houses altogether and turned the whole place into an art gallery.'

'Providing it made money,' said Antoine.'

'Of course,' said Christopher. 'Always providing that.'

Christopher put it to Tom that night. He didn't ask him how he would feel about sharing an exhibition space with Michel. If Tom thought his work would be upstaged and disadvantaged he would either say so or else invent some other reason to veto the idea. But Tom didn't veto it. He said he thought it a very good idea to extend the exhibition area and share it with Michel. He thought, but didn't say, that his own work would be looked at with more interest if it hung alongside the paintings of a more famous artist. That it would be given more respect and more consideration. That Michel's saleability would rub off. 'Has anybody asked Michel what his thoughts are?' he asked.

'No,' said Christopher. 'I thought, better ask you first. Michel would be the next step.'

'Then we'll ask him next time we see him,' Tom said.

Michel and Armand happened to be up in Wimereux that week. They split their time roughly fifty-fifty between the Channel coast and the Dordogne these days. Tom and Christopher both suspected that only Michel's devotion to his mother Sabine, still living in the big house near Boulogne's cathedral and castle, kept him anchored to the north at all. That when she eventually died Armand and he would move down to Nastringues – or somewhere else in the vicinity – for good.

For the moment though they were travelling back and forth about once a fortnight. Tom's opportunity to ask Michel if he'd like to share gallery space with him – a modest wall inside an estate agent's premises – came the following week. Michel seemed unsurprised by Tom's invitation. Perhaps Armand had told him of the over-barbecue conversation he'd had with Antoine. His answer was immediate and unhesitating. Yes, he'd like that very much.

It was the work of an afternoon only to clear a second wall of the Ste-Foy office. A dozen of Michel's framed canvasses joined Tom's and in the evening they invited a few friends round to see the pictures and have a drink. They didn't call the event a private view or *vernissage* – which would have loaded the invitation with the expectation that those invited would put their hands in their pockets and buy a canvas each. But actually two people did that anyway. One of Michel's and one of Tom's pictures went. The two spaces on the wall were filled quite easily the following morning. Both painters had plenty of reserve stock.

Antoine had brought both Patrick and Simon to the office for that informal little event. Afterwards, when they were alone together back at the Vieux Chai, Tom said to Christopher, 'Are we watching the development of a ménage à trois, do you think? I mean over at St Margaret Tyzack.'

'I wonder,' said Christopher. 'It's an interesting thought.'

Christopher actually found the thought so interesting that a few days later he asked Antoine about it when they were together in the office. Though he approached the subject slightly less bluntly than Tom had. 'How are you getting along with Simon?' he said. 'You and Patrick, I mean. Now that he's permanently in the house.'

Antoine's face didn't give a lot away in response to that. Though perhaps the fact that it didn't give much away was a giveaway in itself. 'We get along fine,' he said. 'Better than I'd have expected at first. Simon's odd. Peculiar, do you say in English? But he's not so peculiar that you can't live with him. He's also amusing and very sweet-natured, which helps. Of course Patrick's closer to him than I am.'

Why of course? Christopher wondered. Because he knew Antoine very intimately he decided to ask. 'Not my business,' he began, 'but is there something…?'

Antoine helped him by finishing his question for him. 'Something sexual between them? No. I'm pretty sure there isn't. At least, not in any physical sense. …And there's nothing sexual between myself and Simon,' Antoine added quickly. 'Just in case you were wondering.'

Christopher didn't say whether he was wondering that or whether he wasn't.

Antoine went on, 'Simon's never been very interested in sex – as far as I know. Not since he became an adult. Not since Angelo, I suppose, and he was all screwed up afterwards in the fallout from that.' Antoine didn't just share a house with Simon these days. He'd seen the TV programme; he'd read the book. 'And Patrick… He seems less and less interested in sex as the years pass. Of course he's fourteen years older than me…'

'I'm nineteen years older than you,' Christopher said. 'I'm still interested in sex.' He thought for a half second then said, 'So's Tom and he's three years older even than I am.'

Antoine looked across at Christopher. From desk to desk. 'I'm still interested in sex,' he said.

It was extraordinary how easy it was to be sitting at two desks one moment and standing up, locked in an embrace the next. They kissed each other on the lips, not tearing away for a moment, then each felt the other's hand feeling through his jeans for his suddenly aroused cock. How far this might have gone they would never discover, for at that moment they heard the noise of the handle of the street door and were just able to spring apart in time as a grey-haired couple walked in. They had seen a picture of a house in the window, the woman said in English. They very much liked the look of it.

After the customers had been dealt with and Christopher and Antoine were once again alone together in the office they didn't resume their cuddle. Nor did they refer to it. But Christopher said a few minutes later, 'If things don't work out for the three of you at St-Avit-du-Tizac … well you can always come back and live with us. With Tom and me. At Le Vieux Chai.'

'I'll bear that in mind,' said Antoine. A moment later he added, 'Thank you for what you just said. That was nice.'

Out of the blue Michel got a commission to paint a huge mural on the walls of the main hall of the Chamber of Commerce. It would depict the principal commercial activity of the region: the *vendange*, the annual grape harvest. Michel looked at the area to be covered. It was enormous. He asked if he could share the commission with a friend, another local artist. The officials who had approached him and who were showing him around the building pursed their lips and said maybe. Michel invited them to the estate agency in Ste-Foy and showed them Tom's work hanging side by side with his own. The men from the *Chambre de Commerce* were won over. They agreed to let Michel and Tom work together, splitting the fee between them. Not only that but one of them bought one of Tom's pictures on the spot. Tom was delighted – on both counts.

Michel and Tom began work on the huge mural in the middle of September. They timed this quite deliberately to coincide with the grape harvest that was actually going on around them. All over the Bordeaux region. In the Médoc. In the Entre Deux Mers. Around St-Emilion, Castillon, Ste-Foy, Sauternes, Barsac. Monbazillac… Not a town existed in the region that was not also an Appelation Controllée. Tom and Michel made sketches in the fields of the work that was going on everywhere. Armand sometimes accompanied them, armed with a camera. To give them additional information – the exact details of a picker's basket, say, or the intricacies of the vine-straddling tractors – he took photographs.

Christopher and Antoine envied them this part of the job: the outdoor bit. They would envy them less when they were cooped up for weeks in the hall of the Chamber of Commerce. Meanwhile it was Christopher and Antoine who were cooped up – when they weren't out on the road with prospective clients – inside the office.

They were both in the office one morning at the end of September when Christopher said suddenly, 'Oh, ouch!'

'What?' said Antoine.

'Sudden pain in my back.' Christopher started rubbing at it. 'Oh!' He stood up from his desk.

'Do you want me to…?' Antoine began to say. He too stood up. A second before he had been anxious. Now he was frightened. Christopher fell to his knees on the floor between his desk and the chair behind it. He wasn't saying words now but grunting and gasping. Antoine moved towards him. He knelt beside him. Laid his hand on Christopher's upper back and for a moment stroked it. His other hand was fishing in his pocket. 'I'm getting an ambulance,' he said as he pulled his phone out. But even as he was tapping out the two-digit number

Christopher's body crumpled completely and he toppled sideways onto the floor, unconscious.

Once he'd made his emergency call Antoine wanted to hang up and phone Tom immediately. But they wouldn't let him. They transferred his call to an ambulance crew and asked Antoine to keep the line open. To keep talking to the ambulance men and keep giving updates. Antoine reached for the phone on the desk beside him and got Tom that way.

Holding two phones at once, and two conversations, interrupting himself constantly to check Christopher's pulse – it was racing at first but had now become fluttery and feeble – Antoine managed to tell Tom what had happened. Both of them thought, though neither of them said, that it seemed like a ghastly repeat of what had happened just three months ago to Tom's mother. 'I'm sketching among vines near Nastringues,' Tom told Antoine. 'With Michel and Armand.'

'I'm not sure whether to tell you to come here or head straight for the hospital,' said Antoine. 'The ambulance will be here in five minutes.'

'We'll head towards the town anyway,' said Tom. 'If we're not with you before the ambulance arrives, tell me where they're taking him and we'll follow.'

The ambulance did arrive first. Christopher, still unconscious, was loaded aboard on a stretcher. Antoine climbed in and sat on a small foldaway seat beside him. He checked which hospital they were going to, then phoned Tom – Michel answered because Tom was driving – and told him.

Tom, Michel and Armand arrived almost at a run in the waiting area in which Antoine was standing, looking terribly alone and helpless. Without speaking Tom ran to him and embraced him. 'They've taken him for a scan,' Antoine managed to say, his breath blowing warm against Tom's neck and shoulder. 'They'll probably take him straight from there to theatre.'

'Oh God,' said Tom. Michel and Armand stood nearby: expressionless, mute and powerless.

For twenty minutes they waited. From time to time one of them would sink into a chair, but then a moment later get up again. Then a young woman came to see them. She wore a white coat and a stethoscope. 'Are you the patient's next of kin?' she asked. 'Of Mr McGing?' She looked from one to another.

'I am,' said Tom. He felt his heart beating like a trapped bird's wings.

'I'm Doctor Laval,' the woman said. 'I think you should be sitting down.' She glanced at Antoine, Michel and Armand. 'All of you.' They all sat immediately. As if they'd been playing musical chairs and the music had gone silent.

'I'm afraid I have bad news for you.' The doctor paused. 'Very bad. Actually the worst kind. Your… Mr McGing hasn't managed to make it. He's passed away peacefully. I'm afraid he died before we could operate to try and save him.'

'I can't believe it,' Tom whispered.

'Sorry,' piped up Antoine. 'I have to ask. What was it? What did he die of? I was with him when it happened.'

The doctor turned to him. 'It was an aneurism. A burst blood vessel. The initial pain and shock will only have lasted a moment. Once he became unconscious his death was painless.'

'Oh Jesus,' whispered Tom. And the doctor found herself suddenly having to try and comfort four men who were all older than she was and who were all crying.

The condition, they found out later, was an abdominal aortic aneurism. A triple A or AAA was what the medics routinely called it. For once the acronym read the same way in French as it did in English.

THIRTY

The four men stayed together for the rest of that day. The agency office remained closed, as Antoine had left it, locked, with the *Fermé* notice in the window, before he clambered into the ambulance. There were official routines and form-filling to be got through at the hospital, and a visit to the town hall in Castillon to register the death. Michel made the necessary initial phone call to the undertaker's. Then they retreated to Le Vieux Chai. Tom, whose thoughts were whirling madly, found himself thinking of the apostles, holed up together, numbed with shock, after the death of Jesus.

Antoine had phoned Patrick earlier, while Patrick was at work at the Tourist Board office. As soon as he finished he drove over, bringing Simon, to the Vieux Chai. All day Michel, Armand and Antoine had been thinking separately that Tom should not be left to spend the coming night alone in his house but none of them had raised the subject. But on the arrival of Patrick and Simon that early evening Antoine brought it up almost at once. 'I'm staying the night here with Tom,' he said to Patrick. 'I hope that's all right.'

'Of course it is,' said Patrick. 'I'm glad that's been decided already. Otherwise I would have suggested that one of you should stay the night.' He nodded his satisfaction at his own forethought.

Tom's wishes had not been consulted, but at this point he nodded silently. He wasn't going to reject Antoine's suggestion, evidently. Equally evidently he was still in quite deep shock. Not that the other three were in a much better state.

'Have you got something to eat for this evening?' Patrick asked solicitously. 'Because at some point you'll… I mean, what I'm saying is, if you haven't, I can…'

'It's OK,' said Tom gently. 'Chris and I were going to eat out tonight. We can still do that, can't we? The six of us? I'm sure it's what Chris would want.' Oh dear, Tom thought, hearing himself say that. The dreaded phrase … *I'm sure it's what Chris would want.* Mustn't do that too often. Must stop myself. It'll grate on people. Then it'll grate on myself…

They drove in convoy to St-Emilion and headed for one of the few restaurants in the town where none of them had dined before; where no-one knew them. Nobody was yet ready to announce the death of one of their usual party to familiar waiting staff. When their meal arrived – nobody bothered with starters – Simon unexpectedly said a short Grace in French.

After they had eaten the three pairs of men separated for the night. Patrick drove Simon back to St-Avit-du-Tizac; Michel and Armand followed them most of the way, then turned off to Nastringues; Tom drove Antoine back to the Vieux Chai. Antoine's car was still in Ste-Foy, where he'd parked it when he went to work that morning. Could it only be that morning? Could one single day contain so big an event as the death of Christopher? It felt more like a lifetime.

Back at Le Vieux Chai Tom switched on all the lights. And there was Christopher all around them. Naked and youthful in the canvasses that Gérard and Michel had painted, bare-chested and cricket-trousered in Molly's David and Jonathan. Neither Tom nor Antoine could stop themselves from staring at the paintings. 'I'm so, so sorry,' Antoine said.

'We'll have a glass of wine before bed, I think,' Tom said.

He opened a bottle of Château Fombrauge from St-Emilion. If they were going to drink wine – whether in honour of Christopher or to console themselves – it needed to be a good one.

They sat facing each other on separate sofas, the wine on the coffee table between them. 'You can have your old room,' Tom told Antoine. He didn't add: the one in which we slept together five years ago; the one you slept in with Christopher much longer ago, one night when I was in Paris. He could see from Antoine's face that he was thinking the same thoughts as he was.

'Thank you,' said Antoine.

They managed to talk of everyday things, of life-goes-on things. About the painting that Tom and Michel were working on. About the logistics of keeping the office open. 'I'll be back in there with you, obviously,' Tom said. 'Though it'll be a bit irregular while I'm still working on the mural. Perhaps Armand would help out for the duration.'

Then Tom noticed that Antoine was silently crying and he realised something. 'I'm being very selfish,' he told Antoine. 'Imagining I had a monopoly on grief. That because I loved Chris so much I owned his death as I owned his life. But I didn't own his life. I don't own his death either. You also loved him.'

'So did Armand,' Antoine said.

'Of course,' allowed Tom. 'They lived together for eight years. That was kind of official. They were deeply in love for most of that time and they still love … loved … each other. That's something we all recognised. But with you – well, your love for Chris went almost unseen by others; by me even. You have every right to cry for Christopher. Your grief's as real as mine is.'

'You don't have to…' Antoine began but then stopped, unsure of what it was that he wanted to say. He shook his head from side to side instead. Then, almost breezily, wanting to change the subject, he asked, 'What about Michel? Had he been in love with Chris at some point?'

'Not in love, I think. They slept together sometimes during the short time we were a *ménage à quatre* in Wimereux. And of course they *loved* each other.'

'But were not *in* love,' said Antoine, seeing the difference clearly.

'That doesn't mean Chris's death hasn't hurt him,' said Tom.

'No. Obviously,' said Antoine.

Tom didn't quite let it go at that. 'But for you it's different. You were … the same as Armand.' That was as near as he could get to it.

'Yes,' said Antoine quietly.

When bedtime came they parted with a hug and kissed each other briefly, almost matter-of-factly. But they went to their separate bedrooms and, to the surprise of both of them, a detail which they commented on when they met the following morning at breakfast, slept soundly.

Breakfast was hardly finished when Michel drove up with Armand. Michel was suddenly in charge of the arrangements. 'I'm going to be with you today,' he told Tom. 'We'll do whatever needs to be done in town together and if there's time left over we'll get back into the vineyards and go on with our sketching. Armand will drive Antoine to the office and help him with the business. For today at any rate. Does everyone agree?'

Everyone was Tom and Antoine. They both nodded, glad that, for this moment at least, somebody else seemed to be in charge of things.

Antoine spent that next night at Le Vieux Chai and then the next one. He went back to St-Avit to fetch a couple of changes of clothes and his bathroom stuff. He didn't move in with a suitcase, Tom noticed. Nor did he move into Tom's bedroom.

The next few days were spent arranging Chris's funeral. Dealing with the bureaucratic fallout. The bank.

The death certificate. Chris's will. That last one was quite easy. It only concerned his bank balance and personal effects. His share of the business and the house he'd lived in were already owned by the company they'd set up years earlier. The company, and Le Vieux Chai, belonged now to Tom and Antoine.

Simon worked some magic. He was a *marguillier* – that is, a church warden – in the parish of Ste-Colombe and he persuaded the powers that be to allow a non-religious funeral service to be held for Christopher in the beautiful church that he, Simon, loved so much. No priest would be officiating, and the final committal at the crematorium outside Castillon that followed it would be a secular one. Tom and Chris had talked occasionally about the subject of their one-day, far-off funerals. For once Tom could say that he really did know what Chris would have wanted.

The day of the funeral was beautiful. The sky was a brilliant blue and cloudless. Tom couldn't help looking up at it and, in spite of himself, thinking the obvious. The little church shone golden in the sunshine. The word that kept coming to Tom's mind, though he did his best to shoo it away, was heavenly.

So many people had turned up, whom Tom hadn't presumed to expect. Sabine, Michel's mother, now very fragile, came from Boulogne. Malcolm and Roger came from England as did John and Maisie Moyse. Chris's sister and his two brothers. His own brother Dominic. The contingent from England had all crossed the Channel, made their own hotel arrangements, not hassled Tom with questions about logistics. They had simply arrived at the little church at eleven o'clock in the morning.

Michel had had a service sheet printed. Included on it were some words that Tom had written for Chris many years earlier, and that Chris had read at the time of their writing. They were too intimate to be read aloud in public at the service, but somehow it seemed right to print them.

If it should happen, some time in the years ahead, that the time comes for us to say goodbye – and if we can't be in the same room at the exact right moment, that won't matter. We have no goodbyes to say, except the big 'I love you.' And we've said that, and meant it, and felt it, and lived it, so often, that that's how it'll be for all eternity. My arms are round you, holding you tight, during all bad moments on earth – and then for ever after. And we are joined at the heart for ever.

Love, and love, and love…

Your Tom

Between them Tom and Armand had written a little biography of Chris. Neither of them would risk trying to read it. Anyway it had to be done twice, once in English and once in French. In the end the French version was read out by Michel, and the English one by Malcolm. The short account told of Chris's extremely brief career as a teacher, his days as an amateur actor while at Oxford, the unusual career path he'd later shared with Tom – and for a while with Armand – as variously barman, artists' model, café manager, boatyard manager, builder and estate agent. People smiled as the list was read out. Not everybody knew he'd had to flee England with Tom in a fishing boat at dead of night at the age of nineteen because of a barbaric law long since repealed. Not everybody knew that he'd once jumped into the sea in an attempt to rescue three pilots from a crashed sea-plane off the coast of La Rochelle … or that Armand had then jumped in after him – to rescue him. Not everybody present had known that he'd lived thirty-three years of his life with Tom and eight with Armand. The details of that last case weren't spelled out. But somehow, by the end of the service, it was clear to everyone.

There was music. A life-affirming movement from one of Bach's Brandenburg concertos. A favourite moment of Chris's from Tchaikovsky's Swan Lake. One of the Four Last Songs by Strauss. This one…

We who in joy and hardship have walked hand in hand,
Are pausing on our journey, above the quiet, still land.
Below, the valleys steepen as dusk darkens the air:
Two larks alone still climbing, dream-seeking, heaven's stair.

You couldn't get away from Heaven, Tom thought, as he listened to that – sung in German by Elisabeth Schwarzkopf. However much you disbelieved in it you still wanted it. For yourself. You wanted it for Christopher.

There were readings. Chris's sister Moira read W. H. Auden's Stop all the Clocks – made mightily popular by the film Four Weddings and a Funeral. And Simon had asked Tom if – despite the secular nature of the occasion – he might read the opening verses of St John's Gospel. Tom let him, and he did it in English.

In the beginning was the Word, and the Word was with God, and the Word was God. The same was in the beginning with God. All things were made by him; and without him was not any thing made that was made. In him was life; and the life was the light of men. And the light shineth in darkness; and the darkness comprehended it not. He was in the world, and the world was made by him, and the world knew him not. He came unto his own, and his own received him not. But as many as received him, to them he gave the power to become the sons of God. And the Word was made flesh, and dwelt among us, (and we beheld his glory, the glory as of the only begotten of the Father,) full of grace and truth.

Tom listened to Simon reading that – he did it very beautifully – with the same degree of puzzlement with which he had heard it at the end of every Mass he'd attended throughout his childhood. What was this Word that was a metaphor for Jesus, a metaphor for God? Why a Word? He couldn't help thinking that if the beginning of things was a word, then your life was a string of words too: a sequence of words that struggled in the attempt to make sense of itself. Its punctuation in the earlier part were the commas of your successes and failures, in later life the semi-colons and colons of the deaths of those you loved. Eventually it would come to an end with your own personal full stop.

Tom tried to take the God aspect away from the profound, beautiful St John text. In which case – or was this thought blasphemous? – it seemed to be about Christopher. Was that why Simon had chosen it? For Christopher had been Christopher, or Chris, since time began. There had been no-one like him. His light had lit the darkness. He had come unto his own – his parents – and they had received him not. He'd lived an exile's life in France. But he had been glorious, as glorious as the sun that this morning poured in though the church's windows. He had been full of grace and truth. Tom was shaken out of his meditation by the touch of a hand, reaching and clasping his. It was Antoine's. Antoine was sitting on one side of him, Michel on the other. Tom felt tears running down his cheeks.

The reception that followed was held at Le Vieux Chai. Maps showing how to find the place were printed on the back of the funeral order of service for the benefit of those who didn't know the place and whose cars didn't have satnavs. It was a lively occasion. Even Tom managed to find moments of shared laughter with his and Chris's other friends and relatives. But one thing struck him forcefully; he observed it with wry amusement. Nobody, but nobody, was referring to the deceased love of his life as Christopher. Without exception everyone now spoke of him, evidently now thought of him, as Chris.

THIRTY-ONE

Armed with their preliminary sketches and Armand's photographs Tom and Michel moved into the Chamber of Commerce building. Michel was in charge, up and down step-ladders, dividing the big wall space into squares, deciding which areas would be painted by himself and which by his 'junior' partner. The task ahead required all their attention and powers of concentration, and kept them fully occupied throughout the day. Michel thought the timing of this out-of-the-blue commission could not have been better for Tom: in giving him 'something to do' in the aftermath of Chris's death the sudden job offer had been little short of miraculous. Tom shared Michel's view. Additionally he was immeasurably grateful to Michel for inviting him to share the commission with him. There had been no need for Michel to do that. Inwardly he gave thanks to his one-time lover daily, hourly, from the depths of his heart.

The scene they were painting was a modern take on the famous medieval picture – from the series called Les Très Riches Heures du Duc de Berry – in which cheerful-looking peasants harvest a vineyard under the watchful towers of the castle of Saumur on the Loire. In Michel's concept the castle was replaced by the towers and spires of St-Emilion, rising behind a gentle hill of green vines. In the foreground pickers in modern dress and modern vehicles replaced the medieval peasants and their ox-carts; but in essence they were doing the same immemorial job.

Initially, when Michel was carving the work up between Tom and himself, Tom had said modestly that he would do the bits that didn't matter so much, the endless repeating patterns of leaves, the long perspectives of whitish stony soil and strips of grass.

Michel did not let him get away with that. 'Do some of the people too,' he instructed Tom. 'Do their faces. This is a really big chance for you. You don't need to capture anybody's likeness. You can take a face from the inside of your head – someone you see in the street regularly, someone you remember from your past – and use that as a base. No-one but you will ever know who the face is based on unless you tell them. Only you will know if you manage … or even if you want … to capture a likeness.' Tom accepted his teacher's direction and got on with the job.

In the evenings Tom still had Antoine for company at Le Vieux Chai. They took it in turns to cook. Sometimes Tom didn't feel like eating, let alone cooking, but Antoine made him do both and Tom was grateful for that.

Antoine let Tom talk about Chris and about his feelings, about his grief. He more than let him; he encouraged him: he knew that Tom needed to express what he felt. So Tom told Antoine frankly about the black hole experiences he was having on an almost daily basis. The moments when the world stopped existing and he would find himself tumbling down a bottomless well of emptiness, in terror for those few seconds each time because the floor on which he stood had given way beneath his feet. Antoine said, 'When it happens again, if it happens, and you're with Michel, tell him. Make him stop work and hold you. Then after a minute or two you'll be all right.' He paused. 'If it happens when I'm with you, tell me and I'll do the same.'

'It doesn't happen when I'm with you,' Tom said. 'Or when I'm with Michel. Perhaps I should pretend it does, because the remedy sounds nice. But it always happens when I'm on my own. Sometimes in the car, going to work. Or walking along the pavement in Ste-Foy.'

Tom did take a break from painting sometimes to go and check on things at the office. They seemed to be going fine: Antoine firmly in command of things, dealing with the buyers and vendors and their lawyers; Armand, in his new role as office temp, doing the filing, answering the phone, dealing with emails and the post.

'It's as though there was no Tom before Christopher,' Tom said to Antoine one night. 'It's as if I've lost most of myself. We were like finger and finger-nail – one without the other is no use.' Another time he quoted from Wuthering Heights. '"I am Heathcliff," Cathy said.'

'I understand exactly,' said Antoine. 'I also understand heights. But I've never understood quite what wuthering meant.' Tom laughed and Antoine was glad about that.

Tom and Antoine always slept in their separate rooms. They parted each night with the same brief hug and chaste kiss. They didn't touch each other at other times. But they breakfasted companionably together every morning, then drove off separately to work.

One morning as they sipped their coffee and dunked their buttered *biscottes* in it Antoine said, 'You're not going to like this, but you knew that one day soon I'd have to say it. I need to go back home. To Patrick. To St-Avit-du-Tizac.'

'You're right on all counts,' said Tom in a resigned-sounding voice. 'I didn't want to hear you say it. I was dreading the day you did. But you do need to go back. I can't be selfish with you. You've got to take care of your own relationship.'

Antoine spent one more night at Le Vieux Chai. The next morning he put his things in his car and took them away with him when he went to work.

Tom had told Michel that news within an hour of Antoine's announcing it. He'd relayed it across the space between the two step-ladders they were working from.

'If you want to come and stay with us at Nastringues for a while you'd be more than welcome,' Michel had said.

'That's kind,' said Tom, just then carefully applying a white nose highlight to a face he was painting. 'I'll bear it in mind for the future if I can't hack it by myself. But it's nearly three weeks since Chris died. It's time I learnt to fend for myself. Stand on my own two feet.'

'Have you got food in the house?' Michel asked him when they met again the next day at work at the *Chambre de Commerce*. The day on which Antoine had left. 'I mean for tonight.'

'Yes,' said Tom. 'Antoine went shopping yesterday. He got me a duck breast. He knows I like that.'

As Tom ate his solitary supper that evening he felt, in the clanging silence of the Vieux Chai, in its grand emptiness, that he'd been bereaved all over again. For the third time in less than three months.

Chris's ashes were returned to Tom by the undertakers. Chris hadn't said what he wanted done with them; he hadn't expected to die at the age of sixty. Tom knew what he himself wanted done with them; he had told Chris's sister and brothers of his intentions at the funeral and they had accepted them without argument.

Tom suspected, and so did the others, that it might have been illegal to tip a person's ashes into the Dordogne river. They didn't ask anyone about it, in case they got an answer they didn't want to hear, and they guessed that not even a village mayor like François could legitimise it if it wasn't kosher in the first place. They did it in the middle of the night to save any potential awkwardness. 'They' were Tom and the three of his close friends who had also been to bed with Christopher: Michel, Armand and Antoine. Antoine did tell Patrick where he was off to, slipping out of the house after midnight, but requested that he didn't tell Simon.

That was out of concern for Simon's feelings: he would be fishing the river in the morning.

They chose a place halfway between Ste-Foy-la-Grande and Castillon: a village called Pessac where a bridge crossed the river very picturesquely, with a car-park most conveniently situated right next to it. 'Check the wind carefully,' warned Armand as soon as they were in position by the parapet, and he did it himself immediately with an upraised licked-wet finger. His findings led them to cross the road to the opposite pavement, from where they released Chris's mortal remains over the downwind parapet. It was all done very quickly, and they returned to Le Vieux Chai for a very late, very brief, but much needed, nightcap. Michel and Armand had their car parked there. They took Antoine back to St-Avit-du-Tizac, making a slight detour on their way back to Nastringues to do it.

By the beginning of November the huge mural was finished. A reception was arranged to celebrate its completion in the elegant great hall it graced. That it enhanced. That it embellished... Well, Tom and Michel hoped it did those things. Tom and Michel were invited to sip a glass of champagne at the unveiling. Members of the Chamber of Commerce were invited with their spouses. There was a bit of awkwardness, though, when it came to Michel's and Tom's other halves. Michel's was a man – to whom he was not married – while Tom's, though also of the male sex, wouldn't be considered for an invitation at all because he was dead.

It was François who saved the situation. Tom and he ran into each other by chance in the lane between their two houses and the village. François asked Tom solicitously how he was getting on. Tom told him about the completion of the mural. François nodded. He knew about the mural, and would be going to the unveiling himself. 'Of course Monsieur Armand must have an invitation,' he said when Tom told him about the little awkwardness that had arisen for Michel. 'I shall see to it myself.' Then François thought for a moment. 'But then you have no-one to go with. Since Chris… And that can not be nice. I wonder …' He peered rather closely at Tom in the autumn sunshine. 'Supposing I brought my nephew Antoine along as my guest? Would that be … er…?'

'It would be,' said Tom. 'It would be lovely.'

What had Father Louis said all those years ago? Preaching to a chapel full of terrified children. He'd been talking about mortal sin. 'A terrible perishing awaits you. It is the shrivelling of the soul in this life, and death eternal in the next. Eternal death indeed, but nevertheless – nevertheless – undying pain.' Tom didn't believe in mortal sin these days. He believed there was evil in the world, he believed there was wrongdoing. He believed there was right and wrong, even if in the foggy turmoil of life it was not always easy to see which was which without the benefit of hindsight. But he didn't believe that if you did wrong you went to Hell as a result. And yet the old headmaster's words rang true for Tom now, applied to his own new context. Applied to the misery of his own new life. For Chris had perished, and Tom had perished with him. His soul had indeed shrivelled, like a doll thrown onto a blazing fire. The pain he felt was like nothing he'd ever imagined, let alone experienced. He had no doubt that he would feel it for eternity.

The night before the unveiling of the harvest mural at the *Chambre de Commerce* Tom sat down and wrote a list of adjectives, with which he attempted to encompass Christopher. Fun, funny, handsome, brave, strong, gentle, wonderful, lovely, sensitive, clever, magnetic, bold, wise, loveable, loving, cheerful, sexy, beautiful, nice, gorgeous, adorable, lost.

The champagne was handed round on trays by pretty girls in the livery of a local catering company. Everybody said nice things about the mural, naturally: that was the whole point of the occasion. Antoine had been in to see it a couple of times as a work in progress, but his Uncle François hadn't. François collared Tom at one point. Figuratively speaking, and nicely. 'You still call yourself an amateur, Tom, and your friend Michel the professional. But when I look at this wall…' he spread his hands as expansively as his glass allowed, '…I can't tell the difference between his work and yours. I can't see where one of you ends and the other begins, so to speak. I mean, did one of you do all the figures and the other all the foliage?'

'No,' said Tom. 'That's how I wanted it to be at first. I'd do the leafage and Michel the people, but he wouldn't let it be like that. He insisted we did half the figures each.'

'So which ones did you do?' François asked. 'Can you point them out?'

Tom did.

'Well, now you actually show me I can see a minute difference of style around the faces. And even then I only think I see it, now that you've pointed the figures out. But difference of style or not, yours look just as good.' François thought for a moment. 'Should I recognise any of the faces? Did you think of people you knew when you were doing them? People around Ste-Foy? Castillon…?'

Tom smiled roguishly at François. 'Well, if we did, you'll never know. It's a secret between us. Between Michel and me.'

François laughed. 'Quite right,' he said. 'You're very wise. Better to keep it like that.' He congratulated Tom again, touched his forearm lightly, then walked away to talk to someone else.

Tom was unused to seeing Antoine in a suit, except for during the recent spate of funerals. Tom thought he looked very nice. He 'scrubbed up well' as people said. But Tom had a complex response to the sight of handsome younger men in suits. He always had the feeling that they'd look even nicer in something more casual. In an ideal world he would rip the suits off and re-dress their wearers in something more like jeans and T-shirts. Tightish jeans. He was no fan of the current fad for jeans that sagged and showed the wearer's grubby underpants and threatened to fall down at any minute: a fashion that had been copied from the sartorial necessities of American prisons, where violent or suicide-risk prisoners were deprived of their belts. He liked to see jeans that showed off their contents, both front and back. Though having ripped the suits off, he thought, he might not get as far as re-clothing his imaginary young men. They tended to look even better with their clothes completely missing. Tom might have been going through a major crisis of heart and mind in the wake of his loss of Chris, but it hadn't diminished his appetite for the sight at least of handsome male figures, or instilled a resigned acceptance of a long-term future without sex.

Talking to Antoine this evening, champagne glass in hand, Tom tried not to let his thoughts stray from the general to the particular. He had seen Antoine naked once – had spent the night with him naked and had a second good look at him in the buff the next morning when they were getting up. He didn't want to think about any possible repetition of that. Antoine had made it clear that he still belonged to Patrick by going back to him a few weeks before. And Tom's heart, mind and body were not yet ready for the challenges of sexual congress.

'Chris would have been proud of you,' Antoine said, waving the hand that didn't have a glass in it towards the mural that surrounded them.

'Thank you,' said Tom. 'I do hope so. Right now I'm going through a phase of remembering all the times I was hard on him. All the times I said things that must have hurt him.'

'Did he never say things that hurt you?' Antoine said gently. 'Was he never hard towards you?'

'Over the years… perhaps occasionally. But I don't remember those things…'

'Then forget the others,' said Antoine firmly. 'He loved you unconditionally, just as you loved him.'

'I didn't love him enough,' said Tom flatly.

Antoine caught hold of him by the upper arm. 'Listen,' he said. 'Nobody has ever been able to love anyone as much as they need loving.'

Tom managed to smile in spite of himself. 'That's very clever,' he said. 'Did you invent that?'

'No,' said Antoine. 'I got it from Simon. But I did make up the next bit.'

'Which is…?' Tom asked, genuinely curious.

'That's why God was invented.'

'I see,' said Tom, smiling again. 'You've come along way since you were a jobbing builder's labourer.' They laughed together.

It was good to have Antoine's company this evening, Tom thought. Antoine was still full of solicitude for him, for his well being in his newly vulnerable state. (A hermit crab without a shell was how Antoine thought of him these days. He didn't tell Tom that.) But the unveiling ceremony was not a long drawn-out occasion. The champagne had been drunk, and replacement bottles had stopped coming, by seven o'clock. 'We're going out for a meal,' Antoine told Tom. 'Patrick, Simon and myself. Join us.' Tom said he would.

Then Michel was beside them. 'Armand and I are eating out this evening. Join us?' His question was addressed principally to Tom, but immediately after he'd made it he included Antoine in it with an enquiring look. A discussion ensued. The inevitable result of which was that all six of them went out together to eat – in a newly opened pasta place.

The meal was convivial, companionable, celebratory. But Tom couldn't help thinking that Antoine seemed somehow distracted. He joined in the conversation and the laughter, but something about him seemed different now that he was back in the company of his partner Patrick. He looked ill-at-ease with him. It was the first time Tom had ever thought that. He seemed uncomfortable in his skin, as the French put it. Well, Tom would be seeing Antoine again in the morning. If there was anything Antoine wanted to talk about, he could do it in the privacy of the estate agency office. For now that the big mural project was finished, Tom was going back to join Antoine at work.

Tom returned alone to the Vieux Chai that night. He slept well and dreamt cheerfully. He'd been gratified by the success of the mural, and the compliments that had come flying his way like bouquets – François and Antoine had not been the only people to tell him that his work looked as professional as Michel's did. And he was surprised to find that he was also cheered by the thought of returning to an office to work. It wasn't often, he thought, and it didn't happen to everyone, that you felt cheerful about a thing like that. He drove to Ste-Foy-la-Grande the next morning with the nearest thing he could imagine, these days, to a light heart.

It was good to be back in harness again with Antoine. Even though for the next few days Antoine did seem a little withdrawn and distant. Tom asked him once or twice if everything was OK. Each time Antoine said yes, so Tom didn't pursue it. He wondered, inevitably, if things were difficult between him and Patrick now that Simon lived with them. Perhaps precisely because of Simon. But maybe Antoine was simply finding it difficult to get used to working with Tom in the office again, instead of with Armand as he'd been doing for the past few weeks and, in the weeks before that, just Chris. They would get used to each other again in time, Tom thought.

Tom continued to socialise with the others. Michel and Armand returned to Wimereux for a fortnight but then they came back. October turned to November and the evenings darkened. Lights went on in the streets of Ste-Foy before even the banks shut. It was light at breakfast-time, just about, but it had been dark when you got up.

Grief lasts a long time, and Tom continued to grieve for his catastrophic loss. But he was no longer in shock; the pain of it was growing less raw as the weeks passed. No longer a sharp, knife-wound blaze of hurt it had diminished to a continuous gnawing ache. And he found that by now, two months after the death of Christopher he could interact with other people – with people who were not his close friends and ex-lovers – without it hurting too much. Michel asked him one evening, when he and Armand were entertaining him to dinner at Nastringues, 'Do you think you will … I mean in the fullness of time … be looking for someone else?'

'Hmm,' said Tom. 'I think so. Yes. Even at my age…'

'Our age,' said Armand. That was nice of him. Michel was Tom's age; Armand, three years younger, had been born in the same year as Chris.

'Thank you,' said Tom to Armand with a smile that had something arch about it. He turned back to Michel – his partner for eight years of his distant past. 'A younger version of you would do very nicely.'

'Ha,' said Michel with one of his mini-snorts. 'A younger version of Chris, more like.'

'At Christmas, by the way,' said Armand, changing the subject, 'it's been decided. You're coming to Wimereux to stay with us.'

'Thank you,' said Tom, who had just woken up to the fact that Christmas was approaching and was beginning to have uneasy thoughts about it. 'I'd like that very much.'

One day at work in the office, when December had begun and there wasn't much work about, Tom found himself discussing with Antoine a subject that had been talked about before but then, with the turmoil of Chris's death intervening, dropped and not returned to since. It was the question of changing the nature of the business they were engaged in. Of ceasing to run the Ste-Foy premises as an estate agency and turning it into a picture gallery instead. 'We could turn it into a sort of retirement project,' Tom said. 'For all of us. None of us would have to put in too many hours. If we involved Michel and Armand… Patrick too. Simon…' A thought struck Tom. 'Has Simon said any more about wanting to be a priest?'

'No,' said Antoine. 'Not for months. His thoughts seem pretty far removed from that.'

'But he's still got the religious bug, hasn't he?' Tom enquired. 'Still spends half his life in church?'

'Oh yes, he does all that.' Then Antoine went strangely silent. Tom watched an unaccustomed blush suffuse his cheeks. It reminded him of someone else.

'Are you OK?' Tom asked Antoine gently. 'Are you really OK?'

'I'm fine,' said Antoine, composing himself and smiling. Then he said, 'Tom, would it be all right if I came and stayed with you tonight?'

Tom's heart did something then that it hadn't done in ages. It seemed as though it was going to burst. Not from pain, not from grief or longing. But from things he'd almost forgotten he'd ever experienced or known about. Pure joy. Pure happiness. He wanted to scoop Antoine up with both arms and squeeze him till his ribs cracked. He didn't do that. He said, 'Of course.'

THIRTY-TWO

'Which car shall we take?' Tom asked as they locked the office for the night.

'I don't know…' began Antoine uncertainly, but then changed his mind and said firmly, 'No. Let's take both.'

'We'll park up at the Vieux Chai,' said Tom, 'and then I'm taking you out to dinner. We'll only want one car for that. I'll take you to L'Envers du Décor in St-Emilion. How about that?'

'Oh,' said Antoine, sounding slightly startled. Then, 'I mean, that's great.'

The Envers du Décor (which meant *behind the scenes*, in the theatrical sense) was a place Chris and Tom had tended to go to, over the years, when there was something to celebrate. Tom wasn't sure whether he'd suddenly proposed the venue this evening because he wanted to console Antoine for whatever had gone wrong in his life – as something clearly had – or whether he wanted to celebrate his own happiness at the news that Antoine wanted, or at least needed, his company for this one night.

The restaurant – a wine bar that had grown exponentially over the previous twenty years, and expanded into a whole row of old houses in the town's top square – was a cosy place to enter on a winter's night. They sat opposite each other at a table in a corner and Tom was reminded of an evening in Monpon… That was five years ago now, he thought. He didn't ask Antoine what his problem was, though he could make a pretty good guess. Anyway, he knew that it would come out in due course. He ordered them both a *kir royal* to toy with while they looked over the menu. *'Santé,'* he said to Antoine when the kirs had arrived and they clinked glasses.

'Santé,' said Antoine. Then he said, 'I think I'm losing Patrick.'

Although Tom had thought that might be the case it gave him such a shock to hear Antoine actually say it that he immediately said, 'Oh my darling.' Then, mortified at hearing those words pop out, said quickly, *'Merde.* I didn't mean to say that. Forget it.'

Antoine said nothing. He didn't say that, yes, he would forget it; nor did he say that, no, he would not. Because of course he wouldn't forget it. And Tom wouldn't.

Tom didn't ask, why? or, how come? Antoine would tell him when he wanted to, or when he was ready to, or else not. It was the last thing Tom was interested in, actually. He took a sip of kir and Antoine copied the gesture almost as accurately as a mirror does.

The sommelier arrived to ask them what wine they wanted to drink. 'Château Mangot 2000,' Tom answered without hesitation.

'That's an expensive one,' said Antoine, frowning his concern.

Tom looked back up at the sommelier. 'Ignore him. It's within the budget.' Privately he thought that they might actually be celebrating something. He just didn't know what it was.

'I'll put the radiator on in your bedroom,' Tom said as soon as they got back. The rest of the Vieux Chai was already warm. Thank heaven for central heating and time-switches on December nights. 'The bed's made up. Sheets have been changed since you left in September, you'll be glad to know.'

'I am,' said Antoine and grinned at Tom.

'Do you want a nightcap?' Tom asked a bit uncertainly. Seeing the signs of an imminent no-thank-you in Antoine's face he added, 'Tea? Coffee? Soft drink?'

'Just a glass of water,' said Antoine. 'I'll take it up.'

Which he did. They parted at the foot of the stairs. They said a warm goodnight each but there was no parting hug or kiss. Somehow the balance of everything seemed too sensitive at this particular moment: there seemed suddenly to be a lot at stake, a lot of accumulated capital that, with one wrong move, could go up in smoke.

Tom sat and drank a small whisky by himself in the big downstairs living space. He tried to think but couldn't. He was conscious only of a roaring noise in his head and of the fact that he seemed to be seeing the room he sat in, and the pictures on its walls, through a fog.

They drove to work in convoy in the morning. They busied themselves with replying to emails and dealing with the day's post. For the first hour the phone didn't ring and no prospective customer came in off the street. Neither of them had brought up the question of whether Antoine would be spending a second night at Le Vieux Chai.

Antoine suddenly spoke. 'This gallery idea,' he said. 'I'd still be up for that if you were.' He didn't turn to look at Tom as he said it, but kept his eyes on the screen in front of him.

'It'd be a big decision,' said Tom. 'But there's only you and me who'll be making it.' They were the joint owners of the company these days. If Michel and Armand became involved in the idea at a future date that might be a different matter. But for the moment…

'Worth talking to the others about it?' Antoine asked.

'Michel and Armand?' Tom checked. 'Maybe Patrick, when he retires…' He stopped, realising he'd strayed into an area that Antoine hadn't indicated that he could enter yet. 'Maybe,' he tailed off.

And then the phone rang, Tom answered it, and it was Patrick. 'For you,' Tom said, signalling with his eyes that Antoine should pick up the phone on his desk. As soon as Antoine had done that and Tom had put his own receiver to rest he walked out of the office into the street so that Antoine could have his conversation with his partner in private. Standing outside the door on the pavement Tom found himself wishing, for a rare moment, that he smoked. Smokers had motivation for walking out of rooms and standing about on the pavement. All Tom could do was to stand out there looking like an idiot.

Tom could see through the window the moment at which Antoine put the phone down. He waited a further polite minute, then went back into the office. Antoine looked up at him. 'Patrick wants me to go and have lunch with him near his office,' he said. 'I think it might be quite a long lunch. Are you all right with that?'

'Of course,' said Tom. 'Take as long as you like. And … er … I hope, obviously, that things work out all right.'

Before lunchtime crept round, though, someone did walk in off the street. A man who hadn't come to buy a house he said, but a painting. He had admired Tom's and Michel's work inside the Chamber of Commerce building and had been told, when he'd asked, where he could see further examples of it. He spent some time peering at the canvasses on the walls around him. There were no naked boys among them. Tom didn't paint such things while Michel, who still did, was of the opinion that Ste-Foy-la-Grande was probably not quite ready for them yet.

The customer wanted to buy two paintings eventually. One of Michel's, one of Tom's. Because he was buying a pair, he said, while an eager little twinkle came into his eyes, could he have a reasonable discount? Tom raised his eyebrows slightly, then laughed. 'I'd need to check that with the other artist,' he said. 'He's in Boulogne at the moment – actually Wimereux. I can phone him and get back to you.' The prospective customer seemed quite happy with that and they exchanged phone numbers. As the man left the shop, Antoine checked his watch. Tom saw him do this. 'Get along with you,' he said. 'Go to your lunch.'

After Antoine had gone Tom found himself with nothing much to do. After a few minutes he dialled Michel's number. Michel picked up almost at once. Tom told him about the request for a discount. He told him which picture of Michel's was involved and the amount that the man wanted taken off the price. Michel was fine with it. Then, because he found he was glad of having Michel to talk to for a few minutes, Tom mentioned the possibility of changing the nature of his business – his and Antoine's – and turning the place into a dedicated picture gallery instead of an estate agent's office. The idea caught Michel's interest. He'd be keen to discuss any such possibility when they next met. Then Michel said, 'You sound a bit agitated. *Distrait*. Is everything OK? I mean with yourself.'

Tom told Michel about Antoine. He passed on the bald bare news that Antoine was having trouble with his relationship with Patrick and told him Antoine had stayed the night.

'So will he be staying another night?' was Michel's unsurprising reaction to that.

'That might depend on the conversation he's having at the moment.' Tom told Michel where Antoine was at that moment, and who with.

'Well,' said Michel, 'if it doesn't work out for the two of them, will you be making a move?'

On…?'

'On Antoine, of course. I didn't mean Patrick!'

'No, no, of course not,' said Tom hastily. 'But … hey, it's only three months since Chris died. Isn't it a bit soon…?'

'Soon for you?' Michel cut him off. 'Or are you thinking, what are other people going to think? If it's the first of those, only you can know the answer, but if it's the second – I can tell you nobody's going to give a damn about it. We're not back in the nineteenth century when you had to wear black for a whole year before you were supposed to even think about… I haven't noticed you wearing black. Unless you're doing it secretly. Wearing black underpants?'

Tom laughed but he did do a quick below-waistband check. 'Actually, yes,' he said. 'I am today, as it happens. But that has nothing to do with the death of Chris. It's a pure coincidence.'

'There you are, then,' said Michel. 'You have nothing to fear from anything anyone might think. Follow your heart. And make sure Antoine follows his.'

'Easier said than done,' said Tom. 'Even the first bit. As for Antoine's heart, I don't know what's in it. He won't tell me, and there's no-one else to ask.'

'Oh, I think there is,' said Michel.

'Who?' Tom asked.

'You'll probably find him a couple of hundred metres from your office. Down on the quayside, thinking about God while he catches fish.'

The roadway that twisted its way out of the square towards the river actually ran through the ancient vaulted arcade and under the houses. Before it reached the river it turned away at the last second, leaving pedestrians who wanted to walk by the riverbank to make their way down by a steep flight of stone steps. Tom descended the steps and found Simon a little way along the quay, perched on the edge of it, rod in hand, and with his stall-full of finny produce at his back.

Simon looked up at Tom's approach but showed no sign of surprise. Tom examined the stall first. 'You've got a good selection this morning,' he told Simon. In addition to the usual shad and lampreys there were silver-skinned, orange-finned roach, an olive-striped perch or two, a bucket of eels and one majestic but lethal-looking green and yellow pike.

'Hmm,' said Simon, allowing himself to look pleased. 'Not bad for a morning's work.'

Tom thought it was pretty amazing for a morning's work. He thought of the miraculous draught of fishes. He wondered, did being religious make a difference when it came to catching fish? 'Actually, I came to ask you something,' he said. 'I suppose you know that Antoine spent the night at Le Vieux Chai?'

'I didn't exactly know,' said Simon carefully. 'Nor did Patrick. But we rather guessed.'

'Not that anything happened between us,' Tom told Simon equally carefully. 'Separate rooms, separate beds… Look, you may think it's none of my business, but … what's going on exactly? I mean *chez vous*. At St Margaret Tyzack. Antoine hasn't said, and I don't know where anybody's at.'

Simon looked at Tom earnestly. 'What do you want to know?' he asked.

'Well … OK…' said Tom, 'are you and Patrick an item, for a start? Or you and Antoine, perhaps?'

'We don't all have sex together,' said Simon, looking a bit affronted. 'If that's what you're getting at. And I don't have sex with Antoine or Patrick. We all have separate rooms…'

'Even Antoine and Patrick?' Tom was too surprised not to ask.

'They haven't shared a room for … well, perhaps six months,' Simon said. 'Whether they've had sex together in that time…' He shrugged.

'No, of course,' said Tom. 'I don't think I was asking that.' Although he did wonder privately if perhaps he was. He was silent for a few moments, watching Simon fish. He rather wished that Simon would suddenly get a bite and catch something but he didn't.

'Antoine and Patrick are having lunch together,' Tom resumed eventually. 'Even as we speak. Trying to put things right between them. Well, I suppose that's what it's about.'

'Putting things right between people doesn't always mean their staying together, or getting back together, whichever might be the case,' said Simon. He wasn't looking at Tom now but staring at the point where his fly lay on the river's surface some twelve yards out. 'Actually I never really thought Antoine and Patrick were right for each other.' He said this in a very matter-of-fact tone of voice.

'Oh bloody hell, Simon!' Tom couldn't help showing his annoyance. 'You come into their ménage, like a cuckoo in the nest, and bloody fuck it up. So if Antoine isn't right for Patrick, then who is? Mister Simon Rickman, perhaps?'

Simon did turn and look up at Tom at that point.

'It's not like that,' he said. 'You make it all sound coarse and crass. And simple. Which it's not. You know life's not like that. Nothing's simple. Life's infinitely complex. But God has his plan. He'll sort it out. He always does.'

'For fuck's sake, Simon, you are the limit,' said Tom, and prepared to turn and depart. But then he thought of something. 'Oh hang on. I nearly forgot. Can you sell me some fish?'

Simon got to his feet and they moved to the stall together. Tom bought a roach, an eel and the two perch. Antoine was a whiz at *friture* of mixed river fish. Though whether Antoine would be around to cook it was anybody's guess. If he wasn't, then Tom would do it for himself.

Tom bought a sandwich from the baker's in the arcaded square and took it back to eat, with a cup of instant coffee, in the office. Antoine wasn't back from his lunch yet. There were a couple of messages to deal with, and then Tom phoned the man who had come in to buy two pictures and told him that Michel was OK with the discount. Then the office door opened and Antoine walked in through it. For a second the two men just looked at each other. Then Antoine, walking across the floor to his desk, said, 'Patrick and I are splitting up.'

'Oh no,' said Tom. 'That's awful. I'm terribly sorry to be hearing that.' And part of him really did mean that most sincerely. But another part of him was thrilled to bits.

Antoine sat down at his desk, looked steadily at Tom in silence for a moment – with a very woeful face – then said, 'I wonder… I don't know… Could I come and live with you…? I don't mean live with you… I mean live at the Vieux Chai?'

'Of course you can,' said Tom, trying to ignore the stab beneath the diaphragm that Antoine's backtracking phrase *I don't mean live with you* had given him – cruelly soon after his heart had leapt on hearing the first bit. 'I'd love it if you did. And even if I didn't love it I couldn't stop you. You own half the property anyway. We're joint owners of it. Or had you forgotten that?'

Antoine smiled a bit shyly. 'I suppose I could pretend I'd forgotten that fact. But I hadn't.'

'I'm glad,' said Tom, returning his smile equally shyly. 'I'm glad you're not as innocent as all that.'

It seemed like an action replay of yesterday, Tom thought as, together, they locked up the shop. 'Your car or mine?'

'Let's take both.'

Tom said, 'I've got some river fish…'

Antoine made a maybe-maybe kind of face. Tom said smoothly, 'Or we could save that for tomorrow and eat out again tonight.' He watched Antoine's face perk up at once.

'Same place as last night?' said Antoine. 'I'll pay this time.'

'There'll be talk,' said Tom. He was half joking. He was also half serious.

'So?' said Antoine.

Talk about mixed signals, Tom thought. His feelings were a painful mix of exasperation, disappointment and barbed hope. He kept the thought, and the feelings, to himself. 'L'Envers du Décor it is,' he said.

The sommelier twinkled at them discreetly as he took their wine order. Antoine asked, 'Have you got another bottle of that Mangot 2000? That was good.'

The sommelier found he couldn't help himself. 'Celebration of some sort?'

Antoine's brow furrowed. 'Not quite sure about that. Maybe. But perhaps a bit soon to say yet.' The sommelier bowed slightly, discreetly, and left them to it. Tom would sooner have pulled his teeth out than ask Antoine what his enigmatic utterance meant.

They were back at Le Vieux Chai. Tom put the lights on and once again Chris was everywhere on the walls around them, bare-chested, arm in arm with Tom in the David and Jonathan, naked and frolicking in the sea with

Tom at Audreselles, with Benoît and René, Michel and Armand…

Antoine sat down on one of the sofas. Tom sat opposite him on another one. 'I don't know what to say,' Antoine said.

'Then don't say anything,' said Tom matter-of-factly. 'Just be Antoine for a minute.' They sat in silence for a minute or two. At first they very earnestly scrutinised each other's faces, looking for clues that perhaps only the subconscious could pick up. Then a cautious smile began to appear on Antoine's face. A second later it was mirrored by Tom's. Then Antoine got up and came towards Tom's sofa and sat down next to him on it. 'You know what I said this afternoon…'

'What did you say this afternoon?' Tom stretched out an arm as if without thinking. It landed on the back of the sofa behind Antoine's neck.

'That I'd chosen my words carelessly when I said I wanted to come and live with you…'

'Oh that,' said Tom. He felt his body tense ever so slightly.'

'I was trying to be cautious. Trying not to expose myself.'

'I see,' said Tom. He brushed Antoine's off-side ear lightly with a finger tip.

Antoine said, 'I was afraid of saying too much. Thinking I was going into a place, mentally I mean, where I didn't have a right to… A place you didn't want anyone else to be. I mean, since Chris.'

Tom stroked Antoine's ear a little more obviously. 'You don't need to be careful,' he said encouragingly. He sniggered in advance at the double entendre that he was about to come out with. 'Expose yourself.'

Antoine laughed for a second then became serious again. 'All right. I did mean what I'd said. I was lying when I said I didn't. But I was afraid of what you'd say.

Of what you'd think. So yes, OK. I do want to come and live *with you*. Not just live *here at the Vieux Chai*. That's the truth. Make what you want of it.'

Tom was silent for a second. Then he said, 'Thank you. And I want you to come and live with me. I could want nothing better, nothing other, than that.' They sat silently for a moment, both dazed with the shock of what had just been said between them. Then slowly they leaned in to each other and began to kiss. After a minute Tom slapped Antoine's thigh lightly but in a businesslike manner. 'Come upstairs now,' he said. 'Let's go to bed.'

Months had passed since Tom had felt the warm press of another's tummy against his own, or had handled another man's cock. How long it had been for Antoine he didn't know. He wouldn't be asking that tonight. He would be told one day, obviously: he was old enough to know that at least.

They were careful with each other; they didn't try to behave like horny kids, even though that was exactly the way they both felt. Everything worked, at least. For both of them. Tom heaved an undetectable inner sigh of relief about that. Afterwards they lay together, half in each other's arms, half out of them. 'I hope you'll be OK with me,' Antoine said.

'I hope you'll be OK with me,' said Tom. 'We carry an incredible amount of baggage with us … at our time of life.'

'Most of it being Chris,' said Antoine. '*Merde.* I didn't mean it to sound like that.'

'It didn't sound like that,' Tom said. His fingers triangulated Antoine's right shoulder blade. They'd both stayed slim through the years. Tom was relieved about that … for his part at any rate.

From the darkness Tom heard Antoine's voice just inches from his head. 'I want us to go on forever. To carry on from where Chris left off. Is that very disrespectful to Chris, do you think?'

'No,' said Tom. 'I don't think it's disrespectful towards Chris. You loved him, you slept with him… He'll always be part of us.'

Antoine said, 'There's so many things I want to say. So many things I hope for. I mean, hope for for us. I want to be here for you always. Day and night.'

'Are we planning to spend the rest of our lives in bed?' Tom asked.

'No,' said Antoine. 'Only about half of it. I want to be there for you when you need me in the daytime. And to be there for you when you're frightened in the night.'

'Zut, hey,' said Tom. His fingers ground in among the vertebrae of Antoine's back. 'I should be saying that to you. I'm the older one. By … how many years?'

'Don't go on about it,' Antoine said.

'But all the same…'

'I wasn't thinking of it as a one-way thing, actually,' said Antoine. By now he'd gone into French. *'J'imaginais une situation réciproque.'*

Tom didn't go to Wimereux to spend Christmas with Michel and Armand. He spent it with Antoine at Le Vieux Chai.

THIRTY-THREE

They didn't spend much time planning their journey of the following June. They just decided to go. They had already done this once. Back in January they had closed the office – put the *Fermé* notice in the window – and flown to Tenerife for a fortnight. It had been their first holiday together. A testing time for any new couple. On their return they agreed they'd passed that test. Now they were going to do it again. But this time, at the beginning of summer, they were heading north. They would drive this time. (That had not been an option on the trip to Tenerife.) They packed Tom's car: it was newer and sturdier than Antoine's. Antoine commented on Tom's decision to put his easel and paints and a couple of stretched canvasses in the boot. 'We're not going on a painting holiday. You promised…'

'I still promise,' Tom said. 'It's not a painting holiday. There'll be no leaving you to wander off on your own or twiddle your thumbs while I sit painting. I've packed the things just in case. Just in case I see something I absolutely, absolutely, have to paint. Look. Only two canvasses. Not twenty. Not even six.'

'OK,' said Antoine. 'Fair do's.'

Fair do's? Tom thought. Where did he get that from? Did I teach him it? Surely not. Did Chris?

Tom wanted to take Antoine back to his roots. More precisely, to his and Chris's roots. For there was no Tom without Chris and never would be, just as there had been no Chris without Tom. Antoine had always understood that, he'd known it at a deep level the moment he'd met the pair of them. Having loved the pair of them he had no trouble with the immutability of that fact. No Tom without Chris.

Antoine's roots were easier to get at. They were all in Castillon. For years Tom had known Antoine's Uncle

François. More recently he'd met his mother – he'd got on astonishingly well with her – and a scatter of cousins. All in Castillon. The grandmother, François's mother, was sadly no longer living in Castillon – or anywhere else. But Tom's roots stretched further, geographically speaking at any rate. That's why they were driving north.

They were in no hurry. They eschewed the motorways in favour of the un-crowded, easy, but still fairly fast departmental routes. They drove only a couple of hundred miles the first day, stopping for the night at a small *auberge* in Montluçon. The next day, after they'd taken a walk around Montluçon's graceful streets of medieval half-timbered houses, they travelled another easy two hundred miles to Paris. Though the last bit was not quite so easy. Before today neither of them had driven further into the heart of Paris than the *périférique*, and they were slightly nervous of it. But Tom at least knew where he was aiming for. He'd lived there, and would know the way once they began to get close. To Montmartre.

They had taken the precaution of advance booking a hotel with parking, and once Tom had found his way to the bottom of the butte they had only to drive up the winding Rue Lepic to get to it. With a mixture of pride and humility Tom walked Antoine around to the Rue St-Vincent and showed him the rambling old house in its tree-filled garden that had belonged to Gérard. The house that had then belonged briefly to Chris and himself and whose sale had been the springboard for their subsequent business enterprises. 'The source of my inheritance,' said Antoine with a smile that was only half ironic. He was seriously impressed by its appearance. 'Who lives there now?' he asked.

'I don't know,' said Tom. 'I know who we sold it to, but that was fifteen years ago. We didn't keep in touch. I don't know who lives there now. I don't suggest we go calling.'

'I agree,' said Antoine. After a further minute of squinting in at the house through the shrub-filled, tree-shaded garden, they turned away towards the Place du Tertre where they had a beer among the easel-equipped artists and the silhouette clippers in a café that Tom couldn't have afforded to go into when he'd lived in the neighbourhood.

They drove out of Paris in the morning, still heading north. They reached Boulogne at lunchtime. Tom parked opposite the abandoned ferry port. 'Oh God,' said Antoine, who was sensitive to atmosphere, 'that gives me a creepy feeling.'

The buildings were empty, semi-derelict; the station platforms abandoned and the rails overgrown with weeds and brown with rust. The harbour machinery too was disused and rusting. The link-spans on which cars had boarded ships bound for England were in the upright position, their lattice-work of girders a home to a colony of kittiwake gulls that filled the air around with their snowflake wings and kittenish mewing, and had whitened the old machinery with their droppings.

'The old things … the grids of metal,' said Antoine. 'They look like… What's the word in English? *Herse*…' He made a drawbridge gesture with his forearm.

'Port-cullis,' Tom managed to translate, thanks to the gesture.

'It's sad,' said Antoine.

'And sadly it was Britain that pulled up the drawbridge,' said Tom. 'First the big ferries stopped coming from Folkestone. There was a catamaran service for a time, then that stopped… Now everything this end of the Channel comes through Dover and Calais. Michel tells me all the shops here have become rundown and shabby. Boulogne used to be a wealthy place…'

'La perfide Albion,' said Antoine. He was only half joking.

'There are times in history when England does tend to pull up the drawbridge,' Tom admitted.

'Dunkirk,' said Antoine.

Tom smiled. 'That was different.' He knew that the Dunkirk evacuation was viewed differently on the French side of the Channel. He said patiently, 'I know you see it as the ultimate betrayal – France abandoned to her fate, left at the mercy of the Nazis. But the British see it as the brave rescue of what was left of our expeditionary army. Soldiers – including many French – were pulled off the beaches by brave men in fishing boats. In fact you know one of the men who did that.'

'I do?'

'You're going to be staying in his house tomorrow. Roger. Malcolm's Roger. You'll be able to ask him for his recollections.'

'Ah…' said Antoine. Tom could almost see his brain processing the surprising information.. 'Perhaps I'd better prepare a tactful list of questions.' They laughed together.

Later that afternoon they arrived at Michel and Armand's apartment at Wimereux. Antoine loved the balcony that overlooked the Channel. 'Often you can see England,' Tom told him. 'Today…' he shrugged. 'Despite the clear sky and sunshine it's hazy. Perhaps tomorrow.'

Antoine also liked Michel's pictures – there were some he hadn't seen of Tom and Christopher. 'You see?' he said, waving a hand in the direction of the wall in the living room. 'Chris and you are immortal. Together for ever. Preserved on canvas.'

Michel smiled quietly. Tom's new relationship had his very willing blessing. He was glad that Chris was still a part of it, not just for Tom but also for Antoine. But looking at paintings reminded him… 'Who's looking after the gallery in your absence?' he asked them.

'Simon today, Patrick yesterday. Patrick tomorrow,' Tom told him. It was a light workload when it was shared between the six of them, and rarely was more than one person required to be on duty. They exhibited Michel's work and Tom's, with occasional exhibitions of work by other artists to wake things up a bit.

'We'll be down there after the weekend,' Armand told him. 'Pulling our weight again.' They all knew there was only one reason why Michel and Armand hadn't yet made the Dordogne their principal place of residence.

They had dinner with Sabine that evening. She still kept her big house on Boulevard Auguste Marlette but was no longer alone in it. A woman lived in with her, cooked and cleaned and generally cared for her. She cooked the meal that evening and ate it with them. It was better, Tom thought, than a care home … whatever erosion of Michel's eventual inheritance the arrangement might be causing. At least Sabine still had her wits about her. For the moment. But wasn't that *for the moment* equally true for all of them?

The morning provided Antoine with his first sight of England. From the Wimereux balcony. A braided thread of white and green resting on the water, bright as a jewel in the morning sun. 'It's beautiful,' said Antoine.

'At this distance,' Tom cautioned.

They kept the view with them, glimpsed at intervals between chalky headlands, all the way to Calais. Then little by little it grew closer as their ship made its way out into the Channel. It seemed at moments as though they were not moving towards it but hauling it on slow invisible chains towards them.

Once they'd left Dover the road-signs began almost immediately to point the way to Sandwich. Antoine thought it funny that you could live in a town called Sandwich. Tom reminded him that not very far south of where they lived in France there was a town called Condom.

By the time they arrived in the centre of the ancient Cinque Port, and were sitting in the riverbank garden behind Roger and Malcolm's house, sipping a second glass of newly fashionable Spanish Cava, Antoine had slightly modified his view of the Dunkirk evacuation. It made a difference, he discovered, to find himself talking about it with an eighty-four-year-old who had actually taken part in the rescue of his compatriots and others. Antoine had known Roger for years; he just hadn't known this about him. Roger told the story of how they had set off, a convoy of fishing boats, one among many convoys, theirs shepherded by a destroyer named Sappho; how they had plucked men from the water, shivering and half drowning, and brought them back. 'Many died,' Roger finished, 'but by some miracle none on our boat, none in our little group.'

While Roger told his story Malcolm sat listening with rapt attention. This was his older partner's big story; he wouldn't take away from the moment by uttering a syllable; he would not diminish his partner's brief glory by so much as a heartbeat.

'Right,' said Roger when the story was over. 'Let's go out and eat something. Does Antoine like Indian?'

'Yes,' Tom spoke for him. 'He doesn't know that yet, having never tried it. But yes, he does like Indian.'

Surprisingly, he did.

They stood in a field of mud. A building site on a little windblown hilltop. They'd entered the site through the cross-crowned, Gothic-arched gateway that had once been the entrance to Star of the Sea, the prep school where Tom had been first a pupil and then, returning less than ten years later in his reincarnation as a junior master, had met Chris.

Of the vast building, with its long vaulted cloisters, big chapel, refectory and dormitories; with its routines and smells and memories; with its gardens and playing fields and tennis courts; with its trees and kitchen gardens – not a trace was left. Not one stone was left standing on another stone; not one single brick upon another. All that was left was the melancholy wide open space and its limitless view to westward. 'Level, level with the ground,' Tom found himself quoting, 'the towers do lie Which with their golden glittering tops pierced once to the sky.'

'Two hundred houses,' said Antoine 'That's what the man said they were going to build here. If I understood him correctly.'

'You did,' Tom said.

But the view hadn't changed much. There was the great bay still, the snaking River Stour still pouring its endless waters into it. The long line of Kent across the water. Sandwich – where they had just driven from – and Deal with its leggy pier in the far left distance. The airfield runway still crowned the opposite hillside. But today a massive 747 cargo plane was getting in position for take-off. Tom knew that the scenes of your earlier life appeared smaller when you revisited them later. That didn't apply to the aeroplanes, though. They'd got bigger.

Tom pointed down the slope of mud and rubble, between the JCBs and the bulldozers. 'Somewhere down there I first saw Christopher. He was walking between two trees at the bottom of the playing fields. From where I was looking – from my bedroom window – he appeared to be walking out of one tree and into another. He looked small and young, and very lovely. Very vulnerable. As he was. He was about to start his first … and as it turned out, only … teaching job.'

'It's hard to imagine,' said Antoine. He hastily added, 'I don't mean hard to imagine Chris as a beautiful teenager; that's easy. I meant the buildings here. And all the life within them.'

Tom said, 'It's hard to accept it.'

The acceleration roar of the 747 now reached them, though the plane itself was already well down the two-mile-distant runway.

'You can see the cars approaching for kilometres,' said Antoine.

'Yes,' said Tom. 'And, the other way round, as you approached the building here on its hilltop you could see it – see the chapel and its tower at least – from a huge distance. The distant sight of it made kids returning for the start of term feel very dismal. But now I wonder whether Father Louis … he was the headmaster when I taught here … whether he used to look out across this view on the afternoon before term started, and watch the cars of the returning boarders' parents with similar apprehension. When you're young you don't imagine your own weaknesses and fragility are shared by your elders.'

'Do you share my fragility?' said Antoine. 'I doubt it.'

'I'm not your elder,' said Tom. 'There's barely twenty-two years between us. But my fragility…? I think you know all about that.'

'Kiss me?' said Antoine.

'What? Out here on a building site in front of all these guys on tractors?'

'Et alors? So what?' said Antoine. Tom broke with the habit of a lifetime and kissed his man in public. There were a few whoops and cat-calls from the men on tractors. They both chose to ignore them.

'We'll walk,' said Tom. 'I'll show you… No, on second thoughts we'll take the car there.'

They drove a mile or so. To the far end of the footpath that ran from the demolished Star of the Sea and the still-standing but dilapidated Admiral Digby. They parked in the cliff-top field that did duty as a car-park for visitors to the replica Viking ship, the Hugin. 'Walk along the path with me a little way?' Tom asked Antoine.

The path hugged the edge of the chalk cliff. Some of the way it ran between wind-pruned bushes, some of it gave a full view of the sea, and of France beyond it. 'It seems so close,' said Antoine. 'Though it seemed even closer on the ferry. Are we looking at Boulogne and Wimereux?'

'No,' said Tom. 'They're round the corner.' He pointed. 'The bit on the end there is Cap Gris Nez. But at night you can see the lights of Calais.'

'It's funny,' said Antoine.

'I know,' said Tom. 'But it's actually all just one country.' He thought of telling Antoine about the land-bridge that had joined the British Isles to mainland Europe until as recently as the last Ice Age; how human beings had walked back and forth across it. About Henri Plantagenet who had ruled most of both countries and had crossed the Channel twenty-five times in the course of his energetic administration. In what kind of fragile craft? In what kind of weather? Tom wasn't sure if even he had made that many crossings. 'Another day,' he said, 'I'll tell you the history.'

'I'm sure you will,' said Antoine, rolling his eyes heavenward in mock weariness. He was more than well aware that Tom had been a history teacher.

'Sit for a moment?' Tom invited Antoine. They sat on the cliff top. The calls of birds surrounded them. From the mud-flats below came the calls of curlew and shelduck. Around them flew linnets twittering. 'Look at you, look at you,' they seemed to be calling. At least that was how it sounded to Tom. It didn't strike his French partner in quite the same fashion.

'I sat here with Chris the night we got back together again after the big boyfriend swap,' said Tom. 'It was the night before our birthday…'

'Just as today is,' said Antoine, who knew what was good for him and would have pulled his own teeth out rather than forgotten that.

'And that's the last time I came here. There were oats growing that year…'

'And this year…? Antoine pointed to the field of long thin seed pods behind them. 'I know it in French, obviously…'

'Rape-seed,' said Tom. 'Come on.' He got to his feet and Antoine followed. 'One more thing to do before we leave here. Back to the car park.'

'I was hoping for dog roses,' said Tom. 'But they weren't in convenient places where we've just been walking. He rummaged in the car boot for his oil paints and palette. 'I wanted to do you the way Hilliard painted his Young Man among Roses.'

'I don't know that painting,' said Antoine.

Tom said, 'When we get back we can Google it.' He looked around them, at the same time fishing out a piece of hardboard from beneath his easel.

'No canvas?' queried Antoine. 'No easel?'

'No dog roses, either,' said Tom. He looked at the bushes behind the car, 'We'll have to make do with cherries. Unripe ones.'

'Just as well,' said Antoine. 'Ripe ones might be just a bit too …how do you say? … suggestive?'

'Just sit on the ground in front of the bushes,' said Tom. 'Look ahead of you.'

'At the sea? With France on the horizon?'

'Exactly,' said Tom. 'And can you undo just one more shirt button?' Then he sat down on the grass opposite his lover, resting the hardboard against his raised knees and, in a little over forty minutes, had painted his head and shoulders and the foliage behind him. 'OK,' he said finally. 'You can look now. Be careful not to touch it…'

Antoine got up with a little hesitation. He came round Tom's shoulder nervously, like a wary animal. He looked at the picture and was silent for a moment.

'Well?' said Tom.

'It's … well, you've done it beautifully. But you've made me look much younger.'

'That's how I see you,' said Tom. *'As time takes from you, I engraft you new.'*

There was another few seconds' silence. Then Antoine said. 'It's definitely me. And yet, it also looks like Christopher.'

'Hmm,' said Tom. 'Yes, I can see that too, now you mention it. Would you say I've captured…?'

'Yes,' Antoine cut him off. 'One way or another… I'd say you've captured a likeness.'

POSTSCRIPT

You don't get many birthday cards if you choose to go abroad for the occasion, unless you take them with you. So at breakfast-time the next morning Tom made do with the one he'd brought from Michel and Armand and the one from his hosts, Roger and Malcolm – in addition, of course, to Antoine's. But Antoine had another envelope to add to the ones on the table. 'It's from Simon,' he said. 'He told me to give you this on your birthday... Chris's birthday.'

Tom opened the envelope. Inside was a single sheet of paper, written by hand in Simon's unmistakeable scrawl. That familiar scribble had been the same when Simon was a schoolboy, Tom remembered. There was no address, no salutation, no valediction, no signature. Tom read, and a smile spread over his face as he read, and he looked forward to the moment, just a few seconds from now, when he would share Simon's message with Antoine.

"In principio erat Verbum, et Verbum erat apud Deum, et Deus erat Verbum." Remember when those words came at the end of Mass every day in the Latin days, before Vatican Two? Saint Jerome translated the Bible from Greek to Latin – the Vulgate – because Latin was the language of ordinary people. But time moved on and languages changed. Eventually the Second Vatican Council decreed in 1964 that, starting the following year, the Mass should be said in the vernacular – each country should worship in the language that was its own.

(And the people stayed away in droves. But that is by the way.)

For years I was puzzled by this obscure bit of theology. The words – yes words – seemed to run in a circle. "In the beginning was the Word, and the Word was with God, and the word was *God." What? Even before St John's time the Greek word for 'word', Logos, was used to refer to God's expression of himself in the workings of the world. Then St John used Logos more specifically. The Word, we were told, meant Jesus. Still it made little sense. What was this Word?*

Today I know. I've learnt it from Patrick. It's something you knew already, Tom. Knew by instinct. Knew with Christopher. Knew with Michel. As Michel also knew with Armand. And now you know it again with Antoine. I think by now you've guessed it. The Word is Love.

'Is it a private joke?' Antoine was asking from across the table. 'Or can anyone see it?'

'Anyone can see it,' said Tom. His smile now threatened to turn to exuberant laughter. 'In fact everyone can see it. I think everyone should.'

He handed Antoine the fragile sheet of paper with its precious scribbled cargo.

****

This was the third book in The Dog in the Chapel series. The first two books in the series are **The Dog in the Chapel** and **Tom & Christopher and Their Kind.** All three books in the series, together with other Anthony McDonald titles, are now additionally available as audio-books.

About the Author

Anthony McDonald is the author of thirty-one books. He studied modern history at Durham University, then worked briefly as a musical instrument maker and as a farmhand before moving into the theatre, where he has worked in every capacity except director and electrician. He has also spent several years teaching English in Paris and London. He now lives in rural East Sussex.

Novels by Anthony McDonald

TENERIFE
THE DOG IN THE CHAPEL
TOM & CHRISTOPHER AND THEIR KIND
DOG ROSES
THE RAVEN AND THE JACKDAW
SILVER CITY
IVOR'S GHOSTS
ADAM
BLUE SKY ADAM
GETTING ORLANDO
ORANGE BITTER, ORANGE SWEET
ALONG THE STARS
WOODCOCK FLIGHT

Short stories

MATCHES IN THE DARK:
13 Tales of Gay Men

———

Diary

RALPH: DIARY OF A GAY TEEN

Comedy

THE GULLIVER MOB

Gay Romance Series:

Sweet Nineteen
Gay Romance on Garda
Gay Romance in Majorca
Gay Tartan
Cocker and I
Cam Cox
The Paris Novel
The Van Gogh Window
Tibidabo
Spring Sonata
Touching Fifty
Romance on the Orient Express

—

And, writing as 'Adam Wye'

Boy Next Door
Love in Venice
Gay in Moscow

All titles are available as Kindle ebooks and as paperbacks from Amazon.

www.anthonymcdonald.co.uk

Made in the USA
Middletown, DE
18 September 2018